The
Invisibles

The Invisibles

CECILIA GALANTE

WM

WILLIAM MORROW
An Imprint of HarperCollinsPublishers

P.S.™ is a trademark of HarperCollins Publishers.

THE INVISIBLES. Copyright © 2015 by Cecilia Galante. All rights reserved. Printed in the United States of America. No part of this book may be used or reproduced in any manner whatsoever without written permission except in the case of brief quotations embodied in critical articles and reviews. For information address HarperCollins Publishers, 195 Broadway, New York, NY 10007.

HarperCollins books may be purchased for educational, business, or sales promotional use. For information please e-mail the Special Markets Department at SPsales@harpercollins.com.

FIRST EDITION

Designed by Diahann Sturge

Library of Congress Cataloging-in-Publication Data has been applied for.

ISBN 978-0-06-236351-0

15 16 17 18 19   OV/RRD   10 9 8 7 6 5 4 3 2 1

For Maria
Then, now, and always

The Invisibles

Chapter 1

It wasn't until she reached the corner of Grove Street, where the sidewalk buckled and the pre-dawn smells of yeast and fabric softener perfumed the air, that Nora remembered it was her thirty-second birthday. She stopped abruptly, as if someone had yanked a leash around her neck, and let the information settle along her shoulders. Thirty-two. The number rolled around in her head, and she waited for the onslaught of—what was it exactly: relief? dread?—that was supposed to arrive at reaching the end of another year, but it didn't come. Instead, the first line from a book she had once read occurred to her: *"Once upon a time, there was a woman who discovered she had turned into the wrong person."* Nora could not remember the title of the book or even the name of the author, but the words themselves, strung like so many lights in the distance, felt as distressing now as they had the day she had first come across them. Maybe even more so.

A band of sky behind the rooftops ahead was turning a soft purple. The moon, a lopsided waxing gibbous, was so translucent as to appear glass-like there in the heavens. It would be another forty minutes or so before the sun rose, erasing all traces of the moon for the day. Now, though, it was hers. The September air was sharply cold, the imminent warning of a quickly approaching fall, and the streets were littered with leaves browning around the edges. Alice Walker, her chocolate brown retriever, nuzzled the stiff grass for a few seconds and then turned around, staring up at Nora. She barked once, and then again. It was unusual for Nora to stop during their morning walks, a daily ritual that had become so ingrained in their lives by this point that it was hard to imagine anything preventing it. Even bad weather did little to deter her; Nora made the trek in rain and snow, and once even in a hailstorm, during which she'd had to stop and take refuge under an enormous red-and-green-striped awning until things settled down again. Walking cleared her head in a way few other things could, and she never turned around until she reached the little grove of birch trees by the railroad tracks, where she would sit for a moment and rest before starting back again.

Alice Walker barked again, loudly, the sound reverberating through the stillness, and then cocked her head. *The birch trees,* her eyes seemed to say. *Let's get to the birch trees.* Nora looked away from the dog and stared down at her sneakers instead— pale blue Asics with orange strips on each side. She pressed two fingers beneath her breastbone and took a breath as if to steady herself. A heaviness that was not disappointment or regret or anything else she could identify yet filled her nonetheless. And for the first time in as long as she could remember, she did not want to keep walking toward the birch grove. She just wanted to go home.

"Come on, love," she said, turning around, tugging at Alice Walker's leash. "Let's go."

The dog barked a third time, obviously confused.

Nora's feet moved with a mind of their own, leading her back to the apartment they shared on Winslop Avenue. "Yeah, well, I don't know either," she said. "Come on, now."

She could hear the phone ringing in her bedroom as she unlocked her front door. Alice Walker bolted toward it, barking after each ring, as if the phone might respond. Nora hung back, struggling to get her key out of the lock, which still continued to stick, despite numerous complaints to the landlord. She tugged again. Nothing. Well, she'd have to let the machine get it. It was probably just Trudy or Marion from the library anyway, calling to ask her to pick up some more coffee beans on her way in. Between the three of them, the office coffeepot went through at least four refills a day.

"Hey, this is Nora." The recorded sound of her voice echoed through the empty apartment. "I'm not here, but I will be eventually, so please leave a message." Nora winced, listening. She'd gone through at least a dozen messages when she'd set up the machine, trying her voice out each time—a little happier here, more serious there—until she'd just said to hell with it and settled on this one.

There was a pause and then:

"Norster?"

Nora's fingers froze around the rubber grip of the keys. No

one had called her Norster since she was seventeen years old. And even then, there had been only one person who had ever used that name.

A throat cleared. Then: "Nora Walker? Is this you? God, I hope I have the right number. This is . . ." There was a muffled noise, as if the receiver had just been covered, and then the faint, nearly obscured sound of a reprimand. "I need a minute, Jack, okay? Mommy just needs one minute. Now, *please.*"

No. It couldn't be. Nora gave the key a final furious tug and then let go of it altogether, racing toward her bedroom. It just couldn't be.

"Sorry about that." The voice was back, unmuffled now and slightly raised. "Um, this is Ozzie Randol. I'm just calling to—"

"Ozzie!" Nora snatched the phone up so quickly that she almost dropped it. "Ozzie, I'm here!"

"Nora! Oh my God!"

"Ozzie." Nora said the name a third time, as if the word itself would settle her breathing somehow, stop her legs from trembling. Her windbreaker, unzipped and loose, hung open in front of her like a mouth agape. How long had she been waiting for this moment? She couldn't remember anymore. "Oh, Ozzie. Oh my God. Is that really you?"

Ozzie laughed. "Of course it's really me. You know any other girls out there named Ozzie?"

"No." A giggle emanated from Nora's mouth like a bubble. "No, I've never met another Ozzie." She sat down carefully on the end of her bed, smoothing the edge of the white comforter with the palm of her hand. Ozzie had the same laugh, a bright burst of sound that came out of a mouth so wide and lips so full that

Nora used to wonder how everything fit in there together—and still looked so pretty.

"Shit, Norster, I can't believe I actually found you! Monica told me she thought you still lived in Willow Grove, but . . ."

"Monica?" Nora interrupted. "Our Monica?"

"*Har-Monica!*" Ozzie said, using the nickname they had given her back in high school after Monica had started whistling through her teeth. "Who is doing *great*, by the way. She has a place in Manhattan now—a penthouse, actually, which I've decided not to hold against her. Or the fact that she's managed to snag herself a *bill*ionaire to live there. Can you believe it? Harmonica, living with some Bill Gates guy?" Ozzie laughed. "Anyway, she told me that she thought you still lived in Willow Grove and worked for the library, but she couldn't be sure. When's the last time you talked to her, anyway?"

Nora blinked against the sudden onslaught of information. "Who, Monica?"

"Yeah. You two talk at all?"

"No." Nora paused. "Why, do you?"

"No." Ozzie sounded disappointed. "And I haven't seen her in forever, either. Not since . . . God, I guess not since we all left." She paused. "What about Grace? You talk to Grace at all?"

"No. Not Grace either."

But that had been the deal, hadn't it? They were all going to go and live their own lives and forget everything that happened. Put it behind them. *Leave it in the past,* Ozzie had said, *where it would get smaller and smaller until one day it would just disappear altogether.* Except that it hadn't. At least not for Nora. Twice, just this past summer, she had gotten up in the middle of the night and walked over to the old house with Alice Walker, just to stare at it, to try to remember—or maybe make sense of—all the things that had happened behind those walls. It was an abandoned building now, the yellow paint old and curling off the sides like an old skin, the front porch split in two. But it had once been Turning Winds, a group home for unwanted girls, the temporary residence for Ozzie and Grace and Monica and Nora throughout their last two years of high school, a place that, for a while at least, had afforded them the only sense of safety they had ever known.

After graduation, Nora had been the only one of them to stay in Willow Grove. She hadn't wanted to leave, hadn't felt the tug and pull of the outside world the way the others had. Some nights, though, she wished she had. Some nights she wondered if her life would be different if she'd cobbled together the courage to strike out in a similar way, to carve her own path through the vast unknown. What things would she have seen? What would she have done? Who would she have turned into, aside from the wrong person?

The last time she had gone down to the house and stood there looking at it, she'd had to cup her hands under the curve of her rib cage as her heart beat steadily beneath it. If she didn't hold on to it, she thought, if she didn't gather herself around it and keep it safe, it would split open completely.

"Jesus, time flies, doesn't it?" Ozzie asked. "Can you believe we're in our fucking *thirties* now?"

"Actually," Nora said softly, "I'm thirty-two today."

"What? Wait, what's today?"

"September sixth."

"Oh my God, I totally forgot it was your birthday!" Ozzie

laughed again. "Holy shit, Nora! How weird is it that the day I call you—after all this time—it's your fucking birthday? I mean, how crazy is that?"

Nora smiled. Along with her fondness for cursing, Ozzie had always believed in crazy, inexplicable things—things that had to do with fate and the meanings of names and the way the planets aligned with each other to keep the world spinning. The only facts that made any sense, she used to say, were the ones that we had no answers for. Back then Nora had thought she agreed with her. Now she wasn't so sure.

"So how *are* you?" Ozzie's voice was soft all of a sudden. "What's your life like? Oh my God, do you still collect first lines?"

A flush of joy washed over Nora as Ozzie recalled her favorite thing to do in high school. Nora had still been in the throes of her silent stage when she first arrived at Turning Winds—a period of selective mutism that had begun when she was twelve years old and that, the doctors said, would end only when Nora decided it would end. It had ultimately taken a little over four years. But those silent years had not stifled her in any way. In fact, Nora thought they had actually saved her. She disappeared into books instead of talking, reading whatever she could get her hands on. Her fascination with first lines started almost immediately, after she came across Alice Walker's novel *The Color Purple* and read the first eight words: *"You better not never tell nobody but God."* They had made her suck in air, and she'd given in right then and there, sitting down on the library floor between the fiction stacks to read the whole book from cover to cover. She'd collected over two hundred first lines since then, each of them a small, quiet joy in its own right. There was something about the infinite promise that the first line of a book held, as if the weight of everything that came afterward rested upon it. First lines were one of the bravest things she knew. They toed the line, bent their knees, and jumped—right into the abyss, taking you with them. Good ones did, anyway. Nora had gotten into a bad habit of not bothering to read the rest of the book if the first line failed to measure up to her standards. Which, she understood, probably meant that she had missed out on a great number of wonderful books. But that was the way it was for her.

She still had the same blue and green notebook she'd started her collection with; in fact, she'd taken it out of her underwear drawer just the other day, jotting down a first line she'd found while shelving a copy of *The Chronicles of Narnia* at work: *"There was a boy called Eustace Clarence Scrubbs, and he almost deserved it."* It had made her laugh out loud, and she'd taken the book home with her that night to read. Now, as she stared at the note-book on her bedside table, the whole thing felt stupid and child-ish. Another reminder of the person she still was.

"No," she said. "I haven't done any of that first-line stuff in a long time."

"Ohhh." Ozzie sounded crestfallen. "I used to *love* it when you would tell us first lines! God, I wish I remembered some of them."

"Yeah. Well." Nora heard her voice drift off. "What about you? Where do you live now?"

"Amherst. Up in Massachusetts. The winters'll make your balls turn blue, but my house is the sweetest little thing in the world. We raise our own chickens and vegetables in the backyard. My kids love it."

A string in Nora's heart tugged. "You have kids?"

"Three of them. All under the age of six. Can you believe it?"

Nora stood up. She had not known she was holding her breath until she exhaled, a sudden, forcible movement. "Are you married, too?" she asked, steadying herself against the edge of her dresser.

"Yup."

"No, you're not!"

Ozzie was the only one out of all four of them who had insisted, had *sworn,* that she would never get married. Kids, maybe. But only after she'd gone and seen the world, driven some stake into the ground of a piece of uncharted territory and claimed it for her own. But marriage? Chaining one's self to another human being until you died? Never. What happened? Nora wondered. How did something you had once been so sure of suddenly become negotiable?

"I am." Ozzie's voice got quiet. "Almost twelve years now. And you know what, Nora? I'm still not sure I did the right thing. I mean, I love him and everything, but, Jesus Christ . . . I really don't fucking *know* sometimes." She paused. "Do you know what I'm talking about? I mean, what about you? Are you married now? Kids?"

"No, not married." Nora headed down the narrow hallway of the apartment. Her sneakers made a peeling sound against the hardwood floor as she walked over to the living room window; her fingers closed around the soft pouch of her earlobe as her heart beat a little faster. "But I'm dating a great guy. It's been almost a year now."

This was a lie. A few years earlier, she'd been in a relationship with an accountant named Tom Robertson who had asked her out after finishing her tax return and then went and ruined everything by picking his nose while sitting in her living room one night and, thinking she was still out of the room, wiping the offending extraction on the arm of her couch. In her twenties, she'd gone with a guy named Sinclair Westley, whom she had liked well enough. He was her car mechanic and liked to come over early on Saturday mornings with Boston cream doughnuts and coffee before heading into the shop. She couldn't remember anymore why that one had fizzled out, but it didn't matter. Now, though, there was nothing to tell. Nothing at all.

"Oh, that's great!" Ozzie said. "What's he like?"

"He's . . . sweet. And funny. You would love him."

"Do *you* love him?"

"Yes!" Nora said, too quickly. "Of course!"

"Good." Ozzie said. "Good, I'm glad."

Why was she doing this? What was she ashamed of, still being single after all this time? If anyone would understand the way things were, it was Ozzie Randol. Wasn't it? Ozzie had always been one of those people who said things like it was better to be alone than with the wrong person, that there was no man in the world worth compromising one's self for. In high school, she'd snubbed a senior boy named Linus Worthington, who, despite the fact that Ozzie was only a junior, had pursued her relentlessly, smitten with her brash personality and obvious confidence. She hadn't cared a whit that he was older, or that he was so popular that to get an invitation to one of his legendary house parties was the equivalent of achieving a social status of ethereal proportions; she'd said he just didn't do it for her, period. But had Ozzie ever gone twelve days without talking to anyone in the entire world? Did she know what it was like to hold an animal against her chest, just to feel the soft pulse of breath against her skin, the thrum of a beating heart from inside another living thing? Had she ever gone to bed directly after dinner and prayed for sleep, just so that she didn't have to figure out how to fill one more empty hour by herself?

"Hey, is Turning Winds still around?" Ozzie asked, not seeming to notice Nora's evasive answers. "They still running the place?"

"No." Nora turned as Alice Walker barked from the kitchen, alerting her to her empty water bowl. "It's just an old empty building now."

"Wow," Ozzie said. "I can hardly remember what it even looks like anymore. It's been so long!"

"Fifteen years," Nora said, holding Alice Walker's red plastic bowl under the running faucet.

"Fifteen years," Ozzie repeated. "That's practically a lifetime."

Two lifetimes, Nora thought.

"So I know it seems crazy that I'm just calling you out of the blue like this," Ozzie said, "but I do have a reason."

Nora froze. The water spilled over the top of the dog's bowl and rushed down the sides.

"It's about Grace," Ozzie said. "I mean Petal. She goes by Petal now, you know."

"Wait." Nora shook her head, feeling as though something had drained from inside her chest. She turned off the faucet, set the water bowl down in front of Alice Walker. "Grace goes by Petal now? What are you talking about?"

"She changed her name. I don't think she went and made it *legal* or anything, but her husband says she likes to be called Petal now." Ozzie paused. "It could be worse. She could be calling her-self Stem. Or Root."

Nora didn't laugh. "Why would she change her name?"

"Oh, I'm sure it's part of that whole artist-persona thing she had going on. You remember."

Nora did remember. The four of them had been as close as sisters in that house, but she had shared a bedroom with Grace for two years. Nora knew parts of Grace that Ozzie and Monica did not. Parts they might not ever know.

"Anyway," Ozzie said. "Grace—I mean Petal—"

"Just call her Grace." Nora felt impatient suddenly, and it star-tled her. She rarely got impatient. With anyone. "I mean, at least to me. Petal's . . . I don't know. It's too weird."

"Okay, so Grace's husband called me last night, and we talked for a long time. Over an hour, I'd guess. They live right outside of Chicago now; I don't remember where, exactly. Somewhere in the suburbs, I think. Anyway, the point is, she's not doing so well."

Nora held her breath, as if to block the pinprick of fear rising behind it. "Can you be more specific?"

"She's . . . well, her husband—his name is Henry, by the way—said that she was in the hospital."

"She's sick?"

"Yeah, but not physically sick," Ozzie said. "It was a mental hospital. She tried to kill herself, Nora. Just a few months ago."

The pinprick exploded into a flash of heat that spread out across the front of Nora's chest and down into her stomach.

"And it was no joke, either," Ozzie continued. "You know how some people kind of do it half-assed because they don't know how to ask for help and making a few scratches on their wrist is the only way they can get anyone to take them seriously? Well, Grace wasn't asking for anyone's help. Henry said he found her hanging in the closet. She was blue. Her eyes were bulging out of her sockets."

Nora blocked a cry that was trying to escape from her mouth with the side of her fist. It just didn't seem possible. Grace had always been horrified by death. Once, when the two of them had been walking back to Turning Winds from school, they had come across a dead bird lying on the sidewalk. It was a sparrow, small and brown, with tiny feet that curled up under it like fern fronds. There was no sign of violence, no mark that gave any indication as to how it had died, and for a moment, as Grace sank down next to it, Nora had been sure it would wake up and fly away. It hadn't, of course, and when Grace turned to her, her wide face stricken, and said, "What do you think *happened*?" she hadn't known how to answer.

"*Why?*" Nora asked now. Her voice was a whisper.

"Henry said they've been having a lot of problems," Ozzie said. "I mean, obviously. But I think she's been struggling with depression for a while. And then she just had a baby this past May. Henry thinks it was postpartum depression mixed in with everything else. I guess it made her suicidal." She paused. "If he hadn't come home when he did that day, we'd all be meeting up again at her funeral instead of talking like this."

Just for a moment Nora wished Ozzie had learned not to speak so bluntly. And then, in the next breath, she was glad she hadn't. Ozzie had always been the one who said the things that the rest of them could not.

"She has a baby then?" Nora pulled at the soft skin along her throat.

"Yeah. A little girl. Henry's parents have been taking care of her until he can get things sorted out, I guess."

"Is Grace back home? Or is she still in the hospital?"

"No, she's been home for a while. Since the end of July, I think. Henry said she's really been making progress. But he also said that he was worried she was starting to relapse again."

"Relapse?"

"You know, reverting back to her old behaviors. Crying a lot, not sleeping. Especially in the last two weeks or so. I think he's scared."

"Well, he should bring her back to the hospital!" Nora stood up and raked her fingers through the top of her hair. "What's he doing calling you?" She bit her lip, realizing how that sounded. "I mean . . . you're not a doctor. He should be calling her doctor, right?"

"He's done that." Nora could hear a catch in Ozzie's voice. "Her therapist, too. They upped her meds, and they're monitoring her pretty closely. Henry says rough patches are normal; that they'll come and go."

"Okay," Nora said uncertainly.

"Here's the thing, though, Nora. Henry says that she just wants us. If he said it once last night, he said it ten times. Apparently Grace keeps telling him over and over again that all she wants is to see the three of us."

"The three of us?" Nora repeated. "You mean you and me and Monica?"

"Uh-huh. That's why he called."

Nora let her hand fall from the back of her head. She had been carrying the hope of this—or something exactly like this— around like a stone in her pocket, a toothache that never stopped throbbing, a constant, steady pulse. The stone had gotten smaller, the toothache less painful, but the pulse was still there. It was always there.

And yet . . .

"Nora?"

"God, Ozzie. I don't know."

"You don't know what?"

"Are you going to see her?"

"Well, of course I'm going to see her."

"What about Monica?"

"Monica's in," Ozzie answered. "I called her just before I called you. She already booked her flight, and she's meeting me at O'Hare tomorrow afternoon, which is what I was hoping you would do. Then we could all drive to Grace's house. Together. Like she asked."

"And . . ." Nora walked over to the window and pressed her palm flat against the cold glass. "And . . . do what?"

"What do you mean, 'do what?' " Ozzie sounded indignant. "I don't think Grace is looking for us to take her to the *mall* or any-thing here, Nora. She just wants us to be there. For . . . support." A faint clicking sound came over the phone, and Nora realized that Ozzie was biting her nails. Ozzie had bitten her nails back in high school, so badly sometimes that she drew blood and had to wear Band-Aids over the raw skin. "Don't you *want* to be there for her?" Ozzie's question hung in the air.

"Well, yeah." Nora's voice wavered. "I mean, of course I do.

But I don't think you can blame me for being hesitant about seeing people I haven't seen in almost fifteen years."

"*People?*" Ozzie repeated. "I know it's been a while, Nora, but we're not just people. It's us! We were the best friends of your life!"

"Were." Nora repeated Ozzie's word gently. "We *were* best friends, Ozzie. And then nothing. Not a card, a letter. Not even a phone call. For . . ." Her voice drifted off. It had been a long time, but she wanted to say forever. That was what it felt like. Forever and then some.

A small child's voice wailed in the background. "Mommy! Olivia dumped the flour on the floor!"

Ozzie muted the mouthpiece again with her hand. "Two more minutes!" she bellowed. "Mommy's busy right now!"

There was a short silence. And then, "I . . ." Ozzie's voice was already heavy with apology. Quieter too, as if letting Nora in on a secret. "Shit, you know how we all left things, Nora. After that night. And I know I was probably the most vocal about just forgetting all of it and moving ahead. I know I was. I said those exact words, didn't I? To all of us?"

Nora didn't say anything, afraid that Ozzie would stop talking.

"I did," Ozzie said, answering her own question. "And you know, back then, I really thought that was what we should do. I mean, we were seventeen years old! None of us knew what the hell to do after it was all over. At least I didn't. Shit, the only thing going through my stupid head was how fast we were going to get the hell out of there, and what we'd need to do to forget it."

Nora could hear herself breathing through the line, a desperate sound, muffled like a trapped animal. She wanted to scream, could feel it moving like a living thing from the depths of her belly. "And have you?" she asked instead. "Forgotten, I mean?'

"Mostly." The word entered Nora's ear like a bullet. "What about you? Do you ever think about it anymore?" Ozzie's voice was hoarse, barely audible. "Or are you okay with things now?"

Nora removed her hand from the window glass. A large, damp stain remained, the outline of something that looked as though it might still be breathing. "I'm okay with things now."

"All right." Ozzie swallowed through the phone. "But you know, maybe Grace isn't. I mean, she was a basket case afterward. You remember. Maybe she has some kind of posttraumatic stress thing going on. I don't know. I'm not a shrink. All I know is that she needs us. She needs the three of us to help her get through this, whatever it is. I know we're not teenagers anymore. I'm not asking you to come out to Chicago so we can stand around in Grace's backyard and stare up at the moon. But I think she needs us to be around right now, you know? To just . . . be there for her. *I* need you to be there for her."

"You?" Nora repeated. "Why do you need me to be there?"

"Because it won't work without you. There's no such thing as three of us. There never was. It's the four of us or nothing." She paused. "C'mon, Nora. Please say you'll come."

The pale purple had drained from the morning sky, leaving behind a slate of gray. The sky had been that kind of gray the morning Ozzie left, as solemn and still as Nora had felt. Nora had held her tightly at the bus station, knowing that she would not see her for a long, long time after everything that had happened. She might have held on longer if Ozzie had not pulled back, insisting, "Let go now, Nora. You have to let go." She'd obeyed, unclenching her arms, watching as Ozzie ascended the narrow set of steps into the bus and disappeared into the belly of it.

Now her own belly churned like some kind of lopsided washing machine. Just the thought of reuniting with all of them again made the inside of her mouth taste sour. A rushing sounded in her head, and the tips of her fingers tingled. There was no way she had it in her to go through it again; she'd barely made it through the first time. And yet there was something about hearing her name again—*Norster*—combined with the nearly defunct feeling of being needed that almost made her knees buckle. Two parallel lines of pain began to work their way up the back of her throat. Beyond the red maple tree on the sidewalk, she could see the narrow steeple of Saint Augustine's rising in the air like a pair of folded hands, a perpetual prayer. She'd stopped praying so long ago that she couldn't even remember how to begin anymore. And yet right now, this instant, she knew that one of her prayers had just been answered.

"All right," she heard herself whisper into the phone. "Okay, I'll come."

Chapter 2

She stayed at the window for at least five minutes after Ozzie hung up, her eyes fixed on the horizon, a myriad of thoughts drifting from one thing to another and then back again. In just over twenty-four hours, she was going to be reunited with her girls. Her family. Her life. She could still say those things, couldn't she? It was how she felt. How she'd always felt, even if she'd forgotten she did. Their faces came rushing back at her in rapid succession: Ozzie with the short, cropped hair that she cut herself, dark eyebrows, and wide, fleshy lips; Monica, whose smooth, doughy face was framed with orange curls; and Grace, the beauty of the group, who had long blond hair and a bone structure so delicate that it sometimes looked like porcelain. They would have changed undoubtedly through the years, just as she had; maybe some of them were a little wider around the hips or had a few more wrinkles under the eyes, but she knew she would still be able to spot any of them in a crowded room.

She was glad Grace's baby was staying with her grandparents and that she was not going to be at the house. Seeing Grace was going to be difficult enough, but adding a baby to the mix would ratchet things up another hundred degrees. Nora didn't do well with babies. She never had, and she doubted she ever would. They made her anxious the way little else could. It was not so much their gigantic, wobbly heads that, mishandled at just the right angle, could snap their necks in half, or their rubber limbs that seemed to fold in on themselves like pieces of Play-Doh. It was not even the vague terror that crawled up the length of her arms when she held one, sure that at any moment she would drop it on the floor where it would break apart into pieces. It was the crying that undid her, the sorrowful, helpless sound unraveling some tight ball deep inside her chest when she heard it. There was no way she would have agreed to go if Ozzie had said the baby would be there. No way in hell.

She startled as Alice Walker barked behind her, and, realizing how much time had passed, rushed to the shower. It took her less than ten minutes to get dressed for work, and she raced up the back steps of the library, hoping to slide in through the kitchen before anyone noticed. She was supposed to be at work by 8:30, but the phone call had taken up more time than she realized. It was now 8:46. The library opened at nine.

"Happy birthday!" Trudy and Marion jumped out from behind the wall as Nora turned the corner. Pieces of yellow and white confetti fluttered down around her like snow, and Marion blew on a paper horn. Trudy was holding a cake covered with white icing. The words HAPPY BIRTHDAY, NORA! were scrawled across the top in shaky pink letters.

"Oh!" Nora covered her mouth with both hands, suppressing a giggle. "You scared me!"

Marion blew on the horn again.

"Put that thing away," Trudy said, swatting at it. "It sounds like you're strangling a goose."

Marion blew it once more, this time in Trudy's face.

"A child," Trudy muttered, shaking her head. "Eternally stuck at six."

Marion Hubbard and Trudy Randolph were both in their late sixties. They had known each other for almost thirty years. Between the two of them, they had gone through four marriages, the death of a child (Trudy's), and two cracked pelvises. Trudy, who had actually started the library in her own living room before getting enough federal funding to transfer it to a larger building on Maple Street, was the library director, and Marion, who had been her first hire, was her right hand. It was Marion who had approached Nora with the suggestion of working for them after observing her reading in the corner of the second floor for months on end; Marion, too, who had encouraged her a few years later to apply to the local college so that she could get her degree in library science. Nora had refused outright—the thought of having to immerse herself in yet another close-knit social structure (or being on the outside of one) had literally given her hives—until Trudy mentioned the possibility of doing everything online. It had taken her a little over five years, but Nora had done it, applying for and receiving financial aid every semester, staying up late to make sure her papers were perfect, even asking Marion and Trudy to quiz her some days before a big test. She was twenty-seven when she received her bachelor of arts in library science and media diploma in the mail, and it was one of the proudest days of her life. Marion and Trudy had taken her out to dinner to celebrate, and she had smiled all night long.

Now, Trudy set the cake down on the kitchen table, plopped into a chair, and yanked up one of her knee-high argyle socks. Her wide face was accentuated with bright green eyes and soft jowls. Tufts of her short white hair were clipped into place with a variety of plastic barrettes—two blue butterflies, an orange grasshopper, and several pink kittens. Marion had told Nora once that Trudy had never graduated from the eighth grade, and sometimes Nora wasn't sure if she was kidding.

"You know I'm always glad to see you," Trudy said, looking steadily at Nora, "but for a minute there, I thought maybe you'd decided to live large and were going to play hooky today. I wouldn't've docked you, you know. It is your birthday, after all."

"Oh no," Nora said, "I wouldn't have skipped work. And I'm sorry I was a little late. I just . . . I got a phone call this morning from an old friend. We were catching up. I didn't realize how much time had passed."

"Oh, there's nothing better than a birthday call from an old friend!" Marion clasped her hands together wistfully. "How lovely! Who was it?" The silk triangle of scarf that peeked out from her breast pocket matched her navy shoes. Marion dressed every day as if she were about to begin her own talk show on national TV instead of getting behind the periodical desk at the public library.

"Just someone I used to know in high school." Nora took off her brown barn jacket and draped it around the back of her chair. "She wants me to come out and visit her this weekend in Chicago."

Trudy's finger, which she had just coated with frosting and inserted into her mouth, froze between her lips. "You're going, right? Tell me you're not going and I'll whack you on that empty head of yours."

"Trudy!" Marion scolded.

"I am going." Nora sat down. "I'm a little worried about the money, though. I can't even imagine what a plane ticket might cost these days."

Trudy removed her finger from her mouth with a soft sucking sound. "Round trip to Chicago'll cost you about four hundred dollars. Maybe a little more since it's the weekend and you're booking so late. In the long run, Nora, that's not a lot of money. Do it."

Nora glanced away from the older woman, hoping she didn't look as uncomfortable as she felt. Trudy was always bugging her about taking time off or going somewhere on vacation. It wasn't like she hadn't; just last year, after Trudy had nagged her incessantly, she and Alice Walker had rented a car and driven down to the Jersey Shore, where they stayed for two nights at Trudy's beach house. It had been a nice enough trip—the moon especially, which had been a barely visible crescent, had looked magnificent above the water, like an electric eyelash— and one night she had gotten a bucket of soft-shell crabs that she had eaten out on the deck, but being down there had exacerbated her loneliness, too. She'd left with an empty feeling that gnawed at her all the way home, an ache that did not leave for a long time afterward. It was not something she was yearning to do again.

"I'd have to take tomorrow off," she said. "I'm working Saturdays this month, remember?"

"Oh, I think we'll manage," Trudy replied dryly.

"Hot diggety!" Marion broke in. "Not much else can beat a last-minute plane trip!" She tilted her head, a sly look coming across her porcelain features. "Except maybe cake and ice cream for breakfast! You ready?"

"You brought ice cream, too?" Nora sat forward, grateful that Marion had changed the subject. As bullish as Trudy was, Marion could be equally tactful.

"Of course we brought ice cream!" Marion's heels clicked against the linoleum as she started for the freezer. "Whoever heard of eating birthday cake without ice cream?" She grabbed a plastic sack off the top of the microwave on her way back. "And Swedish fish, too! To sprinkle on top!"

Nora grinned. She knew that her addiction to Swedish fish was something that Marion, who rarely, if ever, ate sugar, considered both appalling and endearing.

"And remember." Marion began cutting the cake. "There is no such thing as calories on your birthday." She plopped an enormous section of cake onto a plate and slid it over to Trudy for ice cream. "Of course, you don't have to worry about things like calories for at least another ten years. Forty is when it really starts to go to hell. And then fifty, well, you may as well just go ahead and burn every girdle you've ever bought, since the only thing they manage to do is leave unsightly indentations around your middle." She patted the front of her skirt gently, as if forgiving her body for such a thing anyway.

"Speak for yourself." Trudy slid her finger down the side of the cake and winked at Nora. "You got any plans for tonight?"

Nora averted her eyes. "No, not really."

"Nothing at all?" Marion repeated kindly. She stuck a single gummy fish in the middle of Nora's slice of cake, and then sprinkled a handful of them around the edges, as if they were swimming.

Nora smiled, trying to hide her embarrassment. "You both know Alice Walker would be offended if I left her alone on my birthday. We'll get some steaks and hang out." She toed the leg of the table with her shoe, knowing how lame this sounded, but the truth was that an evening alone with her dog did not make her want to jump off a bridge anymore. There had been a time, maybe even as recently as a few years ago, when the idea of such a thing created such feelings of dread that she found herself staying late at the library to avoid going home, but not anymore. She'd gotten used to keeping herself company. And Alice Walker, who Nora could swear had been a therapist in a past life, always knew just when to climb up on the couch next to her and rest her head in her lap. No, buying a steak dinner and sharing it with her dog tonight would be just fine.

Trudy, however, did not seem to agree. Nora pursed her lips as the older woman began shaking her head across the table.

"Marion and I would be more than happy to take you to dinner tonight—just the three of us—but why don't you come with us to our salsa class instead? There's lots of young people there; you never know."

Trudy had a variation of invites that she peppered Nora with, but the silent, underlying purpose behind them was always the same: *It's not healthy for a young woman like you to spend so much time alone. You need girlfriends, Nora. Women your own age you can cook with and drink wine with and go to the movies with. Girls you can gossip about sex and love with and bare your darkest secrets to, and know that afterward, they will love you just as much, if not more.*

What Trudy didn't know was that Nora had had all that. She'd had it in spades actually, friendships that had made her feel invincible, whole, complete in a way that defied completeness. And since it had disappeared, she had never had the heart to go out and look for it again. It had been too hard to lose the first time.

She stood up. She wasn't about to get into any of this now. "No, thanks. But listen, thank you for my—"

"Oh, sit *down*." Trudy put her fork down and, with a great display of irritation, reached under the table and withdrew a box wrapped in light blue tissue paper. "For you," she said, sliding it in Nora's direction. "Happy birthday, kid."

Nora sat back down, touching the side of the small box as Marion clapped her hands. "You didn't have to get me anything," she said. "Jeez, the cake was enough." She pulled the tissue off and stared at the cube-shaped box. *Randall's Jewelry* was etched across the top in gilded letters. She looked back up at the women, bewildered.

"Just open the damn box," Trudy said. "And before you get all weird about it, *yes,* it was expensive. But this is what we wanted to do. Besides, Marion and I like to spend our money, not hoard it like some people we know." She raised a thatch of eyebrow. "Don't we, Marion?"

Marion reached out and patted Trudy's hand. "Be kind, dear."

Nora opened the box—and then inhaled at the silver link bracelet nestled in a sea of dark velvet. In the middle of the links was a thick crescent moon, the edges tipped and shadowed in a dark gray. The word *Nora* had been inscribed along the outside curve, a tiny sapphire chip dotting the top of the capital *N*.

"Do you like it?" Marion leaned forward, her forehead furrowed. "We weren't really sure . . ."

"It was her idea," Trudy said, jerking her head toward Marion. A blue butterfly barrette quivered in her hair. "She thought it would be cute and all, 'cause you're always talking about the moon. I have the receipt if you want to exchange it."

Nora shook her head, struggling to retrieve her voice. "I love it. It's beautiful. Thank you."

"Really?" Marion asked. "You're sure?"

"I'm sure." It was hard to get the words out around the mound in the back of her throat. They were so good to her, these women, and had been for so many years. So loving. So attentive. Even if they did feel sorry for her.

She held out her wrist so that Marion could fasten the clasp, and then leaned back, stroking it with a fingertip. "I love it," she said, looking back up at the women. "I really do. Thank you so much."

"You're welcome." Trudy stood up, brushing crumbs off the front of her zippered cardigan sweater. "And now that *that's* over, it's time to get to work."

Chapter 3

Although she had never done it before, booking a plane ticket online was not nearly as difficult as Nora thought it might be. Nora had been on a plane exactly once in her life, when her mother had flown the two of them to Florida to attend her grandfather's funeral. She had only been four years old at the time, and she did not remember much about the funeral or the plane ride. Trudy, however, found her a last-minute deal on some obscure travel website, which shaved fifty dollars off the final price, and had offered to take care of Alice Walker while Nora was gone so that she would not have to pay for a kennel.

"You do want me to come back, don't you?" Nora asked as they locked up the library later that evening.

Trudy laughed. "Only if you promise to go again."

It was dusk when Nora started back home. The sky was awash in a sea of periwinkle, and the moon was brightly visible. She had been too preoccupied with things today to look for a new first line in any of the books she had to shelve, but one came to her now as she gazed up at the sky: *"It was a bright cold day in April, and the clocks were striking thirteen."* She remembered the chill that had descended over her the first time she read that line from George Orwell's book and how a similar sensation—like small, frozen fingertips—tiptoed over the top of her head and down the back of her neck as she thought of the weekend ahead. *Anything could happen,* she thought. *Anything at all.*

She still had to pack and get Alice Walker over to Trudy's, and then call a taxi service to come pick her up in the morning so that she could get to the airport, but right now she needed to walk. She grabbed a handful of Swedish fish, clipped on Alice Walker's leash, and headed toward the east part of town, over a mile away, until she got to Wisconsin Avenue. It was located on the outskirts of one of the more ragged sections of Willow Grove, and the street stuck out from the highway like a dislocated arm. Her head started to pound as she made a left onto Magnolia and stood on the sidewalk opposite the old building, just like it did every time she came down here.

Ozzie would never believe it if she saw what it looked like now, Nora thought; how Turning Winds had transformed over the years from a stately yellow Victorian house with a snake of red ivy crawling up one side into a pale, sagging structure. The wide wraparound porch they used to sit on, Ozzie's legs dangling over the side, skimming the tops of the rhododendron bushes beneath, had almost rotted away to nothing. When Monica had gone through her "I'd rather die than be fat" stage, she used to hook her toes under the railings and do sit-ups until she couldn't breathe. Now the porch floor had sunk to the ground and the railing spindles, formerly delicate white arms, had collapsed into jagged stumps. Behind the house, the grass was waist-high, but back then it had been a lawn, neatly trimmed around the edges and flanking the east side of the river. Nora walked around to one side of the house. She stared past the weeds, tall as grown men, until she could see Grace and herself that last week, before everything happened.

They'd walked to one of their favorite spots, a place where the ground dipped down into a wide sort of basin and three birch trees, their trunks wide as flagpoles, draped the surrounding area in shade. It was a particular spot where Grace liked to sit and draw. A forgotten section of railroad tracks sat less than a stone's throw away, obscured by tufts of weeds, and the bank itself, which sloped toward the water, was sprinkled with blue cornflowers. Nora thought there were more attractive places—just a hundred feet behind them was an entire field full of black-eyed Susans and Queen Anne's lace—but Grace always insisted that the light in this particular spot was perfect. Whole, she called it. Untainted.

The weather had been gauzy-warm, a breeze soft as cotton breathing over everything. Grace was looking at a book of photography, flipping the glossy pages slowly as she examined each face, every picture with a studied intensity. A large sketch pad, which she brought with her everywhere, lay next to her, along with a variety of charcoal pens. She had rolled up the sleeves of her T-shirt, exposing her bony arms, and a lone pencil stuck out from the bun in her hair.

Nora lay next to her, one arm draped over her face to avoid the glare of the sun, the hand of the other arm dipping intermittently into a bag of sunflower seeds. She was reading *Their Eyes Were Watching God* by Zora Neale Hurston, hooked by the stunning first line: *"Ships at a distance have every man's wish on board."* It was already in her notebook.

"Do you think people who die can still feel love?" Grace asked, turning from her book to look at Nora.

Nora cracked a sunflower shell between her teeth. "Yeah, I guess." She was at a good part in the book where the main character—a girl named Antoinette—was about to meet the man she was supposed to marry.

"No, really." Grace's hair, which was the color of corn silk, curled in wisps around the side of her face, and there were dark circles under her eyes. Her bare legs, thin as pins, were crossed at the ankles. "You know, some people think that if we can't get into heaven when we die, our spirits just sort of drift in and out of the universe. Do you think those spirits can feel things? Like love?"

"Uh-huh." Nora kept reading. Grace talked this way a lot—she loved ethereal things like heaven and hell and beauty and God, things, Nora assumed, that must have been passed down by her mother. She kept a picture of the Blessed Virgin Mary under her pillow, a glossy rectangular head shot of a lovely dark-skinned woman with a blue mantle over her head, downcast eyes, and lips the color of an overripe peach—something she had never explained to Nora, and about which Nora had never asked.

"Are you even listening to me?" Grace poked Nora in the ribs.

Nora put the book down and stared at the river. The water was a gunmetal gray for some reason, dark and foreboding despite the sunlight. In one more week, her best friends in the entire world were going to leave Willow Grove forever. Talking had become difficult again. Talking about the future—nearly impossible. "Say it one more time," she said.

Grace sat up and pulled a piece of grass out of the lawn. "Do you think spirits or souls—after we die—can feel things like love?"

Nora thought about this for a moment, hoping it wasn't a trick question. "Maybe," she said.

Grace tipped forward a little as Nora spoke, as if she had been waiting for the answer to tumble like a crumb from her lips. "Maybe?" she repeated.

It was then that Nora understood that Grace was talking about the abortion. Nora didn't know too many of the details other than the few Grace had given them a few days before: it would happen on Wednesday, which was three days from now, and it would be as uncomplicated as taking a vitamin. Grace's boyfriend, Max, who was a sophomore at the university across town, had already obtained some kind of pill called Cytotec, which would make the uterus empty itself of what they had calculated to be a six-week pregnancy. Or at least that was how Grace had described it to them. Max, who was studying premed, said it was going to be a simple miscarriage of unwanted tissue, nothing more. He'd slashed open a medical textbook in his dorm room one night and directed them to look.

"There," he said, pointing to something that resembled a pink lima bean nestled inside a soft blob of tissue. "That's all it is right now. It's nothing. It's not living, it's not breathing; it's not even human." Nora, who was squeezed tightly between Grace and Monica, leaned in past them, peering closely at the image. She thought it looked more like a comma than a lima bean, but she didn't say so. Her eyes drifted to the bedspread alongside the book instead, the dark blue, rumpled material under which Grace had been entwined with Max for months now. What was he like in bed? she wondered. Did the things he did to Grace make her moan? Cry? And what kind of thoughts, after all of them would leave his room again and head back to Turning Winds, did Max himself have about the abortion?

"How long will it all take?" Grace asked.

"An hour," Max answered. "Two, tops. It'll be like a really heavy period. And then it'll be over." Nora snuck a look in Grace's direction. Her mouth was twisted into a painful scowl and she looked pale. Nora already knew that Grace's strict Catholic up-bringing made it impossible for her to believe that any of it was going to be as simple as Max was making it out to be. Grace was pretty sure the whole thing was going to be the equivalent of committing murder.

Nora herself hadn't given the abortion too much thought after the decision had been made, although every so often, after the sound of Grace's faint snoring drifted through the bedroom at night, her mind would wander. There was no reason to doubt him, but she hoped Max knew what he was talking about. He was ranked third academically in his class, but he was still just a college sophomore. Medical school wasn't even on the virtual horizon yet. What if there was something he missed? Something he didn't—or couldn't—know yet? It was frightening to think about.

"Listen," Nora said now, putting her hand on Grace's arm. Fifty feet away, the river roared, the black water churning like a washing machine. "You're starting to overthink things. Don't go there, all right?"

Grace's face darkened. "Don't go there?" she repeated. "Don't *go* there? It's too late, Nora. The pills are in my sock drawer. I'm already there, okay?"

"I just . . ." Nora fumbled for the words she should have said earlier. "All I meant is that it'll be okay. Max looked into everything, and it'll all work out. Really. It'll be fine."

Grace had looked away, staring off at some invisible point in the distance. Nora was sure she didn't believe her, but that had been the end of their conversation.

They had never—not once—spoken of it again.

Now, as Nora stood there staring at the old house, she wished with all her heart that she could go back.

"Yes," she would have said this time, even if she still hadn't believed it, even if she hadn't really known the answer for sure, "yes, Grace, I think dead people can definitely feel love."

Chapter 4

There was a litany of things for Nora to worry about as she sat on the plane the next morning: Alice Walker for one, who would probably never forgive her for leaving for two whole days, who would pretend not to know Nora upon her return, lifting her nose in that snooty-dog way she did sometimes when Nora accidentally ran out of her favorite food. Then there was the cost of the plane ticket, which Trudy had sworn was a steal, but because of hidden costs had actually ended up costing a small fortune. The last time Nora had spent a similar chunk of money was two years ago, when she had purchased a new sofa at Burlington Furniture. It had been a necessity—her old one had gotten so threadbare that Tom (who she had been dating at the time) had come over one evening for dinner and gotten stabbed by a small wire when he sat down—but she had tossed and turned over the purchase nevertheless. She didn't like to spend money. Especially on herself. It made her anxious.

Then there was the whole ordeal about what to wear, which had completely thrown her for a loop. She stood in front of her closet for a full twenty minutes after getting out of the shower, feeling slightly dumbfounded. Nora never fretted about her appearance. Ever. She dressed for work exactly the way she ate—grabbing whatever was closest. Trudy did not have any rules about what they wore to work, which meant that she could indulge in her usual assortment of jeans or khaki pants, a soft long-sleeved T-shirt, and sneakers. Nora had a collection of sneakers that rivaled that of any professional sports player. It was her only indulgence, born out of her necessity to walk, and she took great pleasure in adding to it. To date, she had eighteen pairs, each one labeled and stacked in its original box in her closet.

And yet she'd paused this morning. More than paused. She'd worried. Were her clothes too frumpy? The sneakers too weird? Did she look like one of those stereotypical librarians, whose idea of fashion included forty-two cardigan sweater sets in different colors? She'd settled finally on a black turtleneck, pressed khaki pants, her brand-new gray-and-orange Sauconys that still smelled like wet leather, and the brown barn jacket she wore everywhere. It had a soft corduroy collar, tortoiseshell buttons, and deep pockets. She brushed her brown hair back until it fell in its natural middle part and tucked the ends under with her round brush. A bit of Vaseline on her eyelashes to make them shine, a slick of lip balm, and a spritz of the overly floral perfume Marion had bought her last year for Christmas completed the picture. A final glance in the mirror was not reassuring, especially since a small pimple was just starting to bloom in the middle of her chin, and the faint, C-shaped scar on her forehead, which stood out like a careless scribble mark on her otherwise unremarkable face, seemed to glare at her. But it would have to do.

Now she was settled in the coach section of the plane, squeezed in between an elderly man with a tweed cap pulled down low over his forehead and an enormous woman dressed all in purple. The woman was fingering a plastic sack of peanuts, and the man smelled like old tobacco. Nora turned her head and held her breath. Pungent smells were a surefire way to get her sick in any sort of moving vehicle. She grabbed the white paper bag stuck in the pocket of the airplane seat ahead of her and tucked it in between the seats as the wheels of the plane began to move.

"You get airsick?" The large woman in purple eyed Nora's barf bag as the plane started to move. A black hair stuck out of her chin like an exposed root.

Nora shook her head. Crossing her arms over the front of her chest, she slid down into the seat, tucked her head down low, and closed her eyes. If she could just disappear, she thought—just for a little while—maybe she could make it through. The plane rumbled and lifted, and for three, four, five seconds, Nora's stomach felt weightless.

Grace didn't talk for two days when Nora was first assigned a room with her at Turning Winds. This was fine with Nora. She herself was still in the throes of her own self-imposed silence, and she dreaded the annoyed looks she knew she would get once everyone found out she wasn't a fan of speaking. Grace seemed to be in a state of her own; she stayed in her bed most of the day, curled up like an underfed cat against two purple pillows, drifting in and out of sleep. Her tangle of blond hair framed her face like an angel's, and she had wide, sapphire-blue eyes fringed with dark lashes. Every once in a while, she would lift her arm and examine the inside of her wrist, as if she were preparing to do surgery. Then she would drop it again and sigh. Nora was reading *Swann's Way* by Marcel Proust, intrigued by the first line: *"For a long time, I went to bed early,"* but she was having a difficult time getting through the rest. It was dull and too dense to sustain her attention. She kept her head down and reread the same sentence a third time, trying to convince herself to continue.

"I'm not staying here, you know." It was early evening on the third day when Grace finally decided to speak. Nora looked up, relieved at having been interrupted and curious to hear what this strange girl had to say.

"My mother's at a hospital," Grace said by way of explanation. "But it's totally temporary. She's coming back in, like, a month, and then we're going home." Her arms were wrapped around the purple pillows, her fingers clutching the edges the way a child might hold a favorite doll.

Nora blinked.

Grace waited.

Nora pressed her lips together.

"You don't talk?"

She looked back down at her book, shook her head.

"Why not?"

Nora shrugged.

Grace rolled her eyes. "Great."

The door banged open then, startling both of them. Ozzie strolled in, glancing around the room with quick, eager eyes. Nora had seen this girl at nightly dinner—a requirement for all of them living at Turning Winds—noting how she always sat at the head of the table and directed the conversation. Nora hadn't dared meet her eyes. Now she couldn't take them off her. Ozzie was a picture of nonchalant authority, arms crossed over the front of her denim jacket, long legs encased in a pair of dark brown corduroy pants and heavy black boots. A red cap sat atop her head, trapping all but a few wisps of black hair beneath it, and her ears were pierced with tiny gold hoops. She was pretty, but in a hard sort of way, with deep-set eyes and an angular chin, as if someone might have to take a chisel to get to the soft stuff underneath.

"Hey." Ozzie walked over to Nora and stuck out her hand. "Ozzie Randol. I've been meaning to give you a formal introduction since you got here, but I haven't had the chance 'til now."

"Ex*cuse* me." Grace had raised herself from her mattress and was eyeing Ozzie with an indignant gaze. "Have you ever heard of *knocking*? This is our room, you know."

Ozzie leveled a gaze at Grace and then turned and walked back over to the door, where a chubby pale-faced girl lingered, picking at the edge of the doorjamb with a thumb. Nora had seen this girl before too, hanging around the outside of Ozzie's door, or occasionally sitting on the wicker rocking chair on the front porch, leafing through an old, worn copy of *Madeline* that someone said she'd brought from home. Now, dressed in sneakers and an ill-fitting blue sweat suit, Nora thought the girl looked a bit like a bruised marshmallow. Her orangey hair, braided and secured with rubber bands, hung like tails over her shoulders, and her cheeks were as smooth as a baby's bottom.

Without taking her eyes off Grace, Ozzie knocked once on the back of the door. Twice. And then a third time, with great deliberation. "Better?"

Grace slit her eyes as Ozzie walked back across the room.

Nora suppressed a small smile.

"That's Monica," Ozzie said, jerking her thumb in the marshmallow's direction. "She came last year, two days after me. We're roommates."

"Nice to meet you," Monica said, taking a few steps into the room. Her teeth were too widely spaced, and there was a large bump on the ridge of her nose. "What's your name?"

Nora reached around for the little notepad she kept in her back pocket at all times. It had a blue unicorn on the front and was full of lined paper. "Nora," she scribbled.

"Nora," Ozzie read aloud. Her eyes flicked from the paper back up to Nora. "You don't talk?"

Nora shook her head.

"Why not?" Monica asked.

Nora stared at her the way she always did whenever someone asked her a dumb question. After a few seconds, Monica looked away again.

"Nothing wrong with not talking," Ozzie said. "Shit, I know about a dozen people who should keep their mouths shut at all times."

"Is one of them you?" Grace shot from the bed.

"Depends on who you ask," Ozzie replied without turning around. She settled an arm on top of Grace's dresser, studying Nora for a moment. "So when did you get here? Monday, right?"

Nora nodded. Today was Wednesday. The last two days had disappeared in a blur, consumed with curious stares, endless questions (all of which Nora had answered with a nod or a shake of her head), and forms to be signed. She was glad that part of things was over.

"That's what I thought." Ozzie glanced at the top of the dresser and picked up a tiny figurine a few inches from her elbow. "I thought I saw—"

"*Hey!*" Grace's voice was sharp. "You put that down!"

Ozzie eyed Grace the way someone might regard a rabid animal. "Who *is* it?" she asked.

"The Blessed Virgin Mary," Grace said. "And it's private property. Don't you touch it again."

"The Blessed Virgin Mary?" Ozzie put the statue back. "Who's that?"

Grace's face paled. "Jesus's *mother*?"

Ozzie laughed. "I'm just fucking with you. I know who she is." She raised an eyebrow. "You're Catholic?"

"No," Grace retorted. "I keep a statue of the Blessed Virgin on my dresser because I'm an atheist."

The left side of Ozzie's mouth lifted into a smile, and then she shrugged, as if determining that the ensuing argument was not worth it. She sat down on Nora's bed instead. "So," she said, "Monsie and I always come in and check out the new goods. Ask a couple questions, try and get the lowdown, see what the deal is."

"Could you just leave?" Grace followed her with hateful eyes. "You're really not welcome here."

"Oh my God. Chill. *Out.*" Ozzie leaned back on her elbows and placed the heel of one foot atop the toe of the other. "You've had your panties in a bunch ever since you got here, you know that?"

Grace sat up a little straighter. "What's that supposed to mean?"

"All you do is snarl at people. You give these snotty, one-word answers when we talk at dinner and—"

"When *we* talk?" Grace burst out. "How about when *you* talk? All you do is hog the conversation! No one else *can* talk at dinner."

Ozzie shrugged. "Monica talks at dinner. Ella talks at dinner. Samantha and D'Shawn and Roberta all talk at dinner." She kept her gaze fastened in Grace's direction, tipping her stacked feet in one direction, then the other. Nora still wasn't sure which name belonged to the other four girls in the house, but she had to agree with Ozzie. They had all (except for her, of course) contributed to at least one dinner conversation over the past few days, mostly to tell the others where they were from, what ages they were (almost everyone was in high school; the youngest, Ella, was in eighth grade), and how long they'd been at Turning Winds. D'Shawn, who smoked an endless stream of Newports despite the fact that she was seven months pregnant, had just told everyone yesterday that she'd arrived here when she was twelve. Now, at eighteen, she had only a few months left before she had to leave. She was going to move in with her boyfriend, Frederick, and his mother, who was crocheting a blanket for the baby. D'Shawn's eyes had flashed when she relayed this last bit of information, and Nora couldn't help but wonder what it was about Frederick's mother that had conjured such a look. Whatever it was, she was pretty sure D'Shawn was not going to have an easy time of it.

"Oh please," Grace retorted. "You fire so many questions at them that they don't even know where to start. I wouldn't call that talking."

"At least they answer," Ozzie said. "You just sit there like a prima donna. 'Yes, no, I don't know.' You think you're too good to be part of the discussion?"

"Seriously?" Grace rolled her eyes. "Just leave, okay? Please. Just *leave*."

"I will." Ozzie turned her attention toward Nora. "After I ask the new girl a few questions."

"Well, she doesn't talk." Grace rolled over on her bed so that she was facing the wall. "So good luck with that one."

Ozzie grinned and raised an eyebrow. "But you can write in your little notebook there if you want to answer, can't you?"

Nora nodded.

"Okay, then. I just have two questions. First, do you know what your name means?"

Nora shook her head, puzzled.

"I don't know either." Ozzie looked aggravated. "Usually I know. I know a lot of names' meanings. Like Grace. Grace means 'love.' Monica means 'advisor.' Ella means 'little girl.' Nora, though." She shook her head. "I haven't come across a Nora yet."

Nora bit the inside of her cheek. She felt uncomfortable, as if she had just failed at something she hadn't known she was being tested for.

"Is it just Nora?" Ozzie pressed. "Or is Nora short for something else?"

"Just Nora," she wrote on the pad.

"Yeah, Ozzie's not short for anything, either. Actually, I think my mother may have mistaken me for a pet when I was born." She grinned, a gesture so forgiving of whatever her mother had put her through that Nora just stared. "Okay, second question," Ozzie said. "You get to see her at all? Your mother, I mean?"

Nora shook her head. She hadn't seen Mama since she was twelve years old, after Mama had walked into the kitchen and seen Daddy Ray, her second husband, with his arms around her daughter. Nora had been frozen stiff, eyes shut tight as the syrupy smell of rum drifted out of his mouth, and his dry lips moved along the swell of her neck—*quietquietquietandthenitwillbe over*—but Mama had blamed her anyway. This time, though, she had thrown the remote control so hard at her that Nora's forehead had split open like a peach. When Nora's seventh grade teacher asked her the next day what had happened, Nora told her. It was the last time she remembered talking. She'd been in and out of foster homes since then until three days ago, when a spot in Turning Winds had opened up.

"How about supervised visitation?" Ozzie pressed.

Nora shook her head again, biting her lip until she tasted blood. Mama hadn't wanted visits. None. She'd been firm about that.

"What about Christmas?" Grace turned over suddenly, looking at Nora from the bed. "Or your birthday?"

The edges of Nora's ears had gotten so hot that she was sure everyone in the room was staring at them. She knew it was unusual for a parent to drop completely out of sight like this; most of the other girls she'd run into over the years had, at the very least, been permitted supervised visits, usually hanging out with their mothers and fathers in a large room at the Children and Youth building while a caseworker sat nearby and watched. To be forgotten completely was a rarity as well as a hidden source of shame, another reminder of her unworthiness. But she picked up her notepad anyway. "It's better for all of us if we don't."

"What about your dad?" Ozzie pressed.

"Never met him," Nora wrote.

"Stepparents?" Ozzie's eyes widened.

"No one." Nora underlined the words twice.

"Yes!" Ozzie punched the air with both fists. "Finally! Someone in the house who can be part of our group!" She reached out and slugged Nora gently in the upper arm. "Congratulations!"

Nora's forehead furrowed.

"No visits for Monica and me, either," Ozzie explained, tapping her fingertips against the front of her chest. "At least not until we're eighteen." She slid a knowing look in Monica's direction. "And you can believe when we're eighteen, we're gonna go get our visits. Oh yeah. We're gonna have some accountability questions to ask those motherfuckers on *our* visit."

Nora blinked. Maybe Ozzie wasn't all light and forgiveness, after all.

Ozzie swung her head over in Grace's direction. "Grace over there doesn't get any visits either, but she's too good to join our group. Aren't you, Gracie?"

"Don't call me Gracie," Grace said. "And I don't get any visits because I'm just here temporarily. I don't *need* visits. I'm only going to be here for another month."

Ozzie regarded Grace for a moment and then dropped her eyes. "You could still join for a little while."

Grace picked at the skin around her thumb. "I don't like being anyone's third wheel."

"Well, now that Nora qualifies, you won't be," Ozzie said. "It's just us four. Which means no third wheel and no more excuses."

Grace looked over at Nora and scowled. "If she wants to join, maybe I'll think about it."

"What am I joining?" Nora wrote in her notebook.

Ozzie reached over and put a long arm around Nora's shoulders. "Our secret posse, Norster. It's hard to get in, and it's a privilege to stay. So far, it's only been Monsie and me. We have a meeting once a month. Upstairs, in our secret place. Tomorrow night is this month's meeting. It's gonna be great. Once you become part of us, your life will never be the same again."

Nora hoped the electric exhilaration coursing through her wasn't too apparent; there was nothing worse than coming across as overeager. Or desperate, which was really pathetic. But she had never been asked to be a part of something before: Mama and Daddy Ray had always lived in their own world, deliberately apart from her; each of her three different foster families had all but ignored her after realizing she wasn't going to talk; and so far, there was no one she had even considered wanting to get to know at school. This was the biggest thing that had ever happened to her. This was everything. She glanced over at Grace, hoping she would say something first, but Grace seemed to be enthralled with the inside of her wrist again.

"Few ground rules before you decide if you want to join," Ozzie said. "You have to bring a stick and something of your own to every meeting."

"A stick?" Grace looked up. "Like from a tree?"

"Yes," Ozzie said. "A stick from a tree, Grace."

Grace slit her eyes again. "What do we need a stick for?"

"You want to be part of the group?" Ozzie stood up and put her hands on her hips. The edges of her fingernails were threaded with dried blood.

"Maybe." Grace tossed her head. "I haven't decided yet."

"Then bring a stick." Ozzie headed for the door. "And something of your own. It should be something that shows off a talent of yours."

"What kind of talent?" Nora wrote.

"Whatever you want," Ozzie answered. "Monica's a really good cook, so she always makes a snack."

"I'm thinking something with chocolate for tomorrow." Monica blushed.

"And I'm a good joke teller," Ozzie continued, "so I always start with three great jokes. It can be anything. As long as it's yours and nobody else's."

Nora stared at Grace one last time. She wondered what Grace had that nobody else in this room did. She already knew what she would bring. It was all she had.

She lifted her pencil one last time. "Okay," she wrote. "I'm in."

"Great." Ozzie grinned and looked over at Grace. "What about you, Queenie?"

"Oh." Grace leaned back, letting her head fall between her shoulder blades. "I don't know."

"Don't strain yourself," Ozzie said.

Grace lifted her head again, perusing the group of them with her blue eyes. "All right," she said slowly. "I guess I'm in, too."

Nora didn't panic as she followed Ozzie's slow ascension through what looked like a chimney in the attic of Turning Winds the following night; despite the narrowness of it and the fact that it smelled like a dirty diaper, she already trusted Ozzie for a reason she could not put her finger on, and she knew—she could feel it in her bones—that she wanted to go wherever this girl was going to take her now.

"Almost there," Ozzie said over her shoulder. "Hold your breath until we get all the way through. It stinks." Nora nodded. She wished Ozzie would keep her voice down. It was after midnight and the other four girls in the house were asleep, but God only knew what would happen if one of them woke up. Then there was Elaine, who worked the night shift at Turning Winds, drowsing downstairs in front of another episode of *The Twilight Zone*. Elaine was large and thick, like a tree, and she wore loud T-shirts with sayings on the front like KEEP TALKING; I'M RELOADING. An apple tattoo with an arrow shot through the middle of it adorned her upper arm, and she drew in her eyebrows with a black pencil. Since they were in school for most of the day, Elaine was the one who had the most contact with the girls, but it was quick and brusque, as if she did not want to get to know them very well. "I'm not here to be your friend or your mother," she'd told Nora the first day she'd arrived. "My job is just to make sure you stay out of trouble." Nora hadn't been too sure what kind of trouble she was referring to, but she would bet money now that climbing to the roof in the middle of the night would qualify.

They emerged all at once into fresh air, and it swept over Nora's face like a salve. She inhaled deeply, mouth, then nose— once, and then again. Monica and Grace were already up there, their backs resting against a wrought iron railing, legs crossed beneath them. Truth be told, there wasn't much room to do much else; the entire enclosed space—which Ozzie informed them was called a widow's walk—was about as large as a throw rug. But they were up high. And my God, Nora thought as she stared up at the moon above them—full and yellow as a soft-boiled egg yolk—was this the first time she had ever really looked at the moon? The light around it was a neon blue, enclosed yet again by a thinner, paler line, a pulsing white heat. If she rose up on her tiptoes, she thought, she might be able to touch it. The first line from the novel *Catch-22* flickered across her brain: *"It was love at first sight."* And it was. Right here, right now, she felt something stir inside her that she hadn't even known was there. She'd never seen anything so beautiful.

Ozzie sat down next to Monica, motioning for Nora to do the same. Nora settled in between Grace and Ozzie, her knees touching theirs on either side. "Everyone here?" Ozzie asked. "Monsie, me, Grace, and Nora." She hesitated, looking at Nora. "That reminds me. I looked up your name last night. It's Greek."

Nora felt something tense inside.

"It means 'light,'" Ozzie said. "Isn't that cool?"

Light. Nora couldn't imagine Mama ever feeling anything close to lightness when it came to her. She'd barely used her name at all, in fact, referring to Nora most of the time as "girl" or "you." Nora turned the word over inside her mouth. Light. She liked the feel of it, small and smooth, like a marble. Or a jewel. Something waiting for just the right moment before it exploded into a million fractured pieces of energy. She nodded, smiling shyly at Ozzie.

"What's your name mean?" Grace asked Ozzie. "I don't think I've ever even heard it before."

Ozzie straightened up. "It's a male name." She surveyed the group with a quick glance, as if daring any one of them to laugh. "It's Hebrew," she went on. "And it means 'strength.'"

Monica nodded in satisfaction. Grace raised her left eyebrow and then lowered it again. Nora grinned. As if the word could mean anything else.

"Okay then," Ozzie said. "Let's start. Rules first." She grabbed a notebook sitting off to the side and handed it to Monica. "You want to read, Monsie?"

Monica pushed her orange bangs out of her face and cleared her throat. The light from the moon cast a soft glow over her face, blurring her pudgy features, softening the scraggly edges of her hair. "Rule number one: Never speak of the group outside of this circle. To anyone. Ever. Rule number two: Members must always bring something of themselves to share at every meeting. Rule number three: Stick wishes are private, unless a member wants to discuss them with the rest of the group. No stick wish—no matter how weird—will be judged. Failure to abide by any said rules can result in immediate dismissal." She looked up. "Okay, that's it."

Grace frowned. "What the heck is a stick wish?"

"Hold your horses, jumpy," Ozzie said. "Those come last. Is there anything anyone wants to add?"

Grace shook her head.

"How about you, Nora?"

Nora hesitated, bringing her fingers to her earlobe. Maybe it wasn't such a good idea to bring something up at the first meeting. Especially if you were new. And you didn't talk.

"Go on," Ozzie urged. "I can tell you want to say something. You're part of the group now. You can tell us."

Nora flicked her eyes at Ozzie and then pulled out her pencil. "What about a name?" she wrote.

Monica and Ozzie exchanged a glance.

"I *told* you," Monica said. "Every group needs a name."

"We talked about this before," Ozzie said. "I think a name for the group is a great idea. It's just—I don't want some dopey, sissy name, you know?"

"I still don't think The Velvet Moondrops is dopey." Monica pouted. She looked at Grace and then at Nora. Both girls dropped their eyes.

"If we pick a name for the group," Ozzie continued, "it has to be a really great one. Strong, you know? Determined. Sure of itself. Like us."

"So if you think of anything . . ." Monica sighed and closed the notebook. "All right, rules are done for now."

"Okay," Ozzie said. "Now we share what we brought. Who wants to go first?"

"Me, of course." Monica grinned, passing around a small plastic container. It was full of the chocolate-dipped pretzels she had made in the community kitchen that afternoon. Nora had smelled the melting chocolate in her room and come down, lured by the rich scent. She sat on one of the countertops, watching Monica dip the pretzels into the chocolate and then dust them with cocoa and crushed candy cane. Now everyone got four apiece. Nora ate three of them and then slipped the last one in her pocket for later.

Ozzie leaned forward as they finished eating. "Okay, I'll go next. I only have two jokes tonight. But they're good ones." She cleared her throat and threw back her shoulders. "So once there was a family who was given some venison by a friend. The wife cooked up the deer steaks and served them to the husband and kids. The husband thought it would be fun to have the kids guess what they were eating.

" 'Is it beef?' their daughter Mandy asked.

" 'Nope.'

" 'Is it pork?' the son AJ asked.

" 'Nope.'

" 'Heck, we don't know, Dad!' AJ exclaimed.

" 'I'll give you a clue,' the dad said. 'It's what your mom sometimes calls me.'

" 'Spit it out, AJ!' cried Mandy. 'We're eating asshole!' "

Ozzie and Monica screamed and fell over, and even Nora smiled wide and then covered her mouth, but Grace sat stoically, arms crossed.

"You didn't think that was funny?" Ozzie asked, righting herself again and staring at Grace. "Seriously?"

"No." Grace bit her bottom lip.

"How?" Ozzie demanded. "How was that not funny?"

"I just don't think parents calling each other names like that in front of their kids is funny." Grace shrugged and looked away. "We have different senses of humor, I guess."

"Oh, for Christ's . . ." Ozzie began, but Monica reached out and tugged at her sleeve. Ozzie took a deep breath. "Okay, whatever. I'm sorry if I offended you." She shook her head as she began rolling up her sleeves and then dropped her arms into her lap. "Well, there's no way I can tell the next joke, then. It's filthy."

Nora waited, wondering if Ozzie would back down first or if it would be Grace. They were sitting across from each other in the circle, with no more than a foot of space between them. "Well, I don't have to tell it," Ozzie said. She shrugged, clearly disappointed. "It's not a big deal. I did my thing." She reached out and poked Nora in the shoe. "How about you go next, Norster?"

Nora stared at her feet. She could feel something hot beneath the planes of her face, a slow spreading of blood under her cheeks. She wanted to read it. She knew it was a good one. She'd spent a long time selecting it last night, poring through her notebook for just this occasion. But she didn't move. What if they laughed? Or thought it was stupid? It wasn't an actual *talent,* like Monica's cooking or Ozzie's joke telling. She was just borrowing someone else's words. They weren't even hers.

Ozzie put a gentle hand on the knee. "Come on. Show us what you brought. We really want to know."

Nora looked up. Ozzie was staring at her with a face so full of encouragement that it made something in the back of her throat hurt. She took out her notebook and handed it to Grace, who read aloud: "I collect really good first lines from novels. For tonight's meeting, I chose the first line from the Prologue of *The Invisible Man* by Ralph Ellison. It goes like this: '*I am an invisible man.*'"

Grace looked up from Nora's notebook. "What does that mean? Is he a ghost?"

Nora looked away, mortified. The book, which revolved around a man the world refused to see, had left her pondering the unseen parts of herself, how there were sides of her that she would never, ever show another human being. Was it possible that such a thing could also be true of Ozzie and Monica and Grace? And if it was, might details eventually emerge among them, bruised flowers held in cupped hands, opening ever so slowly for the rest of them to lean in one day and touch? Could it be the reason for a group in the first place?

Or was she wrong?

Maybe she was wrong. It wouldn't be the first time.

Then Ozzie said, "Shit, I love it! You really collect first lines?"

Nora nodded.

"That is the coolest thing ever!" Ozzie said. "God damn, I wish I had thought of something like that! How many of them do you have?"

Nora's deflated heart began to swell back up, a balloon receiving air again. She took the notebook out of Grace's hand. "Seventy-eight," she wrote.

"Seventy-*eight*?" Ozzie sat back in disbelief. "You've read seventy-eight books?"

"I've read hundreds of books," Nora wrote back. "But I only write down the first lines of the ones I like."

"Fuck," Ozzie said. "That is fucking amazing."

"It really is," Monica said. "I can't imagine getting through one book, let alone hundreds."

"'*I am an invisible man,*'" Ozzie recited. She studied the edge of her shoe for a moment, as if puzzling over something. Then she lifted her head. "How about The Invisibles?" she asked. "For a name? Our name?"

"The Invisibles?" Grace repeated the words as if saying them for the very first time. "I don't get it."

"No, no, it's perfect!" A faint sheen of perspiration gleamed from the edge of Ozzie's hairline, and her eyes were bright. "Think about it. We've been invisible to most people for most of our whole lives."

"Um . . . which totally *sucks*?" Monica interjected.

"Which totally sucks," Ozzie agreed. "*Except*"—she stopped

and pointed her index finger at the whole group—"except that now we have a choice. We can choose to be invisible to everyone." She paused dramatically. "Except each other."

"Ooooh." Monica raised her eyebrows. "I like that."

"Yeah." Grace nodded. "Me too."

Nora closed her eyes as the moment swelled around them.

"The Invisibles!" Ozzie crowed, pulling back again and raising her fist in the air.

"The Invisibles!" Monica and Grace echoed, lifting their arms. Nora raised her hand too and made it into a fist.

Fifty feet below, the sound of crickets thrummed in the dark air. A car trundled past, its headlights glowing a lemony yellow against the side of the house, and then faded again. For a split second, Nora felt as though she were in heaven, or at least somewhere very good, somewhere far away from everything else she had known up to that moment in her life. She squeezed her eyes shut so as not to forget it.

"Okay, Grace's turn," Monica said. "What did you bring?"

Grace reached for a soft satchel sitting nearby. Inside was a rolled-up piece of parchment, which, when she unfurled it, revealed a drawing of a girl sleeping in her bed. Nora sat back at first, alarmed to see such a vivid likeness of herself, and then, as curiosity got the better of her, crept forward again. It *was* her. When had Grace even done such a thing? Nora hadn't seen any paper or pencils anywhere; she'd never observed Grace drawing at all.

"I sketch things," Grace explained. "That's really the only thing I can do. I drew you when you were sleeping," she said, looking apologetically at Nora. No one said anything for a moment.

Grace looked down at her knee, touched a small scab. "That's it, really. I didn't know what else to bring."

"Wow," Monica said. "It looks exactly like her." She pointed to the limp cowlick Grace had drawn at the top of Nora's forehead. "Even the hair. It's like, perfect." She turned to look at Ozzie. "Don't you think?"

Ozzie was staring at the picture too. "It's *really* good." She squinted at Grace, as if looking at her with new eyes. "That's a gift, you know, being able to draw like that. You should really consider doing something with it."

Grace blushed and then looked away.

Ozzie clapped once, as if killing an insect, and the moment was over. "Okay, now we do 'Who Wants What?'"

"Yay," Monica said softly. "My favorite part."

"What's 'Who Wants What?'" Grace asked.

"Exactly what is sounds like," Ozzie said. "We go around the circle, and everyone tells the rest of the group what they want. It can be anything, as long as it's not totally ridiculous, like a million dollars or something. And then, before the next meeting, we'll try to find a way to give it to you."

"I want my mother to come get me," Grace sputtered. "But you can't give me that."

"No," Ozzie concurred. "But maybe we can do something close to that. What is it about your mother that you want?"

"I just want *her*!" Grace insisted. "Here. Right now. I want to hold her and hug her and remember what she smells like and . . ." She drifted off, a catch in her throat.

Ozzie arched an eyebrow. "What does she smell like?"

Nora listened, breathless, as Monica described her mother's

scent: a combination of burnt caramel, fresh-cut grass, and Chanel No. 5 perfume. Somehow, she realized, the rest of them were going to find a way to get that smell, or something very close to it, to Grace before the next full moon rolled around. Her heart felt close to bursting, thinking of contributing such a joy to someone else. It was the most wonderful thing she could imagine, like having Christmas every month.

"How about you, Mons?" Ozzie asked. "What do you want?"

"A hug." Monica shrugged, blushing.

"Again?" Ozzie tilted her head. "You said that last time."

"I want three this time."

"You're too easy," Ozzie said, gathering the girl in her arms and hooking her chin over her shoulder. She held her for a good thirty seconds before letting go again. Grace went next, pulling away quickly and ducking her head to avoid Monica's gaze, and Nora did the same thing, but not without noticing that Monica seemed to whimper a bit as she withdrew herself from her grasp. It was strange how such a simple thing could be loaded with complication; awkward in a way that was full of both need and apology.

"Thank you," Monica said, glancing shyly at all of them.

"How 'bout you, Nora?" Ozzie asked. "Anything you want right now?"

Nora's brain raced. How could such a small question be so difficult to answer? Or was the real question that such a thing had never been asked of her before? Maybe an answer did not even exist. She shrugged, fiddling with a shoelace, her mind a blank.

"Nothing?" Ozzie pressed. "You don't want one single thing right now?"

Nora paused in the middle of a shrug and then picked up her

notebook. "THIS," she wrote in large, capital letters, showing it to the group. Ozzie grinned broadly, and Monica reached across the circle and took her hand, just as Grace pressed a palm against her knee. "You got it," Ozzie said.

"How 'bout you, Oz?" Grace asked as the moment passed. "What do you want?"

"Ugh!" Ozzie threw her head back. "I want so many things! I can't decide!"

"Like what?" Monica urged.

"Well, I totally want to get laid."

Grace rolled her eyes. "You're on your own with that one."

"Okay then," Ozzie said. "I want to take a road trip. A real one. With all of you guys."

"What's a real one?" Monica looked nervous.

"Cross-country," Ozzie said. "Or at least halfway. In a convertible. Blue, with white siding, the top down. Full tank of gas, and a case of beer in the trunk."

"I thought you said these things couldn't be totally ridiculous," Grace said. "None of us even has a driver's license if you hadn't noticed, let alone a car."

"We could always steal one," Ozzie looked at her slyly, laughing as Grace gasped. "I'm kidding, tightwad."

They waited as Nora wrote feverishly in her notebook and then held it up for Ozzie to read. "What is it about the road trip that we could give you now?"

Ozzie sat back and tilted her head up. For a long moment, she looked up into the night, as if studying a specific star. "Freedom," she said finally. "The feeling of being able to go anywhere at all with nothing to worry about, nowhere to be, no one to answer to but myself."

A silence descended on the group. It was a tricky one, for sure. But, Nora decided, she would do everything she could to try to give Ozzie something close to that feeling before the next meeting.

"All right, now comes the most important part." Ozzie stood up, turned around, and held her arms up until it looked as though the moon had settled in between them. "We come up here every month during the full moon because this is the time that her powers are at their fullest."

"Whoa, whoa, wait a minute." Grace paused in the middle of rolling up her parchment paper. "Is this gonna be like some voodoo ceremony? 'Cause I'm one hundred percent Catholic. I believe in Jesus and Mary. I'm not into the whole moon- and planet-worship kind of thing."

"Mary is a symbol of the moon," Ozzie said.

"Mary?" Grace repeated. "As in the Blessed *Virgin* Mary?"

Ozzie nodded. "Haven't you ever seen a picture of her standing on the crescent moon? That's because the moon and Mary both represent the same thing: purity."

Grace's forehead crinkled as she considered this. "Well, I guess it'll be okay, then."

Ozzie cleared her throat and began again. "The Invisibles choose to hold their meetings under the full moon because she is the strongest female force in the universe. She is our first mother. The one who will never let us down, who will stay with us always and forever." She grabbed her stick from out of her back pocket, stood up, and faced the moon again. Her hand moved quickly as she traced the air with her stick. "Tonight we ask her to listen to us, to read the wishes we send her for our future, and to answer them someday when the time is right." Ozzie's hand moved faster and faster as she traced her wish in the sky; for a moment, Nora thought Ozzie was joking, because her wish was so long. But then Ozzie's hand grew limp, and when she turned and faced the rest of them, Nora could see the glimmer of perspiration along the line of her nose. Her lower lip trembled and she sat down quickly.

"Your turn," she said to Monica. Her voice was low, hoarse, shaken.

Monica stood up and wrote her wish out for the moon in stick letters. Grace followed, and then Nora, who stood for a full minute under the orb, just staring at the milky glow it cast on the yard below, how the light of it bathed the steeple tip of Saint Augustine's church in the distance, turning it a silvery blue.

"It can be anything," Ozzie whispered behind her. "Anything at all."

Nora moved forward then and lifted her arm and began to write.

She woke with a start as the plane began to descend. Beneath her, she could feel the wheels of it emerging from the belly, its iron legs stretching and creaking like the heavy branches of trees.

The large woman in purple leaned toward her. "We're here," she said. Her breath smelled like salted peanuts. "You slept through the whole thing."

Nora breathed a sigh of relief. Past the old man, out the window, she could see land again, a line of trees, and sheets of pavement as they came closer and closer into focus.

It was time.

For better or worse, it was time.

Chapter 5

Nora!" The voice, soft and slightly hoarse, emerging from the beautiful woman at the top of the ramp was Monica's, but the face, framed with sharply cut white-blond hair and tight, poreless skin, could not possibly belong to her. "Nora!" Monica rolled up on her tiptoes, waving frantically. "Nora, it's me! Over here!"

Nora stared as Monica began to run, her gait steady and pronounced despite four-inch heels, her rail-thin figure accentuating the sharp planes in her face. She was dressed like one of those women Nora had only seen in magazines: a black knee-length skirt secured with a red patent-leather belt, black alligator pumps, and a crisp white blouse. Her legs were gazelle-like, with keyhole-shaped knees and tiny ankles. A silk scarf, smattered with bits of black and red and blue, had been wrapped twice around her neck, the edges dangling in the front, and a handful of thin gold bracelets clattered around her wrist. "Monica?" Nora whispered.

Monica squealed and grabbed Nora all at once, squeezing so

hard that Nora could feel the breath leave her body. "Oh, Nora! I can't believe it's you! I can't believe you're here!" She exuded an expensive scent: good perfume and exotic shampoo, the kind of things Nora found it silly to spend money on and then, for a split second, wished she didn't. A man behind them cleared his throat. They were still in the middle of the ramp, blocking the rest of the plane traffic. Monica pulled Nora to the side with one hand, giggling as she grabbed her bag with the other. Her nails, a perfect square shape, had been painted shell-pink, and a gold ring set with a dime-sized blue stone adorned her right hand. "Baby doll!" she said, bending her knees so that she could make eye contact. "Look at you! You look so wonderful!"

Nora shook her head, still trying to wrap her head around the fact that this was the same Monica who just yesterday, it seemed, had looked like a marshmallowy Pippi Longstocking. Where had the braided orange hair, fleshy frame, and jack-o'-lantern teeth gone? When had she learned how to apply makeup so expertly, the black eyeliner and mascara making her eyes even bluer than Nora remembered? And her nose . . . Nora reached out and touched it with one finger. "Your nose . . ." she said.

Monica laughed. Her teeth were devoid of the previous spaces, shellacked a shiny white. "I got it done," she said. "I got that horrible bump shaved all the way down. Do you like it?" She turned to one side and threw her shoulders back. "What do you think? My boyfriend, Liam, says it makes me look at least ten years younger. Do you agree?"

Nora studied Monica's new nose again. How could the shape of someone's nose make them look younger? Then again, maybe she was right. Now that it was smaller, Monica's face did have a more delicate look to it. Or was it just that there was less of her now? The entire scenario left her anxious and amazed, all at the same time. "You're so . . . beautiful," she said. "Holy cow, Monica."

Monica laughed again, delighted. "Well, you can buy anything these days. Even looks. You know that."

Nora blinked, her anxiety rising again. How much of the Monica she used to know was gone now, replaced by this new, fake veneer? What else about her had undergone such transformation?

"Ozzie's flight should be here in about an hour." Monica slung a brown alligator bag over one shoulder. A large gold buckle gleamed on the front. "I was just on my way to baggage claim when I saw that your flight had landed, so I scooted on over to see if I could catch you." She squeezed Nora's arm. "I love your outfit. Especially your sneakers. They're great. And so practical! I never dress comfortably for flights, and then I always regret it. My feet are killing me." Her eyes were shining despite the complaint. "Oh my goodness, can you believe we're all going to be together again? After all this time? You, me, Ozzie, and Grace?"

"I know." Nora smiled and nodded.

Monica tucked a wedge of hair behind an ear as they started walking. "We're supposed to refer to Grace as Petal now, did you know that?"

"Yes. Ozzie said something about that."

"She's not even responding to the name Grace anymore, apparently." Monica's line-free face darkened. "God. We probably should've come a lot earlier."

"Well, I didn't know." Nora trotted a little to keep up. "I

mean, I had no idea about anything that was going on with her. Did you?"

"I knew she had a miscarriage," Monica said. "But that was a while ago, a few years after she graduated from art school. She called me one night to tell me about it. She was a wreck. Actually, I think she was drunk. I talked to her for a long time, but I don't think anything really registered. I called a bunch of times after that, but she never returned my calls. I didn't even know she'd finally had a baby."

Nora felt a pang as she listened to Monica speak. Had Grace called Ozzie too over the years? And if so, why had she been excluded? Why hadn't Grace called her?

She followed Monica to the escalator, settling in on the step behind her as the machine made its steady ascent to the second floor. Above them, neon signs advertising coffee and cinnamon buns blinked on and off, and a green Starbucks sign shone like an emerald in the distance. Nora's stomach growled as she realized that she hadn't eaten yet.

"Did you know about the . . ." Nora let her voice drift off, unable to meet Monica's eyes. "What she did, I mean," she finished. "Over the summer?"

Monica stepped off the escalator. She adjusted the brown leather strap over her shoulder and winced before answering. "Ozzie told me when she called. I just . . . I still can't believe it. Why wouldn't she have reached out first?" She looked pained, as if her stomach hurt. "To us, I mean. To any of us?"

"Maybe she didn't think she could," Nora said.

"You really think so?" Monica fiddled with the army of gold bracelets, aligning them just so along her thin wrist. "I know it's been a long time, but Grace of all people had to have known we would have tried to help. I would have dropped everything. Honest to God, I would've. In a heartbeat. Any of us would have."

"Maybe it wouldn't have mattered," Nora said.

Monica's fingers stopped moving over the bracelets. "Of course it would have mattered." Nora could hear the hurt in her voice. "It would have mattered a lot."

"Maybe." Nora looked away, feeling as though she'd just been reprimanded.

"Or maybe you're right," Monica said slowly. She reached down and grabbed Nora's hand. "What do I know anymore?"

Ozzie was already at the baggage claim, hauling an enormous duffel bag off the conveyor belt as Nora and Monica approached. She was in blue jeans and hiking boots and an oversize sweat shirt with the words MY MOM ROCKS! printed on the front. A thin ponytail stuck out of the back of a Red Sox baseball cap, swinging from side to side like a tail. She'd put on some weight around her midsection, and her face looked fuller too, but there was no mistaking those mile-long legs, the insouciant swing in her hips as she moved.

"Ozzie!" Monica screamed and darted ahead, arms out straight in front of her. "Ozzie! Ozzie!"

Ozzie looked up, dropped her duffel bag on the floor, and caught Monica around the waist. She spun her around once and then again. Monica shrieked. Her legs flew out like a propeller, and one of her shoes went spinning across the room. Several people still waiting for their bags looked over and grinned.

"Where'd you come from?" Monica said breathlessly as Ozzie

put her down. "I thought your flight wasn't getting in until ten twenty!"

"Who knows?" Ozzie said. "The flight gods were with us. Or maybe we just got a good tailwind." She held Monica at arm's length, her eyes roving up and down the length of her. "Damn, you look good. Holy shit, Monica. What the hell did you *do*?"

Nora had caught up to them now and stood next to Ozzie's other arm, waiting.

Monica giggled. "You mean what *didn't* I do?"

Ozzie noticed Nora then and put her arm around her, enclosing the three of them in a wide hug. "Norster," she said, pulling her close. "Hi, you."

Somewhere nearby, a faint ringing sounded.

"Oh, my phone!" Monica said, pulling away. "I'm sorry, hold on." She dug inside her purse, and pulled out a white iPhone with gold interlocking *C*s on the back cover. "I have to take this," she said, stepping off to one side and putting the phone to her ear. "One minute, okay?"

Nora had not moved. Ozzie's sweat shirt smelled like a kitchen—macaroni and cheese, beef vegetable soup, maybe even a little bit of baby vomit—and she lingered, as if trying to place it.

"I'm so glad you're here," Ozzie said, kissing Nora hard on top of her head. "I can't even tell you how glad I am that you decided to come."

Nora ducked her head, moving in an inch or so more. Ozzie's arm was strong around her, the way it used to be, the way she wished in that moment it had remained—and would always remain—for the rest of her life.

"How are you, really?" Ozzie stepped back, giving Nora a once-over.

Nora pulled on her earlobe, feeling her face flush. "I'm good," she said.

"Yeah?"

"Yeah."

"Okay." Ozzie grinned, chucking her under the chin. "You look good."

"So do you."

"I got fat," Ozzie said. "My husband calls me Chubbers."

"He does?"

"Sometimes." She laughed. "I've probably put on thirty pounds since high school."

"It doesn't show."

"It's all under here." Ozzie slapped the front of her sweat shirt. "Thank God I still have a decent pair of legs. Otherwise I'd look like a doughnut."

Monica came back over and slid an arm through Ozzie's. Her face had lost some of its previous excitement, as if a lightbulb behind her eyes had been dimmed.

"Everything all right?" Ozzie asked.

"Everything's fine." She looked over at Nora and smiled brightly. "You ready?"

Nora nodded. "Let's go."

Chapter 6

Monica's boyfriend Liam had left one of his cars in the long-term parking lot of the airport the last time he was in Chicago and had told Monica to use it for the trip. It was a dark blue Cadillac Escalade with white leather upholstery and a digital dashboard. So many silver buttons ran the length alongside the CD player that it looked like a keyboard, and the windows were tinted. Nora wondered if she would feel claustrophobic behind the darkness of them, or if the strange-smelling, vacuous space would bring on her nausea.

"Jesus!" Ozzie said, hopping into the backseat. "Who exactly are you dating again, Monica? Jay-Z?"

Monica hesitated for a moment on the driver's side of the car and then got in, settling her alligator bag on the seat next to her. "I already told you his name. Liam Sondquist. Besides, you don't have to be a rock star to have money these days. Liam's just doing what at least ten thousand other businessmen in New York City do."

"What, selling coke?" Ozzie leaned back against the vanilla

upholstery and pretzeled her arms behind her head. Three plum-colored marks, each one the size of a dime, dotted the soft skin just above her left elbow. "No, seriously though. Sondquist. I've heard that name somewhere, haven't I?"

"Probably." Monica was staring at the dashboard with a puzzled expression on her face. "He's pretty well known in New York. He's one of the top hedge fund managers on Wall Street. He takes home about a quarter million just for his monthly allowance."

Nora slid into the front seat next to Monica—and immediately regretted her decision. It was much too wide up here. There was an inordinate amount of room to bounce around in, which would make her stomach go haywire. Maybe she should ask to switch places with Ozzie. She turned around—just in time to hear Monica whisper, "Dammit," next to her.

"What's the matter?" Nora asked.

"I don't know where to put the key." Monica kept her voice low. "There's three different holes up here. They all look the same."

Ozzie's feet clunked against the floor as she sat up. "Monica. Tell me you still don't know how to drive. Or that you haven't gotten your driver's license after all these years."

Monica drew the tip of her index finger along one eyebrow and glanced out her window.

"Monsie!" Ozzie pressed.

"Okay, fine, I still haven't gotten my driver's license." The skin along Monica's neck turned pink.

It had been a big joke back then that Monica was the only one of them who would graduate from high school without a driver's license. Even Nora, who doubted she would ever own a car, had gotten hers in her senior year. For years, Monica had insisted that she had just never felt the need to get it. But Nora knew it was because Monica was afraid to take the driver's test. Monica was a terrible test taker. She had failed almost every test she had ever taken. The fact that she had graduated from high school with all the rest of them had been something of a gift—or a miracle.

"For Christ's sake!" Ozzie looked incredulous. "How do you get around?"

"I live in Manhattan!" Monica said. "I walk everywhere. And if I have to go any kind of real distance, Liam's guy takes me."

"You mean you get chauffeured," Ozzie said, grinning. "Gimme the keys, princess."

Monica smiled apologetically and tossed the keys over her shoulder. Ozzie caught them with one hand and then crawled over the seat. Her hiking boots clunked against the ceiling, dislodging bits of dried mud onto the seat.

"Ozzie!" Monica half laughed, half scolded as she pushed her way out of the driver's door. "God, we're not kids anymore. You're a mother now! Use the door!"

"You think I don't crawl around like this at home?" Ozzie asked. "Please. I'm on my hands and knees every day, picking up baby shit or crayons or something. I'm an expert."

The ease with which Ozzie fell into conversation with them filled Nora with a warm, sleepy feeling. The first time she'd ever remembered having that feeling was when she'd stayed late after school to make up a test. Afterward, she had come back to Turning Winds and found the three of them in the kitchen. Ozzie was sitting on the table, her feet resting on one of the chairs, fiddling with a Rubik's cube. Grace was balanced on the edge of the counter, picking at the edges of a pan of lasagna, and Monica was standing in front of the refrigerator, her free arm resting on the open door. They were laughing at something Nora had come in too late to hear. But she stood there anyway, listening to the music of their voices rising and then settling in the way she had come to know so well, and she had felt a swell of emotion that she could not name. Later in bed, she realized that it had been something as close to home as she had ever felt. Now, listening to Ozzie, she felt a glimmer of that feeling again.

Ozzie shot out of the garage, tires squealing, and then came to an abrupt halt at the stop sign on the corner. She looked over at Nora as she gripped the seat rest with one hand and pressed her fingertips against her mouth with the other. "Oh shit, I forgot you get carsick!" Ozzie reached out, her eyes wide, and touched Nora's elbow. "Don't worry, babe. I'll go slow." She eased the car out onto the highway and settled in among the traffic. "Okay, this isn't a real long ride. Henry gave me the directions. We should be there in about thirty minutes if I don't get us lost."

"Use the GPS," Monica said. "It'll tell you exactly how to get there."

"You'll have to set it up," Ozzie replied, swiveling around in her seat. "My husband's got one of those things in his truck, but I've never used it."

Nora grabbed Ozzie's arm as a tractor-trailer sailed past on the left. "Ozzie," she said. "*Please.*"

"I got it." Ozzie turned back around. "It's all good, Norster. Don't worry."

"Here, gimme that little black thing on the dashboard, Nora," Monica said. "It snaps off, right at the base." She turned to Ozzie. "How is it that you've never used a GPS?"

Nora handed the instrument over the seat and sat back to listen.

"I live on a farm," Ozzie said. "If I want to get somewhere, I ride my motorcycle."

"You have a motorcycle?" Nora wasn't sure why this detail surprised her. "Really?"

"Damn straight." Ozzie clenched her jaw as she pressed down hard on the gas. "A vintage Harley-Davidson. I've got to keep something of my former life."

Her former life. She was referring to a part of her life after Turning Winds. Another part Nora didn't know about. Couldn't possibly know about since Ozzie hadn't stayed in touch.

"Where'd you get it?" Nora asked.

"New Mexico."

"New Mexico?" Nora was impressed. "When were you in New Mexico?"

"Oh, I dated this guy for a few years who loved to do road trips," Ozzie said. "We crossed the country twice on his motorcycle."

"Oh, you got your road trip!" Monica said fondly. "Remember how you always wanted to do that?"

"I wanted to do one with *you* guys," Ozzie corrected. "It's a whole different story going on a road trip with someone you're sleeping with. I can't tell you how many times I ended up with dirt and grass in my mouth."

"Ozzie!" Monica looked up, laughing.

"It's true." Ozzie shrugged. "Anyway, I got sick of riding behind him all the time, and he never let me drive the damn thing, and one afternoon, when we were cruising through New Mexico,

I saw this little red beauty propped up on the porch of an adobe house with a FOR SALE sign strung across the handlebars. I told Cesar to pull over, and the rest is history."

"*Cesar?*" Monica echoed from the back.

"Yeah," Ozzie said. "That was his name."

"Was he Latino?"

"Argentinian."

"Mmmm . . . ," Monica said. "Yum."

"You remember the road trip we tried to give you?" Nora asked, turning from the window. "Or the feeling of one, at least?"

"Never forget it," Ozzie said, rearranging her hands on the wheel. "One of the best days of my life."

They hadn't known anyone well enough to ask if they could borrow a car, and for weeks, Nora and Grace and Monica huddled together whenever Ozzie wasn't around, trying to think of something that might suffice as a road trip. The most important thing, Nora had stressed, was that Ozzie feel something like freedom, that she have a day to herself with only the wind in her hair. No rules, no regulations. When a carnival came to town the following weekend, Nora knew she had found the answer. They skipped school, the four of them, and spent all day on the rides. Monica won a stuffed panda with one eye, and Grace and Ozzie had a deep-fried-hot-dog-eating contest, after which Grace promptly threw up. But it was not until they were crammed into a Ferris-wheel car, the large, rotating structure bringing them slowly to the top, that Monica giggled and flung out her arms. "Ah, I feel so free," she said. "Don't you guys? I mean, wasn't this day just so completely *free*?"

Ozzie had squinted strangely at her, not comprehending, and

then all at once, the understanding of what they had done settled across her face. "Is this my road trip?" she asked. "Is that what this was all about?"

"Something like that." Nora flushed as she wrote the answer, wondering if the whole thing had been a mistake. It *was* a stretch when you thought about it. Trying to capture a feeling like freedom was a lot harder than she'd imagined.

"Do you like it?" Grace raised her eyebrows. "It was mostly Nora's idea."

In response, Ozzie had turned her head, staring at the horizon spread out beneath them. From this distance, the green slope of mountain looked half its size, a vast map of the unknown, the streets and houses below like playthings. The sun was beginning to set, and small birds flew overhead, rising and swooping with the wind.

"Oz?" Monica sounded worried.

Nora held her breath as Ozzie leaned over and pressed her forehead against hers. It was something she'd seen Ozzie do only once, after Monica had made a special cake that Ozzie used to eat as a kid. It was a nonverbal gesture that meant simply "I know you. You know me."

"I love it." Ozzie's voice sounded hoarse as she straightened back up, and she cleared it roughly. "I more than love it. It's fucking awesome."

Nora had sat back then, meeting Monica and Grace's satisfied gazes as Ozzie pressed her forehead against each of theirs. She was sure she'd been the only one to see the lone tear that had trickled down the far side of Ozzie's face, and she was glad for it. She already knew it was something she'd keep to herself, tucked deep inside one of her pockets, a tiny piece of Ozzie that she might never see again.

"Okay, here," Monica said, handing the GPS over the seat again. "Now snap it back in. It'll tell you exactly where to go."

"Hell. Oh." A British female electronic voice drifted out from the tiny box. "You. Are. On. Highway. 56. Take. Right. At. Exit. 98."

Ozzie sat back against her seat, clearly taken aback by the electronic voice. "Who the hell's talking? Princess Kate?"

"Take. Right," the GPS commanded. "Exit. 98. Take. Right."

"Okay, honey," Ozzie said. "Don't get your panties in a bunch. I'm heading over to the right." She glanced at Monica again in the mirror. "This thing have a name?"

"Yeah," Monica said. "GPS."

"That's not a name," Ozzie insisted. "Listen to this wench talk. She sounds like that English teacher we had in junior year—you know, the one with the beehive hairdo and the big stick up her ass."

"Mrs. Ditmer!" Monica laughed raucously, clapping her hands. "Oh my God, it *does* sound like her!"

Ozzie grinned. "What was Ditmer's first name?"

"I have no idea," Monica said. "I never paid attention to anything in that class except the back of Jeremy Rindle's neck."

"Myrtle," Nora said quietly, wondering how Monica and Ozzie could have forgotten how much she loved Mrs. Ditmer, how the teacher had taken a special interest in the way she carried a book to read with her everywhere, even letting Nora stay late after school a few times so that she could finish reading her first edition of *Mrs. Dalloway*. The first line, *"Mrs. Dalloway de-*

cided she would buy the flowers herself," was number fifteen in
Nora's notebook.

"Myrtle!" Monica and Ozzie burst out simultaneously.

Nora looked out the window as they laughed.

"Myrtle it is," Ozzie said, wiping her eyes and patting the
GPS. "Myrtle, I'd like to introduce you to the girls. Girls, this
is Myrtle."

Nora blinked rapidly, as if the movement might suppress the
knot ascending within her throat. It wasn't often that something reminded her of Theodore Gallagher anymore, but Mrs.
Ditmer's name was one such reminder. She'd known him as
Theo the way everyone did back then—a tall, thin boy with a
quick smile and an easy, unaffected manner—but it wasn't until
the end of her junior year that she'd actually spoken to him. It
had been in English class after dismissal one day, when everyone
had cleared out of the room and was rushing toward their lockers to retrieve their books. Nora, however, had stayed, settling
into one of the desks in the back of the room with a book, ready
to while away a few hours before leaving for the weekend. Theo
materialized out of nowhere, hovering inside the door, looking
curiously around the room. Nora glanced up from the book
and then looked back down again. "She's not here." Her eyes
skipped over a line. "And no, I don't know where she is or when
she'll be back."

There was a pause and then, "Who?"

She raised her eyes again, taking in his lanky frame, the
caramel-colored hair that stuck out beneath a faded blue baseball
cap, his small, slightly crooked teeth. "Mrs. Ditmer," she said.
"Isn't that who you're looking for?"

He straightened up and leaned against the doorframe. "No, actually. I'm not looking for her at all."

She tucked her hair behind her ear and fiddled with her earring. She'd seen this boy a hundred times in the hallways over the past two years, and yet it occurred to her that this was the first time she'd had a clear, unobstructed view of him. He was always surrounded by a group of people, usually his track teammates, who seemed to enjoy racing from class to class at breakneck speed. He was even more handsome than she realized with his lean, aquiline nose and wide eyes.

"Well, I can't help you," she said finally. "There's no one else in here."

"No one?" The left side of his mouth lifted in a grin.

She bit the inside of her cheek and looked back down at her book. The words swam in front of her. He wasn't flirting with her, was he? No, of course he wasn't. No boy had ever looked at her, much less flirted with her. That kind of thing was for pretty girls like Jenny Packer and Carolyn Meyers, who had big chests and perfect teeth. "Just me," she said, hoping she sounded irritated. "And I'm busy, if you haven't noticed."

She held her breath as he walked into the room. His track pants made a faint rustling sound as he moved, and one of his neon-yellow shoelaces was untied. He stopped at a desk next to the far window, dropped a backpack at his feet, and then plopped down into the seat.

Nora lowered her eyes again and pretended to read as he looked at her. It was impossible. She could feel the weight of his stare on her like some kind of living thing, boring into her skin, whispering through her hair. "Did you need something?" she asked without lifting her eyes. The irritation in her voice was gone.

"Maybe."

She looked up quickly.

"Whatcha reading?"

She held up the book, hoping he could see the cover.

"*Mrs. Dalloway,*" he recited. "Who's that, Virginia Woolf?"

She nodded, secretly pleased by his guess.

"You reading that for fun? Or for an assignment?"

"For fun."

"You must read a lot for fun." He leaned back a little, crossing his feet at the ankles. "Your head's always in a book. Even in the halls."

Her heart skipped another beat. He'd noticed her before? When?

"You like to read more than you like to talk." It was a statement, not a question.

She shrugged, embarrassed.

He laughed, a sweet sound that made its way across the room to her like a bubble. "We should go out some time," he said. "Like to a movie or something."

She raised her eyes, too quickly this time. Did he really just say what she thought he said? Or was he making fun of her?

He stood up and walked through the narrow line between the desks until he was directly in front of her. "I've been wanting to ask you. I just haven't gotten the chance to find you alone anywhere until now."

She tried not to look at the string that clutched at the material in front of his pants, or the way his hips, narrow as a bow, curved beneath it. "You have?"

He nodded.

It didn't seem possible. And yet here it was, finally, for the very first time. A boy who had seen her. Who had not only seen her, but thought about asking her out. Who had, just this minute, gone and done exactly that.

She could have wept.

Here, sweetie." Nora started out of her thoughts as Monica handed something over the seat. "I thought this would go well with your eyes." It was a cobalt blue scarf, threaded with tiny gold filaments that gleamed when the light hit them.

"You brought us *gifts*?" Ozzie asked, glancing over her shoulder. "I didn't bring any gifts. Norster, did you bring any gifts?"

Nora shook her head, her cheeks reddening as she ran her palms over the front of the scarf. "No." She pressed it against her cheek and closed her eyes. "It's so soft," she whispered. "Thank you."

"It's cashmere," Monica said. "I got you one in red, Ozzie, and one for Grace in yellow." She placed Ozzie's scarf in the space between her and Nora. "I'll put yours right here. You can try it on later."

Ozzie glanced down at the scarf. "It's gorgeous," she said. "You shouldn't have, Monsie. Now I feel like a rube."

"Me, too." Nora still had the scarf pressed to her cheek. "I'm sorry."

"Don't apologize," Monica said. "It was just something I wanted to do."

"Heading. North. On. Route. 19." The GPS's voice crackled. "Stay. In. Left. Lane."

"Gotcha, Myrtle," Ozzie said. "I gotcha."

"So." Monica sat forward again, draping her slender arms over the seat. "Is anyone else nervous about seeing Grace?"

"Nervous?" Ozzie eyed Monica in the mirror. "Why would you feel nervous? We didn't do anything."

"I know we didn't *do* anything." Monica settled her chin on top of her hands. "That's not what I meant."

"I'm nervous." Nora almost laughed at how calm she sounded. Monica gave Nora a grateful smile. "It's just been such a long time. I think I'm scared that she's turned into someone I won't recognize anymore. Especially after everything she's been through." A moment of silence passed. It occurred to Nora that Monica could have been talking about any one of them. "What if she cries the whole time we're there?" Monica asked.

"Then she cries the whole time." Ozzie watched Monica in the rearview mirror. "It won't kill us."

"But . . ." Monica rubbed her forehead with her fingers. "I don't know . . . I mean, I don't think I'll be able to handle that."

"Of course you will." Ozzie jerked the car to the right. "It's just crying. It always stops eventually."

"Yeah." Monica looked out the window. "Yeah, I guess you're right."

Nora brought a finger to her mouth and began to gnaw on the edge of it.

She had cried after her first date with Theo. She'd felt it coming as soon as he arrived (two minutes early, no less), a tight lump that pressed against the back of her throat as she noticed that he was dressed in clothes he'd obviously taken time to think about: pressed khakis, a dark blue polo, green-and-white sneakers. It moved her to know that he had wanted to look good. For her. For her and no one else.

"You're early," she said, smiling shyly.

"Punctuality is the politeness of kings." He shrugged, grinning. "Something my dad always says."

The feeling swelled as they sat together in the movie theater, their forearms resting on their individual seat rests, barely touching, and yet creating a heat between them that shocked her. He'd leaned over at one point, his breath already masked with the cloying sweetness of Twizzlers, and asked, "Are you having a good time?" She'd turned, looking at his elongated face in the dark, a narrow column of white perforated with green eyes and pink lips, and nodded. "Do you like the movie?" he pressed. "Or should we go?"

We should go, she thought. *We should go and lie down somewhere soft and press ourselves against each other until we can't breathe.* "I like the movie," she lied, extricating another Swedish fish from her packet. "It's good."

They'd gone to Jitter Beans afterward for coffee. He ordered a frozen mocha drink for himself, a vanilla cappuccino for her, and a gigantic Rice Krispie treat for the two of them to split. The hour had been full of the heady rush of discovery, each of them unearthing themselves one detail at a time. He was the oldest in a family of four boys—all overachievers. He was planning to apply to several colleges early next year, hoping for early admission or maybe even a track scholarship. He had a good shot at one: he'd already set a school record in the 200-meter race and ran the anchor leg in the 400. All of his college choices were far away; he wanted to leave Willow Grove and settle down in a city—Los Angeles, perhaps, or New York—where people could be who they really were and not something others thought they should be. He hoped college would lead him into a profession that helped people, but also afforded him a living—maybe psychiatry or law. His favorite food was his mother's Irish stew, which she served with real biscuits and, on very special occasions, a mug of Guinness. On the rare day when he had nothing to do, he preferred to put a pair of earphones on and walk down to the small pond a short way behind his house, where he would sit and listen to Bruce Springsteen and think about nothing at all.

Nora took it all in, relishing details like the Guinness and the pond behind his house and trying to ignore the pang in her chest when he talked about college and moving away from Willow Grove, but the largeness of his life made her acutely aware of the holes in her own. She felt lopsided as she launched into her own excavation, telling him about her first-line collection, her love of reading, and (without getting into any of the Turning Winds details) her friendship with Ozzie, Grace, and Monica. She didn't have a favorite food unless you counted Swedish fish, and she wasn't very close with her mother, either. That was all there was, really. No, she didn't have any plans after high school. Maybe she would take a few classes somewhere; maybe she wouldn't. Mrs. Ditmer had mentioned something about applying for a scholarship next year at the local college, but she still needed time to figure out what it was she wanted to do first; what it was she *liked* to do aside from reading books. She ducked her head after she stopped talking, praying that he would stop looking at her.

Except that he didn't. He ducked his head down instead until his eyes were level with hers. "What's your favorite first line? Like, of all time?"

She felt a flutter of panic as the line she loved best emerged inside her head: *"Don't never tell nobody but God."* There was no way she could divulge that one. It was private, with a meaning known only to her, sacred by this point.

"Um, 'All children, except one, grow up,'" she lied. It was number eight in her book.

"'All children, except one, grow up,'" Theo repeated. "I like it. What book's it from?"

"Peter Pan."

"No *way!*" His eyebrows arched skyward. "I love that book! Well, I used to love it. My mother read it to me when I was little; the real one, a chapter every night. And I went through a serious, year-long period of wanting to be Captain Hook. Like, I made an actual hook for myself out of tin foil." He stuck his fist out, pointing to the space between his first and second knuckles. "Kept it right in between there, even when I went to bed." He smiled at her, as if they'd just shared something intimate. Which, she thought later, they had, in a way.

He leaned in a little closer. "Why's it your favorite?" His knee bumped hers under the table, and she felt a thrill of pleasure at the contact.

"It says so much," she answered. "Don't you think? Just in those few words? Who doesn't grow up? And why? What happens?"

"Yeah." Theo nodded, looking thoughtful. "I hadn't thought of it that way, but yeah. It's true."

"Okay, now you," she said, desperate to steer the conversation away from herself.

"Now me what? I don't have first lines. I don't think I even remember the last book I read."

"How about your favorite Springsteen song?" Nora prodded.

Theo's face lit up. "Oh, now that's something I can do!" He rubbed his palms together greedily. "Just one?"

"Just one."

"Song? Or album?"

Nora shrugged. "Either, I guess."

"I'll have to do an album. It's impossible to narrow Springsteen's songs down to just one."

"Okay." Nora sat forward expectantly. A vein along one side of Theo's forehead had started to pulse; she'd noticed it before, when he got excited about the movie, too. It looked like a fluid stream of jade beneath his skin, and she restrained herself from reaching out to touch it.

"My top Springsteen album would have to be . . ." Theo sat back in his chair and locked his fingers behind his head. His face took on an anguished expression, as if Nora had asked him to donate a pint of blood instead of recall his favorite music. He rocked back on the heels of his chair and stared up at the ceiling. "Okay!" The word came out of his mouth at the same time his chair clunked back down, and Nora jumped a little. He reached out and touched her arm. "Sorry. Top album of all time would have to be *Darkness on the Edge of Town*."

She watched his mouth as he talked, the way the lines around his eyes eased and tightened at the end of each sentence, and she wanted nothing more at that moment than to lean forward and press her mouth against his. Instead, she said, "Never heard of it."

He looked incredulous. "You're kidding, right?"

She shook her head and pressed a fingertip against a stray Rice Krispie. "Music's not really my thing, I guess."

"Well, we'll have to change that."

She looked up sharply then, as if he'd criticized her.

"If you want to, I mean." He shrugged and looked away.

"Might be fun," she said, hoping her voice sounded contrite.

"Might be." He grinned.

Later he walked her back to the bus, which was where she had told him she would meet him earlier. No need to go into the truth about where she lived; no reason to add anything to the mix that might lead to unnecessary questions and spoil it. It had begun to drizzle, and the metallic smell of rain and asphalt mingled in the air. He'd gone back to talking about the movie, things she had already forgotten, lost and unimportant, but she nodded anyway, and said things like yes, yes, I know. She did not know, not really, was thinking only of the way his fingers felt against her arm when he had rested them there at Jitter Beans.

"Anyway," he said as they reached the bus stop, "I guess it wasn't the best movie we could've seen, but now that we saw it, I'm kind of glad we did."

She stood facing him. Her eyes locked against his Adam's apple, a miraculous thing, she thought, a small and perfectly astonishing thing. She wanted to press her lips against it, to hold the whole of it inside her mouth.

"Maybe we can go see another one sometime."

"What?"

"I mean, if you want to." He laughed, a nervous sound. "Do you?"

She stepped into him instead of answering, pressing her forehead lightly against the cotton material of his T-shirt so that he wouldn't see her cheeks flushing hot, the violent quivering of her lower lip. It was too much, her wanting him. Him wanting her. Making friends at Turning Winds had been more than she'd ever imagined, but this was more than she'd ever hoped.

He laughed again, the nervous edge gone now. "Is that a yes?" He rested his hand against her hair, sliding it down along the back of her head.

She nodded, hoping he couldn't see the splotches that were invariably rising along her neck, and took a slow, deep breath. She wouldn't let him see her cry, no matter what.

"Nora?" He stepped back, tilting his head down so that he could see under her lashes. "You okay?"

She nodded, swallowing the knot, large as an acorn now, in the back of her throat. "I'm fine," she said. "And yeah, I'd like to go. To the movies or something. Again. With you."

"Great." He grinned and shoved his hands in his pockets. "Me too."

Ten seconds later the bus pulled up. She waved from the window, and then, as the bus pulled out of sight, she turned around in her seat, leaned over her knees, and wept. She wept and wept until she could not cry any longer. And when the bus dropped her off in front of Turning Winds twenty minutes later, she knew that she had just traveled a distance no vehicle could ever take her.

She was on her way to being loved.

Which, after a lifetime of not being loved, felt like the first day of the rest of her life.

Chapter 7

"Do you know anything about postpartum depression?" Nora asked as Ozzie sailed past another tractor-trailer. "You said that Grace's husband told you it might've been connected to everything."

"I don't know a whole lot." Ozzie scratched her cheek. Her fingernails were torn and ripped, the edges raw. "I didn't go through it with any of my kids, thank God. But I know it's no joke. Your hormones just go completely off the reservation, apparently. I mean, some women can become homicidal."

"Homicidal?" Monica snapped back to attention. "As in . . ."

"Yeah." Ozzie's jaw set. "You ever hear of Andrea Yates?"

Nora bit her lip so hard that she tasted blood.

"You don't think Grace ever wanted to hurt . . ." Monica started.

"I don't know." Ozzie's voice was edged with a sudden harshness that made Nora's arms prickle. "I would think anything's possible when you're in that state of mind. And Henry said the baby's staying with the grandparents, right? That can't be accidental." She sped up, bypassing a blue Toyota in front of her and then settled back into the passing lane.

"Do you have to keep swerving?" Nora asked.

"I'm sorry." Ozzie looked in the rearview mirror. "There's some asshole in a silver Buick back there who has been driving on my tail for the last ten minutes. I'm just trying to lose him."

"Well, let him pass you." Nora closed her eyes, trying to fight off the rising nausea. "I'm serious, Ozzie. You have to stop flinging the car all over the road."

"Okay." Ozzie rubbed the side of Nora's arm. "I'm sorry."

"Maybe the baby's with the grandparents just to give Grace and her husband a break," Monica suggested. "I can't imagine trying to deal with a suicide attempt and trying to take care of a newborn at the same time."

"Could be," Ozzie said, glancing in the rear view mirror again. "God *damn* it." She swerved across the lane, just missing a white Volkswagen bug. The woman in the driver's seat slammed on her brakes and then gave Ozzie the finger.

"Yeah, yeah," Ozzie muttered under her breath. "Back atcha."

Nora bit down hard on her tongue as the familiar, sour taste of bile pooled in the back of her mouth. "Ozzie," she said, "I'm gonna . . ." She clapped her hands over her mouth, her eyes wide and pleading.

"Pull over!" Monica shouted. "Ozzie, pull over on the shoulder! She's going to get sick!"

Ozzie veered to the right amid a flurry of angry honks and screeches. Nora grabbed the door handle as the popping sound of gravel crunched beneath the tires, and then flung herself out as the car skidded to a stop. She made it just in time, stumbling into the weeds and then falling on one knee as she began to retch. Her whole body seemed to empty itself from the inside out, tears pooling in the creases of her eyes as it shook. A door slammed behind her, and then another, followed by the sounds of gasps and running. She could feel Monica's cool hands as they reached down and pulled her hair away from her face. Ozzie grabbed her around the shoulders as Nora heaved again, steadying her so that she did not fall, and then it was over.

"Okay?" Monica's voice, just a few inches from Nora's face, was a whisper. Nora raised her head. She tried to focus on the tangle of bushes that lined the overhead ridge, but everything looked blurred, as if the Earth were swaying in front of her. A smudged white line, like chalk, split the blue sky in two, and she searched for the plane in front of it. There was nothing.

"Nora?" Monica's mascara was smeared a little around the edges. "Honey? Are you all right?"

For a split second, Nora wondered if either of them remembered the last time she had done this exact thing. They had been driving back from Max's place after he had given them the Cytotec for the abortion. Grace had been in the back with Nora, holding her hand, her eyes closed inside her stricken face. Ozzie was up front, biting her nails and driving too fast. Monica was next to her, twisting the orange braid around her fingers. It was the smell, Nora thought later, that sterile, antiseptic smell from the rubbing alcohol Max had in the room, combined with the warm, salty scent emanating from a half-eaten bag of Doritos on the floor of the car that had turned her stomach. She'd called out, feeling the sourness pooling along the inside of her cheeks, and Ozzie had screeched to a halt.

"Yeah," she gasped now, still struggling to keep herself upright. "Yeah, I'm all right."

"Okay then." Monica helped her back to her feet. "Come on. Let's get you fixed up."

They put their arms around her—Ozzie and Monica both—and like a bridge carried her through the weeds back into the car.

Nora listened to the dull roaring sound of the wheels as she lay in the backseat for the next forty-five minutes. They sounded like thunder in the distance, and sometimes, if she turned her ear just so, like something she'd heard once at the bottom of a body of water.

It was near the end of February in their senior year when Theo asked her to meet him at his house one Saturday. Despite the fact that they had been dating for almost nine months, Nora always insisted that they meet at his house or somewhere downtown. Even though she had finally told him the bare minimum about Turning Winds, the place itself was off-limits when it came to anything social. Having a boy over to a group home was just weird. And if she was being perfectly honest, she didn't want to share him—or their time together—with anyone else, even The Invisibles.

It was an unusually mild day for February, the third one in less than a week. Single-digit temperatures had climbed up well into the thirties, and while there was no chance the balminess would last, the respite had raised everyone's spirits. Nora had unzipped her winter coat on the walk over and shoved her hat deep into her front pocket. She would take her sweater off too once she got inside Theo's house, but she was a little worried about the dampness under her arms. Had she used deodorant this morning? She couldn't remember. Maybe it wouldn't matter. Maybe they'd just go down in the basement again and play air hockey with Theo's little brothers, who without fail jumped all over her when she walked into the house, eager to start a game.

Theo, though, met her at the door, his winter coat already zipped, dark brown gloves on his hands. "Hey." His whole face seemed to brighten when she came into his presence, something Nora never failed to notice, and something of which she would never tire. "You up for a walk to the pond today? I really want to show you something."

"Sure."

He slid his hand in hers, by now a natural, unconscious gesture, and led her down the front steps. He lived in a well-developed wooded area just outside of Willow Grove. A long dirt path wound its way through the development and into a section of woods, ending at a small pond bordered with cattails and scrub pine. Today the path was wet and muddy, the weeks of snow long melted. Dirty slush edged the sides, and tire tracks were filled with icy water. They hopped and dodged their way through it as best they could, laughing as they emerged at the end, breathless and mud-spattered.

It wasn't her first trip to the pond; Theo had taken her two weeks after their initial date to the movies, and almost every weekend during that summer. They would sit on a large, flat stone beneath one of the pine trees and kiss until their lips were numb. More and more frequently, she would let his hands wander beneath her shirt, and once or twice, she had allowed her own fingers to drift along the inside of his waistband and then a little farther down until Theo's breath caught in his throat, and he clenched handfuls of her shirt along her back. Pictures of Daddy Ray sometimes filled her head during these moments, and she would have to squeeze her eyes shut and force herself to breathe, but there was no denying the immediate pulse of physical pleasure in her own body that always accompanied the ugly pictures, and along with the obvious sensations in Theo's, she had tentatively decided she wanted more. She wondered if he had something like that in mind today. She hoped he did.

Today, though, Theo tiptoed to the edge of the pond where the ice was already beginning to crack. Alarm shot through Nora just as a first line came to her: *"Many years later, as he faced the firing squad, Colonel Aureliano Buendía was to remember that distant afternoon when his father took him to discover ice."* The line was from Gabriel García Márquez's *One Hundred Years of Solitude;* she had read the book just last year, during a long, rainy week. Despite the beauty of the first line, the book's strange, ambiguous ending had left her brooding for weeks afterward.

"Don't go any farther," she warned as Theo began to tap the ice with the toe of his shoe. "It's dangerous."

"It's all right." He pressed down again. "I was just here yesterday. Some parts are thin, but it's okay around here."

"You're not really thinking of walking on that, are you?" She shoved her hands inside her pocket. Overhead, a crow floated against the white sky, the only blemish in a sea of pearl.

"Well, maybe not right there, exactly." He drew his foot back as a section of ice splintered beneath it. "Or there."

"Theo!"

But he had already hopped over to another section of the bank and was testing the ice again with his shoe. "It's much thicker in this spot." He beckoned to her with a wave of his hand. "Come on, Nora. Please. It'll just take a second."

"What'll just take a second?" She moved toward him slowly, her heart thumping in her ears. "For us to fall through the ice and drown?" She thought about something Grace had said once, during an Invisibles meeting, when the topic of how they'd want to die if they could choose such a thing came up. Monica and Ozzie had both opted for a gunshot to the head, while she herself had decided that an overdose of sleeping pills would probably be the most painless way to go. Grace, though, had said she'd prefer drowning, optimally beneath a sheet of ice, so that her body could move seamlessly from a state of frozen inertia to one of burning joy.

"Burning joy?" Ozzie had echoed. "What the hell are you talking about? When does anything like that come in?"

"When you get to *heaven*," Grace answered impatiently. "Obviously."

Nora didn't know if she believed in heaven, but she remembered thinking that the idea of moving between two worlds in such a way sounded lovely. Like being asleep one moment and waking up, singing, the next.

Theo cocked his head, hand still outstretched. "Do you really think I'd let something like that happen?"

She didn't answer. The obvious response was no, of course he would never let something like that happen. Still, things happened anyway, whether you wanted them to or not. Didn't he know that yet?

"You don't even have to step on the ice," he said, pulling her in next to him. "Just come here. Just listen. You won't believe it."

She followed his lead, getting down on her knees on the edge of the bank, and leaning the side of her face as close to the ice as she dared. He was stretched out several feet ahead of her, his palms pressed against the glassy surface and his right ear an inch or so above it. His eyes were closed and the edges of his nose had begun to turn pink. "Just wait," he whispered. "Hold on."

She scooched up a little more until he was just in her line of vision, and then she waited, studying the dark curve of his eyelashes and the faint shadows they made against his cheekbone. Up close, his eyebrows were wild and ragged looking in a sexy sort of way, and the slope of his nose, which had a tiny bump at the top of it, was narrow and pronounced.

The sound came all at once beneath them, a long, drawn-out whooshing noise punctuated by splitting pops and gasps, like some sort of broken pinball machine. Nora's eyes went wide and she jerked back, startled, but Theo's hand shot out and rested on her shoulder.

"It's just the ice," he whispered. "It's cracking way, way down below. It's okay. Close your eyes and listen."

The strange sounds that followed were like nothing Nora had ever heard before. She closed her eyes as a screen door screeched, a bullwhip hissed, and plastic bubble wrap snapped and popped with abandon. Some sounds she could not place at all; they were otherworldly, as if aliens had settled beneath the surface and were playing a strange, cavernous symphony on bizarre instruments. And yet they were sounds she recognized, too; she could feel their odd familiarity in a desolate part of herself she had not known existed until this very moment.

She opened her eyes as the faint shrieks faded into the distance, only to find Theo gazing at her. His eyes were so green against the paleness of his skin that she blinked, as if the color hurt her eyes.

"What do you think?" he asked.

Below them, the silence thundered. An unbearable loneliness engulfed her like a wave, followed by the sudden understanding that nothing in this world, not even Theo, who loved her in a way that she had never thought possible, would ever be able to assuage it. The moment hung above her, hollow and hopeless, and then left again. She leaned in and pressed her lips against his. They were cold, almost rubbery. He brought his hand around the back of her head and kissed her back, opening his mouth so that he could move his tongue around hers. She hated being kissed like that, had always considered his insistence of it an intrusion of sorts, but she'd never said anything. Now she pulled away. Beneath them, the ice shuddered and wailed again, a splitting noise reverberating from the depths of what seemed an endless chasm. As if in response, Nora cried out, a single, desperate sound that burst out from her chest, and then clapped her hand over her mouth.

"What's wrong?" Theo looked alarmed.

"I want to go." She was already scrambling back tentatively over the thick, opaque surface. "This is crazy. I just want to go."

He helped her across the rest of the ice and then up the bank. They didn't speak on the walk back, and when they reached his house, she told him she would walk the rest of the way by herself. He'd let her go, not objecting the way he always did, and when she glanced over her shoulder just before she turned the corner, he had disappeared.

Well, here we are." Ozzie braked and turned off the engine. "Suburbia Central."

Monica leaned over the front seat and looked at Nora. "How're you feeling, sweetie?"

"Better." Nora sat up and looked at the white two-story house with red shutters. Buckets of white mums had been arranged on the front steps, and a raffia wreath strung with dried stalks of lavender and eucalyptus hung on the door. White muslin curtains were tied back in the front window; the number 23 had been drilled into the front of a tin mailbox shaped like a cat.

"I like the mailbox," Monica said. "It's adorable. Look how the tail goes into a little figure eight shape."

Nora squinted to see the mailbox more clearly. Had Grace liked cats? She couldn't remember. Maybe it was her husband's thing.

The front door opened, and a short man dressed in baggy blue jeans, a gray V-neck sweater, and dark brown moccasins emerged from inside the house. He was in dire need of a shave—unless he wore his beard purposely scraggly the way some men did these days—and his hair was mussed, as if someone had just reached over and tousled it. He lifted one hand in greeting, shoving the other one into his front pocket.

"That must be Henry," Monica said.

Ozzie turned off the engine and inhaled. "Okay, here we go. You sure you're okay, Nora?"

"I'm fine." Nora ran her hands over her face. They still smelled of vomit. The hand sanitizer hadn't worked; she would have to wash them thoroughly when she found a moment.

Their emergence from inside the car was followed by a flurry of hand shaking and introductions. Up close, Henry had beautiful blue eyes, flecked with little bits of gray. His teeth were small and slightly rounded like Tic Tacs, and a leather watch was fastened around one wrist.

"Thank you so much for coming." He shoved his hands inside his pockets and surveyed them once more, this time with a slight sense of bashfulness. "It really means a lot."

Monica reached out and put a hand on his shoulder. "I'm sorry it's been so hard."

Henry looked startled for a moment and then nodded. "Thank you. We're just taking it one day at a time. It's all any of us can do, right?"

"Yes." Monica nodded.

"Anyway, come in, come in!" Henry grabbed several bags and led them into a small, rose-colored living room. He stood in front of the door as everyone passed him, and then stretched out his arm, indicating two large sofas. They were a pale mauve color, embossed with gold leaves. A wooden table sat between them, decorated with a smooth black bowl. Inside was a blue rubber teething ring, the bubble-like sections of it filled with tiny plastic fish. "Sit down anywhere," Henry said. "Make yourself comfortable. I'll put your bags in the guest rooms and tell Petal you're here. She's just finishing up in the shower."

"Henry." Ozzie adjusted the brim of her baseball cap and lowered her voice. "How is she? Really, I mean."

His eyes swept over the room, as if looking for the answer. "She's doing a lot better. The doctor adjusted her medication, and that's helped a lot. And since she heard you all were coming, she's been . . ." He paused. "Peppy might be a stretch, but she's definitely been more talkative. Sort of like something lifted a little."

"Well," Ozzie said. "Good. That's something."

"Oh, I almost forgot." Henry said. "The baby's here. With us, I mean. She's sleeping now in the back room."

Nora's heart lurched. She reached back with one hand, steadying herself against the doorknob.

"Okay." Ozzie sounded uncertain.

"She was staying with my parents, like I told you," Henry hurried on. "And then my mother got shingles."

"Oh, how awful," Monica said.

"Yes." Henry winced. "It's caused by the chicken pox virus, which is extremely dangerous to newborns. So, obviously, we brought her back here." He raised his eyebrows and exhaled. "She's a very good sleeper."

"It's totally fine," Ozzie said. "Really."

"Yes," Monica chimed in. "My goodness. This is your home. Your child! Don't give it another thought."

Nora smiled her approval as Henry glanced in her direction and tightened her hand around the doorknob.

Henry nodded. "All right, then." He disappeared into a corridor next to the living room. His footsteps sounded down the hall. A door opened and then closed. Nora did not move.

The walls were covered with paintings—three of them, enormous framed canvases of blue, purple, and gray skies. Nothing else. Just dark bruises of sky. The name "Petal" was scrawled in the corner of each one, the *P* a giant loopy letter, the rest of the letters tiny and cramped.

"Jesus," Ozzie whispered. "No wonder she's depressed. All she does is sit around and paint this shit all day?"

"Don't call it shit." Monica kept her voice low, but there was an edge to it, a fierceness Nora had never heard before. "It's her work, Ozzie. Her *art*." She slit her eyes. "And my God, what if she heard you?"

"Yeah, I know." Ozzie took her baseball cap off and shook out her hair, yanking the rubber band from around her ponytail. "It's just . . . God, they all look so *sad*, don't they?"

"They do." Nora let go of the doorknob finally and walked across the room to get a better look. "They look terribly sad."

It was bad enough that the paintings didn't depict any kind of object. The space they occupied was lifeless too, devoid of any light or breath. Even the sections of white, interspersed here and there between swaths of purple and gray, seemed mute. A first line from a Pynchon novel, *"A screaming comes across the sky,"* struck her now as ridiculously appropriate.

"Well, she's been sad," Monica said. "You know that. It's been rough for a while I would think, with the baby and then the post-partum. Maybe this is how she's been getting through it."

"Yeah, that and a rope," Ozzie said.

Monica gasped and then punched Ozzie hard in the arm. Nora was glad. If she'd had the nerve, she would've done the same thing.

"Well, it's true," Ozzie said, rubbing her arm. "I'll tell you something else too, and I don't give a shit if you think it's rude or not. I can already tell she's gonna need us for longer than a weekend."

Monica clasped her bony arms around her waist and stared at the floor. Nora sat back against the couch. The whine of a lawn mower sounded outside. A lazy beam of light floated in through the parted curtains, illuminating a sea of dust motes, swirling like so many stars above the rug. There was no way she was going to be able to stay longer than twenty-four hours, Nora thought. Especially now that there was a baby around. No way at all.

"Hi." The word drifted down from the staircase, soft as a cloud. Nora didn't have to look up to know it was her, but she did anyway, just to be sure. Grace was standing on the third or fourth step, almost as if she was afraid to come all the way down. She was still thin, but without the usual pink in her face; her skin now had a gray, almost transparent quality to it. Her blue eyes were clouded with a heaviness behind them. One hand rested on the banister, the other fiddled with a scarf wrapped around her neck. On either side of it, her still-blond hair flowed down in impossibly long waves. Ozzie and Monica stood up at the same time, but Nora did not move. She was trying not to think about what was under that scarf.

Monica walked over to the stairs and put her hand on the banister. "Hi, baby doll," she whispered.

Grace came down all at once and let herself be swallowed up in Ozzie and Monica's arms. She closed her eyes, leaning into them, as if she had been waiting for such a thing for a long time and now that it had finally arrived, she was afraid it might leave again. Ozzie held her fiercely, cradling the edge of Grace's chin with a cupped hand, while Monica clutched the two of them.

It had been rare for Grace to exchange hugs, even back then.

Physical contact was regarded warily, as if stepping over an unseen boundary. And yet, looking at them now, Nora remembered their second Invisibles meeting, when they had presented Grace with a little cardboard box, complete with a green dental floss bow. Inside were two strips of paper, one saturated with multiple squirts of Chanel No. 5 (for which Ozzie had had to pay Chuck Sullivan five bucks to get from his mother's bureau), the other drizzled with a blob of the burnt caramel sauce Monica had made specially for the occasion. Beneath the two strips of paper, Nora had tucked a few handfuls of the freshly cut grass she'd waited two weeks for until Mr. Richards across the street finally pulled out his lawn mower. Grace had stared stupidly at the contents when they first presented it to her until Ozzie reached over and pushed it under her nose. The patchwork of emotion that stitched itself across her face as she sniffed tentatively at it was like nothing Nora had ever seen before, a mixture of bewilderment, shock, angst, and finally, seconds before she broke down, gratitude. "Oh!" she kept saying, shaking her head and reaching for them with both arms. "Oh! Oh!"

Nora felt something lodge in the back of her throat and then twist a little as she thought of it again. She did not know what it was—until Grace stood back from the other women and fingered the hem of her sweat shirt. "Nora?" Her voice was a croak. Nora stood up and moved toward her. She pressed her nose against Grace's hair—it smelled like pot, for some reason, and potato chips—and held her in her arms.

"I can't believe it." Grace's voice was as thin as a cobweb. "I can't believe you all really came."

Nora knew that their presence was not going to fix whatever

was broken inside Grace, just as she understood suddenly that the brief trip would not, as she had secretly hoped, fill the well within her. But the gratitude in Grace's voice just now was as pure and full of amazement as it had been that day, when they'd given her the little box that smelled like her mother.

And for now at least, that was enough.

Chapter 8

It was during the fourth Invisibles meeting that the subject of their pasts had come up. It had not gone especially well. Nora blamed herself. She should have known that the first line she had chosen to share from Albert Camus's novel *The Stranger* would be too suggestive. It was like setting a match to a bundle of dried twigs; the spark alone was all it needed to burst into flame. Indeed, after Grace read it aloud, the four of them sat there for a moment, muted and motionless.

"*Mother died today.*" Ozzie repeated the line again, the way she always did. Her voice was hard, unrelenting. "God, if only that were true."

"Now why would you say something like that?" Grace asked.

"Why?" Ozzie's eyes flashed. "Because my mother doesn't deserve to live, that's why."

"Well, it's a good thing you don't have a say in those kinds of things, isn't it?" Grace crossed her arms. "Only God gets to decide when people's lives will end. And I'm pretty sure He wouldn't be too happy if He knew you were wishing people dead."

"Oh yeah, right. *God*." Ozzie began to rock back and forth a little. "I forgot about the Big Guy in the Sky. He's the one that gets to decide which ones of us are strong enough to hold on for three days in a locked closet without any food or water, right? Or maybe He figures it'll build character for a kid to have a mother who holds your hand over a lit gas range because you forgot to shut the door on your way into the house."

The color began to drain from Grace's face. "I didn't . . ." she started.

"You're goddamned right you didn't," Ozzie cut her off, the veins in her neck thick as cords. "You didn't anything. So don't tell me that after all the shit that witch put me through that I don't get to wish her dead. And don't ever, *ever* tell me that it's God up there who gets to decide whether or not that feeling of mine is wrong. Because if that's the truth, then fuck God. If my mother died today, I would stand up and cheer. And then I would keep cheering every day for the rest of my life. You want to know why? Because the world will be a better place the day she leaves it. And that's something that doesn't have anything to do with me or you or God. Period."

Nora's mind wandered as the argument continued. How many times had she wished Mama was someone else: Maria from *The Sound of Music* maybe, or the mother in *E.T.* who giggled with her children and allowed them to eat pizza in front of the TV? Anyone except Mama herself with her sharp nose and hard eyes that looked at Nora as if she were some kind of garden slug. And yet she had never wished her mother dead, had never allowed herself to creep up to that final possibility. What would it mean exactly if Mama died? What would that make her? She did not want to be an orphan, left alone in the world to fend for herself. Being sent to a girls' home like Turning Winds for other people to worry about did not make her an orphan, exactly. It just made her unlucky. Or lucky. It all depended on how you looked at it.

A silent moment passed. Ozzie breathed heavily. Grace was silent, tracing the faint map of veins on the inside of her wrist. She rarely pushed Ozzie to her breaking point. It had happened once and ended with them not speaking for nearly a week until Grace finally apologized. Next to her lay the new drawing she had brought to the meeting, this one a still life of the items atop her dresser: a miniature statue of the Infant of Prague, a hair-brush, two Bonne Bell lipsticks, and an old tin can filled with paintbrushes. It was beautiful, Nora thought. Beautiful and solitary and waiting, just like Grace herself, who was already in the middle of her fourth month at Turning Winds. There was still no word from her mother or the hospital.

"I don't really remember my mother," Monica blurted out. "She died when I was two."

"You're lucky," Ozzie said.

"My father killed her." Monica held Ozzie's stunned gaze for only a fraction of a second. Her lower lip trembled. She reached up and tugged on the end of one of her braids. "She was only twenty-eight. My father got a life sentence in prison and I ended up living with my grandmother. Then when I was fifteen, she died, and no one else in the family would take me. Which is how I ended up here."

"Holy shit, Monsie," Ozzie whispered. "Why didn't you ever tell me that?"

Monica shook her head. "I've never told anyone that."

An owl hooted once in the distance, a mournful sound that drifted through the night air like a cry.

"Do you have any pictures of her?" Grace asked.

"I do." Monica smiled wistfully. "Two actually. One that my grandmother gave me, and one that I stole from her."

"I've never seen any pictures," said Ozzie.

Monica shrugged. "I keep 'em in my top drawer, under my socks."

"Why do you keep them there?" asked Ozzie.

"I don't know. I tried putting them on my dresser, but it felt weird. I know she's my mother and everything, but it's like looking at a stranger." Monica paused as a slip of a smile crossed her face. "She has red hair like me, though. And the same bump in her nose. Like, exactly. My grandmother told me she used to read me that *Madeline* book all the time, and sometimes when I read it now, I'll imagine sitting on her lap. Then I'll take the pictures out and look real hard at them, to see if something about her'll come back to me. But it never does. It's like she never existed."

"You were only two," Grace said. "No one remembers that far back. It's not your fault."

"How about your dad?" Ozzie asked. "Have you ever gone to see him in prison?"

"No." Monica shook her head. "Why would I?"

Ozzie shrugged. "I don't know. Maybe he's changed. It can happen."

Monica shook her head. She pulled hard on her bottom lip, trying not to cry. "I don't want to see him. Like, ever."

Ozzie rubbed her back. "Okay," she said. "I know, Monsie. It's all right."

"How about your mother, Nora?" Monica asked, eager to shift the attention to someone else. "What was she like?"

Nora reached up and pulled on her earlobe. She took out her notepad the way she always did, and let the tip of the pen hover above it for a moment. *She liked her husband more than she liked me,* she wrote, and gave it to Grace to read aloud. It was not an inaccurate statement, and she was not going to get into any more detail. What would she say: that Mama had known what Daddy Ray had been doing to her from the time she was ten years old? Mama hadn't actually caught her husband in the act until Nora was twelve, but Nora could tell by the slit-eyed looks she cast her way over the breakfast table, or the way she would sometimes walk behind her chair and pinch the skin beneath her upper arm, that she had known before that. Would she tell them that for as much as Mama had permitted things to go on, she was also violently jealous of the attention Daddy Ray showed her child, so much so that it had taken the remote control incident, leaving Nora's head split wide open, for her to finally be removed from the home? These girls would think she was a freak if she admitted something like that, would probably turn and run screaming in the other direction if she went there. It was too dark. Too gross. Too much.

Around the group, heads nodded in recognition as they read Nora's statement; small grunts of disgust drifted toward the floor.

"So how'd you end up here?" Ozzie asked.

"She liked to throw things too," Nora wrote. "I got hurt."

Another round of murmurs. Monica stared at her the way a child might stare at a parent who has donned a frightening Halloween costume and burst into the room. Grace reached out and rubbed Nora's arm. Ozzie chewed on her nails.

"Is that where that scar on your forehead came from?" Monica whispered.

Nora nodded, running her fingers over the small indentation. There was nothing more to say, nothing else to write. She didn't want to talk about it anymore, either. Maybe ever again.

"You're the only one left, Grace," Ozzie said, taking her fingers out of her mouth. Nora held her breath, but Ozzie didn't allude to the months Grace had been waiting to hear something—anything—from her mother.

They all waited as Grace traced a line on the floor, her thin fingertip collecting a tiny pile of dust. "You already know that my mother's in a hospital."

"You said that before," Monica said gently. "Did she get hurt? Like, an accident or something?"

"No." Grace didn't raise her head. "It's a mental hospital." She opened her mouth and then closed it again. "She gets really depressed sometimes. Like to the point where she can't do anything. At all. Except sleep a little."

"Shit." Ozzie let out a low whistle.

Grace lifted her head quickly, staring at her for a moment, as if trying to determine Ozzie's sincerity.

"I'm serious," Ozzie said. "That sucks."

"It doesn't *suck*," Grace said. "Some people have it a lot worse. And she's been doing the best she can, considering my dad walked out on us three years ago and she doesn't have any money. It's not her fault."

"Of course it isn't," Ozzie agreed.

Grace nodded. "Now that she's in a hospital, they'll treat her and probably put her on some kind of medicine and then she can come and get me."

Nora noticed Ozzie and Monica exchanging glances. She held her breath, waiting for Ozzie to say something about denial or maybe even God, but Monica spoke up first.

"How'd you end up here?"

"One of the teachers at school found out that my brother and I were living with her in her car." Grace scowled. "It wasn't that big of a deal. I think she was more annoyed that we were stealing food out of the dumpster behind the Burger King than anything else. She kept pointing at my pocket and telling the caseworker that I had a freaking hamburger in there."

"What happened to your brother?" asked Ozzie.

"He's with my aunt," Grace dropped her eyes again. "She could only take one of us. It's fine. He's little. I wanted him to go with her. He wouldn't have been able to handle foster care or a place like this."

"How long did they say your mother'd be in the hospital?" Monica asked.

"Two weeks." Grace spoke to the floor. The silence was unbearable. "I know what you're thinking," she said, looking up. "But it's only been a little over three months. She probably just needs more treatment than she thought. She'll get there."

"You *want* her to come back for you?" Ozzie asked.

"Of course I do." Grace looked stricken. "She's my mother."

"That's just a word," Ozzie said.

"Not to me." Grace clenched her teeth. "My mother didn't abuse me. She tried. She did her best. She loves me. And she'll be back. She will. I know it."

Nora wondered if she was the only one who doubted Grace's words that night, or at every Invisibles meeting thereafter when Grace would repeat them again. "She'll be back for me. She will. I know it." It was like a mantra, uttered for the sole purpose of hearing it said aloud. Maybe the words did something to keep Grace's spirit buoyed, a balloon of sorts that she could hold on to so that she did not sink. Nora could not help but wonder too, on Grace's last day at Turning Winds, exactly thirty-one months later, when she finally let go of that balloon and watched it sail away into a silent blue sky, if that had been the beginning of the end for her.

Or the end of the beginning.

Chapter 9

Henry served lunch out on the small enclosed deck behind the kitchen. The green wicker table had already been set with pieces of blue-and-white china, silverware, and white cloth napkins. A bowl of white and yellow flowers was set in the middle on top of a lace doily. Nora watched Henry as he set large bowls of steaming carrot-tomato soup in front of each of them, and then waited as everyone helped themselves to a dish of parmesan croutons. He was equally attentive to them all—passing the pepper to Monica before she asked for it, refilling Ozzie and Nora's water glasses when they got low—but especially to Grace, whose hair he would reach out and tuck behind her shoulder as she leaned in for a bite of soup. Did she like being doted on? Nora wondered. Or did she regard such demonstrations with impatience, the way she used to? Every so often in high school, when Max reached for her in front of the rest of them, he would get his hands shoved away and a dark look, as if he had just done something wrong. It was difficult to tell what Grace was feeling now; her face would revert into a blank, expressionless stare as they ate, and her right foot jiggled against the floor.

Monica got up twice during the meal to answer her phone, disappearing into the back of the house to talk and then reemerging, full of apologies. She and Liam were in the middle of closing on a new apartment, she explained, and things were a little hectic. Ozzie did most of the talking as Henry served the second course—small plates of arugula, roasted chicken, and goat cheese—launching into a story about how she and her husband, Gary, had first met. "It was at a Yankees game," she said. "Something I normally wouldn't be caught dead at since I'm a Red Sox fan, but my friend had an extra ticket and begged me to come. Anyway, Gary was sitting in front of me, and when the other team got a hit, I jumped up and screamed and accidentally dumped my beer all over him."

"You didn't!" Monica's eyes were wide as cornflowers.

"I did." Ozzie looked around the table. "I felt terrible, of course, and ran to the concession stand to get a bunch of napkins. And then, after he had gotten himself all cleaned up, he asked me out on a date."

"Oh!" Monica squealed and clapped her hands. "I love it!"

"Now every year on our anniversary, at the very end of the night, we pour a bottle of beer over each other's heads," Ozzie finished, laughing.

Henry laughed a little too loudly along with her, glancing over at Grace to see if she thought it was funny. She smiled and fiddled with an arugula leaf.

They talked a little bit, each of them, about their work: Monica, who did not have a regular nine-to-five position, spent whatever free time she had planning and participating in fund raisers with other women in her new tax bracket. The events were all the same, she said. "Lots of wine, expensive outfits, and high heels, all disguised as assistance for the needy. And boring, to boot." Nora talked about her job at the library and the degree she'd earned online, unable to hide the pride she still felt for her milestone achievement. "Oh, Nora, that's so fan*tas*tic," Monica said, placing a hand over hers. "That's one thing I will always wish I'd done. I'm so proud of you."

Ozzie was equally effusive, winking at Nora over her salad. "You were always the brains of our outfit. Goddamn, girl. Good for you." Ozzie ran an egg-and-vegetable-selling business out of her house and also did palm readings in her kitchen.

"You wouldn't believe how many people out there want their readings done," she said. "I get them from all over the place—people on road trips who stop just because they're bored, townies who've lived in the area for thirty-plus years. I don't think I've had a single day in the past three years—except maybe Christmas—when I haven't done at least one reading."

"I've never had anything of mine read," Monica said. "Or my fortune told, or anything like that. I've always wanted to, but I'm scared."

"Of what?" Ozzie asked.

"I guess of hearing something I don't want to hear," Monica answered. "What if I went to some lady who looked into a crystal ball and told me I had six months left to live? Or that she sensed the relationship I was in was coming to an end? It would change everything, hearing something like that. I would live my whole life differently just because of what someone said."

"But who's to say that what you'd been told was right?" Nora said, glancing over at Ozzie. "I'm sure the readings *you* do are accurate, Oz, but you don't know who else is out there. They could be telling you anything."

"Real palm reading is an art, just like painting or writing or photography." The defensiveness in Ozzie's voice had left, replaced now with an urgency that Nora had not heard before. "You've got to really believe in it yourself for it to work. It can't just be a way of making money." She raised an eyebrow in Monica's direction. "And just to put your mind at ease, Mons, if someone you've paid a hundred dollars for a palm reading says that your life is coming to an end in six months, ask for your money back. No one can ever know when your life will end. No one."

A silent, ponderous moment passed. Then Ozzie said, "Do you work, Grace?"

Grace's face blanched. She lifted her napkin and dabbed at the corners of her mouth.

"She's been painting up a storm," Henry blurted out. "I don't know if any of you saw the pictures in the living room . . ."

"We did see them." Ozzie nodded.

"They're lovely," Monica added.

Grace forced a smile.

"We're thinking of showing them," Henry said. "You know, in a gallery. There are a few buyers who've already expressed interest."

"A gallery?" Monica repeated. "How fantastic!"

A noise that sounded like static floated out from somewhere in the living room.

"That's the baby monitor." Henry stood up. "Let me just go check on her. I'll be back in a minute."

Nora put her spoon down. She pressed two fingers against the bottom of her breastbone and took a breath. She could do this. She could. She looked over at Grace, who was picking at the lettuce on her plate. "Congratulations, by the way, Grace." She was forcing herself to talk, dragging the words out of her mouth with a rope. "What's her name?"

Grace winced, as if Nora's eyes were burning a hole through her skin. "Can you please call me Petal?" She swept her eyes over Monica and Ozzie; it was a request for all of them. "Please. I've been Petal for three years now. I really, *really* don't like to be called Grace anymore."

"Oh." Nora dropped her eyes, embarrassed. "Of course. I forgot."

"Thank you." Grace's voice was soft as she looked back at Nora. "Her name is Georgia."

"Oh, that's a beautiful name!" Monica burst out. "I love it! What made you choose it?"

"For Georgia O'Keeffe?" The name was out of Nora's mouth before she realized it had formed in her brain.

The tightness in Grace's face eased, a loosening of strings beneath the skin. "That's right," she said. "My favorite artist of all time. Remember, Nora?"

Nora nodded. Of course she remembered. She remembered all of it.

"Why was she your favorite?" Monica asked.

"Oh." Grace dismissed the question with a wave of her hand, as if it were unanswerable. "Just her . . . way with everything. I can't even remember specifically anymore."

"Light," Nora said. "You used to love her way of working with light. You said once that all her pictures, even the dark ones, had some source of internal light, which generated through the colors."

Grace looked at her blankly. "I said that?"

Nora nodded. "And another time you told me that on really good days, when you drew something well, you felt as though you were borrowing some of that light."

Grace locked eyes with her, and for a moment Nora thought they were back in that little room, Grace curled up in bed, her charcoal pencil making little *skitching* noises on a pad, Nora huddled against the wall, reading a book. Hours could go by like that, whole afternoons, without a sound or a word from either of them. And it had been enough, the easy understanding that hovered there between them like some kind of warm air. It had been more than enough.

Grace's brow furrowed. "I guess what I really loved about her was that she didn't copy anyone else. She trusted her own instincts, which were way off the beaten path, not like anything anyone had really seen before. She said in an interview once that it took courage to create your own world. And I guess what I like most about her is that she dug deep enough to find that courage."

"Wow." Monica ran a hand through her hair. "I love that."

"Can I ask you a question?" Ozzie interrupted the moment. "Where'd you come up with the name Petal? For yourself, I mean. I'm curious."

Grace lowered her eyes and stared into her salad. "I just like it. I think it's pretty."

"It's beautiful," Monica said. "It fits you."

Grace rested her chin against the heel of one hand. Nora stared at the tiny white lines that ran across the inside of her wrist in sordid little tic-tac-toes. Had there been another attempt earlier? Maybe even before Henry? Had life really seemed that unbearable?

"I guess what I mean is, where did the whole idea to change your name come from?" Ozzie shifted a little in her chair, crossing one leg over the other. "Why would it even occur to you? Most people don't do that."

Grace tossed her head. "I told you. I don't like the name Grace. I've never liked it."

"Really?" Ozzie pressed. "You never said anything about it before."

"Ozzie," Monica said gently.

"Okay." Ozzie took a swallow of mineral water and set the glass back down on the table. "I don't mean to pry. I was just wondering."

Henry came back in then, smoothing a hand along the nape of Grace's neck and down along her shoulder before sitting in his chair. "Snug as a bug," he said. "She should sleep for another hour or so before her next feeding."

Grace looked away distractedly, as if the information about the child pained her. Nora couldn't help but wonder if Henry tended exclusively to the baby. Did Grace ever hold her or pick her up? Did she look at her, even from afar, or had the postpartum depression made even that difficult?

Grace pushed her chair back and stood up. "Excuse me. I have to use the restroom."

Henry watched her go, his eyes anxious. Then he looked back

at the women. "That's my cue to get dessert," he said. "Sit tight. I'll be back in a jiffy."

"Well." Ozzie tossed her napkin on the table and folded her arms across her chest as Henry disappeared. "What do you think?"

"She's like a . . . shell." Monica reached inside her purse as her phone went off again.

Ozzie glared at the phone as Monica brought it into view. "Is there any way you can turn that thing off for a while?"

Monica glanced at the screen, bit her lip, and then pressed a button on the phone before sliding it back into the bowels of her purse.

"I think she's less than a shell," Ozzie said. "She's like a zombie. I know I said that she was going to need us for more than a weekend, but there's nothing we're going to be able to do even if we do stay longer. I think she needs to go back into the hospital. Seriously. She needs really intense psychotherapy, or something. The woman is walking around like she's half dead! I mean, who are we kidding?"

For a moment, Nora agreed with her. This was too big for them. There was nothing any of them could do. None of them were trained in any sort of psychology or counseling, and Nora herself didn't have the slightest idea about medication or how any of it worked.

But.

"Do you remember how I was when I first came to Turning Winds?" she asked.

"Of course I remember." Ozzie took her hat off and rubbed her hair.

"You didn't talk," Monica said fondly. "You wrote everything down in that little unicorn pad of yours."

"*I* was a shell of a person," Nora said. "And then I met you. And you brought me back to life. All of you." She paused. "Remember when I talked for the first time?"

"Meeting Number Six," Ozzie said, winking at her. "Never forget it."

"Me either." Monica's eyes glistened.

It hadn't been a "moment," or even anything special. Certainly nothing wrapped in dramatics. There had been no scene or yelling, nothing yanked out of her by force. It had simply been another Invisibles meeting, her turn to share another first line that she'd already chosen and written down carefully in her notebook for Grace to read aloud. And yet for some reason she didn't pass the notebook to Grace that night. She'd stared at the cover of it instead, studying the swirl of blues behind the rearing unicorn, the narrow, conchlike pattern of the animal's horn, and realized that she didn't need it anymore. That part of her life was over. It was time to go on, to open another door.

"Nora?" Grace had prodded. "You want me to read it?"

She had shaken her head and placed the notebook down next to her. And then she'd opened her mouth. "I want—" she started. The words came out slowly, haltingly, a baby bird pecking its way out of a shell, and she cleared her throat and tried again. "I want to do it."

For a moment, no one moved. The silence, combined with the weight of the girls' stares, felt intrusive, as if she'd done something wrong, and she felt a catch in her throat.

"Go," Ozzie said before Nora could take another breath. "Go, Nora."

Monica and Grace leaned forward just as eagerly, and Nora straightened up a little bit, feeling for the first time in as long as she could remember that nothing in the entire world could hurt her in this moment.

"'When I . . . stepped out into the bright sunlight . . .'" She paused here, amazed at the slight trilling sensation that emanated from the back of her vocal cords, dusty strings stretched thin across a violin, and pressed her fingers against her neck.

"Keep going," Ozzie urged. "Keep going, Nors. You're doing great."

She swallowed. "'From the darkness . . . of the movie house, I had only two things on my mind: Paul Newman . . . and a ride home.'"

Ozzie let out a whoop and clapped her hands. "From *The Outsiders*! Nora, you did it! Oh my God, you fucking talked!"

They crowded around her, drawing her in close under their arms and pressing their cheeks against hers. Monica cried a little, Grace hid her mouth behind a pair of cupped hands, and Ozzie laughed, punching the air with a fist. Over Grace's left shoulder, Nora caught a glimpse of the moon, round as a coin, white as milk. It was brighter than she'd ever thought possible.

"But you opened up after five or six months," Ozzie said now. "We've got two and a half *days* to work with here."

"We don't have to change her," Nora pressed. "Maybe all we have to do is give her something to hold on to. That's what happened to me. Right after our first Invisibles meeting. It was like something that had been sealed off for years and years opened inside and let the air in, after that first night when we all sat under the moon and shared our stuff and did our stick wishes. And I know it was just a start. But that start changed everything for me." She shrugged. "It helped me find my voice again. And maybe that's all we can give Grace now. A start. But it's something."

"You're absolutely right." Monica reached out and took Nora's hand. "It is something."

Ozzie scowled. But, Nora noticed, as Monica took her hand in her other one, that Ozzie pressed it gently.

Something was better was nothing.

And sometimes, Nora thought, if you got very lucky, maybe even a little more than that.

Chapter 10

Another ten minutes passed before Grace returned from the bathroom. She had pulled her hair up into a knot and loosened another button on her shirt. Stray tendrils fell down like wayward roots along the side of her face, and her skin had a just-washed look, as if she had splashed water over it.

"Hi, angel," Monica said. "Everything okay?"

"Yes." Grace sat back down heavily. "I'm sorry I took so long. I just needed a moment."

"No need to explain," Ozzie said.

The corner of Grace's eye creased ever so slightly at Ozzie's statement. Nora wondered if the old tension between the two of them was building. Or if it was already back.

"Listen, I don't want to jump the gun or anything on our plans," Monica said. "But Liam made reservations for all of us tonight at a beautiful restaurant in the city."

"He did?" Ozzie turned her baseball cap around and settled it backward on top of her head. "Wow, that was big of him."

Monica looked hopefully at Grace. "Have you ever been to a place called Tru? Right in downtown Chicago? Liam says it's one of the best restaurants in the country. He's so excited to be treating us."

"Oh, Monica." Grace looked alarmed. "I wish you had said something first. I think Henry was planning on making a special dinner for all of us tonight. I don't think we should . . ."

"Absolutely not." Henry appeared in the doorway, holding a tray of miniature éclairs on small glass plates. "Don't even give it another thought. You girls go out on the town tonight and have fun." He put a hand on Grace's shoulder. "It'll be great for you, sweetheart. You haven't done anything like that in a long time."

"You're sure?" Grace looked up at him anxiously.

"I'm positive. I'll be perfectly fine staying here at home. Besides, after Georgia goes down for the night, I can catch up on my boat."

"Your boat?" Ozzie repeated.

"Henry's building us a rowboat in the garage out back," Grace said. Nora could hear the pride in her voice. "We're going to take it out on Lake Albeena on summer nights. Especially when the moon is full. Henry and I love being out on the water under the full moon."

Nora wondered if it was a slip of the tongue that Grace had mentioned going out on full-moon nights. She'd been sure that she was the only one who still took an interest in it, but did any of the rest of them ever think about their meetings and stick wishes up there on the roof? Did any of them still regard the moon as the strongest female force in the universe, under which anything was possible? Maybe she wasn't the only one, after all. The thought made her feel light inside.

"Oh, how wonderful!" Monica slid an éclair in front of her, running her index finger over the flat wedge of chocolate on top. "I've always wanted someone to row me across a lake. That sounds amazing!"

"It will be." Henry leaned down and kissed the top of Grace's head. "Now who wants tea?"

"Where in God's name did you find him?" Ozzie stared at Grace as Henry left again.

Grace smiled. "He's sweet, isn't he?"

"Sweet?" Ozzie repeated. "He's a goddamn saint!"

Grace smiled. "We met at a wine-tasting party a few years ago. It was random seating and we were next to each other."

"Was it love at first sight?" Monica sounded breathless.

"No." Grace's voice was soft. "Actually, I didn't even really look at him until I overheard him tell the maître d' he couldn't drink red wine. The guy looked at him like, *What the heck are you doing at a wine tasting, buddy, if you can't drink red wine?* but I understood perfectly. I can't drink it either. The tannins make me break out in hives. But I love all different kinds of white. Anyway, that's what started us talking."

"What was the first thing about him that you liked?" Ozzie picked up her éclair and took an enormous bite. Nora watched her eat, Ozzie's mouth moving up and down voraciously the way it always had. Ozzie ate things the way she did everything else— quickly and without much thought of the consequences.

Grace considered this for a moment, her fingers touching a tiny vein along the side of her neck. "I think his kindness. He was kind right away, from the first minute we started talking. He asked me if I was comfortable where I was sitting or if I wanted him to move over." She paused. "That and his lips. He has very sexy lips."

"You like being married to him?" Ozzie's jaws were still working, pulsing with every chew.

"I do." Grace nodded. "It's very . . . what's the word I'm looking for? Comforting, I guess. I feel comfortable being married to Henry."

"I know exactly what you mean," Monica said.

Ozzie stopped chewing. "Oh, really? Is that really how you would describe your relationship with Liam? Comfortable?"

"Absolutely," Monica replied. "I'm the most financially comfortable I've ever been in my entire life." She threw her head back and laughed. Her ivory teeth glittered against the late afternoon light. Nora got the feeling that Ozzie and Monica knew something she did not. Maybe they knew a lot of things she knew nothing about. It wouldn't surprise her. Not anymore.

Ozzie snorted and tossed the last of the éclair into her mouth.

"How *did* you and Liam meet?" Grace asked.

Monica folded her hands in her lap. A coy smile spread across her lips as she took the clip out of her hair and shook it out. "Well," she sighed. "I used to have this fabulous job as a bike messenger in the city."

"A *bike* messenger?" Grace repeated. "*You?*"

Monica laughed. "I know! Can you believe it? I've always been such a klutz; I never even considered trying to balance on top of a bike. But my first roommate was a bike messenger, and after I quit the whole nanny scene—which was a nightmare, by the way—I needed a job, and her company was looking, so I just said to hell with it and tried it out." She leaned forward, as if letting everyone in on a secret. "And guess what? I was good at it! I could shoot in and out of traffic, up and down those long, wide streets, like you wouldn't believe. God, I'd get such a rush going places at that kind of speed. And that's how I finally, finally lost the weight! You girls wouldn't believe it. I mean, I turned into a lean, mean bike-riding ma*chine*." Her voice sounded wistful for a moment, and Nora wondered when the last time was that Monica had been on a bike, how long it had been since she'd done anything so plucky, just for herself. "Anyway, one day I had to deliver a big manila envelope to this address on Park Avenue. Liam opened the door and . . ." She paused, flicking her wrists out on either side. "The rest is history."

"He asked you out right there on his stoop?" Ozzie asked. "Right there, while you were standing there in your bike shorts?"

"They were *really* cute shorts," Monica said.

Ozzie laughed. "I bet they were."

"And now you're married?" Grace asked.

Monica blushed and fiddled with the edge of her plate. "No. We're not married. Just . . . together. We've been together for three years and have a place right off Central Park West." She smiled again. "And two cats. Coco and Chanel." She nodded, as if the picture was complete. "We're very happy."

Nora thought back to a day at Turning Winds when she and Monica had been lying outside in the backyard. They were quizzing each other on vocabulary words for an upcoming test (the prospects of which looked bleak for Monica) when the conversation turned to the future. "I don't care about being smart or getting any kind of real important job when I grow up," Monica said. "I just want to be happy. And pretty. I want to be happy and pretty more than anything else in the whole world."

She'd certainly cornered the market on pretty, but was she happy? Really?

"How about you, Nora?" Ozzie asked. "You said something to me yesterday about a guy in your life, but you didn't really get into any details. What's his name?"

"Oh." Nora's fingers went up to her earlobe. "Joel. His name's Joel."

Joel was the name of a man in his late seventies who had been coming into the library every day for the last six years to read the *New York Times*. Nora knew his name because once, in all that time, he had checked out a book—*The Life and Times of Winston Churchill*—and had to hand her his library identification card.

"And . . . ?" Ozzie encouraged her with a wave of her hand. "How'd you meet?"

"Oh, he came into the library." How many lies did this make since her first conversation with Ozzie yesterday? Three? Four? But how could she not lie? How could she sit here and be the only woman who not only wasn't in a relationship but had decided that she didn't want to be, that she wanted instead to live a life alone with her dog, her walks, and the moon? How did you go about explaining something like that? To anyone? Including herself?

"What's he look like?" Monica asked.

"He's . . . um, tall." Nora coughed. "Dark hair. Nice looking."

"Is it serious?" Grace asked. "I mean, do you think he's the one?"

"Oh no," Nora said. "We're just . . . I mean, we just started . . . it's new, you know? We only met a little while ago."

"I thought you said you'd been together a while." Ozzie leveled her eyes. "When we talked on the phone?"

"Yeah, well . . ." Nora smoothed the front of her pants with the heels of her palms. "You know. It feels like a while to me. But it actually hasn't been so long." She dropped Ozzie's gaze, unable to hold it.

"Just take your time." Monica nodded her head. "There's no need to rush anything."

"You can say that again," Ozzie said. "I just jumped in—feet first. It didn't even occur to me to wait." She pointed to Nora's untouched éclair. "You gonna eat that?" Nora shook her head. Ozzie popped it into her mouth, chewing with the same voracious movement as before.

"Do you think you rushed it?" Monica asked.

"I *know* I rushed it." Ozzie's mouth was full of chocolate and pale cream again, all mixed in together. "I married Gary when I was twenty years old. Who the hell knows who they are at twenty?"

"Whatever happened to your Argentinian lover?" Monica raised an eyebrow.

"Cesar?" Ozzie rolled her eyes. "Best sex I ever had, but he had a really mean drug problem. I couldn't take all the people constantly coming in and out of our apartment. It was like living at a zoo."

Nora looked down at the table. It was not hard to imagine Ozzie doing drugs or having sex; both things seemed as natural as breathing when it came to her. Still, she felt guilty as the sudden images flooded her head, as if she'd opened the wrong door by accident.

"You say no one knows who they are at twenty," Grace said slowly, "and I'd have to agree with you there, but does anyone ever know who they are at any age?"

The question slowed Ozzie's chewing. "Well, *yeah*. I mean, I hope we do. Isn't that the whole point of getting older? To find out who you are, what you want?" She leaned forward. "Or, more importantly, what you *don't* want?"

"But who's to say that happens at a specific age?" Grace asked. "I mean, isn't this whole 'finding ourselves' thing a lifetime process? Something that changes all the time? Look at me. I would have never thought I'd want a child as badly as I've wanted one this past year. And now I have one . . ." Grace's mouth began to quiver. Around the table, breaths were taken in and held, fingers closed in reverence. This was the reason they were here. It was time to be quiet now and listen.

"How do things work like that?" Grace said. "Why does it happen that way?"

"What things?" Ozzie asked. "What way?"

"It just doesn't make any sense." Grace shook her head. "I mean, when I found out that I was pregnant, I was ecstatic. I started taking those horrible prenatal vitamins and stopped eating sugar. I didn't exercise at all except for the occasional walk, I stopped drinking coffee, I didn't even *look* at wine."

Inside the house somewhere, Nora could hear a clinking noise. It was probably Henry fumbling with the teacups, setting them neatly inside another tray with fresh napkins. *Stay inside,* she thought to herself. *Don't interrupt this.* And then, in the next breath, she thought, *He probably already knows all this. He probably knew it first.*

"I was so excited about it," Grace continued. "So thrilled. And then I had her. And a few weeks in, I just . . ." Her voice drifted off, a boat fading on the horizon. "I don't know what happened. But I don't feel that way anymore. Not even a little bit. It's just . . . gone."

"But it'll come back," Monica whispered. "Won't it?"

"I don't know." Grace's eyes shimmered. "It's so far away from me right now that some days I really don't think it will."

Ozzie leaned forward. "But you know it's not real. You just feel this way because of the postpartum depression."

Grace's face contorted, a map crumbling in on itself. "Just *because*?" she repeated. "Are you really going to kick all this down to a 'just because,' Ozzie?"

"I'm not trying to diminish it, Grace," Ozzie protested. "I'm just saying it's a feeling. It's not reality."

"It's *Petal*," Grace said firmly. "And until you've been through some of the things I have, please don't talk to me about how real or unreal my *feelings* are."

"I didn't mean . . ." Ozzie blinked rapidly, at a loss.

Grace shook her head. Her mouth was still twisted, as if she were sitting on a nail. "Please stop, okay? Please. Henry and I have been over all of this already." She inhaled through her nose and placed her hands flat out in front of her. "Maybe it's not about having a child. Maybe it's that I realize now that I don't—and haven't ever—deserved to be a mother."

"What do you mean, sweetheart?" There was a catch in Monica's voice. "Why would you say something like that?"

Grace raised her eyes, moving them over each face around the table, as if looking for something she had lost long ago. She opened her mouth and then closed it again.

It was then that Nora understood why Grace had needed them to come. It was because she wanted to be absolved of the sin she felt she had committed so many years ago. And she wanted them—the only people in the entire world who knew about that sin—to somehow grant her absolution. As bizarre as it sounded, it wasn't so crazy. Not really. If they couldn't do it, who could? And maybe, just maybe, if they could figure out a way to put it all to rest, once and for all, the remainder of them would be absolved as well. Even her.

"Of course you . . ." Ozzie started, but Grace cut her off with a raise of her hand.

"I can't talk about this anymore. Not right now, okay?"

Ozzie glanced down, defeated.

Monica rubbed Grace's pinkie finger. "Listen, why don't we all go lie down for a while? Ozzie and Nora and I have been traveling all day, and you look like you could use a little rest, too. We'll all take nice long naps. Then we can freshen up and go for dinner."

Grace nodded wearily. "That would be nice."

Nora followed, rising from her chair as Grace stood up. Her heart was beating fast, like the wings of a hummingbird, and her face felt hot. She would welcome the chance to be alone for a while.

The three of them turned to look at Ozzie, who was the only one still seated.

"Ozzie?" Monica asked. "You coming?"

Ozzie stood. "I have to call Gary. And then I think I'll take a walk. I need a little fresh air."

"But you don't know the neighborhood," Grace said. "You might get lost."

"That's okay." Ozzie grinned and put her baseball cap back on. "I always get lost. I'll find my way back."

Nora stared at Ozzie for a moment, and then grabbed her windbreaker from the back of her chair. "I'll go with you," she said, turning around in her chair as Ozzie opened the porch door. "Come get me when you're done with your phone call." She waited as Ozzie let the screen door slam behind her. "Ozzie!" she called again.

"Got it." Ozzie raised her hand without turning around. "Gimme two minutes."

Chapter 11

Nora stayed in her chair on the porch as the other women dispersed, held in place by an anxiety that pressed against her chest like an oversize hand. How was all of this supposed to be working, exactly? Had they really come all this way just to bicker and argue with one another? Or was it necessary, like brushing cobwebs out of an attic before settling in to open the boxes? She knew she'd be annoyed—devastated, really—if she went back to Turning Winds after a weekend in which they'd all sat around exchanging banal pleasantries and acting their politest selves. The bickering was hard to listen to, harder to still to be a part of. But it also meant they were being honest. Which brought her back around to herself. Was she really going to keep up the fake boyfriend story? There was bound to be more talk about everyone's significant others as the weekend progressed. Could she really keep it going? Did she want to? If she had to come clean to anyone without worrying about judgment, it was these women. None of them would care that she was single. So why did she?

She got up from her chair and began walking around the room. They hadn't even laid eyes on her yet, but what would she do if Grace's baby started in on some inconsolable crying jag? They'd only been here a few hours, and it was still early. Nora knew first-hand that there was something about the lateness of the day that seemed to throw kids off balance. She'd seen babies as young as two weeks old have meltdowns in the library; one cried so loudly and for so long that Nora had to leave the building altogether, sitting on a side bench across the street until the helpless sound faded in her ears. It was strange how that particular time of day seemed to unleash some kind of weird energy over kids. Trudy called it the "witching hour." She said her own children had been the same way when they were little, falling apart at the seams as soon as the sun started to set. It was almost three o'clock now, which meant that they had a good two or three hours until dusk rolled in, but Nora wasn't about to take any chances. She had to get ready. She had to be prepared.

Behind her, Ozzie stalked across the yard as she talked on the phone. Her voice rose and fell as the conversation dragged on; Nora could make out snippets of it through the screen door—words like "until" and "absolutely." Suddenly Ozzie stopped and looked straight up into the sky. Nora could see the tips of her fingers turning white as she clenched the cell phone against her ear.

"Please don't make me feel like I have to ask your permission here, okay, Gary? I'm thirty-two years old, not a kid." She paused, shading her eyes with her free hand, as if studying something overhead. "I already told you. I'm planning on coming back to-morrow. I'm just putting it out there, in case we need an extra day or two. That's all. Yes. Yes. I *told* you that, *yes*."

Nora walked into the living room. Eavesdropping made her uneasy. And for some reason, the voice Ozzie was using now—the pleading one—didn't sound like her at all. She thought about what Ozzie had said before, that her husband called her Chubbers since she'd put on weight. She knew there were all kinds of fond little nicknames that couples shared between themselves, but that one didn't seem cute. In fact, it sounded rude to her.

She made her way down the hall, pausing outside the last door where Henry had said the bathroom was. Monica was inside, leaning toward the mirror, plucking her eyebrows with a pair of tweezers in one hand and holding her iPhone in the other. The interlocking *C*s on the back of it had small jewels at the tip of each one. "Wait, who?" She arched her eyebrows and tilted her chin as she regarded her profile in the mirror. "What'd he say?" Her voice dropped an octave as she stood up straight. The tweezers fell to the floor. "Did he say *why?*" She listened for a moment, her back rigid, the fingers of her other hand creeping around to clutch the front of the phone. "No, I have no idea." She glanced in the mirror, catching Nora's gaze, and reached out with one hand to shut the door.

Nora moved quickly back down the hall, embarrassed at having been seen. She passed Henry and Grace's room; just inside the door, which was partially ajar, they were embracing. She pulled on her ear and headed for the front door. The center of her chest ached, and a roaring sounded in her ears. But she was the one, she reminded herself, who had ended both of her relationships in the past few years, who said no every time a man had asked her out since. There hadn't been many offers—maybe three or four—but she'd always said the same thing. No thanks. Not up for it. And she hadn't been, not really. If there was someone who had been interested in just keeping things platonic, she might have responded differently. But things never changed, no matter who it was. Eventually, after enough time had passed, they always expected her to sleep with them. It was just the way it was, the natural course of events. Tom had held out the longest—almost two months, and she'd given in to Sinclair after one because she was so physically attracted to him—but the suffocating feeling she'd felt with both, the stifling sensation that overwhelmed her as soon as their bodies began to rise and then arch over hers, was always the same.

She would shut her eyes and count to ten, force herself to think of fields of yellow tulips or of walking down the street with Alice Walker, but inevitably as they began to push her legs apart and slide their way inside her, the feeling would overpower her until everything inside her head had disappeared into a roaring sea of white noise. *Quietquietquietandthenitwillbeover.* Until they finished, it was all she could do not to scream at the top of her lungs. She never did, of course, clenching her fists and biting the inside of her cheeks, but afterward she would excuse herself and retreat into the bathroom, where she would lock the door and crawl under the sink, holding her knees to her chest and pressing her forehead against the silver drainpipes until the panic subsided.

Theo had wanted it too, of course, something that Nora held against him for a while until she reminded herself that he was a normal seventeen-year-old boy and not Daddy Ray. He loved her too, which would make it okay, wouldn't it?

Maybe if he hadn't tried so hard, she thought later, if it had just happened quickly, naturally, a sensible progression instead of one long, drawn-out plan involving candles and new sheets, even a special Springsteen soundtrack he'd put together for the first time, maybe then it would have been better. She might not have felt so hopeful. Except that deep down, she knew this was a lie, too. Nothing anyone could have done would have made it better.

Theo had had the house to himself that weekend since his parents and younger brothers were away visiting relatives. There was a track meet the next morning that he couldn't miss; he was running the anchor leg in the 400-meter relay to try to qualify for districts, and he had to get to bed early. Still he'd made a special dinner for the two of them—hamburgers, baked potatoes with sour cream, and a salad. He'd even bought a peach pie for dessert, one of Nora's favorites, and served it up to her with a big scoop of vanilla ice cream on top. They'd eaten slowly, nervously, and then after they put the dishes in the sink, he led her up to his room.

Nora could smell the faint scent of pine and musk against his sheets and she wondered if he had sprayed them with cologne. There were white votive candles on top of his dresser, and she could see his hands trembling as he lit them. She was nervous too, but it hadn't occurred to her that he would be. *Tunnel of Love* played faintly in the background, the soft pulse of it thrumming between them. She kissed him hard as he took her in his arms, hoping he didn't notice the tremor in her lips, and helped him pull off his shirt. Shadows from the candles danced across his bare chest and the same familiar longing she felt when he held her close stirred again.

They lay naked for a long time, pressed together, kissing. She was acutely aware of the slenderness of his arms wrapped around her back, how the faint hair on his legs tickled against hers, and of his hardness against her stomach. When the time came, she closed her eyes, but for some reason, she hadn't thought it would hurt as much as it had with Daddy Ray, and the pain, combined with a nearly suffocating apprehension at this point, triggered other dark pictures inside her head. She squeezed her eyes and willed them to leave, but they only got worse, growing more and more vivid as Theo began to move in and out of her, until by the time he gasped and shuddered, she was weeping silently. He'd rolled off her, trying to pull her hands away from her face so that she could tell him what was wrong, but she could not look at him. Despite his continued protests, she begged him to take her home, and after a while he did. They'd tried twice more, but each time, it ended similarly. After the third time, they'd broken up. It had been a mutual decision, initiated by Theo, who seemed both horrified and helpless by Nora's reaction to him. They'd only spoken once afterward, and when he'd left for college, she'd never seen him again.

Yes, it was her fault she was thirty-two and alone. Her choice. And yet right now, the thought of calling Trudy and Marion—who were the only people in the entire world who knew of her absence—made her want to scream. Or kick something.

Instead, she took her cell phone out of her purse and dialed the library.

"Well, hel*lo* there!" Trudy said. "How's it going? And why in the world are you calling me so soon?"

Nora blushed. "Oh, I just wanted to let you know I made it okay. And to see how Alice Walker's doing."

"Oh, she's fine. Actually, she's more than fine. Marion is coming over tonight with three T-bone steaks. Two for us, one for Alice Walker. She's never going to want to leave me, you know."

Nora felt a pang of something inside her chest. "Tell her I miss her, will you? And tell her the moon is going to be a waxing gibbous tonight. It's one of her favorites."

"A waxing what?" Trudy repeated.

"Just take her outside when it gets dark. Out in the backyard or something, okay? And point at the moon so she can look at it. It'll be almost full. She likes to stare at it for a while."

"Done." Trudy's voice was soft. Nora wondered if the older woman thought she was crazy. Or maybe just weird. Did it matter?

"So how's the friend?" Trudy asked. "You all reconnecting?"

"Yeah. There's three of them, actually."

"*Three* of them?" Trudy repeated. "All from high school?"

"Yep."

"How come you never mentioned any of them before?"

"I don't know." Nora let herself out the front door and sat down on the brick steps next to one of the potted chrysanthemums. "I guess it just never came up."

The chrysanthemum plant was enormous, like a gigantic cloud, but up close, Nora could see the individual blossoms, small and tight, with pale yellow centers. She ran her fingertips along the surface of one, cradling the tip of it. She had never told Trudy or Marion about Turning Winds, or about any of the girls she'd met there. It wasn't important—or relevant—to anything.

"They're . . . okay people, though, right?" Trudy asked. "You'll be in good hands? No nuts in the bunch?"

Nora smiled. "We're all a little nuts, I think. In the same kinds of ways, though. Sort of like you and Marion."

"Okay," Trudy said. "Just making sure."

"Okay, then." She did not want to hang up for some reason, did not want to lose the connection just yet. "You know, I'm the only . . ." She stopped mid-sentence, biting down hard on the tip of her tongue. What was she *doing*?

"Yeah?" Trudy asked. "The only what?"

Nora cleared her throat. She looked up as a car drove by, some kind of blue station wagon with wide windows and rusty wheels. The driver, who didn't look much older than Nora, kept alternating glances between the road and the keypad on her phone. In the backseat, a young girl was reading a book. Her head was pressed up against the window, and she held the book out in front of her, as if to get the best light from outside.

"Nora?"

She blinked. "I'm the only single one," she said in a rush. "Everyone else is either married or in some kind of long-term thing. Which isn't the end of the world or anything. I don't even know why I'm saying this. I guess it just makes me feel . . ." She stopped talking again, leaning over the front of her knees and tracing an invisible line on the step beneath her. "God, I don't know." She closed her eyes. The silence on the other end was unbearable. Mortifying.

"It makes you feel . . ." Trudy encouraged. Her voice was soft. Almost gentle.

"Like a failure." Nora sat back up. "Which is stupid, of course. There isn't anything wrong with being single at my age. Or any age. I guess just being the only one . . ."

"All right now, you listen to me," Trudy said. "There's a reason you're not attached to someone yet, and that reason is no one's business but yours. I know I fret and worry about the whole situation, too, but the truth is, it's none of my business either. And it *certainly* doesn't mean you've failed at anything. My God, how many idiots are locked in some kind of sad, pitiful relationship just so they can say they're in one? Now *that's* failing, in my opinion. You relax and enjoy yourself, all right? The last thing you need to do right now is to start fretting about the fact that you don't have some *man* hanging off your arm. God Almighty."

Nora smiled, despite herself. She could always count on Trudy to set things straight. Even when she hadn't asked her to. And even if she insulted her in the process.

"You have yourself a good time, you hear?" Trudy was on a roll now. "Have some real fun! Let yourself loose! Spend some of that goddamned money you work so hard for. I want to hear all about it when you get back!"

Nora plucked one of the tiny flowers off the stem. It looked so fragile apart from the rest, so solitary and unsure. She put it back among the others, where it stuck out at an awkward angle. "I'll try," she said. "Thanks, Trudy."

Chapter 12

"I still can't believe Grace flipped out on me like that," Ozzie said as she and Nora started out on their walk. "All I did was suggest something about the things she's been going through. I mean, I know it's a sensitive topic, but God."

"I wouldn't say she flipped out, exactly," Nora replied. "She did have a strong reaction. But are you surprised?"

"What do you mean?" Ozzie pointed to the left as they reached the corner. The cross street read Maplethorpe Road. "Okay if we turn here?"

"Sure." Nora followed Ozzie's lead. "All I'm saying is *you* might think you just suggested something, but maybe Grace took it as you being judgmental." Nora chose her words carefully, not wanting to agitate Ozzie, whose tension level seemed to have rocketed even further since she had talked to her husband on the phone. "She's in a really fragile state right now, Oz. I think she kind of needs you to go—"

"I know, I know." Ozzie cut her off. "I can't even imagine what she's been through in the last few years. But then I think about that poor fucking kid, and it's all I can do not to start screaming at her."

"You mean Georgia?"

"Yes, Georgia! It's all well and good that Grace feels like she doesn't want to be a mother, but where does that leave her baby girl? God, even if Grace is depressed, doesn't it all sound just the slightest bit selfish?"

"She feels like she doesn't *deserve* to be a mother," Nora said. "That's a lot different than not *wanting* to be one."

"With the same result." Ozzie stared ahead stonily, unwilling or unable to cut Grace any slack. "Both of them leave Georgia up shit's creek. Just like our mothers did to us. I mean, Jesus. After two and half years of waiting for her own mother to come back for her in that fucking place, you'd think Grace'd know what being absent might do to a kid. Maybe even more so than the rest of us."

Nora pondered this for a moment. It was possible for women to reject their own children, whatever the reason. Mama had been so vocal about all the extra work Nora's raising required that it almost felt like a blessing when she was finally taken away. Still, something didn't sit right when it came to Grace's rejection of Georgia. Nora could understand the added physical stress a newborn might place on an already fragile psyche. But Grace had said that she wanted the baby. Desperately. And she was one of the most loving people Nora had ever known. After they had come across the dead bird on the sidewalk that day, Grace had scooped up the animal inside the hem of her skirt and carried it home. She fashioned a makeshift coffin out of an empty roll of toilet paper, wrapped the bird inside, and stuffed the whole thing into a Q-tip box filled with cotton. They'd buried it on the riverbank, near the water, and Grace had marked the spot with a tiny plastic figurine of Mary.

"It's just a bird," Nora had said gently as Grace knelt next to the spot and crossed herself. "Seriously, Grace. You really don't have to do all this."

"Of course I do," Grace answered, clasping her hands together in front of her chest. "It's one of God's creatures. Besides, if I don't, who will?"

That inherent willingness to love was, at least in Nora's opinion, one of the most beautiful things about Grace. It might have even been one of the most beautiful things she had ever come across in a human being. It was not something that could just disappear, even if her brain had gone temporarily haywire. Could it?

"Maybe she can't help it," Nora said now. "Maybe on top of the postpartum, there's too much other stuff that she hasn't started to deal with yet."

"Well, she needs to start dealing with it," Ozzie said. "And fast. Because that little baby of hers is going to end up with serious mother issues if she doesn't."

Nora didn't particularly disagree with Ozzie's assessment. But she wished that Ozzie didn't sound so irritated when she said it. It made her nervous. People like Grace, who had suffered for most of their lives, didn't just "get better." At least none that she knew of. It took time. Months, years. Maybe even a lifetime.

"I think she needs us to be patient. Grace always did better without people breathing down her neck."

"Maybe." Ozzie sounded resigned. "No, you're right. And I

shouldn't be so quick to judge all the time. Shit, she's been to hell and back." She slowed a little. "Remember when she found out that her mother had been released from the hospital? That she'd been living in that little apartment in the next town over for almost six months?"

Nora did remember. The news, which Grace had stumbled upon accidentally, after a friend's mother from school mentioned it, had flattened her. She'd stayed in bed for four days, staring at the wall, refusing to eat or drink. And then she'd snapped out of it, adopting the same mantra she'd used when she first arrived. "She'll come for me. She will. She just needs to get settled. To feel her way around in the world again. I'm not worried." Nora had marveled at Grace's ability to hope, how not even the endless days that stretched before her seemed to extinguish it. She wondered if all children possessed such a gift, if she herself might have it, even if she could not feel it.

Now Ozzie grabbed her arm. "How much of this do you think is actually about that night? You know, with the abortion and everything?"

The question caught Nora off guard, so much so that one of her knees buckled and she stumbled.

"Whoa," Ozzie said. "You all right?"

"Just tripped." Nora smoothed her hair back off her face.

"I think she might be still killing herself—or wanting to, anyway—because of her guilt about that night," Ozzie said. "You know? You think that's it?"

"Maybe," Nora heard herself say. "But there—"

"I know she's Catholic and everything," Ozzie interrupted, "but she acted like she'd actually gone and shot someone. Remember? How do you get someone to get over guilt like that? It's like trying to save the *Titanic* by bailing the water out with a paper cup. I mean, Jesus."

Nora didn't answer. She could feel a trickle of sweat, light and small as a sequin, sliding down the middle of her chest. She hadn't expected Chicago to be so warm in September. There was nothing short-sleeved in her suitcase, not one weather-appropriate item she had packed for such weather.

"This whole visit sounded a lot more manageable when I was talking about it on the phone with you the other day." Ozzie laughed. "Now I don't know what the fuck to do."

"I guess it's like what we said earlier," Nora said after a moment. "We just have to be here for her. And then maybe the rest will start to take care of itself." Even as she said the words, she wished she could yank them back, put them somewhere where no one would ever find them again. Her earlier belief in their validity had vanished; now they were just ridiculous things to say, juvenile thoughts, Hallmark-card mantras. *Just be there for her.* Please. Real life didn't work that way. Everyone knew that.

"Yeah, well." Ozzie sighed. She wasn't buying it, either. "It is what it is, I guess. Come on, let's see what's around this place."

Grace's neighborhood was small and neat, the tree-flanked streets dotted with bright blue recycling bins and stacks of newspapers. Flags bearing watercolor pictures of autumnal leaves and overflowing cornucopias stuck out from the front porches, and a few wisps of smoke curled out from the tops of chimneys. A first line by William Faulkner came to Nora as they made their way around a corner: *"Through the fence, between the curling flower spaces, I could see them hitting,"* and she tilted her face up toward the sun. It was warm against her skin, and she closed her eyes, feeling the heat of it against her lids.

Theo had been waiting for her in Mrs. Ditmer's room the day after they'd had sex for the third and final time and had asked her to come out into the empty hallway so he could tell her something. She did, but timidly, with her shoulders hunched, her throat tight, as if she'd done something else wrong besides dissolving into sobs (again) during sex. He stood next to her as she pushed up against the row of gray lockers and rested his hand on the metal door sticking out just above her head. She could smell the faint spiciness of his deodorant, the clean, aloe scent of the shaving cream she knew he used every morning, and she pushed down the stirring inside.

"Nora," he said softly. "Please look at me."

She shook her head. She couldn't look at him, couldn't even raise her eyes to stare at his Adam's apple.

"All right." He shifted his weight to his other foot, readjusted his hand on the locker. The faint smell of a cinnamon Life Saver drifted down from his mouth, and she wanted to raise her mouth and press it against his, to inhale the taste of him one final time. "I know I apologized for things last night," he said. "But I just want to make sure that you're really hearing me. I shouldn't have pushed. Especially after that first time. And definitely not after the second. I shouldn't have made you feel like you had to try again. I'm sorry."

His words were unexpected, and the shock of hearing them combined with their kindness brought tears to her eyes. She shook her head, the floor blurring beneath her feet.

"I know people have hurt you, Nora."

She raised her head warily, on guard. All he knew was that she lived in a group home. She hadn't told him anything else. Not about Mama, and certainly not about Daddy Ray. There was no way he knew any details about her past. Nobody did.

He shrugged at the question in her eyes. "I can just tell. I can feel it. And that's . . . I mean, I think it's better if we break up. I just . . . I don't want to add to that. Not in any way. Not ever." He kissed her on the cheek and then paused, his face inches from hers. "I couldn't take it, you know? Graduating next month and leaving you behind, knowing that I hurt you, too. I just can't do it."

She realized in that moment that she had been bracing herself for such a thing, more or less, since their very first date. But hearing the words out loud was unbearable, more painful than anything she'd imagined. He might as well have been staring at her from the banks of the pond as she slid under the ice.

"It's fine," she heard herself say, turning her face away from his. "You got what you wanted. I didn't expect any more from someone like you anyway."

The look that came into his eyes then reminded her of the time Mama had come into her room and without a word slapped her across the face. There was no reason for the blow, and as Mama turned around and walked back out again, Nora had caught a glimpse of her own face in the mirror across the room. She'd looked both shocked and crushed, a humiliated fragment of herself.

"Nora." Theo's voice broke in the middle of her name, and he reached for her, but she pushed his hand away and strode down the hall away from him. She could feel his gaze making its way into the center of her spine, through the red-and-white-striped shirt she was wearing, the one he had always said she looked good in, the one she had put on purposely this morning just to please him, and she knew that he was willing her to turn around, to look at him a final time, to say that she hadn't meant what she had just said, not a single word of it, but she did not. She would not.

She squared her shoulders instead, and kept going.

Here we are." Ozzie pointed to Grace's house up ahead. "See, I always find my way back. No matter where I am. God, I'm exhausted all of a sudden. I think I will take that . . ." Her voice faded as her phone began to ring. She pulled it out of her pocket and glanced at the screen. Her jaw clenched as she punched at a button and held it to one ear. "What now, Gary?"

Nora began to walk on ahead, wanting to give Ozzie privacy, but she heard her name being called. "Nora, wait! It's my kids!" Ozzie jogged up next to her and pressed another button. "They're on speakerphone. I told them all about you before I left. Say hi!"

"Hello?" Nora spoke tentatively into the phone.

"Hello?" A little boy's voice came through the tiny microphone. "Is this Norster?"

Ozzie laughed out loud, and Nora couldn't help but smile. "It is," she said softly. "What's your name?"

"Alec," the boy said. "I'm four. Are you on a walk with my mom?"

Nora glanced at Ozzie, who was nodding gleefully. "Yes, we just walked around the neighborhood. It's nice to talk to you, Alec. I like your name."

"It means 'defender.'"

"My name means 'God is gracious!'" An older voice cut over the younger one. "I'm six!"

"Don't interrupt, Jack!" Ozzie leaned into the phone.

"Nice to meet you too, Jack," Nora stepped back, unsure what to do.

Ozzie leaned into the phone again. "Where's Olivia, guys? Does Daddy have her?"

"Listen to me, you cunt." The voice hissed through the phone like a serpent. It was a calm, weighted sound, the tone so horrifyingly matter-of-fact that Nora felt her whole body freeze, as if getting ready for battle. "What'd I tell you before about hanging up on me? I swear to God, I'll fucking . . ."

Ozzie turned away, stabbing at the speaker button with one index finger, and then stalked on ahead, pressing the phone to her ear. Nora could hear her replying, using her own vulgar language, sounding appropriately outraged, but for some reason, this fact did nothing to assuage her horror. She stood there for a moment, as if rooted to the ground. Who was this man, talking to Ozzie in such a way? And even more flabbergasting, why was Ozzie letting him? It could hardly be the first time he'd used such vile language; they'd been married for twelve years. Did Ozzie really put up with that sort of thing? Or even consider it acceptable?

And if she did, when had that happened?

And what else in God's name was she hiding?

Chapter 13

Ozzie was pacing around the living room when Nora let herself in the front door. A vein, wide as a shoelace, was pulsing in the middle of her forehead, and her jaw was thrust so far forward that it looked disjointed. The only other time Nora could remember seeing her in such a state was when they had talked about their mothers back at Turning Winds. And even then, Ozzie's anger had been fleeting, a sudden release of something that she had been able to bottle again, like water. This was bigger. And this time, Nora wasn't sure if she was going to be able to put a cap on it.

"Hey." Nora tried to keep her voice steady. "Oz. You okay?"

"I'm fine." She threw her phone on the couch and walked over to the window. "Goddamned motherfucker."

"Ozzie." Nora walked toward her. Ozzie's hand, clenching one end of the curtain, was trembling. Nora put a hand on her shoulder. "Oz. Please. Talk to me."

Instead of answering, Ozzie dropped the curtain. She scrubbed her face with her hands, the skin along her fingertips turning pink and then white, and then sank into the couch, shaking her head.

"Does he call you names like that a lot?"

"Oh, he was just worked up." Ozzie's fingers were clenched so tight that the knuckles were turning white. "We both get like that. We fight a lot. Obviously. He's pissed that I came and left him with the kids."

Nora blinked, still uncomprehending. The Ozzie she knew would never stand for a man who would call her such disgusting names or deny her freedom. It didn't make sense. What was going on?

Ozzie's eyes filled with tears, and she brushed them away with two brusque flicks of her fingers. She got up again from the couch and yanked the curtain back once more. "Fucking asshole. Goddamned motherfucking asshole. The only other time I've gone away in twelve years—in twelve goddamned *years*—he did the same thing. Called the whole time and made me feel like shit about it. I should've known better." Without warning, she reached out and pounded the wall with the side of her fist. "I should've never come." Her voice was barely above a whisper. "I should've stayed home and never fucking left."

"What is it that . . . he . . ." Nora struggled for the right words. "Is it that he doesn't trust you?"

"Probably." Ozzie's voice was dull now, resigned. "Or he doesn't have a goddamned life of his own, so he resents me having one." She turned, taking Nora's hands. "Listen, I'm sorry I got you involved in this. It's not fair to you, and it was never my intention. It's not even that big of a deal really, okay? I have a husband who gets a little crazy sometimes. That's all. But I'd appreciate it if you wouldn't say anything to anyone else. About the call, I mean. Or what I just said about him. All right?"

Nora opened her mouth but didn't say anything.

An exasperated noise came out of Ozzie's mouth. "The last thing I need right now is anyone else knowing this shit and getting all worked up about it. Especially with everything else we've got going on with Grace. Come on, Norster. This weekend is about her, okay? Not me. And especially not my marriage."

Nora swallowed.

"Nora." Ozzie squeezed her hand a little too hard.

"Okay." She took a breath. "But you know, it's not okay that he calls you names like that."

"Oh, I know." Ozzie sighed. "Believe me, I call him worse." Her eyes searched Nora's as if peering at something in deep water. "I gotta go lie down," she said finally, dropping Nora's hands. "I'll see you in a little while, okay? For dinner?"

"Okay." Nora's voice was small. She watched Ozzie walk from the room, and she didn't move until she heard the door to Ozzie's bedroom close. Then she headed upstairs.

She needed to lie down, too.

The entire right side of the room that Nora and Monica were sharing, a neat, small space with yellow walls and white trim, was almost completely taken up by Monica's luggage—two enormous Louis Vuitton suitcases and a Gucci carry-on bag. Eyelet curtains tied back with pieces of yellow fabric hung over a single window, and the beds had been made up with patchwork quilts and matching pillows. There was a bureau too, and a throw rug on the floor that matched the colors in the quilts. Another one of

Grace's paintings hung above the bureau, this one framed with gold edges. Another bruise, although not as dark as the ones downstairs, with the same scribbled moniker in the corner.

Nora lay down on one of the twin beds and pressed her hands over her eyes. They were trembling. She felt drained inside, exhausted, like the time she'd tried to swim too many laps at the pool and emerged from the water breathless and shaking. So much had already happened in such a short span of time. Grace getting so angry at the lunch table. And now the scene with Ozzie and the phone. Nora shuddered as the sound of Gary's voice drifted through her head again, the way he'd emphasized the *t* in that awful word, as if spitting it at her. Then there was everything else still waiting on the horizon. How long was it going to take for that final, dreadful night at Turning Winds to be addressed? Because it would have to be, wouldn't it? That's what this trip was ultimately all about—coming to terms with their actions that night, and somehow, in some way, making peace with them? Nora wasn't sure if she could do it anymore, if she possessed the physical or emotional strength to withstand what was to come.

She sat up as her door opened.

"Hi," Monica said. "I thought I heard you come in. I was just getting myself organized in the bathroom. How was your walk?"

"Nice," Nora said, lying back down. Did Monica know anything about Gary? Had Ozzie let anything slip during the few conversations she'd had with her over the last few days? Or was Nora really the only one who knew?

Monica walked over to the other bed, taking in the room with a few sweeping glances as if seeing it for the first time. She had changed into white cashmere sweat pants and a matching hoodie, revealing just the slightest edge of a pink camisole beneath. Her hair was swept up, held in place with a tortoiseshell clip, and her heels had been replaced with delicate leather thongs.

"You guys weren't arguing just now, were you?" Monica asked. "I heard Ozzie down there. She sounded pretty loud."

"No, no." Nora wondered if Grace had heard anything. Or Henry. "You know Ozzie. She talks like that about everything."

"Yeah." Monica laughed. "So what'd you guys talk about on your walk? Anything about me?"

"No, nothing about you." Nora folded her arms behind her head and tried to smile. "Grace, mostly. And Ozzie's husband."

"Oh, Gary." Monica sounded disgusted.

"Why do you say it like that?"

Monica shrugged, running a fingertip over a line of stitching on top of the quilt. "I don't know. Just that I don't think Ozzie's all that happy with him."

"She said that?"

"No. Not exactly." Monica's finger paused. "It's just a feeling, really."

"What kind of feeling?"

"Oh, just something inside." Monica looked up. "Ozzie never wanted to get married in the first place. Remember?"

Nora nodded.

"You gotta wonder, you know? What was it about this guy that convinced her to do something that she'd always been so against? I mean, we're talking about *Ozzie* here. He must've been pretty . . ." She shook her head, letting the room swallow up the rest of the sentence. "I don't know. It's none of my business, anyway. It's her life."

Pretty what? What word would Monica have used just now if she had let herself? Nora wondered. "I heard him on the phone," she heard herself say, immediately wishing she could put the words back in her mouth. Not ten minutes ago, she had given Ozzie her word that she wouldn't talk about it with anyone else. And yet the admission had come so naturally, as if by instinct. A red flag had just been thrown into the ring. The others needed to know.

"When?" Monica turned. "On your walk?"

Nora nodded. "He was awful to her."

"What do you mean? In what way?"

"He called her a . . ." Nora could not bring herself to say the word out loud. "You know, the *c* word."

Monica went rigid. "He did not!"

Nora dropped her eyes, as if she had been the one to commit the offense.

"Why?"

"I don't know. She had the phone on speaker, and we were talking to the kids, and he just came on all of a sudden and started cursing at her."

"In front of their kids?" Monica sounded incredulous.

"I guess so. They must've still been around."

They looked at each other for a moment, waiting, it seemed, for the other to provide a perfectly reasonable explanation for the incident. Except of course there wasn't one.

"Well," Monica said finally, shaking her head. "Honestly, if it was anyone else, I might worry."

"But it's Ozzie," Nora concurred softly.

"He shouldn't be calling her anything even remotely close to that. But she's got a mouth of her own that she uses. I'm sure she can handle it."

Nora nodded. She hoped so. Whatever "it" was.

Monica kicked her sandals off and lay back on the pillow, positioning the heel of her right foot on top of the toes of her left. "Are you tired?" she asked.

"A little."

"Do you want to sleep? I'll leave."

"No," Nora said. "Stay."

"I'm not that tired after all. And even if I were, I don't think I could sleep if you gave me ten Ambien. My brain is just racing."

"About what?"

"I just can't stop thinking about all of us back at Turning Winds. It seems like yesterday, doesn't it? And now here we are, all these years later, and everything from back then is still so much with us. Maybe even more so."

Nora couldn't go into all of it again, just after the discussion with Ozzie; if she did, something might explode inside her head. Instead, she turned so that she could look at Monica's profile. She stared at the perfect arch of brow above her black eyelashes, the alabaster skin that barely moved, even when Monica rested the tips her fingers against it. "What's it like being beautiful?" she asked softly.

"What?" Monica looked startled.

"Is it fun? Being so pretty?" Nora could feel her neck getting hot. "I just . . . I always wondered what it would be like."

Monica sat up. For a few seconds, her eyes roved over Nora's face, as if trying to figure out where her voice had come from. "Don't you think you're pretty?"

Nora muffled a laugh with the back of her hand. "Come on, Monica."

"No, really!" Monica got off her bed and sat down next to Nora. She pushed Nora's brown hair off her face and tilted her head, studying it.

"What're you doing?" Nora said.

"You have gorgeous bone structure," Monica said. "And everything is so natural! So real! I'd give anything to have that back, you know that? I've been pulled and pinched so many times now that my skin's natural elasticity will probably never be the same."

Nora pulled back. "Well, why'd you get pinched and pulled, then?"

"Oh, all the women in New York do it. Getting your face done is the thing to do these days. I haven't had that much done. A brow lift, some Botox. I got my nose done too, but that was more because of my deviated septum than anything else. I can actually make it through the night now without snoring. And my teeth. Liam offered to get my teeth done." She shrugged, a little pink rising along the swell of her cheeks. "God, remember how my teeth used to look? Like a jack-o'-lantern! And those horrible whistling sounds I used to make when I talked? You guys didn't call me Har-Monica for nothing. Seriously, how could I say no?"

"Do you like it better?" Nora asked. "The way you look now?"

"Oh my God, yes!" Monica touched the edge of her hair. "There's no comparison! I looked like a little gnome back then!" She shivered. "All that dry, orange hair, that horrible pimply skin. And chubby too. God, I was always at least fifteen pounds overweight." She looked out the window. "No wonder no one ever asked me out in high school. Ugh. I was just a dog."

Nora thought she saw something flit behind Monica's eyes when she said that. Boys weren't the only ones who hadn't wanted her in high school. She'd had no siblings, and after her grandmother died, there was no one else who had ever put Monica first again. Maybe not even until she met Liam. Maybe Monica wasn't the only one who fought so hard to hold on to love. No matter what shape it took.

"Well, I'm glad for you," Nora said now, touching the sleeve of Monica's hoodie. "Really, I am."

"Oh, Nora," Monica squeezed her hand. "God, you were always so sweet. You still are, baby doll. You're just the sweetest thing." She gazed at her for a moment and then said, "Do you wear any makeup? At all?"

"A little bit of Vaseline on my eyelids."

"Will you let me do your makeup? For dinner tonight?" Nora opened her mouth to object, but Monica pounced. "Oh, don't say no! Please! Let me put some makeup on you—just a little, I promise—and then you can see if you like it. If you don't, you can just take it off again. No hard feelings. Okay?"

Nora hesitated only a moment more before relenting. It had always been hard to say no to Monica, who rarely if ever asked for anything. She'd always been the one who insisted that Grace and Nora share the umbrella on rainy mornings as they walked to school, or let Ozzie have the last chocolate chip brownie after dinner, even though they were her favorite. And she had never, not once during their entire stay at Turning Winds, asked for anything else but a hug during every Who Wants What part of their Invisibles meeting. It took a lot for Monica to ask for anything really big for herself, although that had changed apparently, now that she could.

Nora sat still as Monica pushed her hair back with a black headband and tilted her chin toward the light from the window. "Okay," Monica said. "Let's start with a primer." She picked up a thin cylindrical bottle from an enormous pile of makeup she had dumped on Nora's bed and squirted a small amount onto the tips of her fingers. "This is going to set your foundation and make you glow."

Nora pulled back. "Maybe just do some mascara." She twisted her fingers in her lap. "I just . . . I don't want to look stupid, Monica. You know, like I'm all spackled. I'm really just a jeans and sneakers kind of person."

"Nora!" Monica arched her back. "You're going to have to trust me. I know what I'm doing, okay? I promise, you will not look *spackled*." She ran the tip of her finger lightly down the bridge of Nora's nose. "Not even remotely."

Nora closed her eyes then and let Monica do her thing. She could wash it off if she didn't like it, she told herself. Monica had said she could. No hard feelings. Monica's fingers across Nora's forehead, along her cheekbones, under her lips, were as smooth as marble, as soft as light. It occurred to her that this was the first time in a very, very long time that someone had touched her like this. This, Nora thought, was what might happen someday when someone she loved again brushed the tears off her cheeks or ran his fingertips over the planes of her face just before he kissed her. The thought alone made the inside of her nose prickle and the side of her neck flush hot, until, when

Monica asked her to open her eyes for the mascara, they were wet and glistening.

"Oh, honey!" Monica said. "What's the matter? Am I upsetting you? Do you want me to stop?"

Nora shook her head, mortified and grateful at the same time at Monica's reaction. "No, no, no. Go ahead." The words came out in a whisper. "It's okay. I'm fine."

And she was, she thought.

Right now she was perfectly, inexplicably fine.

Chapter 14

"Say cheese!" Henry pointed Ozzie's camera at the group of them posing in front of the fireplace.

"*Cheese!*" Nora was in between Ozzie and Grace, their arms clutched around her waist. Monica was on the other side of Ozzie, jumping up and down like a little kid. Nora held in her stomach again, hoping that a sudden burst of laughter wouldn't split open the back of Monica's black silk pants. She had on a blouse of Monica's too—a sheer peach thing with ruffles in the front that pulled a little across the front—and a pair of very expensive pearl stud earrings. The only thing she'd refused to try was Monica's high heels. Her dark gray New Balances with the pink stripes would do just fine. And when she had come downstairs in Monica's clothes, her face done up with Monica's makeup, both Ozzie and Grace had gasped in amazement.

"Oh, Nora!" Grace breathed. "You look spectacular!"

Nora bit her lip, smoothed down the front of the blouse. She looked over at Monica, who was beaming. "It's just . . . you know, for going out tonight. I don't usually get dressed up like this."

"Well, you should!" Ozzie said. "There's a friggin' bombshell inside that frame of yours, dying to get out." Ozzie did not look as if she had rested; on the contrary, the shadows under her eyes were darker, and her mouth lapsed every so often into a scowl. But she was trying, Nora thought. Despite everything else, she was trying. Just like she always did.

She got into formation with the rest of them as Henry prepared to take their picture. They were all done up: Ozzie in soft wide slacks and a purple V-neck sweater, Monica in a tight black dress and heels, her perfect face punctuated with a swipe of deep red lipstick, and Grace in a flowy skirt and blouse, her blond hair pinned up in a twist. A different scarf than the one she'd had on earlier had been looped several times around her neck and knotted neatly on one side. As awkward as she felt on the outside, Nora could feel a warmth rising in her belly too as she stood there, an assuredness she had not felt in a long time.

"Cheese!" they said in unison.

"Okay!" Ozzie said. "Enough already. Let's go eat!"

The white-gloved maître d', a thin man with wire spectacles, confirmed Monica's reservation for four and then led the women to their table by the window. Nora had never been to a restaurant like Tru before, had never even *seen* a restaurant like Tru before. The few times she'd accepted Trudy's repeated Friday night dinner invitations, they'd gone to a seafood place that was decorated with white-and-red plastic life preservers on the walls or a steak joint where peanut shells littered the floor. Here there were candles everywhere, some nestled in small coves along the walls, others in copper candelabras, their tips glowing in the dimmed room. Gold drapes framed the rectangular window at one end, and an enormous Warhol painting adorned the west wall. The carpet was a plush cream, the tablecloths stark white, and the chairs a smooth black satin. It was like something out of a magazine.

"So, what do you think?" Monica grinned as the waiter, dressed in a dark blue designer suit, left with their drink order. Nora had followed Monica's lead, ordering a glass of sauvignon blanc, while Ozzie ordered a Jack Daniel's, neat. Grace asked for a club soda with lime.

Nora shook her head and looked around anxiously. "I can't even imagine what a drink in a place like this is going to cost, let alone a meal."

"Let alone *four* meals!" Ozzie echoed, pointing to the menu. "Look at the appetizers!"

Nora's eyes roved over the tissue-thin paper anchored with gold ribbon inside her menu, trying to take in the strange words— *langoustine, carpaccio, foie gras*—without giving away her ignorance. But when she saw the prices—$260.00 for a trio of caviar samplers—she closed it again and put it to the side. Paying that amount of money for any kind of food, no matter how rich someone was, did not make any sense.

"Are you sure Liam is okay with this?" Grace asked. "I mean, he's never even met us."

"He doesn't have to meet you to treat you to dinner," Monica said. "He already knows how much you mean to me. Besides, he likes doing things like this. It makes him happy."

"He likes spending his money, eh?" Ozzie asked.

Monica arched an eyebrow. "On certain things, yes."

"Like you."

Monica nodded. "Yes. Like me. And really good food. Come on, girls, don't worry. I mean it. Besides, when will we get the chance to do something like this again?"

"Well." Grace still sounded unsure. "It certainly is generous of him. You'll have to make sure to leave me your address, Monica, so I can send him a thank-you note."

Monica smiled. "You don't have to do that. I'll tell him."

"Absolutely not," Grace scoffed. "It's the least I can do. My goodness."

"You know, I never think to do things like that." Ozzie closed her menu and looked at Grace over the top of it. "You'd think now that I'm all grown up with kids and everything, sending thank-you notes would be something I'd be doing all the time. God knows I should. Gary's parents probably spend a thousand dollars on Christmas presents alone for my kids." She pressed her lips together. "But I always forget. And then when I do remember, it's too late. Like, embarrassingly late. It's just one of those things, you know, where I wonder . . ." Her voice trailed off. "Oh, never mind." She opened her menu again, scanning the inside.

"What?" Grace asked. "That if someone had taught you to do that when you were younger, it wouldn't be so hard to remember now?"

Ozzie closed her menu again, slowly this time. "Yes," she said. "Exactly."

The women moved back a little as the waiter appeared with

their drinks. Nora took a sip and then placed the glass—which was the size of a small fishbowl—back on the table. The wine warmed her belly, but left a slightly sour pool on the back of her tongue.

"I used to have that problem with going to the dentist," Grace said. "It literally took me years to remember that I should probably be going on a regular basis to get my teeth cleaned and checked for cavities." She shrugged, stirring her drink with a slender stick. "She just never took me."

She. She meant her mother. Nora remembered a story Grace told them once about her and her brother going weeks without brushing their teeth because their mother couldn't afford brushes or toothpaste. Another time they had toothbrushes but had to rinse them in the Dunkin' Donuts restroom since they were out of bottled water.

"Well, Liam's the one who taught me how to eat properly." Monica's voice was soft, as if she was ashamed of this fact. "The first time he took me out and I looked at all that silverware on either side of the plate, I got so anxious about using the right one that I almost burst into tears. And then there were three different glasses!" She reached up and fingered one of her diamond earrings. "I caught on eventually. But I felt like a little animal for a while, until I did."

"Or like Julia Roberts in *Pretty Woman*," Grace said forgivingly. "Remember that scene with the snails? Where she sends one of them flying across the room because she doesn't know how to use that weird little fork?"

Nora nodded, listening. There had been a lot for her to learn on her own too, things Mama had never shown her, such as eating three meals a day instead of whatever you could find before bed. Taking a daily vitamin. Flossing. Changing her bedsheets every two weeks instead of every six months. Dusting. For real, with a cloth and lemon oil, instead of with the back of her hand. She'd picked up a lot of things by reading what other people did in books, such as getting an ob-gyn and following up once a year for a checkup. Even managing her periods had been an exercise in futility; the first time she had started to bleed, she had been sure she was dying. It was only when she went to the woman on duty at Turning Winds and confessed what was happening that she got the full story—and a box of pads, to boot. Once, when Trudy had observed her in the library kitchen, eating yet another lunch of saltine crackers and grape jelly, she'd put her hand on her hip and asked: "Don't you ever get sick of eating those every single day?" The question had startled Nora, who had taken to preparing the jelly crackers for lunch without even thinking about it. Now, though, as she thought back, she realized that they were exactly what she had prepared for herself back in grade school, when Mama had forgotten to pack her a lunch, and crackers and jelly were the only things in the pantry. Old habits were hard to break. Some more than others.

"I try hard," Ozzie said. "God, I try so hard to give my kids everything that monster didn't give me." She clenched her teeth. "But I still fuck up. The thank-you notes are just one example. I still forget so many things. Like just the other day, Gary had to remind me to turn the lights on when the kids were doing their homework." She shook her head. "It's ridiculous, you know? You'd think that getting used to working in the dark because my mother was spending her money on drugs instead of the electric bill would have worn off by now! But I still do it! After all this time!"

Monica reached over and touched Ozzie's cheek. "It's okay, sweetie. It's just the way it is."

A muscle pulsed along Ozzie's tight jaw. "No, that's the way it was. That's the way it *was,* Monica. It's not the way it is. And I don't want the way it was to keep being an excuse for the way it *is.*" She grabbed her whiskey glass, took a slug, and grimaced as it went down. Next to them, a woman with a beehive hairdo and frosted pink lips looked over as Ozzie plunked her glass back down. Nora stared across the table until the woman looked away again. She watched as the woman said something to the man across from her and then patted her lips with a cloth napkin.

If she were braver, she would stand up now, right at this moment, and walk over to the other table. She would tap the woman's thin shoulder, watch as the beehive turned, the painted eyebrows arched skyward. *Can't you see that my friend is peeling back her skin and laying herself on the table for all of us to see? Turn around. Cover your eyes. Show some respect,* she would say.

But Nora did not say anything.

She put her head back down and took another sip of her wine instead.

The meal lasted a good three hours. They shared multiple hors d'oeuvres, tiny plates of bizarrely shaped creatures—snails, mussels, chunks of squid—all drizzled with squirts of neon green liquid, and small dishes of white sherbet served in crystal wineglasses, something the waiter called palate cleansers. Nora spooned it carefully into her mouth, letting the bitter, sour taste melt along her tongue, and then asked for another one. The main courses came next. They had each taken a long time to decide on what to order and shared bites of their selections. Nora settled on what she thought would be a relatively benign piece of fish, only to sit back, shocked, as the waiter placed a gold-rimmed plate in front of her, heaped with a tangle of translucent noodles. The pile was drizzled with brilliant squiggles of green and a bright red poppy, complete with a stem, tucked in along one side.

"Oh, I just ordered fish," she said. "I don't know if this . . ." She paused, embarrassed, as the waiter nodded.

"The fish is under the noodles," he said, smiling. "You can eat all of it. Even the flower!"

Even Ozzie seemed a bit flummoxed. "Well, shit," she said, surveying her dish. It was some kind of venison braised in wine, bedecked with an enormous variety of green leaves and purple and yellow pansies. "Should I eat this or frame it?"

Nora poked at her pile of noodles with her fork, but they didn't budge. They had a shellacked appearance to them, smooth and glossy, as if they had been sprayed with Aqua Net. She stuck her fork into the middle of it, cracked off a section, and put it inside her mouth. To her amazement, the noodles turned soft and salty against her tongue, the crispy veneer a thing of the past.

"What do you think?" Monica was simultaneously watching her and texting on her phone.

"It's good," Nora said happily. "Really good."

"Mine too!" Ozzie's mouth was full, but she grinned, talking anyway. "Really fucking good!"

"Ozzie." Monica's voice was low as she put her phone back. "You gotta keep the vocab in check here. Please."

"Oh God, I know." Ozzie was still chewing. "Sorry."

Grace ordered some kind of chicken that had been freeze-dried and then flash-fried. It was settled atop a glistening puddle of cherry compote. Small green gooseberries dotted the sides, and an enormous pink orchid filled the other half of her plate.

"You gonna eat your orchid?" Ozzie asked, still grinning. "I dare you."

Grace took a small, careful bite of one of the petals and chewed. "It doesn't taste like much of anything," she said. "It's kind of bland."

Ozzie shivered. "They really shouldn't serve flowers to people. It goes against every rule of nature I've ever learned."

"What's a rule of nature?" Grace asked.

Ozzie shrugged. Her plate was almost empty. "Flowers are to be admired, not eaten."

"Point made." Grace nodded. "What else?"

Ozzie stopped chewing then and put her fork down. She looked at all of them around the table and then lifted her napkin and wiped her mouth. "The moon is the strongest force in the universe," she said slowly. "The moon is our rightful mother, the one we should have had from the very beginning." Monica looked over at Nora. "Children are to be loved and cherished," Ozzie went on. "We are to be loved and cherished."

A silence descended over the table. No one moved.

It was, Nora thought later, one of Ozzie's finest moments.

Then, and now.

Chapter 15

It was unusual for Nora to have a second glass of wine, but she did, urged on by Ozzie, who was on her third Jack Daniel's, and Monica too, who said that the sky—and the bill, apparently—was the limit. By the time they left the restaurant, Nora had to steady herself against the edge of more than one chair, and the periphery of the room seemed to swell and then close in on itself. She didn't like the feeling; it made her uneasy, as if the tight edges she was trying to keep aligned were loosening.

"It's a beautiful night," Ozzie said as Grace turned the car turned into the driveway. "What do you say we sit out on the back porch for a little while? Have a nightcap before we turn in?"

Nora waited. The mood on the drive home had been unusually somber; Monica had yammered on and on about some trip she and Liam had taken to Greece last year, but no one had commented on any of it. It wasn't that any of them were uninterested, just that their individual thoughts were elsewhere. She herself, for instance, was still thinking about the conversation at dinner, about the thank-you notes and the dentist. Were they still chained to the events that had shaped them throughout childhood, or had any of them—any single one of them—broken through and crossed over to the other side? She couldn't be sure about the rest of them, but as for herself, she knew the answer.

"Oh, that's a great idea." Monica's eyes swept the group eagerly. "I'm in." Her pupils looked too bright, as if they had been dilated. She'd had three glasses of wine at dinner, maybe more. Nora had stopped counting after the fourth course was served.

"Sure, that's fine." Grace sounded resigned, as if the choice had been taken out of her hands. "Henry always keeps a few bottles of wine in the fridge. Help yourself. I'll join you, but I'm going to run and get a sweat shirt. I always get cold at night."

Ozzie headed for the refrigerator as Monica and Nora went out to the back deck. They sat down at the wicker table, the same one Henry had served lunch on, and settled in. It looked strangely bare now without all the requisite china and dishes on the table; a wide green candle in the middle was its only adornment, centered atop a fresh white tablecloth. Crickets thrummed in the dark outside, and the faint smell of woodsmoke hovered in the air.

"You know, I think this has been good after all." Ozzie reappeared, an uncorked bottle of wine in one hand and three glasses in the other. "I don't know what I was hoping for exactly, but I think it's okay. At the very least we've gotten together and really talked, you know?"

"I agree." Monica traced an invisible line along the edge of the tablecloth. "I just hope we've talked about the things that need to be talked about."

"Like what?" Ozzie began filling the goblets with the amber-colored liquid.

"Well, like the real stuff," Monica said quietly.

"Like *what* real stuff?" Ozzie pressed, setting the bottle back down on the table. "You don't think the conversation we had at dinner was real?"

"No, of course it was." Monica reached out and slid her fingers around the belly of her wineglass. "It just wasn't everything."

"Well, we have all night." Ozzie pushed the cork back inside the bottle. "So shoot."

Monica took a careful sip of her wine. Nora watched the muscles move up and down along her throat as she swallowed, like the sides of an accordion. "It's not always that easy."

"What's not always that easy?" Ozzie squared her shoulders. "God, Monica, you don't always have to talk in code. It's us, okay? Just fucking say it."

"You don't always have to be such a bitch, you know that?"

The skin on Nora's neck prickled as Monica's words slashed through the air. For a moment, the only sound she could hear was the rush of something inside her ears and then the steady chirp of crickets again outside the screen door.

"A bitch?" Ozzie's fingers froze around the stem of her glass. "I'm not—"

"Yeah, you are, Ozzie." Nora wondered if it was the wine that was giving Monica her nerve. Or maybe this was just a part of her that had blossomed, something that had finally emerged after years and years of being so subservient to everyone around her. "You don't always have to say everything so rudely. Or like you're the boss of everyone. Those days are over, in case you hadn't noticed."

For a split second, Ozzie's face blanched. And then the second passed. She set her mouth. "What are you talking about? All I'm saying is that I thought we *were* talking about real stuff. If I said it too *stren*uously, then I apologize."

Monica exhaled loudly. She was on the verge of responding when Grace appeared. A small army-green satchel was in one of her hands, and she had donned a gray hoodie with the words WEST POINT on the front. A quirky look decorated her pretty face as if she had tasted something strange. "You guys okay?" she asked.

"Oh yeah." Monica waved the question away with her hand. She sounded weary. "We're fine. Little on edge is all. Long night, I think."

"Long *day*," Ozzie muttered. She lifted her glass and downed half of it.

Grace sat down, watching Ozzie carefully. "You found the wine."

Ozzie nodded and gestured with her chin. "What's in the bag?"

Grace didn't answer right away, taking her time instead to place the bag on the tabletop before her and run a hand lightly over the top of it. "Well, I can't drink, as all of you know. But I do have other ways to relax."

Monica, who had raised her own glass to her lips, froze. Her eyes moved from Grace to the satchel on the table and then back to Grace again.

Nora felt something flip-flop in her stomach.

Ozzie set her glass down on the table, surveyed the satchel for a moment, and then burst out laughing. "Can we join you?" she asked.

"Of course you can." Grace's eyes flitted about the table without making eye contact with any of them. "Why do you think I brought it down?"

It only took three inhales on the joint, the last one of which Grace coaxed Nora to hold and hold and hold until she thought her lungs might burst, before she realized she was high. It was a different sensation than the wine had produced, a deeper, thicker feeling that seemed to embody her cells and make time slow down to just the faint, steady ticking of something that might have been a clock or even just a watch. She was lucid in a way that she had not known she could be, a state of being in which everything was altered and then heightened. The crickets especially, with their incessant chirping, held a particular fascination; she found herself wondering whether, if she went outside and cupped one in her hand and then held it to her ear, the sounds it made would in fact manifest themselves into a kind of singing word. Maybe even a message.

She was brought back suddenly by the sound of her name.

"You don't ever hear anything from that Theo guy anymore, do you, Nora?"

She thought it was Ozzie at first, but she was mistaken. She stared at Grace again and then said, "What?"

"Theo," Grace repeated. "Theo Gallagher? I was just wondering if you ever saw or heard from him again. After we all left, I mean." The tightness around her mouth was gone; her lips were slack as rubber bands.

"No." Nora stared at the tablecloth, wondering how a thing could get so white. "He left too, you know. The same time you did."

"Yeah. I figured. I guess I just hoped . . ." Grace stopped, biting her bottom lip.

"What?"

Grace shook her head. "Oh, I guess I wish someone had stayed. For you, I mean. Especially after everything . . ." She let the words trail off, where, Nora imagined, they were encapsulated by a bubble, drifting somewhere in the night air. Maybe it would be there in the morning, and she could put it in her bag, tucked in among her sneakers and clothes, and take it home with her.

"What made you think of him?" Nora asked.

"I don't know," Grace said, trailing her fingers through her hair. "I guess just thinking about things in general." She let her head fall back and then rolled it up to attention again. "Didn't you tell us once that he wanted to be a lawyer?"

"Yes," Nora said. "In L.A. or some other big city. Definitely a city." She could feel her thoughts unfocus again, strands unraveling.

"I wonder if he ever made it," Grace said. "As an attorney, I mean. You don't know?"

"Me?" Nora touched her chest. "How would I know?"

"Oh, I forgot." Grace's eyes were at half-mast. "You said you didn't stay in touch with him. Still. It'd be fun to find out. You should Google him. Or Facebook him! See what you could find!"

"You couldn't pay me to be on Facebook," Nora said, and then, as Grace opened her mouth to object, "because it's annoying! Why people feel the need to document every breathing moment of their lives is beyond me. If someone has really significant news, tell them to pick up the phone the way it's always been done."

"You don't need to do anything like Facebook anyway," Ozzie

said. "I can tell you about Theo myself. He did make it. As an attorney, I mean."

Nora felt something firing inside her brain, like a distant firecracker. She sat up, eyes wide as quarters, and stared at Ozzie.

"I actually ran into him a while back," Ozzie said. "God, it must be eight or nine years by now, way before I had the kids. Actually, I can't even remember if Gary and I were married yet. No, we must have been married. I remember Theo saying something about my wedding ring."

Nora struggled to sit up straighter. "Where'd you see him?"

"Somewhere in Hoboken. You know, in New Jersey. Gary and I drove down for the weekend to visit some of his friends, and we went to this little dive bar after dinner and goddamn if Theo Fucking Gallagher wasn't sitting on a bar stool right there, in the middle of the place, drinking a pint of Guinness."

"All by himself?" Monica's eyes were wide.

"No, he was with some girl. His fiancée, I think. If I remember right. Maybe they were already married. I don't know. It was a while ago."

Nora felt a question rise inside her chest and then float off again. "And then what happened?" she asked instead. "Did he recognize you?"

"Well, *yeah,* he recognized me." Ozzie sounded insulted. "Geez, Norster, it's not like I went and shriveled up into some prune." She ran a hand lightly over the front of her face, as if to reassure herself. "Anyway, we had a blast catching up. I kind of felt bad for the wife, or fiancée, or whoever she was, if you want to know the truth. I mean, the two of us must've talked for an hour straight. I don't remember her saying a single word. He told me he'd passed the bar a little while back, and that he was working for some guy in Jersey. He hated it, though. He said he was biding his time until he could strike out on his own, maybe open his own practice." Ozzie looked at Nora. "He asked about you, of course."

"He did?" Nora could feel her breath coming in shallow spurts.

"Of course. He wanted to know how you were, all that. I told him I hadn't heard much . . ." Ozzie's voice drifted off. "You know, that we had sorta lost touch."

"Yeah, well." If she had some kind of device that enabled her to look inside her chest at that moment, Nora was sure she would have seen her heart deflating. Or maybe it was already flat.

"He really was such a nice guy," Monica said. "And so cute!" Her eyes had a dreamy quality to them too, half lidded and drowsy. "I remember he was in my senior English class. He had a sweet smile even with those little crooked teeth in front. Great hair, too."

Nora wasn't surprised that the girls remembered Theo. He had been her boyfriend, after all. But calling out details such as his crooked teeth caught her off guard, since for a long time, it had felt as if they were the only two people in the world. She had shared little things here and there with them, of course, such as the movies they went to see, the gold hoop earrings he'd bought her for Christmas, and the cake he'd made himself for her seventeenth birthday, but she'd kept most of it to herself. None of them knew, for example, about the first line she'd written down for him—"*Whether or not I shall turn out to be the hero of my own life, or whether that station shall be held by anyone else, these pages must show,*" from Charles Dickens's *David Copperfield*—or that he tucked it inside his shoe on race day because he said it brought him luck. Nor had she shared the little wooden box he'd given her on Christmas, the edges etched with clouds and stars, a picture of Peter Pan carved on top, in memory of their first date. She'd never breathed a word about telling him that she loved him, and she had never even considered saying anything about the disastrous sexual part of their relationship.

Still, how could she have forgotten the number of times Ozzie and Monica had crept into her room after one of her date nights so she could giggle about it with them? Monica liked to hear the details about the movies they'd seen, or who they'd run into at the theater, and Nora could still remember the look on Ozzie's face when she told them about the extraordinary sounds they'd heard beneath the ice. They'd given her space too, after the romance ended, letting her mourn alone for a while, and then sitting with her when the solitude felt too large to hold by herself.

"Holy shit!" Ozzie burst out suddenly. "Look at the moon!"

Three heads swiveled around, following Ozzie's pointed finger. A lopsided egg, wide as a nickel, huddled against a cape of blackness. For a moment, Nora thought, it looked as though it were breathing, the swell of the vast, pale stomach falling and then rising again.

"A waxing gibbous," she said. "Two more days, and it'll be full."

"A waxing what?" Ozzie asked.

"A waxing gibbous," Nora repeated. "That's what it's called at this stage. It won't be completely full until Monday."

"Huh." Ozzie sat back, obviously placated. "You know, for all my screaming and yelling about the moon back then, the only phase I ever got around to learning anything about was the full one." She shrugged. "Pathetic. So obvious. Well, whatever it is, it's fucking gorgeous."

"Oh my God, I have a great idea." Monica clapped her hands together. "We should have an Invisibles meeting!" She opened her eyes wide, as if letting everyone in on an enormous secret. "I know the moon's not completely full, but we're leaving tomorrow, and when are we going to have the chance to do this again? Let's go out in the backyard and do one. Just for old times' sake."

Four pairs of eyes drifted from face to face, gauging one another's reactions. Nora could tell their interest was piqued. She herself felt like her heart would burst.

"But we don't have anything," Grace said. "To share, I mean. You know, of our own."

"What're you kidding me?" Ozzie's eyes opened wide. "You've got about ten original paintings hanging twenty feet away! Go take one of them off the walls and bring it out here!"

Grace laughed, and for a moment Nora thought she had only imagined the sound. But then Grace stood up and laughed again. It resonated under the pale light, fragile and melodious. "All right," she said. "I will."

"Well, I *really* have nothing to bring to the meeting." Monica looked mournful. "I mean, I don't even cook anymore, much less bake. Liam and I either go out every night or order something in."

"Who says it has to be the same thing you brought to our old meetings?" Ozzie said. "Shit, we were teenagers back then. You can't tell me that in all this time, you haven't figured out something else that you can do well." She caught herself, and Nora could see her mentally backtracking on her choice of words. "I mean, look at you, Monsie. There's gotta be twelve million things you're an ace at these days."

Monica looked up at the ceiling. "Well," she said slowly, "I guess there is one thing I could share."

"Perfect." Ozzie turned her head. "What about you, Norster? You in?"

Nora nodded. "I guess so. I'll have to—"

"And even if you want to share something else of yours, can you give us a first line, too? Just because I love them so much and because this whole visit will have been worth it if I can hear one again?"

Nora blinked, her heart swelling. "I told you I don't do that anymore."

Ozzie leaned in close. "I don't believe you," she whispered.

Nora paused, studying the vibrant starburst pattern around Ozzie's pupils. Then she leaned in, pressing her forehead against Ozzie's and closed her eyes.

"All right," she said softly after a moment. "I can probably come up with something."

It was lie number six.

She had thought of a first line for a possible Invisibles meeting before she even boarded the plane.

Chapter 16

The women settled themselves in a circle on the far right-hand side of Grace's yard; the spot itself, with its soft grass, an overhanging lilac tree bough, and an uninterrupted view of the moon, seemed to have been waiting just for them. A small pile of sticks had been arranged next to the candle Ozzie brought out and centered in the middle of the circle. Monica and Grace giggled as they crossed their legs and then giggled some more. Nora wondered if they were too high to be participating in such a solemn affair, if in fact all of them were. Ozzie withdrew a lighter from inside the breast pocket of her shirt and lit the candle. The light from the flame danced over the women's faces, alternately shadowing and illuminating their features. Around them, the crickets chirped ceaselessly, as if trying to relay a message.

Ozzie straightened up and looked around the circle. "We are here to commence the thirty-first meeting of The Invisibles."

"The thirty-first?" Monica echoed. "Where the hell did you

get that number?" She had brought the bottle of wine out with her; it rested against her hip, corked and slightly tilted.

"I'll tell you exactly where I got that number." Nora wondered if the look Ozzie shot Monica was the same one she used on her children when she was trying desperately to be patient. "We had an Invisibles meeting every month when we lived at Turning Winds. Twelve months for two and a half years makes thirty meetings. That means that this makes our thirty-first."

Monica and Grace exchanged a look and then dissolved into giggles again.

Ozzie rolled her eyes. "Can we begin now?"

"Yes."

"Yes."

Nora nodded.

"All right." Ozzie gestured with her chin. "Monsie, do you remember the rules?"

"Of course I remember the rules." Monica grinned and then grew solemn. She closed her eyes and rested both hands on her knees. Ten seconds passed. Twenty. Thirty. Monica was still silent.

"Monica?" Ozzie pressed.

"Hold on!" Monica didn't open her eyes. "I just need a minute. It's been a long time."

Ozzie dropped her head. It was the second time, Nora thought, that Monica had put her in her place.

"Rule number one." Monica raised her head and spoke in a loud, clear voice. "Never speak of The Invisibles outside of this circle. To anyone. Ever. Rule number two: Members must always bring something of themselves to share at every meeting. Rule number three: Stick wishes are private, unless a member wants to discuss it with the rest of the group. No stick wish—no matter how weird—will be judged. Failure to abide by any said rules can result in immediate dismissal." She opened her eyes on the last word and gasped. "I remembered all of it, didn't I? I can't believe it! I remembered every freaking word!"

All of them laughed, including Nora.

"Great job." Ozzie gave her a wink across the circle. "Okay, now we have to share something of ourselves. Who wants to go first?"

Grace raised her hand, only to lower it and then raise it halfway again. "I guess I'll go." She reached next to her, centering a small framed print in the middle of her lap. Even in the dark, Nora could tell it was one of the bruises.

"This is *Melancholy*," Grace said. "It's the first of a six-part series I did a while ago."

"There are six *Melancholy*s?" Ozzie asked.

Grace turned the painting around. The expression on her face darkened, as if she were seeing it for the first time. "This is the only *Melancholy*. There's also *Staid*, *Pulse*, *Mania*, *Spiral*, and *Void*."

A chill ran over the tops of Nora's arms, and she shivered.

"What do they all mean?" Ozzie asked gently.

"Nothing, really. Just what I was feeling at the time."

"Where does *Melancholy* fit in with all the rest of the series?" asked Monica. "I mean, what number is it?"

"Second to last," Grace said. "Number five."

"Are the other ones in the series hanging up in the house?" Nora asked.

Grace nodded. "There's one in every room. Henry framed

them all for me and hung them up. He says they're work to be proud of."

"It *is* work to be proud of," Nora said, fighting off her alarm. She knew now what bothered her. The paintings had such different names. But every one of them looked the same: a pulsing bruise in a white, screaming sky. Every one of them was "Melancholy." She had a feeling that Grace had been depressed for a much, much longer time than any of them knew. "You've always had a way of being able to transfer what you feel onto the canvas, Grace. It's amazing."

"Petal," Grace said softly, placing the painting back down on the grass. "Please."

Nora stared at the grass, her cheeks burning. An owl hooted somewhere in the distance, and out in front of the house, a swath of headlights swelled and then dimmed as a car sped by.

"Okay," Ozzie said. "Who's next?" She raised her eyebrows in Monica's direction. "Mons? You up?"

"All right." Monica began to giggle. She slid the bottle of wine into her lap. The cork made a bright popping noise as she pulled it out of the neck, and she laughed again. Nora tensed. There was more than half a bottle left. She wasn't going to chug the rest of the wine in front of them, was she? Surely Monica was above fraternity tricks.

"What the hell are you up to?" Ozzie asked.

Instead of answering, Monica raised an eyebrow. Slowly, she lowered her face over the top of the bottle. It took Nora a moment to realize that the entire neck of the bottle was in Monica's mouth, and then another twenty seconds before she understood what Monica was actually doing. Up and down, up and down.

Monica's lips and tongue moved over the glass neck so smoothly that Nora might have been in awe if she had not first been so disgusted.

"Oh. My. God." Ozzie guffawed. "Monica Ridley. *Really?*"

Grace giggled hysterically. "Keep going, keep going! I could use some pointers!"

Nora tried to giggle as well, to prevent suspicion, but it came out awkwardly, like a cough. On and on Monica went, saliva dripping from the corners of her mouth now, her eyes locked in a heavy, glazed state as the minutes ticked by. Nora shut her eyes as the women continued to scream and laugh. It was not their fault that she had never told them about Daddy Ray. They were the last ones to blame for what she was feeling inside and she knew—she knew this to her core—that if she had ever told them the truth, none of them, not one single one of them, would be doing this in front of her now.

After a lifetime, it was over. Monica finished with a flourish, removing her mouth with a loud, sucking sound, and then raising the bottle high in the air.

"Bravo!" screamed Ozzie.

"Encore!" giggled Grace.

Nora clapped and tried to smile.

Monica wiped her mouth with the back of her hand. "I know it's not very ladylike," she said, "but it's also something I'm really, *really* good at."

Grace and Ozzie laughed again. "No one said we had to be ladies here tonight," Ozzie said. "I, for one, am duly impressed."

"Ditto!" Grace clapped again.

The three of them glanced over at Nora, and from the expression on their faces, Nora got the faint impression that they had forgotten she was there.

She tried to laugh, but it came out like a squawk. "Way to go, Mons." Her voice caught in her throat, squeezed up like a dishrag.

"Nora Walker." Ozzie straightened up from her slouched position. "Tell me you've never given a guy a blow job."

Behind them, the crickets screamed.

"Ozzie," Grace said. "Don't."

"You don't have to be so vulgar about things all the time, Ozzie," Nora said. Wait, had that been her? Had those words actually come out of her mouth? From the look on Ozzie's face, they had. And they'd registered, too.

"I'm sorry." Ozzie looked as if Nora had just slapped her. "I didn't mean to be rude, Nora. Really."

Nora put her hand on top of Ozzie's. She left it there for a moment and then took it away again. "How about you? Are you going to tell us a joke?"

"Oh, I've graduated a little bit from jokes." Ozzie's face relaxed itself again. "I thought I'd use another skill I've honed over the years."

"Ooooh!" Monica clapped her hands. "Are you going to read our palms?"

"I thought I would. Although I can't do everyone's. We'd be here all night. But if someone wants to volunteer . . ." She grinned as Monica stuck her hand up and began waving it back and forth. "I thought you said were afraid of things like this, Monsie."

"I am," Monica sounded slightly out of breath. "But I trust you."

"All right." Nora and Grace leaned in as Ozzie took Monica's hand in her lap and held it up by the wrist. "Okay, first we'll look at the size of the whole hand." The candle flame illuminated Monica's thin fingers and beautiful nails; they shone in the light like tiny pink shells.

"It's small," Grace volunteered. "And so feminine. God, Monica, every single part of you is just exquisite."

"Oh, honey, thanks." Even in the dark, Nora could see Monica beaming.

"A very small hand," Ozzie conceded. "Especially in relation to the rest of the body, which is incredibly long."

"Is that a good thing?" Monica sounded worried.

"None of this is good, and none of this is bad," Ozzie said. "It's just what is. That's all."

"Well, what does a small hand mean?" Monica insisted.

"Generally, a small hand means that a person is more active, that they spend less time thinking about things and just go do them instead. It also means you're emotional, and a little bit naïve. Especially when it comes to money issues."

"Oh." Monica looked thoughtful. "Well, I guess that could be me."

"Okay, now we'll look at your palm lines." Ozzie pointed to the three most obvious lines running the width of Monica's palm. "You've got a nice long life line, which is always good. Your head line isn't as long as it could be, but then . . ." Ozzie paused, maybe unwilling to say more.

"The head line is for intelligence?" Monica asked.

Ozzie nodded, pressing her lips together.

Monica sighed. "It's fine. Keep going."

"All right. This top horizontal one is your heart line." Ozzie winced and then ran her fingertip up and down the length of it. "From the length and deepness of this one, I can tell you that you have not met the real love of your life yet. But you will later."

Monica pulled her hand away as if she'd just been burned. "What are you talking about? Liam is totally the love of my life. Are you saying we won't last?"

"No. What I said was that you haven't met the real love of your life yet. The length of your love line indicates that you won't meet him until you're older. Whether or not that turns out to be Liam remains to be seen."

"But then how could it be Liam?" Grace asked. "I mean, if you said she hasn't met the real one yet?"

Ozzie shrugged. "Maybe they'll meet up again later. Maybe Liam will be different somehow. Changed. I don't know. I'm just reading the lines. And that's what your love line is indicating."

Monica rubbed the inside of her palm with her thumb, as if trying to erase the lines. "Damn it," she whispered. "That's exactly why I've never done any of this crap before."

"Here's the thing about palmistry," Ozzie said. "All it does is clarify things that we already know. Even if we aren't one hundred percent conscious of knowing it." She tapped the side of her head. "Our subconscious minds already hold more information than we can understand. Whether or not we dig deep enough to excavate that information is something we can decide—or not decide—to do."

"Sort of like deciding whether or not to listen to your gut," Nora said.

"Exactly." Ozzie put a hand on Nora's shoulder. "Exactly like deciding whether or not to listen to your gut."

"But that still doesn't make any sense." Monica's voice shook around the edges. "I love Liam. I love him more than I've ever loved anyone in my entire life. I can't imagine loving anyone more. Ever. Anywhere."

"Things don't happen or not happen just because you can't imagine them," Ozzie said. "Look at 9/11. Did you ever imagine even once that someone would use a plane as a weapon of mass destruction?"

"No." Monica sounded slightly panicked.

"I'm not saying Liam's going anywhere, Monsie." Ozzie reached out and grabbed her hand again. "Palmistry doesn't predict the future. It just reads your lines and interprets them. You do the rest. How your future plays out will always be up to you. Always."

"Okay." Monica nodded, her shoulders sagging. "Thanks. I think."

"Nora's turn!" Grace chirped after a moment. "Norster, you ready?"

Nora blinked a few times, trying to focus, realigning the first line in her head. It was a good one. She wanted to say it just right, to give it just the right amount of emphasis.

The three women stared at her expectantly, waiting.

"Well, it's a first line," she said. "From a book called *The End of the Affair.*"

"A first line!" Monica clapped her hands together once. "Oh, Nora! I was hoping you'd do one!"

Nora sat up straighter and cleared her throat, a vague excitement rising in her chest. It was then that she heard the noise, faintly at first, but gathering strength, as if someone were dragging it closer. She pulled at her earlobe once and then twice, as if to ward off the sound, but it only got louder. She couldn't be one hundred percent sure what it was, but something about the way her heart clutched and unclutched itself told her she didn't have to be certain; that the look on Grace's face told her everything she needed to know.

"Norster?" Ozzie obviously hadn't heard it. She cocked her head. "Come on, babes. You ready?"

Instead of answering, Nora stood up. She moved toward the sound, which was coming from inside the house. Maybe it was the weed, she thought quickly. Maybe she was imagining things, hearing something that wasn't really there. Did that happen when you were high? Could you actually start to hallucinate?

"Nora! Where are you going?"

"Honey, what's the matter?"

Ozzie and Monica called out behind her, but Nora kept moving. There was no mistaking the sound any longer, but the knowledge of this fact did nothing to ease her angst. She felt a hand close around hers suddenly, and she jumped.

"Henry'll settle her down." Grace's eyes were huge, and Nora thought she could see the moon reflected in them. "It'll be okay. It won't last long."

Nora inhaled shakily. Even Grace's inherent understanding of what she was feeling at this moment did nothing to ease the growing panic she was feeling inside; the yard around her felt as if it were closing in and even the sky seemed to drop closer, a mantle falling over her head. She would suffocate if she didn't get out of here; she would drown in a sea of sound.

The baby's wails went on and on, a rending of something deep inside, some bottomless pain that nothing would fix.

Nora pressed her hands against her ears and shut her eyes. "I have to go," she whispered, even as she realized that she still had not gotten around to making any kind of plan to prepare herself for this very moment. Somehow, with everything else going on, she had forgotten. Again.

"Go where?" Grace clutched at her sleeve.

"I don't know. Just for a walk. I'll be back."

"Honey, it's after midnight. And you don't know the neighborhood."

"It's okay." Nora increased her pace as she angled around the house. "I'll be fine."

"Well, at least let us go with you." Ozzie and Monica had caught up to Grace; Ozzie was pulling on the back of Nora's sweater.

"No!" She whirled around, facing them. "I don't want any company. Not now. Please. Just let me walk for a little bit and then I'll be back, okay?" She backed up, holding her palms out in front of her. "Please. Just stay here. I'm fine, okay? I just need a minute." She turned around before any of them could object and disappeared into the night.

Chapter 17

A light wind whipped the hair along the top of her head and rustled the leaves in the trees, but the silence that descended as she moved through the streets was so still as to feel almost sacred. It was the sort of stillness that had draped itself over her that last terrible night, after everything was over, as if the world around her had stopped breathing. She broke down all at once as she felt it and leaned against the thick trunk of an oak to steady herself. There was no telling how far she'd walked or even where she was exactly, but she was not worried. She longed for Alice Walker, her silent, faithful companion, who had only to push her nose into the space between Nora's ear and shoulder for her to feel that everything off balance had once again aligned itself. She felt an ache now, thinking of it, and sat down against the tree. For a long time, she sat very still, her eyes closed against the world, and breathed in and out.

Her watch said 12:45 a.m. God, was it that late already? She had to get back. She winced, thinking of it. The women would still be up, waiting for her, probably sitting in a row on the couch, hands on their knees, rushing fearfully toward the door when she came in. Even if they didn't push her to talk, the strain in their faces would be evident; they would have already discussed the situation in her absence, weighed in on her mental state (and here Grace was supposed to be the one with problems!), maybe even devised some other kind of secret hand signal or eye movement the way they used to do at Turning Winds whenever one of them needed to talk.

No. There was not a single person in the world who needed to treat her with kid gloves. She was beyond this. Past it. The fact of the matter was that Grace had a baby now, a real, living, breathing child. That was just the way things were. She needed to be stronger, to steel herself when the child inevitably cried. Because that was just what babies did; they cried. They wailed too, when their needs were not being met fast enough. And if her reaction to hearing it brought her to her knees, she would let herself fall, but only on the inside. This would be the last time she crumbled in front of them. In front of anyone. She was an adult now, thirty-two years old, for God's sake. It was time to act like one. She got up quickly, pushing herself off the trunk, and headed back to the house.

Breakfast the next morning was a somewhat somber affair, although Ozzie tried her best to keep things light with her goofy jokes, and Henry served perfectly poached eggs atop English muffins, each one dolloped with a lemony hollandaise sauce. There were individual mixed berry compotes too, and good, strong coffee, all served out on the back deck again as the sun peeked through the blinds. Monica, who had been preoccupied with another phone call, seemed on edge for some reason, and Nora kept her own eyes down, the remnants of her mortification still lingering around the edges. She'd been wrong about the women sitting on the couch or rushing for the door when she returned; only Grace, whose bedroom was on the first floor, poked her head around the corner as she heard the door lock, to ask her if she was all right. Nora had nodded, mumbling something about needing to sleep, and Grace had let her go, watching as she walked up the steps, and then giving her a little wave as she turned into her room. Monica had been in Ozzie's room, sitting on the edge of her bed, and they'd both turned, their faces tense and expectant.

"I'm fine," she volunteered wearily. "See you in the morning."

Some time later, after she'd brushed her teeth and slipped into her pajamas, she heard Monica opening the door and sliding into her own bed. The brief silence in the room was followed by a whisper. "Nora?"

She closed her eyes, which had been wide open, staring at the ceiling.

"Nora, you awake?"

"No."

"Okay." Monica sighed. "Well, I just wanted to tell you that I love you."

Her heart swelled then in the dark, a sea anemone expanding in the darkest recesses of the ocean. "I love you, too, Mons."

Somehow she had slept, but lightly, uneasily, one ear subconsciously tuned for the baby. It was, she thought later, quite possibly the longest Saturday night of her life.

"So what time's our flight?" Monica asked, spooning a bite of the hollandaise sauce into her mouth. "It's not 'til later, right? What should we do this morning?" She picked up her coffee, spilling some on the tablecloth, and then put it down again.

"Mons?" Ozzie was looking at her strangely. "What's the matter?"

"Nothing." Monica picked up her spoon to stir her coffee.

"Why's your hand shaking?" Ozzie asked.

Monica glanced at her trembling fingers and set her spoon back down. "Oh, I'm a little overtired, I guess."

"You don't look good," Ozzie said bluntly. "I mean, you look like something's eating at you."

"You do look a little anxious," Grace joined in. "Is something wrong?"

Monica pressed her lips together and shook her head. Without warning, a single tear welled out of her eye and slid down the front of her face.

"*Honey.*" Ozzie reached across the table and put a hand over hers. "What is it?"

Monica dropped her head and shook it from side to side.

"Is it because you're leaving today?" Grace tried. "I don't want you to leave either. But it'll be okay. Now that we've gotten back in touch . . ." Her voice trailed off as Monica shook her head again.

"Does this have anything to do with the phone call you made in the bathroom this morning?" Ozzie asked.

Monica's shoulders caved in on themselves as she gave way to the sobs, and for a moment, Nora was afraid she might fall face first into the plate of eggs still in front of her. She reached out and steadied one of her arms, but the gesture seemed to undo Monica completely. Her sobs drifted out from under her blond hair as she clutched at her face and began to rock back and forth.

"Jesus Christ." Ozzie pushed her chair behind her with the backs of her knees as she stood up and came around the other side of the table. "Monica Ridley! What the hell is going on? Talk to us!"

"Oh, God," Monica blubbered behind her hands. "Oh, God, I can't."

"You can't what?" Ozzie exchanged a bewildered glance with Nora and Grace.

Monica rocked harder.

"Who'd you call this morning?" Grace asked. "Liam? Is something wrong with Liam?"

Monica shook her head.

"Monica." Ozzie put a hand on her hip. "Please. We don't have time here for twenty questions. Please just talk to us."

"Oh, God, I can't," she moaned. "I've done a terrible thing. I'm a terrible person."

"You're not a terrible person." Ozzie squatted down next to Monica's chair. "Stop being so melodramatic and just tell us what's going on."

Grace gave Ozzie a withering look and came around to the other side of the chair. Kneeling down next to Monica, she smoothed her hair with one hand and patted her back with the other. "Honey. Try to calm down, okay? That's it, deep breaths.

In. Out. Okay, good. Now, can you try to tell us what's gotten you so upset?"

Monica pressed her fingertips against her mouth. "I'm in trouble," she whispered.

"What kind of trouble?" Ozzie asked. "What'd you do?"

Instead of answering, Monica began to cry again.

"Oh, for God's sake," Ozzie burst out, standing up again. "What'd you do, kill someone?"

Monica's head jerked as she stared up at Ozzie. "*No!*" Her voice, tremulous as it was, sounded furious.

Ozzie seemed unfazed. "Okay, well, good. Murder would be a tough one. Anything else I think we can deal with."

Monica's face eased a fraction of an inch. "You mean it?"

"Of course we mean it!" Ozzie looked at Grace and Nora. "Right, girls?"

"Of course," Nora echoed.

"Absolutely," Grace said.

"It's bad," Monica whispered.

"It's okay." Ozzie sounded grim.

"I . . . took . . ." Monica pressed her napkin into the corners of her eyes. "I mean, I stole . . ."

"What?" Ozzie encouraged. "A Prada purse? That tacky cell phone cover? What'd you steal?"

"Money." Monica dropped the napkin from her face and stared at a spot on the table. "I stole a lot of money. From the treasury. I mean, I'm the treasurer. For the fund-raising committee I'm on. For the charity. And I stole money. Other people's money. A lot of it."

Ozzie steadied herself on the back of Monica's chair and licked her lips. "Let's take this one step at a time. What's a lot of money? What are we talking here?"

Monica steadied her lower lip with her teeth. "A lot."

"Monica."

"Forty thousand dollars."

Ozzie inhaled sharply through her nose. Nora, who had started to sweat, could see Monica's shoulders trembling through the thin material of her blouse.

"Forty thousand dollars?" Ozzie repeated. She sat back down in her chair. "Are you serious?"

Monica nodded.

"Why?" Grace gasped.

Monica shook her head.

"*Why?*" Ozzie pressed.

"I don't know!" Monica cried, snapping her head up. "I don't have an answer, okay? I just did!"

"Did you need it?" Ozzie pressed. "I mean, was Liam not giving you money? Were you saving up or something? You know, trying to get away from him?"

"No, no, no." Monica shook her head back and forth. "No, it was nothing like that."

"Then what?" Ozzie said.

"I told you." Monica looked up helplessly. "I don't have a reason. I just did it."

There was a moment of silence around the table. Nora could not think of a single thing to say next that had not just been uttered. She stared at the top of Monica's white-blond hair instead, wondering how anyone just stole forty thousand dollars.

Especially if they didn't need it. What exactly went through someone's mind before they did something like that?

"All right, well, who were you on the phone with this morning?" Ozzie asked finally. "Liam?"

"No." Monica's voice was frantic. "He doesn't know. He can't ever know. He'll leave me if he finds out."

"Then who were you talking to?" Ozzie's voice was eerily calm.

"A detective." Monica choked on the word. She swallowed and fiddled with the ring on her finger. "From the Manhattan police department. He left a voice mail for me yesterday. Said I had to call him back no later than this morning."

"Which you did," Grace encouraged. "And then what?"

"He said they found out. That they know. The police, I mean. They know what I did. They've known for a while." Her face crumpled in on itself. "He said that I have to turn myself in before noon tomorrow at the Nineteenth Precinct."

"The *police* station?" Nora found her voice. "Why?"

"Because they're going to . . . press charges." Monica's upper body heaved under a fresh sob. "And arrest me."

"Holy *shit*." Ozzie's face was pale. "Well, of course they're going to arrest you. I mean, they have to, I guess. Right?"

Monica nodded helplessly.

"Can you try . . ." Ozzie began pacing around the room. "I mean, Monica, you live with a fucking millionaire! What the hell are you stealing that kind of money for? *Any* kind of money for?"

Monica closed her eyes against the question and shook her head.

"Monica!" Ozzie clenched her hands.

"She said she didn't *know*, Ozzie," Grace said firmly. "Now might not be the time to start analyzing the reasons why she did it. Especially if she's not ready to talk about it."

Ozzie's face was turning pink. "Well, when is the time to start talking about it, Grace? You want to tell me? Because she's going have to come up with some sort of decent explanation so that after she gets arrested, she doesn't end up in *jail*!"

"Why are you yelling?" Monica looked frightened.

"Why am I yelling?" Ozzie's voice veered sharply. "You've just admitted that you stole forty thousand dollars from a fucking charity for no reason at all, and that you're on your way to the Manhattan police station to turn yourself in, and you want to know why I'm *yelling*?"

"Stop." Nora's voice quavered as she stood up. Ozzie stared at her, her nostrils white around the edges. "Just stop it. You're making things worse, Ozzie. Now quit yelling."

Ozzie dropped her eyes and inhaled. She strode around the other side of the table, yanked her chair out, and plunked down in the middle of it.

The room was silent save for the faint thumping sound of Ozzie's butter knife as she turned it over and over against the tablecloth. Monica stared down at her lap as Grace remained kneeling next to her, looking down at the floor. Nora glanced at her half-eaten breakfast, which, with its smeared egg yolk and stained berries, now had a vaguely lurid appearance. She pushed it away.

"Why didn't you tell us anything earlier?" Grace asked.

"I was embarrassed," Monica whispered.

Nora bit her lip. She wouldn't have told anyone either.

"So what now?" Ozzie asked. Her voice was hard, unforgiving. "You have an attorney, right?"

204 CECILIA GALANTE

"Yeah." Monica nodded.

"Have you talked to him?"

"A little."

"You gotta tell him everything, Mons. You might be too embarrassed to tell us the truth, but you're gonna have to lay your cards on the table for him. Seriously. Lawyers can fix anything. I mean, maybe he can claim mental distress or something and you can just get probation."

"What do you mean, mental distress?" Grace asked. "Monica's not mentally distressed." She looked at Monica. "Are you?"

"I am now," Monica whispered.

"I mean before," Grace said. "When you . . . stole the money."

Monica shook her head.

Grace turned back to Ozzie. "You can't seriously be advising her to make something up . . ."

"She doesn't have to make anything up," Ozzie retorted. "She can use her background card. Lay it all out on the table. You know, horrific childhood, raised in a group home, yada yada yada. Took a toll on her mental health. She wasn't thinking straight. Got her—"

"That's disgusting," Grace interjected. "Her *background* card? Seriously, Ozzie?"

"You got any better ideas?" Ozzie threw a sideways glance in Monica's direction. "Besides, it's probably the truth. Or at least part of it. Even if she doesn't know it yet."

Nora considered this as a silence enveloped the room again. Could Ozzie be right? How much of their upbringing directly affected the decisions they made now? And how much of it was nothing more than an excuse?

"I'm so sorry," Monica said suddenly. Her voice cracked. "God, I'm so sorry." She buried her face in her hands and wept.

Nora went over to her, putting an arm around Monica's thin shoulders. "You don't have to apologize to us."

"Yes, I do," Monica sobbed. "I let you down. All of you. And what's even worse is that the only thing I want right now, even though I've done such a terrible thing, is for all of you to come with me tomorrow."

"Come with you?" Ozzie repeated.

"Yes," Monica's blue eyes leaked more tears. "I'm more scared right now than I've ever been in my life. And I don't want to walk into that police precinct tomorrow morning by myself."

"You won't be by yourself," Nora said. "You'll have your attorney."

"I want you!" Monica burst out. "All of you! Please."

"Monica, we can't," Grace objected. "I mean, we don't have anything to do with this. Seriously. This is a big deal. We can't just traipse in after you like some kind of support group. They'll probably just tell us to leave." She looked around the room. "Don't you think?"

"Definitely." Nora agreed. "This is something that just you and your attorney should handle. You can't fool around with the law."

Nora realized that she and Grace were both looking at Ozzie, whose face was scrunched up into a knot. She wondered if Ozzie felt the same sort of hesitation that she did, not because of the reasons she'd just given or the ones she hadn't, but because this was a knee-deep issue involving people who were still only ankle-deep with one another. There had been a time when none of them would have hesitated at Monica's request, when the only possible wrinkle might have been finding someone to drive them to New York City. But that time was over. Long over. And, Nora found herself realizing wistfully, that fact was never more apparent than right now.

"Yeah, I mean it sounds nice, but I think they're both right," Ozzie said slowly. "You can't fuck around with stuff like this, Mons. Seriously. Just let your attorney handle it. It'll work out."

"All right." Monica ran both hands roughly through her hair. "Okay."

"You're not angry, are you?" Grace took her hand.

"No, of course not." Monica squeezed it back. "You're right. You're all right. I'm the one who isn't thinking clearly."

"Will you let us know?" Nora asked. "I mean, how it all turns out?"

"Of course." Monica choked on the last word. She looked around the room wildly for a moment, as if trying to place herself. "I still have some last-minute packing to do. Upstairs. I'll be down in a little bit."

They watched her walk out of the room, the heavy soles of her Gucci loafers making a clunking sound against the floor. Nora sat back down and took a sip of her coffee. It was barely warm. She felt shaky inside, as if the floor had just lurched suddenly beneath her feet. Ozzie remained standing, occupying her foot against the leg of the chair, and Grace began stacking dirty plates.

"You know, fifteen years ago, none of us would have blinked if she'd asked us to do this," Ozzie said without lifting her head.

Nora closed her eyes, but she wasn't surprised. Not really. Maybe they were a little more than ankle-deep after all.

"I know." Grace set a plate down. "But it's not fifteen years ago anymore. We're different people now, Ozzie."

"Are we?" Ozzie lifted her head.

"Yeah." Nora looked directly across the table, holding Ozzie's gaze. "We are."

For a moment Ozzie stared back, as if deliberating her answer. "Well, so what?" she said finally. "People change. Life happens. That's how it goes."

"We're not kids anymore, Ozzie," Grace said. "This is serious business."

"Are you telling me that the things we dealt with as kids weren't serious business?" Ozzie asked. "How about that last night at Turning Winds? You can't tell me that that wasn't some of the most serious business we've ever encountered in our whole lives."

Nora stood up. "It's not the same thing."

"Why not?" Ozzie challenged.

Why not? Was she kidding? Comparing an abortion to a person with legal woes? Had Ozzie lost her mind completely?

"The circumstances are different," Ozzie said, "but the feelings are the same. Monica'll be going through one of the most frightening experiences of her life tomorrow. And she'll be doing it alone. Or at least without us."

Nora and Grace exchanged a look.

"Well, even if you're right, I can't go," Grace said plainly. "I just can't. It's impossible for me right now, with ev—"

"We didn't get to do Who Wants What at the meeting last night," Ozzie said quickly. "We already know what Monica wants, so I'll go next." She paused, looking first at Nora and then at Grace. "I want my road trip. With all of you. Chicago to New York."

"You're not listening." Grace was shaking her head, fiddling with a loose curl. "I can't leave, Ozzie. I just can't. With the baby, and trying to get myself back on a regular schedule . . ." She closed her eyes. "It would just—"

"Just answer the question first," Ozzie said. "What do you want?"

Grace exhaled softly and put a hand on her hip. "What I want and what I need are two different things."

"I didn't ask you what you needed," Ozzie persisted. "I asked you what you wanted. Why is that so hard to answer?"

Grace examined the nail on her thumb for a moment and then began nibbling the edges of it. "I want to go." Her voice trembled. "But I can't! Things are different now. We've all—"

"We came for you." Ozzie's nostrils flared. "You told Henry that was what you wanted, and we came."

Grace squinted. "That's not fair."

"Why not?" Ozzie squinted. "You needed us, we came. We wanted to come. Now Monica needs us."

Grace pulled on her lower lip.

"Don't push her," Nora pleaded, looking at Ozzie. "She can't right now. It's not—"

"No." Nora stopped talking as Grace dropped her hand from her mouth. "No, it's okay, Nora," she said. "I'm in. I'll go."

"That just leaves you, Norster." Ozzie waited, biting her nails.

"I have work tomorrow," Nora said.

"You can't call in?" Ozzie asked. "Explain the situation?"

"You wouldn't have to explain the situation in detail," Grace offered. "Maybe just tell them it's some kind of emergency."

Nora dropped her eyes.

"What do you want right now, Nora?" Grace asked.

She was surprised that deep down, past her fear, the desire to go with them churned like some kind of glowing lava. She wanted to spend more time with all of them, to wring out every last second that she could before they all went their separate ways again. Or was that something she thought she'd wanted? The truth was that spending the last twenty-four hours with these women had been one of the hardest things she could remember doing in a long time. And they hadn't even scratched the surface yet, not really. No, she had to get back. She longed for her walks and the library and Alice Walker, the things in her life that centered her. That needed her. This? This was a little bit of madness. Maybe even insanity. Why would she put herself in a situation like that?

And yet Monica needed her. Monica needed her now in a way that each of them had needed the others at one time or another. And she wanted to give her that. She wanted to be there with her. After all these years, Monica had finally told them something she wanted besides a hug. She needed Nora now maybe just as much as Nora had needed her once.

"Nora?" Grace's face was peaked, and her mascara had smudged beneath her eyes.

Maybe just as much as Nora needed all of them still, whether she liked it or not.

Chapter 18

Grace and Ozzie and Monica left the table to pack, but Nora headed out to the backyard and took out her phone. The empty wine bottle Monica had used last night was lying on its side, the blue-green glass littered with fingerprints, and the candle they had set in the middle of their circle had melted down to a nub. She walked over to the other side of the lawn and sat down in one of the chairs. She noticed she was pulling on her other ear nervously and forced her hand into her lap as the ringing started.

"Marion?" Nora startled as the familiar voice picked up on the other end. "Is that you?"

"Nora?" Marion's voice went up three notches.

"Yes, it's me. Marion, why are you picking up Trudy's cell phone? Is everything okay?"

"Oh yes, darling." Marion sighed with gusto. "I came over last night, and we had a few glasses of wine, and we must've both fallen asleep. Her cell phone is so loud; it just woke me up. Hold on a minute." Nora could hear a faint patting sound and Marion whispering outside of the receiver. "Wake up, Trudes. It's our Nora."

Our Nora. Her heart swelled at the words.

"Nora!" Trudy's voice barreled through the phone as she cleared her throat. Nora held the receiver away from her ear and winced. "My God, what time it is? What's going on? The three amigos not treating you well?"

Suddenly she felt foolish. Here she was, a thirty-two-year-old woman, calling two old ladies before they'd even had breakfast because . . . Because why? Because she was unsure of something? Because she was afraid of making another decision that might alter the rest of her life?

"I'm sorry," she said. "I shouldn't have called. I didn't realize how—"

"It's fine, it's fine." Trudy cut her off impatiently. "The dog's fine too, by the way, although I hope to God that's not why you're calling. I did take her out to look at the moon last night. Like you asked. She howled, the damn thing, like some kind of werewolf. Scared the living daylights out of me."

A scuffling sound came through the line, followed by Marion's voice, hissing and muted.

"Nora." Marion's voice came back on the line all at once. "Talk to me, darling. What's going on? What do you need?"

"I was wondering if I could take tomorrow off." Nora stammered. "I mean, I know it wasn't really planned, but—"

"She wants to take tomorrow off," Marion whispered loudly.

"Take the week!" Trudy yelled in the background. "Hell, take the month if you need it!"

"I don't need a week. I'll be back on Tuesday. I just wanted to make sure—"

"We're completely sure," Marion said kindly. "It's no problem at all."

"Okay," Nora said. "Thanks."

"Is that everything, dear?"

No, it was not everything. She hadn't even started.

"Well, I . . . I was hoping I could . . . I just need to talk. To you. To both of you." Nora took a deep breath and then let it out. "Can you hold the phone so Trudy can hear, too?"

"Of course." More rustling and then: "Okay, darling, we're ready. We can both hear you."

"But speak up anyway!" Trudy demanded. "My ears are shot!"

She told them about Monica and the stolen money. And then because she wasn't quite sure they understood how important Monica was to her, she told them about Grace and Ozzie too, and a little bit about Turning Winds: how they had all grown up together there, how they had become women under thirty full moons. She told them about the just-cobbled-together road trip to New York City, and how frightened she was to go on it with them because . . . well, she didn't have a because really. Maybe she wasn't strong enough. Maybe the expectation and the happiness and the sorrow and the pain of the last twenty-four hours had wrung her dry.

Or maybe she had nothing left to give.

There was a long silence on the other end of the line after Nora stopped talking. She did not know when she had started to cry, but she could feel the tears sliding down her face. She wiped at them with the back of her wrist as they collected at the bottom of her chin and then blew her nose. "Hello?" Her voice was faint. "Are you still there?"

"We're here," Marion whispered. "Don't worry, we're here."

She felt something lift at Marion's words, a sudden easing of a burden that until that very moment she had not known was so heavy.

"I think you already know the answer." Trudy's voice was gentler than Nora expected, and it brought new tears to her eyes. "You're calling us for our take on things, but I think you know exactly what you need to do."

Henry appeared in the yard just then, looking frightened. Nora held up one finger and he nodded, leaving again.

"But what if it's a mistake?" she whispered into the phone.

"Then it's a mistake!" Trudy's voice barreled through the phone. "Is the world going to end if you make a mistake? Hell, I could fill an entire book with all the mistakes I've made in my life."

"Me too!" Nora couldn't help but smile as Marion's voice drifted faintly through the phone. She could picture her standing on tiptoe, trying to make her voice heard. "Mistakes are how we learn, Nora."

"But . . ."

"But *what*?" Trudy sounded exasperated.

Nora opened her mouth and then shut it again. What could she say? That it might be too big a mistake? That another twenty-four or forty-eight hours with Grace and Ozzie and Monica could change her, maybe irrevocably this time? That it might take her another ten years to recover from it?

"Listen to me, Nora Walker." Trudy's voice was stern, uncompromising. "I don't know who or what taught you to be so afraid of everything in your life, but I'm telling you right now, it's no way to live."

"Gentle," Marion whispered.

"It's no way to live!" Trudy barked. "If you keep tiptoeing through every situation that comes your way, you know what you're going to end up with?"

Nora blinked.

"High arches!" Trudy hissed.

"High arches?"

"High arches!" Trudy repeated. "And a bad back. Not many people I know can make progress with high arches and bad backs."

"Do you even *know* anyone with high arches and a bad back?" Marion whispered.

"Shhhh!" said Trudy. "For God's sake, I'm trying to make a point here, Marion!"

Nora bit her tongue so that she wouldn't giggle. She loved these women. Both of them could have been part of The Invisibles back then and held their own in the group. And yet she was glad they hadn't been. Right now, the two of them felt like another kind of family—one she needed just as much as The Invisibles.

"My *point*," Trudy started again, but Nora interjected gently.

"I know what you mean, Trudy."

"You do?" Trudy sounded wary.

"I do," she whispered into the phone.

"Don't be afraid." Trudy's voice was vehement. "Go with your girls, Nora. Take the trip. See what happens. You might be surprised."

She hung up a few seconds later, Trudy's words reverberating in her ears. She would go. She would see where it took her. Even if it just brought her to a place she never expected. Which could even end up being the reason she went in the first place.

"Nora." Henry stepped out into the back porch. "I'm so sorry. I don't mean to bother you. But Petal just told me what happened. And she's a nervous wreck about it, but she's *going* to New York. I told her it wasn't a good idea, since it's completely out of the regular routine we've been trying to establish for her, but she's absolutely insistent."

Nora nodded, examining him up close, maybe for the first time since she'd arrived. Grace was right. He did have a quiet, innate kindness about him. And very beautiful lips. She blushed as he pressed something in her hand. "Please, will you just make sure she takes her medicine?"

Nora looked down at the orange bottle in her hand; the white band on the outside was encrypted with dark lettering:

GRACE FALCHECK: RISPERDAL.
Take two times a day with food.

She'd never heard of Risperdal, had no idea what it was for. But the frightening feeling she had earlier when Grace was explaining her paintings was back. This was more than postpartum depression. A piece of the puzzle was still missing. Something was off.

"She . . . she doesn't take it?" she asked. "On her own?"

"Well, I'm sure she would." Henry sounded desperate. "It's just. . . . well, since July when everything happened, I've been making sure she takes it. She's used to me giving her a pill at breakfast and then again at dinner. I just . . . with the sudden change in circumstance . . . I'm afraid she'd forget." He stopped all at once, pressing a clenched fist against his forehead. "I know it must sound weird, like I'm treating her like a child. I don't mean to. I know she's an adult . . . perfectly capable . . ." He pressed his lips together as his voice drifted off, and for a moment Nora thought she might have caught a glimpse of what he had endured—and continued to endure—throughout his life with his wife. Grace was not perfectly capable at all, had not been even close to capable for probably much longer than any of them knew. He was the one who had to pick up the slack. He was the one who had picked up the pieces. "This medication is the only thing that's going to keep her well." Henry said this last statement with finality, as if the discussion was over. "If you could just make sure she takes it at breakfast, and then again with dinner, I'll be able to get through the next few days a little more easily."

She closed her fingers around the thin bottle. It was so light in her hand, such an inconsequential thing in the scheme of all that had become so urgent. Maybe it didn't matter if she didn't know all the details. Maybe the details were secondary. The most important thing was Grace. Just the way she was right now, at this moment.

"Of course," she said. "I'll take care of it."

Chapter 19

It was ten a.m. by the time everyone got into the car. Nora pretended not to watch as Henry and Grace said their goodbyes in front of the house, but it was hard to look away. Despite his anxiety, there was an ease to the way he touched her, smoothing the palm of his hand over her forehead and then letting it slide down the small of her back until hooking it along a belt loop on the outside of her jeans. Even the way he kissed her seemed easy; full on the mouth, with no hesitation at all. *You are mine,* his movements seemed to say. *And I am yours.*

Theo had never kissed her in front of anyone; they had never gotten comfortable enough for that. In private, though, he had kissed her with such confidence and sometimes with such urgency that she felt as if he were sucking the breath out of her body. It was an alarming feeling at first, but it morphed quickly into a deep pleasure, one she would return to again and again as she lay in bed at night and thought of him. Now, watching Henry with Grace, she felt that same kind of longing pulse through her and then settle like a stone in the pit of her stomach. She needed to get hold of herself, bring herself back to reality. She wasn't really shocked to hear that Theo had gotten married; it would have been odd if he hadn't. He probably had children now too, maybe a boy that looked like a miniature version of him, or a girl that had the same eyelashes as his wife. It was a good thing, him being married, moving on, creating a life. It was what people did, how life worked.

Grace had offered to drive the first leg since she knew the surrounding area best, and Monica, whose mascara had started to run despite washing her face and applying new makeup, got in the front with her. Monica had been sitting on the edge of her bed when they came up to tell her about their decision, her fingertips pressed lightly on either side to keep herself upright. Her back was to them, and Nora had marveled at the length of her neck, the narrow, rectangular shape of her shoulders, how beautiful she was even from behind. Monica didn't say anything right away when Ozzie blurted it out—"Well, we're going"—and at first Nora wasn't sure if she had even heard her. Then she exhaled, a low, hoarse sound, and Nora realized that Monica had been holding her breath since she'd first heard them ascending the steps behind her.

Ozzie, who had been surprisingly quiet since they all emerged from the house, was in the back with Nora. She reached over the front seat as soon as she got in and placed a steady hand on Monica's shoulder. Nora couldn't help but think how different this trip was going to be from the one they had taken in from the airport; how much more was riding on all of their shoulders this time around. There was no telling what might happen, no way of knowing what would come next. Especially when they got to Manhattan. She'd never been inside a police station before, let alone one in New York City.

"So I was thinking we would take I-90 to 80 East and just go straight through," Grace said. "It's the fastest route."

"Sounds good." Ozzie let go of Monica's shoulder. "What's the time frame?"

"About twelve, thirteen hours with stops," said Grace. "Give or take."

"I'll get us a hotel room," Monica said, turning around weakly in her seat. "For tonight. I'd have you all at my place, but I don't . . ."

"Want Liam to know," Ozzie finished. "We know."

Monica blushed and turned back around as Grace started the car.

Henry stood in the middle of their front yard, his left arm raised as Grace pulled out of the driveway. Nora watched as he got smaller and smaller under the eave of the small porch roof, his lined face a mixture of fear and hope and something else she could not place.

She wondered if she'd ever see him again.

No one spoke until Grace aligned the Escalade into a stream of traffic along Interstate 90. Nora had already taken two Dramamine; now she prayed silently that it would not have some kind of adverse effect on her system since she was sure, when she woke up this morning, that she was still vaguely high. Remnants of the night floated around like torn pieces of lace in her head: the dinner at Tru, the joints, Monica's palm reading, the baby crying.

The baby crying. Just the memory of the noise hurt, like pieces of glass moving around inside her chest, cutting the softest parts of it into jagged shards. She'd been sure she could handle it; there was no telling what the women thought of her now that she hadn't. She pressed her forehead against the cool sheet of window glass and closed her eyes. At least something else had taken center stage; now the attention would be off her.

"All right," Grace said after a while. "We're pretty much out of the city. We have to take 90 straight for about five hours and then switch over to 80 East. That'll take us right into Manhattan."

Monica, whose silent, intermittent weeping had ceased for the moment, took out her cell phone for what must have been the tenth time and dialed. "Nothing," she said after a moment, flinging the phone onto the seat. Her voice was desperate. "I don't know where he could be."

"Who?" Ozzie said.

"My attorney." She raised an eyebrow. "I've left him at least three messages since I talked to the detective."

"It's Sunday," Ozzie reminded her. "Maybe he's doing something with his family and turned his phone off. He'll probably check tonight and then call you back. All you need is him there with you tomorrow, right? To take you through the precinct? Get you to the next step?"

"Yes," Monica said absently.

Nora watched her from the backseat. For the first time since she'd laid eyes on her, Monica's beautiful veneer seemed fragile. Tiny lines perched like quotation marks along the corners of her eyes, and her mouth was pinched together. The gorgeous plume of blond hair was in a state of wild disarray, as if she'd clutched at it numerous times, and pieces stuck out in back like misplaced fingers.

Ozzie glanced over at Nora, who gave her a look. No one had said anything more about the theft since Monica's admission at the breakfast table, but Nora could tell by the way Ozzie sat forward a little on the seat and gathered a piece of Monica's hair in her fingers, that she wanted to. "Do you want to talk a little bit more about it?" she asked. "It might help."

Monica's shoulders tensed as she looked out the window. "Not right now." Her voice was faint.

"Okay." Ozzie didn't move. "Whenever you're ready."

Nora watched Ozzie's fingers trail through Monica's hair, remembering how Ozzie had used to do the very same thing at Turning Winds as Monica sat pressed up against the side of her bed. Monica had even fallen asleep once, and Grace, who had been talking, hushed her voice and pointed. "She's asleep," she whispered, obviously impressed. Ozzie, who continued to run her fingers through Monica's hair, just grinned. "Magic fingers," she said, raising one eyebrow. Now though, Monica reached back with one hand, and pushed Ozzie's fingers away. Ozzie sat back, stung, and looked out the window.

Grace, who had noticed the gesture too, sat up a little straighter in her seat. "I'm confused about something," she said, looking at Monica. "All weekend you've been telling us how amazing Liam is. He arranged for you to use this car, and then he treated us to that beautiful dinner. I don't know what the rest of you think, but he seems to me like a really great guy."

"He is a really great guy," Monica said dully. "The best."

"So why don't you want him to know about this?" Grace pressed. "I mean, if he really loves you, he'll understand. He'll—"

"Oh, he loves me," Monica said. "But he won't understand. He'll never understand." Nora could hear the despair in her voice.

"You sure you're giving him enough credit?" Ozzie asked.

"We've been together a long time," Monica said. "Almost four years. Liam's the one who took me in when I was a nobody. A bike messenger!" She spit the word out. "He's the only one who's ever really believed in me, the only person in my entire life who made me feel like someone. If I—"

"Hey!" Ozzie's voice was tight. "*We* believed in you first."

"And then you *left*!" Monica turned around in her seat, her eyes filling. "You built me up, all of you, and then you left! No one ever called to see how I was doing or where I ended up, or what was happening to me! Not one of you! Ever!" She was looking at all of them, her head moving from side to side, her mangled hair whipping around her face.

Nora felt her breath catch in the back of her throat.

These were her words.

Her cry through the years.

It had never occurred to her that any of them might feel the same way.

Not once.

"That was the deal!" Ozzie planted a hand on Monica's shoulder again. "That's what we said we would do!"

"No!" Monica pushed Ozzie's hand off her shoulder, glaring at her in the harsh light from the window. "That's what YOU said, Ozzie! That's what *you* said we would do!"

Ozzie opened her mouth and then shut it again. She let her hand drop against the backseat. It lay next to her like a stone. She slumped back against the upholstery and stared out the window.

"I can't go through that again." Monica's voice quavered. "He *loves* me. I can't lose that."

For what seemed like an eternity, they sped on in silence. The air inside the car was so thick with emotion that Nora could feel it along the tops of her arms, a light, prickling sensation shot through with electricity. She pressed the back of her hand against her mouth so that she would not cry and stared out at the flying scenery. Ozzie had sagged to the other side of the car, slung into submission, while Monica cried silently up front and dabbed at her eyes. Only Grace was still upright behind the wheel, her shoulders squared, chin set like a brick. Every few seconds, she would glance over at Monica, peek at Ozzie, and then position her eyes back on the road.

"All right," she said suddenly. "I have something to say." No one moved. "Monica's not the only one who came here this weekend with secrets. I have one, too."

Ozzie's eyes fluttered open. A whimper froze halfway out of Monica's mouth. Nora could feel the hairs prickling on the back of her neck as she lifted her head away from the window.

"I'm sick." Grace laughed once, bitterly. "Like for real. I'm a total nut job, just like my mother. After all those years of waiting for her to come back, she finally did, in the form of a mental illness. I'm just like her." She bit her bottom lip.

For a moment, no one said anything. There were no words. And then Monica said, "So you're . . . ?"

"Bipolar II." Grace recited the term deliberately, as if she'd been forced to memorize it. "A spectrum disorder characterized by at least one episode of hypomania and at least one episode of major depression." The corner of her lips twitched, as if the words had scratched something soft inside her mouth. "It's what she had, too, although we didn't know it back then. Basically it just means that my brain is completely screwed up. I used to think that staying up for four days so that I could paint was something everyone did." She winced. "It was the crash-and-burn part of things I didn't do so well with, although thank God I didn't have two kids to deal with at the same time, the way my mother did. No wonder she went off the deep end."

"Did you have to go to the hospital, too?" Ozzie asked.

"Twice. Right before graduation from art school I checked myself in at a place in Atlanta for about twelve days. It wasn't much help; as soon as I got stable, I stopped taking my medication and was off and running again. After the second episode, though, they put me in a long-term psych unit." The lines in Grace's face softened. "That one was longer. Almost three months."

"What do you mean by an episode?" Monica echoed.

"Oh, there's high ones and low ones." Grace rubbed her forehead impatiently. "Being in the middle of a high one felt like I'd just chugged fourteen Red Bulls and then snorted a line of cocaine. I'd act like a crazy person, bouncing off the walls, talking gibberish, running all over the place. Sleeping was impossible because my feet twitched all the time and my head raced, so sometimes I'd go out and walk around town until the sun came up. Or lock myself in my room and paint." She shook her head disgustedly. "The really ironic part about a manic episode is how much painting I could get done. Good stuff, too." She squinted, as if trying to bring a thought into focus. "Things I couldn't summon up now if I tried. My brain was working on a completely differ-ent level when I was manic, even creatively. E*spe*cially creatively."

Nora thought back to the paintings in Grace's house, the titles she had given each one. Staid. Mania. Spiral. Melancholy. Void. Blackness. Each of them a window into her beautiful, defective brain. Each of them a step on the ladder of her mental illness. She was starting to understand.

"So those paintings you have in your house . . . ?" Ozzie started.

"Yeah." Grace's jaw tightened. "Henry hung those. He says they're art, but I think he likes to keep them up so that I don't forget."

"Forget what?"

"The episodes, I guess. What it feels like to be inside them. He told me once that seeing where I used to be helps me stay focused on where I am now."

"Do you like having them up?"

"Not really." Grace gnawed the inside of her cheek.

"Is that a yes?" Ozzie pressed. "Or a no?"

Grace glared at Ozzie in the rearview mirror. "It's a 'not re-ally.' Sometimes I look at them and they don't bother me. They're just paint on a canvas. Other times, though, they bring back the memories of those places in my head, and I just want to go hide in the basement. Or rip them off the walls and bash them over Henry's head."

"Well, I don't blame you for feeling confused about it," Ozzie said finally. "Art should be a celebration of something, not a re-minder of your illness."

"Have you ever told him how you feel?" asked Monica.

"Oh, yeah," Grace sighed heavily. "He means well. I know he does. It's not some dark, heavy, in-your-face kind of thing. If I told him to take them down, he would." She tucked a strand of hair behind her ear. "You know, if Henry hadn't been willing to stick around all these years, I doubt I'd still be here. He's the one who finally convinced me to stay on my medication so that I could have a normal life. And after another year of complete mayhem, I did." She paused, staring out at something in the horizon. "It changed everything. For the first time in my life, I felt as though I was living inside a relatively quiet mind."

Monica's hand moved up and down the length of Grace's arm. "And then what?" she asked. "What happened last summer?"

"I got *pregnant* is what happened." Grace spit the word out. "It wasn't supposed to happen. After I got diagnosed, I decided I was never going to have a child. I was on the pill! But there it was. Life, pushing through, despite all the odds." She bit her lip, her eyes swelling with tears. "Henry and I talked about it. You know, all the options. But I couldn't get rid of it. I just couldn't. Not after . . ." Grace wiped at her eyes with the back of her hand. "But every day that baby grew inside me, the more I realized that it was only thing I had ever really wanted in the entire world. The only thing maybe I'd ever wanted. And when she was born, and I looked at her for the first time, I also realized that it was also the single most selfish decision I had ever made in my life."

"Selfish?" Monica whispered.

"I've given her the worst gift any person could ever give to another human being." Grace was speaking through gritted teeth, her words chopped and precise. Nora had the feeling that she had said these words before—to Henry maybe, or just to herself—a hundred times. "I've passed on my own defective genes, just like my mother did to me. It won't take long for Georgia to realize that her mind doesn't work the way other people's do. And when she's in high school or college or maybe later when she finds someone and settles down, and she's so exhausted from trying to balance herself between two worlds, she'll try to eliminate herself. Just like I did." Grace was choking now over her words, her fingers so tight around the top of the steering wheel that the knuckles protruded sharply beneath the skin. "I did that to her. I gave her that."

"But, Grace!" Ozzie sat all the way forward in her seat. "You can't—"

"PETAL!" Grace screamed. "My name is *Petal*!"

"No, it's *not*!" Ozzie barked back. "Your goddamned name is Grace! What, was Petal something that you grabbed on to during one of your manic phases? Something you thought sounded cute or even made sense back then?"

Grace's eyes narrowed.

"Was it?" Ozzie demanded.

"So what if it was?" Grace shot back. "Why does it bother you so much that I went and changed my stupid name?"

"Because it's not *you*," Ozzie said. "Don't you see, Grace? It's a symptom of your illness. And for some reason, it's one you're hanging on to."

"Why would I want to hang on to my illness?"

"Maybe you don't really want to get better." Ozzie shrugged. "Maybe you don't think you deserve to, or that you're holding some torch for your mother, who never got a chance to get well. I don't know. But this is your life. You have other options. And if you want to keep dancing the crazy dance, you're gonna have to do it by yourself, Because I'm not gonna play along anymore."

By the time Ozzie had finished talking, Grace's face was another shade of pink. Her lower lip was trembling and her nostrils flared. "You've always thought you were the one with all the answers, haven't you?" Her eyes strayed dangerously from the road, locking on Ozzie's in the backseat. "Well, you know what?"

"Let's pull over," Monica said, tapping Grace on the shoulder. "Pull over, honey. Someone else can drive now. Please. You're so upset. Please just pull over."

To Nora's relief, Grace slowed, easing the car along the side of the road and then bringing it to a stop. The silence crackled, charged like an electric cord. Grace raised her fingertips and pressed them along the edge of her forehead.

"I'm sorry," Ozzie said, although the tone of her voice said otherwise. "I don't think I have all the answers. And I really don't want to make things any worse than—" She stopped as Grace raised her hand.

"Please," Grace whispered. "Please just stop talking."

The car fell silent, the engine humming beneath them. For a moment Nora wondered if it too was running on nervous energy.

"Monica, you stay put," Ozzie said, yanking at the handle of her door. "I'll drive."

Grace lowered her hands and whipped around in her seat. "Who the hell ever died in your life and made you the boss of everyone else's?"

Ozzie froze.

"I just took a huge risk telling you that I'm sick." Grace's eyes swept the inside of the car. "Telling all of you. I'm *ashamed* that

I'm this way, okay? I don't want anyone to know that I'm fucked up, or that I have the crazy kinds of thoughts that I do. But I told you because it's us, and because . . . because you used to be people I could tell anything to." She glanced at Ozzie before lowering her eyes again. "Don't make me regret that. Please. After everything else, I don't think that's something I could bear right now."

Chapter 20

A long moment passed. Nora knew exactly what Grace was talking about; her own shame was probably the one thing still keeping her from opening up about anything real or legitimate. It wasn't so much that any of them would judge her; it was that they would want to fix her. And right now the last thing Nora wanted to feel was any more broken than she already felt.

"I'm sorry." Ozzie repeated her apology, blinking rapidly, struggling to hold Grace's gaze. "Really, I am. I don't mean to come on so strong. And I don't mean to act like some kind of . . ." She paused, looking for the right word.

"Steamroller?" Grace's voice was still icy.

"Yeah." Ozzie's shoulders sagged. "I guess I can steamroll. You've got to know I don't mean it, though."

Grace ran a finger down the bridge of her nose. "It's jus . . . I don't think I was looking for any real feedback." She glanced at Nora. "From anyone. I just needed to say it, I guess. Especially to you guys. After Monica came clean, I decided that I wanted to be

straight with you, too. Not have any more secrets." She shrugged.
"That's all."

"That's a lot," Nora said softly.

Grace smiled sadly. "Anyway. We should get going."

Ozzie reached for the door, but Nora stopped her. "I'd like to drive if it's all right. It's good for my motion sickness."

"Are you feeling sick?" Monica asked in alarm.

Nora shook her head. "I took Dramamine before we left. But the driving'll help, too." She wasn't sure if this was entirely accurate. She was slightly drowsy, too. But she did have an urge to drive just now, despite the fact that she'd never even been seated inside a car this big until yesterday. She wanted to get behind the wheel, to take this vehicle somewhere, put some distance between what they'd left behind and where they were headed. She got out of the backseat and walked around the back, bracing herself as a tractor-trailer sailed past.

Grace slid out of the front seat, stumbling as she underestimated the drop to the ground, and Nora caught her arm. For a split second, as they locked eyes, Nora saw the girl who, weeks after her breakup with Theo, would slip into bed next to her and stroke her hair as she cried. The one who told her, night after night, that it would get better eventually; she didn't know how exactly, but it would; she believed it with her whole heart and soul. There were some things, she told Nora, that the brain just couldn't comprehend, things that had to be taken on faith. How could any of them—least of all Grace herself—know that her own brain would stop comprehending even the most basic of things, that it would become the sole enemy in a war she would have to fight for years and years to come? Nora wanted to weep, thinking of it.

"You okay?" she asked instead.

"I'm good," Grace said, avoiding her eyes. "Thanks."

Nora's uneasiness about the vastness of the backseat was nothing compared to the huge array of buttons spread out before her now. It was like a cockpit of some kind, a virtual dashboard island all its own. Monica and Ozzie had also switched seats, with Ozzie up front now next to Nora. For some reason, this little detail comforted her. Ozzie may not have been the world's best driver, but with her verve and confidence, she could be Nora's copilot any day of the week. The engine was still running too, which helped. She had no idea where the key went or if the car even had one, but she was relieved that she didn't have to fiddle with it.

"You ready?" Ozzie asked.

Nora nodded and put the car into drive. A slight touch of her foot, and the car roared back onto the highway. She scrambled to keep control of the wheel, swerving for a good twenty seconds or so before aligning the vehicle into traffic.

"It doesn't need much," Ozzie said, watching her out of the corner of her eye. "You can probably ease up a little on the gas if you want."

Nora lifted her toe an inch or so and the car hummed back down. She could feel her shoulders unclench themselves as she settled in among the stream of cars. All right, then. She could do this. She could definitely do this. She could feel her heart slowing beneath her shirt, the dull hammering of it still pounding in her ears.

"Nice job." Ozzie's fingers were clutching the dashboard. "Great work."

The previous tension in the air had dissipated, replaced now with something that Nora did not yet recognize. Something was shifting though, among all of them. Something big.

"Should we put Myrtle on?" Monica asked from the backseat.

"If Nora wants her," Ozzie answered. "Nora, do you want Myrtle on?"

"I think I'm okay," Nora said. "It's just straight, right? Until we hit 80?"

"That's right." Grace paused. "Who the hell is Myrtle?"

Nora looked out the window again as Monica explained the navigation system to Grace.

"And her name is Myrtle?" Grace asked.

"We gave her that name," Ozzie said. "Because she sounds exactly like Mrs. Ditmer from senior year. Wait'll you hear the voice." She unclipped the GPS from its stand and handed it over the seat. "Here, Monsie, turn it on, just for a minute. Just so she can hear."

Monica fiddled with the GPS for a moment and then gave it back to Ozzie, who set it back on the pedestal.

"Hell. Oh," the British voice uttered. "Where. May. I Take. You. Today? Please. Insert. Destination."

Ozzie and Monica smiled at the sound, but Grace frowned.

"You think that sounds like Mrs. Ditmer?" she said. "Nora's favorite teacher?"

Without thinking, Nora turned around and flashed a wary grin in Grace's direction.

"Wait, was Ditmer really your favorite teacher?" Ozzie asked.

Nora shrugged. "She was nice to me."

"I never knew that." Monica was draped over the back of the front seat, her chin resting on her elbow. She looked exhausted. A thin piece of her hair had been braided on one side and the gold strands caught the light from the dashboard. "Why was she your favorite? What'd she do?"

"She let me borrow books. And stay after in her room sometimes, so I could read them."

"She wouldn't let you take them home?" Ozzie asked.

"They were first editions," Grace said. "Right, Nora?"

Nora nodded. "She had her own collection of them. They were very expensive. I was lucky she even let me touch them."

"Boy, that was nice of her," Monica said. "I never knew that, either."

There was a lot that the rest of them hadn't noticed during school, mostly because they'd barely made it through. In English class for example, which they all had together, Monica and Ozzie tuned out completely whenever Mrs. Ditmer started talking, passing each other notes or flirting with Chad McGovern, who was almost nineteen and wore so much Polo aftershave that it made Nora's eyes water. Grace made more of an effort, taking diligent notes and asking questions, but more often than not, her notebooks were covered with cartoon doodles or sketches of horses. With the exception of Nora, none of them had managed to get any grade above a C in the class.

"So how come she was nice to you?" Ozzie sat up a little and rested her knee against the dashboard. "She was always a first-class bitch to me."

"Probably because you were a first-class bitch to her." Monica laughed, a hollow sound. "You gave everyone a hard time in school, Ozzie. Especially the teachers. You were always screwing around."

Ozzie scowled, but Nora could tell from the expression on her face that she knew Monica was right. "Yeah, well, I never did take very well to authority figures. Especially the ones who told me I had to write papers. God, I hated writing papers." She smacked her hand off the seat rest. "I am so glad I never have to write another fucking paper for the rest of my life, I can't even tell you!"

"Oh my God." Monica rolled her eyes. "Me, too."

"What are you two talking about?" Grace shifted her gaze between Monica and Ozzie. "Neither of you wrote a single paper in high school, and you know it. Nora wrote them."

It was true. Nora had written all their papers—even Grace's—not because they wanted her to, but because *she* wanted to. She had been the one to offer, volunteering herself over and over again whenever a term paper or essay assignment came up. The honest truth was that she liked researching odd topics, liked reading about things she didn't know, such as the way volcanoes formed beneath the Earth's surface, or how the biggest hurdle that sea turtles faced as babies was during the moments right after they hatched, when they had to run from their nest into the ocean before getting eaten by a gull or a sea lion. She'd sit for hours after discovering things like this, lost in other worlds as she wrote about them for her friends. Books—and the imaginary worlds they placed her in—were easier to be in than anywhere else. Sometimes, even with them. Or with Theo.

"God, Norster, what would all of us have done without you?" Ozzie sighed. "I probably never would have graduated."

"And I *definitely* wouldn't have." Monica's wide eyes were serious. "My gram used to say I was as dumb as a bag of hammers.

'Course, she said a lot of mean things to me, but she was right about that one."

"Oh, you just think you're dumb," Ozzie said. "There's nothing dumb about you, Monsie. You're just not street smart."

"Or book smart." Monica snorted. "Which basically means I'm just a little bit higher up on the scale than a moron."

"Don't say that," said Nora.

"It's true." Monica shook her head. "Look at this whole mess I got myself into."

Ozzie, who was biting her nails, paused mid-chew.

Monica gestured with her hands, waving them loosely at the wrists, as if they were broken. A tear welled up and then spilled over the rim of one blue eye. "I still honestly don't know why I did it," she whispered. "Maybe I did want my own money instead of having to ask Liam all the time. Or maybe I just wanted to see if I could get away with it." Her eyes widened. "It was just so *easy*. I mean, everyone walked in during those meetings and handed me their checks. *Me!* Eight-, nine-, ten-thousand-dollar checks! I remember my hands shaking the first time I held them, thinking to myself, 'They have no idea who I am, do they?'"

"What do you mean, 'who I am'?" asked Grace.

"Me!" Monica stabbed at her chest. "The dumb fat girl that nobody wanted."

"That wasn't who you were," Grace protested. "That's just the way you felt as a kid."

"Oh yeah?" Monica asked. "Then why do I still feel like her on the inside? Every single morning when I wake up, I get a sinking feeling inside my chest because I know I'm going to get out of bed and put on a mask." Her voice broke as she glanced out the window. "God, I sound pathetic."

"No you don't." Ozzie put a hand on her shoulder. "Keep going."

Monica stared out the window for a few moments. "I don't know . . . I think I was just flabbergasted that none of these people on the charity committees ever saw through me, that they couldn't tell that I was this . . . this *fraud* who'd barely made it through high school and somehow managed to snag one of the hottest hedge fund managers in the city." She shook her head. "Getting a new face, dressing up, driving out to the Hamptons, those were the easy parts. I kept playing the role, putting on a smile. But being put in charge of all that money . . . I don't know. I guess . . . I mean, I think it did something to me."

"What?" Ozzie cocked her head.

"They *trusted* me," Monica said. "They really believed I was the person I was pretending to be. And it got too hard, living like that. I wanted to get back to the place where I recognized myself. Where it wasn't fake. Where that little girl whose father murdered her mother still lived." She pulled on her lower lip. "It's crazy, but when I started stealing that money, it felt like destiny. As if all the things that I was born to become had finally materialized, right before my eyes. It didn't matter that it was illegal. It was just who I was, who I'd always been."

"And who was that?" Ozzie asked.

Monica paused. "A criminal. Just like him."

The car sped on silently. Nora imagined it as a bullet, cutting through the void ahead, swallowing up everything in its path. A part of her wanted to turn and shake Monica, to tell her that her explanation was bullshit, that it was just an excuse for something for which she had only herself to blame. Honestly, how could you live thirty or so years and still point to your parents for the stupid mistakes you made in your adult life? It was just another way of passing the buck. She should know better. As should the rest of them. Including herself.

Maybe especially herself.

"Do you still feel that way?" Grace asked.

Monica didn't answer right away. But when she did, her face set itself into a kind of deliberation. A finality. "Yeah," she said. "I do."

"Well, that's just great." Ozzie glared at her. "I'm glad it's been so easy for you to embrace your dark side, Monsie. Do you feel all warm and fuzzy about jail, too? Because you know there's a distinct possibility that that's what you might be facing when we get back to Manhattan."

"God, Ozzie," Grace said. "What did we just talk about?"

"I'm sorry if it's too harsh!" Ozzie protested. "And I don't mean to steamroll anyone here, either. But who's it gonna help if we start pussyfooting around? I mean, come on! She thinks it's her destiny to become her father? I just want to make sure she knows that—"

"I didn't say I *became* him." Monica whipped her head around. "I said there's a part of me that's like him."

"Of course there is," Ozzie answered. "But you don't know what part that is, Mons. You've just assumed it's the bad one be-cause that's the only thing you know about him. You've never taken the time to go talk to the guy, to learn anything else about the kind of person he is, what he—"

"Don't start." Monica's index finger trembled as she pointed at Ozzie. "That man shot my mother. And then, because she was taking too long to die, he went over and finished her off. Do not criticize my decision to never lay eyes on him. Ever."

"I'm not criticizing it." Ozzie's voice softened. "I'm telling you that there is more to him than the part that did those horrible things. No one's born all bad. We've all got light and dark parts to us. Which means you got some of the shit genes belonging to your dad. And you also got some of his good ones. But assuming that the shit choices *you* made are because of him isn't only unfair, it might also be way off base. Maybe you got some bad traits from your mother, too. Did you ever stop to think about why she got involved with a man who was so cruel to her?"

Monica held Ozzie's gaze for a long while. Her lower lip trembled as she absorbed her words, and Nora could tell from the way the color drained from her face that she had never considered such a thing before. Grace was quiet too, her left eye twitching. It was a fine line with Ozzie: on the one hand, she could be pushy and judgmental; on the other, honest in a way that forced you to look at yourself in a way you'd never quite done before. Would maybe never do if it wasn't for her.

"You can't honestly be blaming my mother for anything," Monica said.

"I'm not blaming your mother *or* your father for anything here," Ozzie said. "I'm pretty sure the ball's in your court, Mons. Yeah, your parents gave you a crap deal. Neither of them were around long enough to give you any of the tools you needed to navigate through this life. But that doesn't mean you spend the rest of your life blaming them for it. And it certainly doesn't mean you relinquish your responsibility for things because of it. That's just cowardly, babes. I'm sorry, but it is."

"I'm not *relinquishing* anything." Monica's eyes darkened. "I'm in a car heading back to Manhattan right now. I'm going in to stand in front of a judge and face what I've done."

"And I applaud you for that," said Ozzie. "Now you've got to do the same thing up here." She tapped the side of her head. "Inside." She paused. "Maybe we all do."

"Okay then, how about you?" Monica asked Ozzie. "You never feel like you're the way you are because of your mother? Because of what she did to you?"

Ozzie ran a hand roughly through her hair. "I think I've gone the opposite way. I think I've been so desperate *not* to turn into my mother that I turned into someone I don't even recognize anymore."

"In what way?" Grace asked.

"Well, I know it's hard to believe, since I'm still so bossy around all of you . . ." Ozzie laughed, a loud, nervous sound. "But the truth is, I'm pretty much a doormat at home."

Nora braced herself.

"You mean with your kids?" Monica asked.

Ozzie shook her head. "With Gary."

"Yeah, right." Grace snorted. "Like you'd ever—"

"I told you it's hard to believe." Ozzie's voice was sharp as she cut Grace off. "But it's the truth."

Grace crossed her arms over the front of her chest. "How are you a doormat?"

Nora watched Ozzie out of the corner of one eye. She was

gnawing again on one side of her thumb, and her breathing had shifted.

"How?" Ozzie repeated.

"Yeah, how?" Grace challenged. "What, does he set all the rules in the house or something? Order you around? You can't really expect us to believe—"

"He's mean, okay?" Ozzie's eyes blazed. "He's mean and possessive, and a few times during some of our worst fights, he's hauled off and hit me so bad I've ended up in the hospital."

Grace gasped and then clapped her hand over mouth. Nora thought back to the bruises she'd seen under Ozzie's arm at the airport, how quickly she'd dismissed them as something her children had inadvertently done, how terribly wrong she'd been.

"Ozzie, no!" Monica's voice broke and Nora thought that if she or Grace had spoken just then, each of their voices would have cracked too.

"Oh, don't worry, I fight back." Ozzie stared down at her fingers, pulled at a cuticle. "It's not like I'm a battered woman here or anything. Believe me. He's stronger than me, but I've gotten a few right hooks in." She snorted. "I've even given him a few black eyes. And once he had to get his lip stitched up in the ER."

"But, Ozzie!" Monica pleaded with her. "You . . . I mean, you've never taken shit from anyone! Anywhere! I . . . I just don't understand!" She shook her head, begging for an explanation.

"I don't really know how to explain it, either," Ozzie said. "I had a million things going on in my head the first time he hit me, you know? It was right in the middle of this stupid fight; I'd glanced at some guy at a bar and Gary wanted to know what the 'story' was between us. There was no story; I'd just looked at the guy, and he'd looked at me, and that was the end of it. But Gary kept putting his finger in my face, over and over again, insisting that I tell him, that I 'own up,' and finally, I just slapped it away and told him to go fuck himself." She inhaled deeply and then let it out all at once, as if breathing fire. "He decked me so fast that I barely even felt it. I mean, it was that quick. It took a few seconds for it to register, but as soon as it did, I was like a crazy person. I wanted to kill him." She jabbed at her chest with a finger. "I mean it's me, right? Ozzie Fucking Randol." She began to cry, her face contorting into a strange dissolution of everything that had ever held her up. "The girl who always stood up to everyone. The one who called all the shots, who led all the meetings, who got in everyone's face. Always."

"Yes," Grace whispered, putting a hand on her shoulder. "*Yes.* So what happened?"

"You mean that night?" Ozzie asked.

Grace nodded.

Ozzie shrugged and pulled hard at the loose cuticle, ripping it finally from the skin. "I went home with him and fucked his brains out. He fell asleep right after, but I remember lying awake for hours and wrestling with all of it. Trying to figure out what had just happened, what I was still *doing* there. Logically, I knew I couldn't stay. That even though he hadn't hit me all that hard, it was still unacceptable. I knew that, you know? Kind of like I knew what two plus two was. Or what color my eyes were. No-brainers. But then I remembered feeling something on top of all that that I hadn't felt in a long, long time."

"You liked it." Grace's voice was flat.

"I didn't *like* it." Ozzie's face twisted. "I'm not a masochist. But

I knew it. It was familiar, you know? Terrain I could navigate. Living with Cesar was fun and wild, but I never knew what was going to happen when he got angry. Sometimes he'd laugh it off; other times he'd yell. Once he drove off on his motorcycle and didn't come back for three days. I thought I was going to lose my mind, trying to figure out where he'd gone, if he'd come back. With Gary, I knew what to expect. I'd already done it for half my life. And I was so good at it. God, I was so fucking good at it." She shrugged. "So I stayed. A few years later, I married him. And now it'll be twelve years in June." She stared into her lap. A tear dropped onto her pants, but she did not move to wipe it away.

Nora reached over and took Ozzie's hand. Despite the warmth in the car, it was cold, the fingertips icy. The great Ozzie Randol. Broken not by a man finally, but by her decision to stay with the wrong one. Nora squeezed her hand and kept it inside of hers.

"Well, you know you can't stay," Grace said. "I mean, you have to leave him, Ozzie."

"I don't know what I know anymore," Ozzie said.

"What about your kids?" Monica asked.

Ozzie's head shot up. "What about them?"

"They see everything, don't they? With the fights, I mean. Gary hitting you?"

"No." Ozzie picked at her cuticle again. "Well, maybe a few times. Nothing too terrible, though."

Nora and Monica exchanged a glance. "Maybe not too terrible to you," Monica said. "It's a different story for them."

"Their only story," Nora said softly.

For a while, no one spoke; it was as if Ozzie's information, on top of everyone else's, had sucked the last bit of life out of the car.

Ozzie stared out of her window while Monica and Grace looked out of theirs. It was hard to know, Nora thought, if each of them was trying to come to terms with the information they had just shared, or with hearing someone else's.

"That just leaves you, Nora," Ozzie said suddenly, turning her head from the window.

"Leaves me what?" Nora's ears got hot. Even from the backseat, she could feel Monica's and Grace's eyes on her neck, waiting.

"I don't know." Ozzie sounded dangerous somehow, as if she was daring Nora to say something. "You tell us. Are things really as great in your life as you've said?"

"Well, yeah." Nora shifted uncomfortably in her seat. "I wouldn't use the word *great* per se, but they're okay." She pulled on her earlobe as Ozzie's eyes bored into the side of her head.

"No secrets?" Ozzie pressed.

"Ozzie, stop," Grace said from the back. "You don't always have to *harangue* people."

Ozzie inhaled through her nose and set a foot against the edge of her seat. Nora pressed down hard on the gas, maneuvering the car around a large white Lexus, and then settled in behind a red Honda. A bumper sticker on the back read: *The village just called. They're missing an idiot.* Perfect. Just what she needed to see right now. She looked out the side window, bit down hard on her lower lip. Keeping things to herself at Turning Winds had been a necessity, a primitive need born out of fear. Letting those secrets out would have meant not only baring herself but also risking the loss of the most important people she had ever known in her life. Besides, those memories were the only things she had left of herself, the last threads that still connected her to Mama. As strange as it was, she wasn't ready to sever them. She still hadn't let go. And so she had shared the barest minimum of information when their questions arose, answering just enough to keep any more prying at bay.

But things had changed. She wasn't a teenager anymore. They were far from Turning Winds. And despite the fact that all of these women, every single one of them, had just revealed a horrific truth about their own life, she understood that she still loved them. Maybe even more than she had loved them back then. And it was *because* of their weaknesses, because of their secrets. Why couldn't the same be true for her?

"Okay, you know what, they're not," Nora heard herself say.

"Who's not what?" Ozzie looked at her.

"Things," Nora said. "In my life. They're not as great as I said they were. I don't have a boyfriend. I actually haven't dated anyone in about three years. I just said I did because . . ." She stopped, wondering what else she could say that would not make her sound any more idiotic than she already did. "I don't know. I guess I was embarrassed. Everyone here has someone and I . . ." She shook her head. "It was stupid. But there you go. I'm single. No boyfriend. Not looking. Not even interested."

The ensuing silence was deafening. Nora tried to swallow, but something felt as if it had gotten caught in her throat.

"Okay," Grace said encouragingly. "Well, my goodness. There certainly isn't any hard-and-fast rule about being attached. Especially these days."

Nora didn't move.

"Why would you feel embarrassed at being single?" Ozzie asked. "Shit, I envy you."

Nora had gone this far. Maybe she'd try another step. "I don't really *like* dating. It gets too . . . complicated."

"Tell me about it." Ozzie snorted. "And then they want to fuck you."

Nora's stomach tightened. "Actually, that's what I'm talking about."

"What, the sex?" Ozzie said. "It's been a while since I've been out there." She nudged Nora in the side. "Catch me up. What makes it complicated?"

Oh God. Ozzie had misunderstood. But of course she had. Nora had said too much, opened the door too wide. She backpedaled frantically, trying to figure out how to end the conversation.

"Do they get all *Fifty Shades of Grey* on you?" Ozzie pressed. "That reminds me, this one friend of mine who just got divorced signed up on a Christian dating website and wound up going out with some guy who asked her to be part of a threesome. On their first *date*!"

"No, God, no." Nora shook her head. "It's nothing like that. Really. I don't even know why I brought it up. It's honestly nothing."

"Oh, don't do that, Nora!" Grace protested. "Tell us what you're talking about! What makes things so complicated?"

Nora closed her eyes briefly and then opened them again. It was mortifying that she still had issues with sex, that things got to a point where she'd rather not have it at all than have to deal with the memories that surfaced once it started. Real women didn't deal with that. Or at least none of these women did. She was sure of it.

She took a deep breath. Screw it; what did she have to lose by telling them? Or maybe that wasn't even the question. Maybe the real question was, what did she have to lose if she didn't tell them?

"It's not that the sex is complicated," she said slowly. "It's that *I'm* complicated. With sex in general."

"It's hard for you to be intimate with someone?" Monica's voice was so kind that it brought tears to Nora's eyes.

She nodded instead of responding and readjusted her hands on the wheel to stop them from shaking.

"Because?" Grace sat forward in the backseat.

"I guess because I had a bad experience with it," she said. "A long time ago."

"You mean with Theo?" Ozzie asked.

Nora felt her face flush hot. "*No,* not with Theo. With someone else. And that's really all I want to say right now. Okay? I'm sorry. I'm not trying to be dismissive or go back into my shell or anything, but can we please change the subject?" She drew a hand over the front of her eyes as if might erase the shame that was rising behind them. "Please?"

"Of course we can." Grace squeezed her shoulder. "I appreciate you saying anything at all, Norster. I know how hard it is for you to talk." She sat back in her seat, but not before catching Nora's eyes in the mirror. She winked.

"It's hard for me talk about things, too," Monica said. "If I hadn't been here this weekend when I got the call from the detective, I probably wouldn't have told another living soul what I'd done."

"I only opened up about Gary because you did first," Ozzie admitted, looking at Monica. "If you'd asked me before I came out here whether or not I was going to tell you girls the truth about my marriage, I would have laughed in your face."

"I knew you knew some of the gory details about me," Grace said softly. "But I hadn't planned on saying anything else. Not until Monica spoke up first."

It was funny how that worked, Nora thought as the car raced on. How they borrowed strength from one another, leaning on it for a while until the next one needed it. It might have been the only thing from those Invisible days that hadn't changed.

It might have been the only thing that wouldn't change, the last, single thread that held them all together.

Chapter 21

There's a Burger King up ahead at the next exit," Ozzie said a few minutes later. "Anyone hungry?"

"Starving!" Grace said.

"I could eat," Nora agreed. "And pee."

"Me too." Monica grimaced. "I've had to go for over an hour now, but I didn't want to say anything."

"Why not?" Grace asked.

Monica shrugged. "I'm always afraid public restrooms aren't going to be a single room. I hate it when there's someone in the next stall."

"You still have bathroom hang-ups!" Ozzie said, slapping the backseat. "Don't you guys remember? She couldn't go if she thought we were being too quiet in our rooms. She always thought we were listening!"

Nora smiled as Ozzie laughed out loud. She'd forgotten that part about Monica, but now as she thought about it, she remembered how Monica would turn on the water in the tub to drown out any noise she might make, how she would emerge red-faced, mortified by the fact that the girls knew what she'd been doing.

"God Almighty." Monica smiled faintly at Ozzie as they pulled into the Burger King parking lot. "You've got a memory like an elephant."

For a little while, after they'd eaten their burgers and slurped the last of their milkshakes, the women slipped into a silent, sated state, leaving Nora alone with her thoughts. She had already put over two hundred miles behind her and the distance was wearying. She could feel her eyelids getting heavy even though she'd had an extra-large Coke, and her arms felt waterlogged. The pot had worn off long ago, although remnants of it combined with the overload of everyone's personal information had left her emotionally exhausted. The sides of the highway were bleak and dusty, but farther back, a wash of red and yellow trees lit up the landscape, and small flocks of sparrows dipped and sailed over the tops of them. For as much as she loved the moon and its phases, daylight never failed to disappoint Nora. Each morning, as the light seeped back into the world during one of her walks with Alice Walker, she felt the same assurance rise inside her chest, as if something dark had split open and revealed something new to her. Life pushing through, despite all the odds. Now she felt the same way, except with an intensity that made her tremble.

A first line from *A Tale of Two Cities* came to her: *"It was the best of times; it was the worst of times, it was the age of wisdom, it was the age of foolishness, it was the epoch of belief, it was the epoch of incredulity; it was the season of Light, it was the season of Darkness, it was the Spring of Hope, it was the Winter of Despair."*

Here, today, was all of these things, she thought.
And more.

One by one, the women dozed off as it began to rain, the land-scape darkening under a thick clot of clouds. Nora stared through the slosh of the windshield wipers, admiring the just-washed colors of the trees, and wondered what Alice Walker was doing. Maybe Trudy had just gotten back from taking her for an afternoon walk. She hoped so. Alice Walker was used to getting up early for their daily treks to the birch grove and over the rail-road tracks, but she doubted if Trudy or Marion would have man-aged to rouse themselves at such an hour. Still, if Alice Walker didn't get out at least once a day, she would start to howl.

If she were home now, she would be on the couch probably, having just returned from the grocery store. Alice Walker would be nestled up against her, and Nora, who would have showered and gotten into sweats and fuzzy socks, would be reading, maybe finishing up the Sunday crossword from the *New York Times*, or flipping through the Book Review, which was her favorite part. The afternoon light would be coming through the living room window at a slant, warming the hardwood floor, touching the tips of her small ficus tree in the corner. Every so often she would look up from the paper and study the patterns on the floor, leaf-shaped movements dancing to and fro like small hands. After a while, she'd get up, go to the refrigerator. Maybe take out some cream cheese, toast a bagel, drizzle a little honey over the top of it. A glass of root beer too; and a few gummy fish from the bag she kept in the bread drawer. Then back to the couch, where she'd turn on the TV, find a *Law & Order* marathon, drift in and out of sleep in between episodes, while Alice Walker readjusted her position, trying to get comfortable.

It wasn't such a bad life, she thought.

It couldn't be.

If it was, she wouldn't be missing it the way she was.

Next to her Ozzie snored, a long, rumbling sound that careened off into a high-pitched whine. Grace, who was curled up like a cat in the backseat, her thin legs tucked under her, muttered under her breath, while Monica, whose head was flung back on the seat rest, sat perfectly still. Nora's eyes got heavier, and after another few moments, she reached across the seat and shook Ozzie awake. Ozzie recoiled at her touch, a rattlesnake ready to strike.

"Hey," Nora whispered. "It's just me. I have to stop or I'm going to fall asleep at the wheel. Can you take over?"

"Yeah." Ozzie's eyes, momentarily disoriented, focused once more. "Yeah, of course. Where the hell are we? What time is it? Did I fall asleep?"

"You slept for a while." Nora jerked her thumb toward Monica. "She conked out. And Grace, too. It's almost four-thirty. We've got another seven or eight hours or so, I think. We're in Pennsylvania."

Ozzie rubbed her eyes and yawned. "Okay, pull over. I got it."

Nora stopped the car and let herself out, sliding to the ground. The backs of her knees were stiff, and something in her back cracked. The headlights of the car were clotted with dead insects and the windshield was covered with a thick film of dust.

"Mmmm . . ." Ozzie said, rolling her head between her shoulders. "My head feels like a bag of rattlesnakes, but I'm glad I got a little shut-eye. Thanks."

As if on cue, Grace lifted her head from the backseat and yawned. "Where are we?" she asked. "Did we get to Manhattan?"

"Not yet." Ozzie eased the car back onto the highway. "I'm driving. Nora has to rest for a while."

Nora sprawled out on the enormous leather seat next to Ozzie, the top of her head touching Ozzie's thigh, and closed her eyes. She could feel the muscles in her back and then her neck relax, as if she had been clenching them for hours.

The wheels spun and then squealed a bit as Ozzie lurched the car forward.

Monica sat up like a shot at the noise and looked around. "We're there?" she cried. "Already?"

"No, doll." Ozzie reached over the seat and patted Monica's arm. "Just switching drivers. We still have about seven more hours."

Monica rested her head against the window. She stared through the glass, not moving. "Oh my God, I still can't believe this is happening. I'm so sorry to drag all of you into all this."

"You don't have to be sorry," Ozzie said. "And you didn't drag any of us into it. We wanted to come, remember? I just hope that when we get there, you can fix things, Mons. I really do."

Monica's teeth pulled at her lower lip. "Yeah, me too."

"Any word from your attorney?" asked Ozzie.

"No." Monica sounded stoic. "I left him another message a while back."

"And? Nothing yet?"

"I don't know. I didn't check."

"Well, check!"

"My phone's out of juice."

"Well, plug it in!" Ozzie sounded irate. "We're driving a fucking Escalade here, Monica! This goddamned thing has everything in it except a toilet. It must have—"

"I left my charger at Grace's." Monica looked away as Ozzie stared at her in the rearview mirror, openmouthed.

"I have one!" Grace leaned over and dragged a duffel bag across the back. "Actually, I might have two. Henry's always worried I'll lose one."

"What are you doing here, Monica?" Ozzie was looking at her dangerously.

"What's that supposed to mean?" Monica asked.

"You do realize that you have a right to try to get out of this, don't you? That you don't have to punish yourself any more than the law already will? For whatever mistake you made?"

Nora sat up. It was going to be impossible to sleep. And as exhausted as she was, she didn't want to sleep. Not really. Who knew, after Manhattan, where they would all go, where any of them would end up? What if she never saw any of these women again? What if, after everything came to a close, it would be the end for them? The real end this time?

"I'm not trying to punish myself." Monica sounded uncertain. "I'm on it."

"Doesn't sound like you're on it."

"I'm *on* it, Ozzie."

"You sure?" Ozzie asked.

"Positive."

"Okay." Ozzie sat back again. "If you say so. Sorry for waking you up, Norster."

"It's all right." Nora shrugged. "I've got a lifetime to sleep." She slung an arm over the seat and watched Grace, who was looking at a baby picture of Georgia inside her wallet. "When was that taken?"

"Few weeks after she was born." Grace seemed lost in thought. "I was in the hospital. Henry took her to JCPenney."

"It's so cute." Monica leaned over. "God, she's adorable. Like a little pea in a pod."

"Yeah." Grace closed her wallet abruptly and dropped it back inside her purse.

The same pained expression she'd had earlier when Henry had mentioned the baby crossed her face again. Did she really not want to have anything to do with the child? Nora wondered. Or was it something that would pass, a long, terrible mood that she would snap out of eventually?

Monica was watching Grace carefully, too. "You know, I lost one of the pictures I used to have of my mother." Her voice was wistful.

"Oh, no!" Nora said. "The ones your grandmother gave you?"

Monica nodded. "I can't tell you how long I've spent looking for it. It's like it just disappeared. I don't know if I lost it at Turning Winds or later, when I came to the city. It still makes me crazy when I think about it. Thank God I still have the other one."

Nora didn't have any pictures of Mama. Not one. She wondered sometimes if the absence of them, which, in a way, denied Mama's very existence, meant that something was wrong with her. But then she would close her eyes and look at the litany of images Mama had left behind. They were more than enough.

Ozzie turned on the radio, pressing the buttons at random. She fiddled with the tuner, skipping station after station until the sudden unmistakable sound of Cyndi Lauper's "Time After Time" filled the car.

"Oh!" Monica sat back, mouthing the words. "Remember this song?"

"One of our favorites," Grace said, smiling at the memory. Nora wondered if any of them were thinking about the same day she was thinking of now: the four of them crammed in Ozzie's car as the same mournful lyrics drifted through the side speakers. It was the day after graduation; the heat was a slick, oppressive weight on the skin. Cicadas buzzed relentlessly outside, as if protesting the high temperatures, and birds perched motionless in the heavy green of the trees. They were sitting at the Willow Grove bus stop, where, in less than half an hour, Monica would board and leave for New York City, where she had just been hired as a full-time nanny for a wealthy family on Park Avenue. Grace would get on one of the Greyhounds a half hour later, headed for art school in Georgia. And after Ozzie had hugged Nora goodbye, she would get on the third and last bus in line, headed for a horse farm in Montana, where she had found work as a ranch hand.

Nora knew that the tears sliding down each of their cheeks that afternoon were real—just as hers were—but she hated them anyway. She hated them equally and without guilt, a small, black snake coiled in the deepest recesses of her belly. She could not, no matter how hard she tried, shake the feeling that she was being left behind in the worst possible way, that she was being abandoned all over again by people who were supposed to love her. Worse, they were leaving her with a secret—a secret she alone knew about, a secret she knew she would take to her grave—the weight of which made things nearly unbearable, like being forced to walk around underwater with a tire around her neck. She knew it was none of their faults; they had graduated, and this was the most logical next step. No one could help the fact that she wanted to stay. Life went on, and they were going with it. But still she blamed them, waiting in vain for one of them to turn and say, "Just come with me, Nora. Come with me, and we'll figure it out together," or "You know, maybe I'll stay. Just for another year. Just 'til you're feeling okay again."

But none of them had.

And Nora, in her own inimitable way, had stayed silent, too.

Chapter 22

They pulled off again, this time at a mini-mart in Clarion, Pennsylvania, to refill on gas, drinks, and snacks. Ozzie, who had volunteered to buy the food, returned with a gigantic package of Nutter Butter cookies, four strawberry yogurts, string cheese, and six bottles of water.

"Oh my gosh, all this junk food reminds me of the Chore Chart at Turning Winds." Grace said suddenly. "Remember all those jobs we had to do?"

"Yeah, because Elaine didn't feel like doing any of it herself." Ozzie peeled open the package of cookies. "Fat slob. She probably sat around all day and ate potato chips while we were at school. I don't remember her picking up a broom even once when we were there."

"She ran the place!" Monica said. "And she was the only one there half the time, remember? Everyone else worked part-time. Besides, she wasn't so bad. I remember she sat up one night with

Ella after she'd come back from visiting her dad. I don't know what happened, but the poor little thing wouldn't stop crying. Elaine stayed in her room for most the night, until she fell asleep again."

"And I remember she crocheted a huge baby blanket for D'Shawn," Grace piped in. "It was all these different colors. Just beautiful. It must've taken her months."

"D'Shawn," Ozzie murmured, looking out the window. "My God. I wonder whatever happened to her."

"She was going to move in with the boyfriend and his mother," Grace said. "Remember?"

"I'm sure that went over like a lead balloon," Ozzie said. "She was constantly bribing me with her Newports to get me to do her jobs on the Chore Chart. She hated doing any kind of house-work."

"What job from the Chore Chart did you hate the most?" Monica asked. "Mine was cleaning the bathrooms." She shud-dered. "Ugh. All that hair in the drains, and the crud around the bottom of the toilet?"

"Do you mind?" Grace asked, holding up a piece of cheese. "I'm eating here."

"Well, that was my worst," Monica said. "What was yours?"

"Cooking dinner." Grace's response was immediate. "I used to break out in hives when it was my day to cook. I thought I was going to have a heart attack."

"You did fine!" Ozzie insisted. "We all did, considering. I don't remember very many meals I didn't eat."

"I do!" Monica said. "And a lot of them were yours."

"*Mine?*" Ozzie looked shocked. "What're you talking about?

I was a great cook! I'm still a great cook. Maybe not as skilled as Henry yet, but close."

"I'm with Monica," Grace said, stifling a giggle. "You did get a little weird when it came to food combinations. Admit it."

Ozzie put a hand on her hip. "Give me an example."

"Scrambled eggs with cut-up Slim Jims," Grace shot back.

"It's the same thing as sausage and eggs!"

Nora raised an eyebrow.

"Fine, gimme another one," Ozzie demanded.

"Peanut butter toast with sliced tomato and bacon." Monica stuck a finger in her mouth. "Blech!"

"My BPTs?" Ozzie looked hurt. "You didn't like them at all?"

"Horrifying," Monica said, shaking her head. "Nightmare-inducing."

"Peanut butter and tomato do not go together," Grace added. "Under any circumstances. Ever."

"What about you, Norster?" Ozzie looked pleadingly at her. "You liked my BPTs, didn't you?"

"I don't remember the BPTs," Nora said, spooning the last of her yogurt. "But I do remember the time you made something called Popped Cereal."

"Oh my God, Popped Cereal!" Monica and Grace began to laugh wildly. "Popcorn and milk! Ozzie, you were nuts! How did Elaine ever let you get away with that one?"

"Oh, I told her it went way back." Ozzie was finding it hard not to smile, too. "Which it did. Growing up, those were the only two edible things in our house half the time. Elaine was all tickled, though. She thought I was trying to share a piece of the old family heritage."

Their laughter filled the car, and Nora thought as they sped along that it was still one of her favorite sounds in the world.

I still have no idea if my parents are even alive, but has anyone else been in touch with theirs?" Ozzie asked as the car raced on. "Any phone calls maybe, or sudden encounters?"

"My father called me once at Liam's place." Monica's voice was tentative, almost fearful. "I almost fell over when some guy told me I had a collect call from the Richmond State Prison and asked if I would accept charges. I have no idea how he even found me."

"Wow," said Ozzie. "What'd you do?"

"I hung up," Monica answered. "I said no, that I wouldn't accept the charges, and I hung up."

Ozzie nodded. "What about you, Grace? You ever hear anything again from your mother?"

"I saw her once."

"Your *mother?*" Ozzie sounded as flabbergasted as Nora felt. "You did? My God, after all that time! Where?"

"I'm still in touch with my little brother," Grace said. "You remember me telling you about Sam? He lives out in Arizona, right near the border." She smiled. "He's married now, has three kids, and owns his own construction company. He's doing so well. Anyway, he called and told me that she was in some asylum out there, receiving electroshock therapy."

Ozzie whistled through her teeth.

"Sam said he thought the shock treatments were working, but that she kept asking for me. Over and over and over again. He said she just kept repeating my name, and nothing else." Grace stared into the horizon at something and then refocused. "Anyway, he begged me to come see her and I went. More for Sam, I think, than for her. I flew out there, it must be two years ago now, and I met Sam, and we went together to go see her." She pressed a finger against the bottom of her throat and left it there, but her eyes were blinking rapidly, as if she were trying to dislodge a wayward thought inside her head. "It's funny, the expectations you carry around when it comes to certain people, isn't it? I hadn't seen my mother in almost thirteen years by then, but for some reason I was still holding on to the same ridiculous reunion scenario I'd had when I was a teenager. You know, her freezing for a split second when she saw me, eyes filling with tears. And then rushing over, screaming my name, and throwing her arms around me."

"She didn't?" Ozzie looked perplexed.

"She refused to believe it was really me," Grace said. "She just kept saying, 'You're not my Grace. You don't even look like Grace. Grace is much shorter than you. And skinnier.'" Grace brushed the top of her arm with her fingertips. "She even pinched me, like she was trying to make sure I was an actual person."

"Why?" Monica sounded pained.

"Sam said she was probably waiting for that sixteen-year-old girl she'd left behind to walk into her room." Grace shrugged. "Who knows what shape her brain was in, after all those years? In and out of treatment. On and off drugs. Maybe she was just stuck back there, you know? Back when I was younger."

"Oh, doll," Ozzie said. "How awful."

"In a way it was good for me to see," Grace said. "It made me realize how sick she was, how sick she'd always been. I think it even helped me forgive her for everything she put Sam and me through."

Outside, the sky looked endless, a pale blue color shot through with clouds. Nora couldn't help but wonder if it had been Grace's meeting with her mother that had triggered her last suicide attempt. Grace blamed it on the pregnancy, but what had she really thought, having her mother, who had abandoned her so many years ago, deny her existence yet again? What did something like that do to an already fractured mind?

"What about you, Nora?" Ozzie asked. "You ever hear anything from your mother?"

Nora thought back to the letter she'd received twelve years ago. It had been from Mama, postmarked from some seaside town in Maine and mailed to Turning Winds, which in turn had forwarded it to her at the library. The letter had been long and sloppy and rambling, but the gist of it was that Daddy Ray had died and Mama was all alone, living in a little house by the sea. She hadn't asked Nora directly to come and visit, but Nora could feel the request implied there between the lines. She'd crumpled up the paper after reading it and thrown it away. Later, just before she locked up the library for the night, she'd gone back over to the trash can and fished it back out again. It was still in her dresser drawer, hidden behind her old running socks.

"I got a letter once," she said. "She's somewhere up north."

"What'd the letter say?" Monica asked.

"Nothing much. She moved to Maine after her husband died. She wanted me to come visit."

Silence.

"What was her husband's name?" Grace asked. "I don't think I've ever heard you say a word about him."

"George," Nora said. "But I had to call him Daddy Ray."

"Why Daddy Ray?"

"That was his last name. It's what he wanted to be called."

"You never said much about him," Ozzie said. "You know, back then."

"There wasn't much to tell."

"Did you go to Maine?" Ozzie asked.

Nora shook her head. "I'll never go. I have nothing to say to her." She hadn't realized she had even felt such a thing until it came out of her mouth.

Ozzie nodded. "That's kind of how I feel now, too. I used to think that I'd go back and rage and scream at my mother. Maybe even throw something at her. But what would that do?"

"It might make you feel better," Monica offered.

"I don't think so. Or maybe it would, but just for a few minutes. And then afterward, I think I would feel even worse."

"Why?"

"Because I want to be better than her," Ozzie said. "My mother's way of handling things and dealing with people was to scream and yell and then beat them to a pulp if she could. I know I'm in a relationship right now that says otherwise, but I don't want to scream and yell at anyone anymore. Not even her. I want to figure out another way of communicating. And if I ever go back there and have it out with her, I want it to be done in a decent, respectful way. I want her fucking jaw to drop open, listening to me talk. I want her to see that she spent her life stepping on me and that I got up anyway, and walked away from it with my head held high."

Not me, Nora thought.

Not ever.

Ozzie's plans were respectable, even admirable, but Nora knew that if she arrived at her last day on Earth without laying eyes on Mama again, she would be just fine.

Chapter 23

They had driven a few more hours when Ozzie suddenly pulled off at an exit that read Stroudsburg, and said that if she couldn't find herself a bathroom, she was going to ruin the front seat of Liam's beautiful car. The sun was long gone, and the sky was dark. The clock on the dashboard read 9:57 p.m.

"Oh, thank God," Monica said. "I didn't want to ask again."

Ozzie rolled her eyes and pulled the car into a rutted parking lot. She parked in front of a small store with a dirty red and white awning over the front door. The inside was lit with a bright, almost garish sort of light, and Nora could make out a tall figure standing behind a counter. The scrawled missive WE SELL BEER AND ICE CREAM was taped in one of the windows, and another sign, scratched out in the same cryptic handwriting, was tacked to the front door: RESTROOMS IN BACK.

"Ewww." Monica sat forward on the seat, perusing the building with a worried expression. "Nothing in that place is going to be clean *or* have a single room. Can't we go somewhere else?"

"Oh, for the love of Pete." Ozzie had already opened her door and was stretching her arms and legs outside the car. Grace and Nora followed. "We're the only other people around. And if you're worried about germs, just put some toilet paper down on the seat. Or squat above it. It's not a big deal."

But Monica held back, her fingers gripping the front of the dashboard. "I don't know if that'll be enough. You can pick up anything on a dirty toilet seat these days. Even STDs."

"Well, we can go somewhere else," Grace said. "But the sign back there said the next restroom isn't for another thirty-four miles. Do you think you can wait that long?"

Monica let out a small whimper.

"I'll go first," Ozzie said, leaning in Monica's window. "Okay? I'll go first and then wipe everything down, and then you can go. All right?"

Monica dug inside her purse. "Use this," she said, handing Ozzie a plastic bottle of lime-coconut-scented hand sanitizer. "For when you wipe down the seat."

Ozzie studied the plastic bottle and then raised her eyebrows as Monica got out of the car. "Okay," she said. "Whatever floats your boat."

Nora moved quickly inside the dirty restroom after Monica and Grace were finished, being careful not to touch anything she didn't have to.

"Where's Ozzie?" Monica asked as she emerged back outside.

"Probably getting something to eat," Grace said.

"Inside?" Monica looked horrified as she glanced at the store again. "She won't find anything edible in there."

"Let's wait in the car," Nora suggested. "She'll be out in a minute."

Thirty seconds later, Ozzie reemerged, not from inside the building, but from the right-hand side of it. She walked toward them with long, quick steps, her eyes riveted on something inside her cupped hands.

Monica rose up a little on the seat, staring through the windshield. "What happened? What's she holding?"

Ozzie trotted up to the car and motioned for Monica to roll down her window. Monica looked at her fearfully and then lowered the glass pane.

"Look what I just found," Ozzie said, opening her hands.

Monica screamed and drew back, nearly pinning Grace against the side of the door. Her feet scrabbled on the seat in front of her, and her arms flailed helplessly on both sides.

"What?" Grace yelled. "What is it?"

"Oh my God, it's a rat or something!" Monica shrieked. "Get it away, Ozzie! Get it out of here!"

Nora leaned over the backseat and stared into the well of Ozzie's hands. Inside was the tiniest creature she had ever seen; no bigger than a dinner roll and covered with soft brown fuzz. It had ears, but just barely, and its tiny slits for eyes were squeezed shut.

"It's not a *rat*," Ozzie said. "It's a baby rabbit." She lifted her hands up, turning the small creature to the right and then to the left. "I can't believe none of you noticed it. It was just a little ways from the bathroom." She nodded toward the animal. "Look at the little white blaze on its forehead. That means it's still too young to survive without its mother. It must've fallen out of the nest somehow and then crawled toward the bathroom."

"Well, put it back!" Monica was still clutching at Grace behind her. "Please, Ozzie. It's probably carrying all kinds of diseases. Go put it back."

"Oh, I *will*." Ozzie made no effort to hide her annoyance. "There's a field right behind the store, which is where the mother probably is with the rest of the litter. I just wanted you guys to see it first. Have you ever seen a wild rabbit? They're a lot different than the domestic ones you can raise at home."

"No, I've never seen one." Monica's voice was a whimper. "And thank you for thinking of us, but you can go return it to the field where it belongs."

Ozzie rolled her eyes. "It's a *rabbit,* Mons, not a cobra. Relax."

"I'm relaxed." Monica nodded her head. "Go ahead now. The field's right behind you."

Nora was still staring at the tiny animal. Its nose had begun wiggling ever so slightly, as if just catching wind of her scent, and the tip of its right ear was bent forward, as if it had been creased somehow. She opened the door on her side of the car. "I'll go with you," she said as Ozzie turned back around.

"Me, too." Grace got out of the front of the car.

"Wait, you guys are *leaving* me?" Monica leaned halfway out of the window, a horrified look on her face. "All alone?"

"Get out of the car and come with us!" Ozzie called, not turning around.

Nora trotted back to the car and leaned in Monica's window. "Come on," she said. "It'll be like an adventure."

"I don't *like* adventures," Monica whimpered as she stepped out of the car. "Especially when they involve wild animals. My idea of an adventure is looking at *pictures* of animals. Preferably on the wall of a spa."

They followed Grace and Ozzie toward the back of the building, stopping as they rounded the corner.

"Good Lord," Monica said. "It's like *Little House on the Prairie* out here."

Nora didn't disagree. Even in the dark she could make out the stretch of field, full of waist-high brown and green grass and dotted with black-eyed Susans and Queen Anne's lace. Not a building was in sight. Just grass and flowers and more grass and flowers. Above it a star-spangled sky loomed, wide and endless as the ocean.

"Shhh!" Ozzie said, looking at Monica. "You have to be real quiet or we won't be able to find the mother."

"You want to *find* the mother?" Monica's voice went up a notch.

"Monica." Ozzie turned around, her steepled fingers parted at the top. "We have to find the mother. That's the only chance it'll have of surviving."

Monica gripped Nora's arm. "Okay. But what if . . . what if the mother's mean? Like what if she charges at your leg or something because you have her baby? And then she bites you?"

Ozzie bit her lip, suppressing a smile. "Really?"

Nora patted Monica's hand. "It'll be okay. Wild rabbits don't usually charge at humans."

Monica nodded and stared out at the field. She did not look convinced.

"Why don't you and Nora go left?" Ozzie suggested. "Just walk along the perimeter of the field and look for any movement in the grass. Grace and I will go this way and do the same thing."

"Movement?" Monica repeated. "What kind of movement?"

Nora pulled on her arm. "Come on. And don't worry; I won't let anything happen to you."

"Fine." Monica clutched at her hand. "But if I see anything move in that grass, I'm running like hell."

The left side of the field was behind the store. A large metal dumpster sat at the opposite end of the building, filled to overflowing with black plastic bags. Flies swarmed over the tops of it in tight, dark clouds, and then separated again, like loose threads. A heap of smaller white bags had been thrown haphazardly around the bottom of the dumpster, and their contents—old watermelon rinds, orange peels, dirty Q-tips—spilled out from the gnawed corners.

"It smells like summer in New York back here," Monica whimpered. "I don't like it."

A hiccup of a movement next to one of the white garbage bags caught Nora's eye. She paused and then squinted, wondering if she had just imagined it. But there it was again, a slight kick, almost like an afterthought, from behind the garbage bag. "Stay here," she said, holding Monica lightly around the wrist. She concentrated on keeping her voice as normal sounding as possible. "I just want to go see something."

"What?" Monica's voice pleaded behind her. "What is it, Nora?"

Nora knew it was the mother rabbit even before she got up close. She knew it was in the very last stages of death too, in the same way she understood that the tiny balls of fur around it were the other babies, and that they were already dead. A fox, perhaps, or maybe even a cat must have stumbled across the nest and dragged it out here. Or maybe the mother rabbit had gone in search of food and been mortally maimed before the attacker had turned its attention to the babies. Whatever the situation, they were too late. There was nothing anyone could do.

"Don't come over here," Nora said, holding her hand out in Monica's direction. "Just stay right where you are."

Monica stood frozen to the spot, watching as Nora grabbed an empty paper bag and laid it gently across the lifeless carcasses.

"It's the mother?" Monica whispered as Nora came back over.

Nora nodded. "And the rest of the babies."

Monica stared at the paper bag, her stricken eyes filling with tears. "That's terrible," she said.

"It is terrible." Nora took Monica's hand again. "But it's life too, Monica. Come on. Let's go get Ozzie and Grace and tell them."

Monica put up a fight for twenty whole minutes after Ozzie announced that she was keeping the orphaned rabbit, but Ozzie didn't budge. "For Christ's sake, Mons, the poor thing's entire family has just been obliterated." She crawled into the backseat of the car, still holding the animal in her hands. "At the very least, we can keep it safe during the remainder of the trip. Look at him! He's shaking like a leaf."

Grace climbed into the driver's seat, but made no move to start the car. "I think he might be shaking so much because we've taken him out of his element."

"Do you know anything about wild animals?" Ozzie's voice was dangerously close to sounding rude.

"No, but—"

"Well, I do," Ozzie said. "We've raised two baby foxes at our house and a porcupine."

"A porcupine!" Monica, who had crept into the front seat next to Grace, drew back in horror. "Ozzie! You cannot be serious."

"They're adorable. You would love them. My *point* is that I know what I'm doing here. You've got to trust me."

"Well, I may not have raised any wild animals from birth," Grace said, "but I've read enough to know that taking them out of the nest when they're this little isn't a good thing. He's not an infant, Ozzie. I bet he has a good chance of making it if we just put him back where we found him."

"In the nest?" Ozzie sounded incredulous. "Did you forget that his mother was torn to pieces back there? It won't take ten minutes for some fox or badger to smell this little guy and finish him off, too. If we put him back now, we're just bringing him back to die. But if we keep him, we can give him some food, keep him warm and comfortable. We can at least give him a chance."

"To do what?" Grace's eyes flashed. "We're on our way to *Manhattan*, Ozzie. We have to go to a police station in the morning and God knows where else after that." She reached out and put a hand over Monica's. "I don't mean to project, sweetie. We just don't know what else is going to happen yet."

"What's your point?" Ozzie asked.

"My *point* . . ." Grace paused, rolling her eyes. " . . . is what are you going to do with the rabbit? Put him in your pocket? Dump him in a shoebox and set him outside the police station until everything's over? And then you have to take a plane home. Do you really think you can pass through security with a wild animal in your hands?"

"I don't need to take him all the way home." Ozzie sounded less convinced. "I'll . . . I don't know, I'll find a vet somewhere. In Manhattan. There's got to be a million of them there."

"Ozzie, come on." Monica's pleading voice was back. "We don't have time to do that. We're barely going to get into the city as it is, and we still haven't found a hotel room!"

"I agree." Grace set her jaw. "Now come on, Oz. You're the one who's always yelling about being realistic about everything, so let's get real here, okay? As sad as it is, we can't bring the rabbit. We just can't. It doesn't make any sense. You have to put him back."

"I can't." Ozzie turned away from Grace and Monica, resting her head against the side of the seat. "Besides, I've already given him a name."

"A name?" Nora asked. "What is it?"

"Elmer," Ozzie said.

Nora and Grace exchanged a look. "Why Elmer?" Nora asked.

"Oh, you know, Bugs Bunny, Elmer Fudd. One just sort of segued into the other." She shrugged. "Listen, we're not letting him out to die, okay? Please just start the car. Give me a minute, all right? I'll think of something."

"What if it has fleas?" Monica tried as Grace started the engine. "Seriously, what if it has fleas and we get them and bring them home?" Her eyes were opened so wide that Nora could see tiny red streaks zigzagging across her pupils. "If I get fleas on top of everything else I have to deal with right now, Ozzie, I will seriously lose what's left of my mind. I'm not kidding."

"Oh, please," Ozzie said. "Fleas are not a big deal. I got them last summer from one of our dogs, and it was nothing a good medicated shampoo didn't fix."

"I Don't. Want. To. Get. Fleas." Monica was semihysterical, pounding her words against the back of the seat. "I don't care if there are ten million medicated shampoos out there! I don't want to get them! Now, please, Ozzie! I'm serious!"

"Elmer doesn't have fleas." Ozzie's jaw pulsed. "The poor little thing is only a few weeks old. He hasn't even had time to get fleas." She opened her hands a little and peered inside. "Look. If it makes you feel any better, I'll check him out. Right now."

"What do you mean, check him out?" Monica leaned back until she was almost flat against the dashboard as Grace pulled the car back on to the highway. "Can you actually *see* fleas? Will they jump out at you if they're in there?"

"Hmmm hmmm . . ." Ozzie ran an index finger through the rabbit's fur. Nora settled herself sideways against the seat and watched. The animal was shaking so hard that it looked like a battery-operated toy. She could see the faint outline of its spine as Ozzie ran her fingertip up and down the length of it, and its tiny nub of a tail was no bigger than her fingernail. "Nope, all clean."

"Nothing?" Monica bit her lower lip. "Not one flea. You're sure?"

"Positive. And look." Ozzie opened her hands a little, moving them toward the front seat. "He's shaking like a leaf. He's scared out of its mind. He *needs* us."

"Okay, okay." Monica moved back even more. "You can put him back now. I believe you."

"Can I hold him?" Nora asked.

"Really?" Ozzie looked surprised. "You want to?" Nora nodded and held out her hands. "Okay," Ozzie said. "But just for a few minutes, all right? Wild animals aren't like pets. They don't do well being passed around. Human scents are too overwhelming to them. It can just cause more stress."

Nora didn't breathe as Ozzie deposited the tiny figure inside her palms, staring in amazement at the utter perfection of it. It was so tiny! Like a breath! A whisper!

"Have you ever held a wild rabbit before?" Monica asked, looking nervously at Nora's hands.

"Never," Nora whispered. "He's so *light*. Like a little pincushion."

"Well, he is light." Ozzie fiddled with her wallet, opening the Velcro pouch and counting out single dollar bills. "They only weigh a few ounces when they're born. Elmer probably still weighs less than a half pound." She tossed her wallet aside and leaned in close to Nora. "He's sweet, right?"

Nora could feel something rising within her, and she swallowed it forcefully. "So sweet," she whispered. "Perfect."

"Poor little guy." Ozzie reached out and ran her finger down its back again. The pink ears twitched, and its nose wiggled like a button. "Oh, Nora, he's shaking even more. Give him to me now, okay? He was just starting to settle down a little in my hands, which means he's already gotten used to my smell. I think he's freaking out from the switch."

Nora bit the inside of her cheek and turned away from Ozzie.

"Come on, Norster. He's really stressed."

"Not yet." She clutched her hands around the rabbit and moved a fraction of inch farther away from Ozzie.

Ozzie pulled on Nora's arm and then moved her hand as if to grab the rabbit. "Nora. Seriously. Give him to me."

"I will." Nora turned even more, so that she was almost facing the window. "Just let me hold him for a little while longer." She knew how ridiculous she sounded—like a child or maybe even some kind of crazy person. But she didn't care.

"Nora." Ozzie's voice was slow, dangerous. "Please give me the rabbit. He needs to relax. I know a lot more about animals than you do. Babies can have heart attacks if they feel too anxious. Now, please."

"No." Nora turned all the way around now, so that Ozzie could see the back of her head. "I just want to hold him for a few more minutes. He's all right." She could feel Ozzie's eyes on the back of her neck, hear the frustrated sounds of her breath going in and out behind her. Well, it was too bad. She would have to wait. Nora clutched at the animal, pressing it to her. She wanted to feel it against her chest, its pea-sized heart thrumming beneath its silky fur. She wanted to feel his breath, the shaky movements of him, the staggered breathing. She did not want to give him up. No matter what.

"Okay, fine." To Nora's relief, Ozzie sat back against the seat again. "The poor thing is probably on the verge of a heart attack right now, but you hand him over when *you're* ready."

Nora gripped the tiny animal beneath her shirt; she could feel the pitter-patter of its heart slowing, even as she held him closer and closer still. Nothing Ozzie could say right now would make her give him up.

Not a thing in the world.

Chapter 24

It was Grace who spotted the sign for the pet supply store in Hopatcong, New Jersey, an hour later. It was hard to miss with its neon yellow siding and HOPATCONG HONEY'S spelled out in electric-green letters across the front. A plastic palm tree, set in a terra-cotta pot, leaned to one side, and a long, red-and-white-striped snake had been painted along the blacktop in front of the building. Nora could see its pink forked tongue from where she sat, the stripes beneath its belly. For some reason, despite the lateness of the hour, the lights were on inside.

"How about in there?" Grace said, pointing out the window. "It looks like someone's around. We could ask them, you know, whoever it is, if they'd take Elmer. And keep him even, until he's well enough to be released again into the wild."

"Yes!" Ozzie leaned over toward the window, nearly crushing Nora's arm in the process. "That's brilliant, Grace. Brilliant!"

"It's worth a shot." Grace pulled into the parking lot and turned off the engine.

Ozzie yanked open her door and came around to the other side. She opened Nora's door and stood there, waiting. Nora was still holding Elmer close to her chest.

"I gotta take him, Norster," Ozzie said. "You want to come in with me?"

Nora met Ozzie's eyes, but she did not move. "Just one more minute, all right?"

"Yeah." Something in Ozzie's face flickered. "Okay."

Nora lifted her hands close to her face. She could make out the warm scent of dirt and fur from between her fingers. Inside, the rabbit trembled and quaked, a minuscule bag of bones and skin and nerves. She could imagine its tiny heart inside there, banging away like some kind of piano key, alerting its whole body to danger. "You'll be okay," she whispered. "Hang in there, little guy, and you'll be okay." She leaned down and kissed him on the nose. "And don't worry; somebody'll come for you."

Ozzie waited as Nora lifted her face again. She extended her hands this time and nodded. "All right?"

Nora nodded as she handed the animal over. But she was not all right. She felt as though part of her was disappearing somehow, drowning in a void of memory and loss.

"I'll go with you," Monica said, sliding out of the car next to Ozzie. "I mean, since we are giving him away and everything. I'm not *totally* coldhearted."

Nora watched as the two of them disappeared inside the store. For the first time since she had arrived, she was alone with Grace. Nora could feel her eyes on her from the front seat, but she did not raise her head to meet them. She had a feeling that she knew what Grace was thinking, and she did not want to go there. She could not bear it just yet.

"I thought she was going to tell us the name Elmer had some kind of meaning," Grace said. "You know, like 'abandoned one' or something."

Nora tried to smile, but it came out quivery and fake; she could feel it on her face like a plastic thing. "Yeah, who knows? You know Ozzie and names. I bet it means something."

Grace hunched forward a little over the seat, tucking a loose strand of hair behind her ear. "Maybe it means 'lucky.'"

"Or unlucky."

"Why unlucky?" Grace asked.

"What if it dies?"

"Well, then." Grace's voice was slow, as if moving through a great body of water. "He'll have died with someone. And not alone out there in the field."

Nora didn't answer, not because she didn't want to, but because she could not. Her voice had vanished, maybe lodging itself somewhere inside the trembling rabbit, like another rapidly beating heart. The seconds ticked by in a weighted silence. The clock on the dashboard read 11:03 p.m. They'd been on the road for eleven hours and it already felt as though an entire year had gone by. But then, that was the way it had always been with the four of them. You could give The Invisibles an afternoon or an evening, and they could have the world—and the universe—at their disposal.

"Are you glad you came?" Grace's voice drifted over the seat.

Nora lifted her head. "On this trip or out to Chicago?"

"Both, I guess."

"Yeah."

"Me, too." There was a pause and then: "It's so good to see you again, Nora. It's been too long."

"Yes. It has."

"Tell me some more about you." Grace reached out and touched Nora's sleeve. "You've hardly said anything since you arrived."

"That's not true!" Nora suppressed an annoyance. "I told you about the whole . . . you know, fake boyfriend story." Her face felt hot, thinking of it again. "So stupid."

Grace's hand moved over Nora's. "Tell me more about the other stuff. You know, that you started telling us. Sex is supposed to be one of the most amazing feelings in the world. What happened that ruined it for you?"

Nora shrugged and looked out the window. They were sitting in a rental car in a pet store parking lot in Hopatcong, New Jersey. A painted snake with googly eyes and a forked tongue stared out at them from the pavement. Did Grace really expect her to get into this right now? Here?

"Nora?"

"Oh, it's a long, boring story. Seriously. It's not even worth—"

"I think it's worth it. No matter what it is." Grace rubbed a thumb over the top of Nora's hand. "Can you try to tell me? Even just a little bit?"

For a moment, Nora felt so embarrassed that she thought she might cry. And then she did cry, not out of embarrassment, but because the thought of sharing such an enormous burden she had been carrying alone for so long took her breath away. It was a moment before she found her voice, and then another moment until she could use it again. "It was my mother's husband," she said finally. "He's what ruined it."

"Daddy Ray?" Grace whispered.

"From fifth grade to seventh." Nora stared out the window. "At least once a week."

Grace bit her upper lip. Her eyes filled with tears, and the edges of her nostrils turned white. She put her other hand over Nora's, clasping it between both of hers, and then she dropped it and slid her arms around Nora's neck. "Oh, Nora, I'm so sorry," she whispered. "I'm so, so sorry."

"It's okay." Nora pulled away and stared at her feet. She felt humiliated. Naked. As if she had just pulled down her pants and exposed herself, right there in the car. And why was Grace looking at her like that? God only knew what kind of images were going through her head, probably some X-rated monstrosity involving a grown man pushing his way between a little girl's legs. Nora covered her face with her hands and leaned back against the seat, breathing into her palms. Her breath was hot and rancid; a roaring sounded in her ears.

"Nora?"

"Just give me a minute," she said behind her hands.

The car was quiet, the only sound the echoed breathing inside her own palms. *Quietquietquietquietandthenitwillbeover. Quietquietquietandthenitwillbeover.* Except that the quiet mantra wasn't working. In fact, she thought suddenly, maybe it had been one of the problems all along.

She lowered her hands. Grace was still watching her, her big eyes wet and glossy. "I need to get out and walk," Nora said.

"You got it." Grace was out the door before Nora could

straighten back up. She opened Nora's door and stood there waiting. "Come on. We can walk around the parking lot for a few
minutes."

The air was cool against Nora's face, a much-needed respite
from the stifling temperature inside the car. Or was the heat
coming from inside her own body? No matter. She was already
breathing easier; her heart had slowed down inside her chest, and
the terrible anxious feeling was starting to lift.

They set off, moving away from the painted snake and the fake
tree toward a mass of shrubs opposite the store. The trucks on the
highway rushed by less than fifty feet away, their headlights cutting narrow swaths through the darkness.

"Walking's good," Grace said as they turned around and
started back across the lot again. "Remember the walks we used
to take together? Next to the railroad tracks? That little birch tree
grove?"

"I still go there," said Nora. "With my dog. It's only about four
miles from where I live now."

"Wow." Grace was staring at her. "You walk all that way?"

"Every morning."

"*Every* morning?" Grace whistled softly. "Man. I wish I had
that kind of discipline."

"I wouldn't call it discipline." The tightening sensation was
back. "I like it. I wouldn't do it otherwise."

"Why do you go there?" Grace asked.

Nora sidled a glance at her. "Why?"

"I mean, is it just your regular route? Or . . ."

"Yeah," Nora heard herself say. "It's just my regular route."

There was silence for a moment. Nora felt as though something inside of her might burst—might literally explode—if she did not say something else, and so she lifted her head and said, "Grace?"

"Yeah?"

"Why didn't you ever call me? After you left, I mean?"

Grace looked down at the ground. Her eyes moved back and forth between her shoes, as if determining their size. "Oh, Nora, I was such a mess. I told you earlier in the car. After that last night at Turning Winds, I was so out of touch with things that I just walked around in a stupor. For months. Then . . ." She shook her head. "I didn't realize the bipolar stuff was starting up. I was manic for months, and then I'd crash. Up, down, all over the place." She paused, fiddling with her wedding band, a thin ring of silver etched with tiny leaves. "I'm sorry I didn't call you. I didn't even have the wherewithal to call my boyfriend half the time back then, and I was *living* with him."

They had stopped walking, were facing the traffic now. "But I was going through it too," Nora said stubbornly. "Not the bipolar stuff or anything, but God, Grace! Not a word? Not a call, a letter? Just to check in? You knew what I—what *we'd* just been through. I just don't understand."

Grace nodded. She rolled her teeth over her bottom lip to stop it from trembling. "I'm so sorry."

"You don't have to apologize. I don't need an apology. I just want to know why. I think in some ways not hearing from any of you was even worse than that night."

"No one called?" Grace asked. "Not even Ozzie?"

Nora shook her head.

"Ever?"

Nora shook her head again. "Ozzie said the reason she didn't was because she wanted to forget it, leave the whole thing behind."

"Yeah." Grace's voice was barely audible over the scream of traffic. "I guess that was true for me, too."

"But that included forgetting *me*." Nora's voice rose. "I was part of that night, remember?"

"I do remember. God, as much as I try to forget it, Nora, I do remember. Every single day." Grace's blue eyes were as big as dimes. "It was wrong of me not to call. I was protecting myself when I should have been more concerned about you. Can you ever forgive me?"

"Yes." The word came out of her mouth automatically, a learned response, like some kind of Pavlovian dog. She was too afraid to say no, that she couldn't forgive her, that she didn't even know how to go about doing such a thing. What she did know was that it had hurt too much and been too long for a few words in front of a highway to erase it all now. Still, if Grace needed to hear her say yes, she would do it. Maybe it was a start. Besides, what would it hurt?

She turned and started back across the parking lot, shoving her hands inside her pockets. Something bumped against her fingers, and she pulled out Grace's bottle of medication.

Grace peered at the bottle, a funny look coming over her face. "Is that mine?"

"Yeah." Nora shook the bottle, as if to remind Grace what was inside. The pills made a rattling sound, dried seeds inside a gourd. "I'm so sorry. I totally forgot to give you one when we ate back there."

"Give me one?" Grace looked confused. "Since when are you doling out my medicine?"

Nora blushed. "Henry asked me to make sure you took it." She bit the inside of her cheek as Grace's face blanched. "He said you probably wouldn't remember."

"He *told* you about me?" Grace's eyes narrowed.

"No. He didn't get into any details. At all. He just asked me to keep track of when you took your medicine." She winced. "Which I already screwed up."

"It's okay." Grace shook her head disgustedly. "I'll eat a little something in the car and take one now. It won't mess anything up." She took the pill bottle out of Nora's hands and studied the cryptic writing on the side, as if examining it for clues. "I don't know why I'm surprised. He's always on me at home, too. Like some kind of ward nurse. I should have known he was going to ask one of you to keep an eye on me."

"You're not angry, are you?" Nora asked. "He's just trying to take care of you."

"I don't need to be taken care of!" Grace snapped. "I'm not a fucking child."

Nora thought about Grace's old boyfriend Max, how she used to smack his hands away when he reached for her, how sometimes, when Grace talked to her at night, she complained how "ridiculously nurturing" he acted. "You'd think he was my father instead of my boyfriend," she said one night. "All he ever does is fuss and worry and ask me if I'm okay. It's pathetic." Nora couldn't help but wonder if Grace's harshness toward the people who wanted to care for her was purposeful. Did she resent them for trying to fill the void her mother was supposed to fill? And would she punish them ever after because of it?

"No, you're not a child," Nora said now. "You're sick."

"Well, I know how to take care of myself."

"Do you?"

"Yes, Nora." Grace raised her eyes. "I do."

"Then why'd you try to kill yourself?"

The fingers on Grace's right hand curled slowly into a fist, and for a moment, Nora thought she was going to take a swing at her. "I knew one of you would throw that in my face eventually," she said instead.

"I'm not throwing it in your face. I'm trying to make a point. You had to take care of yourself for a long time, Grace. And you did a pretty good job of it. It's not your fault that you got sick. And there isn't anything wrong with needing people to help you through it."

"It *is* my fault." Grace's voice cracked.

"What is?"

"Being sick. Being so . . . screwed up like this."

"How is it your fault?"

"I don't know!" Grace stared at a point in the distance, past Nora's shoulder. "Because it's my head! I'm supposed to have control of it, aren't I? I'm supposed to be a better person than this! Stronger or something."

"Being bipolar doesn't mean you're weak," Nora put her hands on Grace's arms, holding them just above the elbows. "Actually, I think it means the opposite. You have to be stronger than anyone I know to withstand something like this."

"Maybe."

"And another thing."

Grace lifted her head.

"Just because you have this doesn't mean that Georgia will."

"You can't know that."

"No." Nora shook her head slowly. "But neither can you."

"Nora." Grace raised her eyebrows. "There's a sixty percent she'll have some kind of mental illness. It runs in my whole family. These things are genetic."

"Okay. So the chance is there. Which means you'll get her help if it happens. You'll help her through it."

Grace stabbed at the ground with her shoe. "It just sucks. I wanted to give her everything. Except this."

"But everything of you *includes* this," Nora said. "Which isn't the end of the world. You're going to miss out on her whole childhood, Grace, because you're so worried about what might come up from the past and damage her future."

"But what if it does?"

"Then you'll deal with it! Remember what you told us about Georgia O'Keeffe? About how she was brave enough to go out there and create her own world? That's what you've got to do, Grace. You've got to create a life for yourself and your little girl. It won't be perfect. And it probably won't be easy. But it'll be yours. It'll be your light. And no matter what happens, you can always be proud of that."

Grace stared at her without blinking. Her eyes moved over and around Nora's face, as if seeing it for the first time. Maybe, Nora thought later, she was trying to memorize something, the shape of her face perhaps, or the way her eyes looked there so that she could take it back with her again. Or maybe she was just listening to her talk.

Hearing her words, the way Nora herself was for the first time.

Chapter 25

Our boy is all set!" Ozzie announced, emerging from the store with her arms over her head. She yanked open the door on the driver's side and climbed inside.

"You want to drive?" Grace asked.

"I want to drive!" Ozzie clapped her hands and rubbed them together. "I am re-fucking-energized!"

"Great." Grace climbed into the passenger seat while Nora and Monica got in back. "I'm exhausted."

"You should have seen Ozzie," Monica shook her head. "Like some kind of Doctor Dolittle in there. They were eating out of her hand!"

"I still can't believe anyone was even in there," Ozzie said. "They said they were working late, doing inventory." She stuck the key in the ignition. "Actually, the one guy seemed kind of thrilled. He hooked Elmer right up to a little feeding tube and put him in an incubator. That's what took so long. I was just hanging around, making sure they got everything working right."

She revved the engine. "But he's going to be fine. He's going to make it, Norster."

"That's such good news," Nora said, leaning back against the headrest. She was exhausted suddenly, too. "Good for you."

Ozzie placed her hands on the wheel and sighed. "I haven't felt this good in a long time. Seriously. In a long, fucking time." She turned around in the seat, surveying the lot of them. "You all could ask me anything right now and I'd give it to you."

"Well," Monica coughed nervously. "Since you put it that way." She fiddled with her ring. "We're only about an hour or so from New York. And I know it's . . ." She checked her watch. "God, is it really midnight already?" She bit her lip, glanced at Nora and then Grace.

"You want to find a hotel out here?" Grace tilted her head. "Call it a night?"

"No." Monica was holding Nora's gaze now. "I was thinking maybe we could take a little detour. Say, an hour or so south? I mean, if you all feel up to it. It's crazy late, I know."

It took a moment for the suggestion to register.

Nora caught on first. "You want to drive down to Willow Grove?"

Grace gasped. "We could see Turning Winds!"

"Oh, it's just an empty, rotted-out building now," Nora objected. "It's not—"

"I know." Monica cut her off. "But I really want to go back one last time and see it. I don't know what's going to happen tomorrow, and it might be the last time I can do anything like this for a while." She pressed her fingers against the middle of her chest.

"And maybe . . . you know, it'll help reconcile things. With all of us."

"Damn!" Ozzie smacked her hands off the steering wheel. "Now this is what I call a *road* trip!"

Nora felt her body lean back into her seat with a will of its own. Despite the terror she felt, she also understood that she had known something like this might happen. Willow Grove was just under eighty miles from Manhattan, after all; it was not so unusual that one of them might have thought of it. But now the moment was here. And it was more than just a whim, bigger than a wistful suggestion made in passing. It was a chance, Monica had just said, to turn around.

To try to reconcile things.

Maybe once and for all.

Nora studied the white circles from the oncoming headlights across the highway—pinpoints of light followed by wide bands of darkness. Every so often, her clotted thoughts would disperse as she thought back to the conversation she'd had with Trudy and Marion: *Go with your girls, Nora. Be brave. See what happens.* They were small words, but the meaning behind them felt colossal. As if what might happen next rested upon whether or not she decided to keep abiding by it.

Ozzie was pressed up against the steering wheel as they pulled into Willow Grove ninety minutes later, peering at everything from behind the windshield, but there was a weariness about her too, as if she was starting to fray around the edges. Grace leaned against her own window, pressing her fingertips against the glass. "There's Jitter Beans!" she said as the car drifted past the old coffeehouse. "Holy cow, I can't believe it's still there."

"It's all still here," Nora said, feeling strangely defensive.

"Oh my God, it's just like I remembered," Monica whispered, her fingers pressed lightly against the window. "Like we never left. Except that everything looks a little bit . . ."

Nora held her breath, waiting.

"Smaller," Monica finished.

"Nothing's smaller," Ozzie chuckled. "You're just bigger."

"Yeah," Monica said softly. "Yeah, I guess that's right."

The car rolled down South Main Street, making a right on Stuyvesant exactly the way they used to on their walks back from school, iced coffees in one hand, a Reese's Peanut Butter Cup cookie in the other, until it turned finally into Magnolia Avenue.

"Oh my God." Monica exhaled as the old house came into view, and sat back hard in her seat. "There it is."

Nora stared at it, taking in the familiar wretched structure, the four walls barely visible under the dim streetlights and thick carpet of vines. She felt an odd need to protect it from the rest of them, which made no sense at all. It belonged to each of them, this place, and then to the girls who had come after them. Or it had, once. And yet it had been just hers for the past fifteen years. She had been the only one of them to stay and keep it company, to make the occasional trek on dark summer nights and stand there across the street, listening for the ghosts inside.

"It looks so . . ." Monica was trying not to cry. "Old. So beat up."

"It is old," Nora said. "It's been twelve years since they closed it for good. Three years after we left."

"And then what?" Ozzie was massaging her temples. "God, it looks condemned. Is it condemned? It should be if it isn't."

Nora was embarrassed that she didn't know the answer to Ozzie's question, but the truth was that she had never taken the time or the effort to inquire further about the property. She didn't want to know the details about why it had closed, or who might buy it one day in the future, or if it might even be razed eventually. There was nothing more to know, nothing anyone else could tell them. Everything they needed to know about the house was right there in front of them, behind those tattered walls.

"Do you think we can go inside?" Grace had a glint in her eye.

"Oh no." Nora's heart began to pound. "I mean, look at it. It's all boarded up."

"Let's try," Monica whispered. "I'd love to see the inside again. Our rooms upstairs? Let's go in. Just one more time."

"We can't," Nora stalled, her fingers already starting to tremble. It was one thing to park across the street and look at their old haunt, maybe even creep around the backyard a little bit, but it was a whole other deal to go inside, where, despite the years, all the old ghosts still lingered. "The place is a wreck. We'd probably fall through a floor or something. Besides, we couldn't get in there if we tried. I'm sure it's all locked up."

"I'll bet money that one of us could probably get us into that house right now," Grace said, avoiding Nora's eyes.

"How much money?" Ozzie turned around in her seat.

"Yeah." Grace laughed. "That's what I thought."

It was Ozzie's idea to go around back. There was no need to attract any attention should someone drive by and catch sight of them at this hour, and God only knew what might happen if the police were called. Besides, the back door, which was rotting off its hinges, would be much easier to kick in.

"Kick in?" Nora was horrified. "There's no reason to des*troy* anything here, Ozzie. We're not trying to rob the place."

"Hey, what's this?" Monica strode over to the cellar door and began tugging at the handle.

An old, familiar dread began to take hold as Nora caught sight of the door. The wooden planks were cracked and splintered along the edges now, the curling wisteria vines wrapping themselves like an embrace around the rusty handle. They could probably get in that way, but there was no way she could go down there. Not now, not with them. Not ever again. Her eyes roved frantically over the rest of the building, searching for another entrance. The chimney was definitely out. Too dirty, ridiculously high, and except for Grace maybe, too narrow for any of them to squeeze through anymore. There was nothing else, except for the windows—which Ozzie would have to break—and the door, which she seemed all too eager to kick down. "Whatcha got, some door?" Ozzie moved toward it now too, standing by as Monica continued to pull. "Maybe to the basement? I don't think I ever came down to the basement when we were here. Did any of you?"

"I did," said Grace. "Elaine was always sending me down for cardboard boxes whenever somebody was getting ready to leave. Remember that Goth girl who came during our senior year? Tamara something? It was right around Christmas."

"The one who never took the dog collar off her neck?" Ozzie raised an eyebrow. "Even when she went in the shower?"

"Yeah. She had something like five thousand heavy metal CDs.

It took at least ten boxes to get them all packed up." Grace shook her head. "God, what a nightmare. I wonder whatever happened to her?"

"Let's hope she got rid of the dog collar," Ozzie said. "Or found herself a pet."

Nora didn't move as the door creaked open a few more inches and then gave way as Monica strained a final time. The vines made a light ripping sound as the door swung wide, and Nora blocked the cry coming out of her mouth with the side of her fist.

"Nice job, Mons!" Ozzie patted her on the back.

As if on cue, all four of them leaned over the gaping hole and peered into it. At least ten cement steps led down into a low-ceilinged room and then vanished in a sea of darkness.

"Oh God, it's pitch-black!" Monica wailed. "We don't have a flashlight or anything, do we? How're we going to find our way around?"

"We'll hold on to each other's shirts and feel around until we find the door that leads to the inside." Ozzie sounded matter-of-fact. "It can't be that hard. It doesn't even look that big."

Nora didn't say anything. She had been in the basement only twice in her life, but she knew that it was the exact same size as the living room above it, and that the door on the inside led to the kitchen. She wondered if the old lawn furniture was still propped up against the east wall, if the folding chairs with their yellow and blue linen seats were tucked under the white wicker table. Did the shelves built into the opposite wall still hold the same sloppy array of discarded baskets, the haphazard collection of empty canning jars and tin cans? The jars had been arranged by size, the largest on one end, gallon size, its glass belly protruding far above the rest. It was flanked on the opposite side by the smallest one, no bigger than a salt shaker.

"Come on, Mons." Ozzie grinned. "You lead."

Monica's eyes widened as she took a step back. "Uh-uh. I did my part. Now I get to hide behind all the rest of you as we make our way in." She shivered. "God only knows what kind of vermin is down in there. Maybe we'll find a nest of skunks. Or opossums." She brought her hands to her face. "Oh, God. What if there really is a nest of skunks down there? Or opossums?"

"Listen, chiquita," Ozzie said. "You're the one who brought us here in the first place."

"I know." Monica wiped her forehead with the back of her wrist. "I know. Just give me a minute to put on my big-girl panties, okay?" She inhaled sharply through her nose and then released it again. "Okay. Let's go."

The four of them descended into the darkness: Ozzie first, then Nora, Monica, and finally Grace. Nora's fingers were hooked around Ozzie's belt loop; behind her, Monica clutched the edge of Nora's pants so tightly that she could feel the button on the front digging into her stomach. Ozzie's hand moved back and forth as she swept cobwebs out of the way, and every few seconds, she let forth another stream of expletives. They moved farther into the space, and a familiar scent filled Nora's nostrils. Dirt and grape jelly. Tears sprang to her eyes. How, after all these years, could the same smell still be there? *How?* She squeezed her eyes and held her breath. She could do this. She could. Another few moments and it would be over.

Ozzie came to an abrupt standstill, as if she had just walked into a wall.

"What?" Monica shrieked once, a high-pitched sound that made the hair on the back of Nora's neck stand up.

"It's nothing." Ozzie's voice was thick with impatience. "I just can't *see* anything. I don't know if I'm leading us down a set of stairs to break all our necks or into a nest of rattlesnakes."

"*Rattlesnakes?*" Monica clutched so hard at the back of Nora's pants that she lost her balance.

"Relax," Ozzie said. "There's no *rattlesnakes,* all right? Jesus Christ. All I'm saying is that not knowing what's ahead of me is extremely disconcerting. It's like being blind or something. Hold on. I think I might have a lighter in my backpack."

Nora let go of Ozzie's shirt as she squatted down and began rummaging through her knapsack. The darkness itself didn't bother her; it felt familiar, in fact, like an old worn-out shirt she had lost once and then found again. It had been just as dark that night, and she'd been glad for it. Relieved, even. Now, though, the darkness did not afford the same kind of security. It felt strange, otherworldly, as if she were on a different planet.

She reached her arm out and felt around. Her fingers brushed against a cobweb and she pulled them back, wiping the vague stickiness of it against her pants. She took another few steps to the right and reached out again. This time, her hand came into contact with a wall. She let it slide down the length of it—until it bumped into an object.

"Nora?" Monica's grip was so tight that it was getting hard for Nora to breathe. "What are you doing?"

"Let go, okay?" Nora extricated Monica's fingers gently from her pants. "Just for a second. Hold on to Grace." She reached out again and slid her hand toward the object. It was some kind of rough material, slick with dust and dirt, rolled up tightly into a narrow column. She could feel hard, slender rods beneath it and a larger, thicker stick at the bottom. The picnic table umbrella. She almost smiled, thinking of it. Green, with little tassels that bobbed and swayed in the wind. They used to prop it up sometimes in the grass when it got warm and crawl under it, eating tuna fish sandwiches on white bread and potato chips, the sun slanting across their bare legs, warming their painted toes. The table couldn't be much farther away, and the chairs were probably here too. Which meant they were facing the east wall. Twenty more feet or so to the right, and they would be standing in front of the steps that led up to the kitchen door. She turned, the information poised on her lips, when Ozzie let out a whoop.

"Found it!" Nora froze as Ozzie's thumb rolled over the lighter. She was doing okay down here in the dark, she realized. She wasn't ready to see any of it, to have any of the things she was remembering come rushing back—even under the light of a tiny flame.

Ozzie worked the lighter once more, and then again. "Come *on*." Another attempt failed. "Are you kidding me? Seriously? This thing decides to run out of juice now? *Now*?"

"Forget it, Oz." Nora stepped forward. "I think I know where we are. Put your stuff back in your knapsack and follow me."

Ozzie threw the lighter back into her backpack. "How do you know where we are? We're in total fucking darkness. I can't even see you, and you're standing three inches away from me."

"Come on." Nora dodged the question. "This way. Let's just get out of here. It'll be much lighter upstairs."

"Upstairs where?" Grace's voice quavered a little in the back. "Do you know where the steps are?"

"I think so." Nora moved forward, placing one foot in front of the other. They were so close. She could feel it. Still, there was nothing to see, nothing in front of her except an entire world drenched in black. She stopped as the front of her foot bumped something hard and reached out. "Here!" she said, still feeling along with her fingers. "They're right here. Come on. This way!" She reached out to the left, nodding as her hand came in contact with the wooden railing. Inch by inch, she led the rest of them upward. Her hand was slick with grime, and she could feel her fingers trembling, the edges of them like ice. She felt the door before she saw it, looming in front of her like some unseen presence, and she reached out carefully, patting around. Her hand closed around the knob all at once and she twisted it and pushed. Behind her, a collective sigh of relief sounded. The door swung open, the hinges moaning from the sudden exertion, and a faint scrabbling sound drifted from the right side of the room. Nora winced at the sudden onslaught of moonlight, filtering through the shattered glass windows. It looked electric somehow, as if it had been plugged in somewhere in the heavens, illuminating everything within.

She stepped through the doorway, swiping a clot of cobwebs blocking her way, and wrinkled her nose as the cloying odor of dust and old urine filled her nostrils. The floor was barely visible beneath the layer of dirt, but she could just make out the lemon-and-white tiles they'd walked over so many times, littered now with tiny paw prints and piles of droppings. She shuddered. It was impossible to guess just how many rodents had taken up permanent residence in here since the property had been abandoned, but it was probably in the hundreds. She didn't want to think about it.

"All clear?" Ozzie paused, resting a hand on Nora's shoulder, and glanced around. "Jesus, look at that moon. Wait, is this the kitchen?"

"Yeah." Nora raked at a cobweb stuck in her hair. "And I'm pretty sure the entire mice population just bolted when they heard us." She pointed to several pea-sized piles around their feet. "Looks like they've been having a regular party up here."

"Did you say mice?" Monica's face paled as she peered through the door.

"Yes, Mons, she said the *m* word." Ozzie grinned and held out her hand. "An abandoned building is a mouse and rat's dream house. There's probably five thousand of them living inside this shack right now."

Monica whimpered, recoiling at Ozzie's outstretched hand.

"Do you honestly think saying things like that is going to encourage her to go any farther?" Grace linked an arm through Monica's and pulled her into the kitchen. "Seriously, Oz."

Monica still held back. "You don't actually *see* any mice, do you?"

"Not at the moment." Ozzie put an arm around her shoulders. "Come on, babe. You can do this. We're all here with you." She strode around the room with ease, undeterred by the filth. "God, remember all the time we used to spend in here?"

"You mean when we had to." Grace rolled her eyes. "I hated the kitchen."

"Oh, I *loved* the kitchen." Monica sounded mournful. "It was the one place in the whole house that made me feel like I was in a real home. This kitchen could've been anywhere, you know? In any family's house." She glanced at the dilapidated cupboards along the wall, some of which were missing entire doors, and the countertop, which had rotted from the inside out, cleaved neatly down the middle. "Let's go upstairs," she said. "There's nothing down here to see, and it's depressing the hell out of me. Besides, I really just want to look at my old bedroom again."

The group of them traipsed behind her, clouds of dust rising with each step. The old staircase groaned beneath their weight, and Nora held her breath, wondering if the whole thing might give way. But then they were on the second floor, another dimly lit corridor cluttered with dust and droppings. Nora paused, taking in the old familiar wallpaper on the walls, a pale green background dotted with pink cabbage roses and gold scrolls. A few times, after Ozzie and Grace and Monica had left that summer, and before Nora herself left a few weeks after that, she found herself sitting in the hallway, unable to go back inside her room, which still smelled like Grace, and counting the roses on the wallpaper. It was a way to pass the time, to keep her mind occupied with something—anything—other than their absence. One night, she had gotten to 642 of them before Elaine had come up and told her she had to go to bed.

"Come on, Mons!" Ozzie barreled through another horde of cobwebs. "Our old bedroom's right down here!"

"Wait!" Monica yelped, trotting a little to catch up with her. "Oh God, don't leave me! It's dark!"

Nora looked over at Grace as Monica and Ozzie disappeared down the hall. Grace met her eyes and then motioned with her head in the opposite direction. "You want to go see ours?"

Nora hesitated, touching her neck with the tips of her fingers.

"Just for a minute?"

There had been other girls, of course, who had occupied the room after their departure, but the bones of the little space were exactly the same as Nora remembered: the sloped alcove under which she had arranged her bed, the window against the far wall where Grace had placed hers, the strange little closet next to it shaped like a lopsided rectangle. The same cracks still snaked across the top of the ceiling, including the one that looked like a web of lightning, and the one above the window that used to remind Nora of a skeletal hand. Grace walked over to the far wall, where her bed had been, and smoothed her hand over the dusty surface. "I remember wishing I could fade into this wall when I first got here," she said softly. "That I could merge with it some-how and then disappear."

Nora thought back to those first few days, the silence of them, as Grace lay in her bed, staring at nothing, while she'd struggled to read Proust. She'd felt similarly, having overheard Sally, her last foster mother, a tall blond woman with bad teeth, telling Elaine that she was some kind of "weird mute." She remembered think-ing that day, as Elaine had shown her to her room and introduced her to Grace, that none of it really mattered anymore. She could be taken from place to place, introduced to twenty more people, and shown to one room after another, but it was all right. She'd found a way to hide from all of them, had figured out how to become—and stay—invisible in any sort of surrounding. Until the day came, of course, when the opposite of that had presented itself, upending everything she thought she understood about the world. And herself.

A scream sounded suddenly from the opposite end of the hall, causing both of them to jump.

"Was that Monica?" Grace was wide-eyed as they rushed out of their room and felt their way down the corridor.

"*Why?*" Monica's voice was tremulous with rage. "Why would you ever do such a thing?" She was on one side of their old room, which faced the far side of the building. The moon peeked out from the upper right-hand corner of the window, casting a watery column of light across the floor. Ozzie had the fingertips of both hands pressed against her mouth, and a large red blotch had begun to form on the side of her neck.

"What's wrong?" Nora asked. "Who screamed?"

Neither woman looked at her. "Answer my question." Monica stared deliberately at Ozzie. Her mouth was tight.

"I don't know." Ozzie sounded hoarse. "It was stupid."

Nora glanced around the room, trying to figure out what they were talking about. The floor was dirtier than she could have ever imagined, with piles of dust and so many animal droppings that it was impossible to distinguish the hardwood beneath. A single board next to Ozzie's feet had been dislodged and Nora thought she could see papers inside the shallow hole of it.

"No one's hurt, are they?" Grace held back a little, watching from the doorway.

In response, Monica thrust her hand out so that Grace and Nora could see what she was holding. They both gasped.

"The picture of your mother!" Grace whispered. "Oh, that's

incredible, Mons! You were just saying how you lost it! How you—"

"I never lost it." Monica looked at Ozzie again with the same accusing stare. "Ozzie *took* it." She glanced down at the floorboard opening. "And then hid it down there. All these years."

"Took it?" Grace looked confused. "What do you mean, took it? Why?"

"I don't *know,*" Monica said. "Why did you take it, Ozzie?"

"You had two of them." Ozzie spoke quickly, as if her words might overtake Monica's anger. "And she was beautiful and so perfect . . . I don't know . . . I thought I needed one, okay? Especially during those last few months. I was starting to freak out, thinking of all of us leaving and . . ." She stared at the floor, as if trying to reconnect the dots, and then looked up again. "I remember you saying she was like a stranger to you, that you couldn't remember anything, and I just . . . I guess I thought you wouldn't mind that much. I needed something extra to hold on to, okay? Something to look at, maybe to pretend that I had a mother out there who gave a shit. Even if it was all just in my head."

"So how'd it end up in the floor?" Monica's voice was hard as steel. "If she meant so much to you, why'd you . . ."

"I slept for weeks with it under my pillow," Ozzie interrupted. "But I was afraid you'd find it, so every morning, when you got up to go to the bathroom, I'd jump up and put it back in the floor. And then everything started to get really crazy, you know, with graduation and moving and everything else. I forgot I put it down there. I just totally forgot until we walked in here today and I saw the floorboard."

Nora could see the color returning to Monica's face as she absorbed Ozzie's explanation. "Those pictures were all I've ever had of her. You took that from me."

"Yes." Ozzie closed her eyes as a tear rolled down her face. "I did. I'm so sorry."

"I would have shared her with you," Monica said, her voice splintering. "Especially when things got hard. All you had to do was ask."

"I was too embarrassed," Ozzie snatched at her eyes. "I didn't want anyone to know I was even thinking of my mother, let alone someone else's."

Nora could feel her insides clenching as Ozzie's words from the very first Invisibles meeting came back to her: *We'll choose to remain invisible. To everyone except each other.* But they hadn't, had they? For as thick as the walls they'd built around themselves to keep the rest of the world out, there had been cracks. Despite all their best efforts, doubt and shame had seeped through, nibbling at the edges of their fortress, letting the cold in. *I didn't want anyone to know.* It could have been their rallying cry, she thought later, their group motto. Each and every one of them.

Monica walked across the room and enfolded Ozzie in her arms. Ozzie sagged against her, her whole body absorbing the acceptance of her apology. Nora stared, trying to understand. How was it that, in the span of a single heartbeat, Monica was able to embrace someone who'd just betrayed her? Why couldn't she be more like that herself? What was it that kept her from letting go finally, and forgiving?

"Can I see the picture?" Grace asked as Monica and Ozzie let go.

Nora moved in too, looking at the picture over Grace's shoulder. It was a head shot, taken when Monica's mother was in high school perhaps, or a few years later. She wore a black cardigan, buttoned up to her collarbone, and pearl earrings that were only slightly smaller than her earlobes. Her eyes were the same as Monica's, round and widely spaced, and they shared the same curve in their chins. A tangle of red curls had been pulled back neatly with a silk scarf, and the ends of it hung over her right shoulder.

"She's so beautiful," Grace breathed. "Absolutely gorgeous. Just like you, Mons."

Monica traced the outline of her mother's face with the tip of her finger. "It's funny," she said. "I don't remember anything about her. Not one single thing. But I miss her more than any other person in the world."

The moment was shattered by the sound of a bang downstairs. Monica screamed. There was another bang, and a third, followed by a loud male voice. "Police!"

Monica gripped Ozzie's arm as Nora and Grace held their breaths.

"*Fuck,*" Ozzie said. "Now what?"

Chapter 26

"What do you mean, now what?" Grace hissed. "It's the police, Ozzie. We can't screw around here. We have to go down and explain ourselves."

"Do you realize you're trespassing on private property?" The cop's voice hurtled up the stairs. Nora wasn't sure if the question was rhetorical or if he was just stalling for time until they showed their faces. Either way, it wasn't good.

"He won't arrest us, will he?" Monica looked like she might faint.

Ozzie rolled her eyes. "*No,* he's not going to—"

"I'll give you three seconds to get down here before I come up there and arrest you!" The cop put extra emphasis on the word "three," his voice louder than before.

"I knew it!" Monica lunged for the door, stuffing the picture of her mother inside her shirt. "Come on!" She raced down the hall, her leather thongs slapping against her heels, and turned too quickly, tripping at the top of the stairs. A high-pitched scream sounded through the house as she tumbled down five or six steps, one hand flailing wildly for the railing as her feet flew up in the air. It was, Nora thought later, like watching the scene of a movie play back in slow motion as the railing splintered and collapsed, and then the staircase, with a horrible groaning sound, gave way in the middle, swallowing Monica beneath it.

"Holy shit!" Ozzie grabbed Nora from behind as they both skidded to a halt and stared down into the cavernous opening. "Monica!" There was no response.

"Oh God." Grace clutched at Nora's sleeve. "Oh my God."

"Monica!" Ozzie bellowed again.

The police officer, who Nora assumed had been standing inside the still-open front door, was nowhere to be seen, and for a split second, the only movement in the house was the faint trail of dust that made its way up through the hole in the stairs.

"Monica!" Ozzie yelled a third time, her voice hoarse.

"She's okay!" It was the police officer, grunting under the weight of something. "I got her!"

Ozzie sagged against the wall, and Grace buried her face into Nora's shoulder. They could hear Monica moaning softly, followed by the sound of something being dragged. Nora wondered how badly she was hurt, if any of her arms or legs were broken. It couldn't have been more than a ten- or fifteen-foot drop from the middle of the staircase to the floor below, but anything was possible when you took into account the direction she had fallen, along with all the nails and splintered wood she'd landed on. She stared back down at the hole, hoping to catch a glimpse of Monica's blond hair or a splayed leg, but it was treacherously dark, a gaping void.

"How bad's she hurt?" Ozzie yelled.

"I'm all right." Nora could hear the fear in Monica's voice. "I'm okay, guys. Really."

"You sure?"

"Her foot's hurt," the policeman said. "And it looks like she's scraped up a little. I'm going to call an ambulance."

"No!" Monica shrieked. "No, please don't. I'm fine. It's probably just a sprain. Look." They could hear her struggling to get up, small whimper-grunts forcing themselves out of her mouth. "See? I'm fine. There's no need for an ambulance. Really. Besides, we're actually in kind of a rush. We have to go."

"You're in a rush, huh?" Nora imagined the cop shining the flashlight directly into Monica's eyes. "If you're in such a rush, what're you doing here?"

There was no answer.

The policeman appeared at the foot of the steps, tipping a flashlight in their direction. "Anyone hurt up there?" He was a short, stocky man with big arms. Nora could see the outline of his gun in its holster, the dull shine of his belt buckle beneath his waist.

"No, we're not hurt," Grace said. "But . ." She stared disbelievingly into the hole again. "How are we going to get back downstairs?"

Ozzie was already pacing up and down the hall, looking around wildly, as if trying to recall a secret staircase or a hidden panel. The only one Nora could think of was the one in the chimney, and there was certainly no point in going up there. "We'll have to climb out a window," Ozzie said finally. "Maybe the one in Monica's and my old room."

The cop narrowed his eyebrows. "Is that how you got in?"

"No, we came in through the basement," Grace said. "See, we used to live here. A long time ago, when we were teenagers. We just wanted to see it again."

"You used to live here?" the cop repeated.

"Yeah," Grace went on, a little too eagerly. "When it was a girls' home. Turning Winds? It was kind of a while back. You might not remember it. There was a whole bunch of us living here. Anyway, we're in the middle of a road trip, the four of us, from Chicago, and we just got carried away, you know, thinking back, remembering how it used to be, and we were—"

"All right." Ozzie elbowed Grace in the ribs. "Jesus. He doesn't need the annotated version." She put a hand on her hip and stared down at the cop. "Is it okay if we try to climb out the window? There's one in the bedroom on the far side of the house. The moon's shining right into it, which'll give us some light, and if you have some rope or something in your car, we might be able to rappel ourselves down the side."

"*Rappel* ourselves?" Grace echoed. "I don't think I—"

"Relax," Ozzie murmured. "It'll be fine."

The cop seemed to consider this for a moment, moving the flashlight over each of their faces as if they were trying to get something past him. "All right," he said finally. "Stay right there. I have some rope in my car." Nora watched as he picked his way carefully through the rubble. He moved with an odd sort of daintiness, sidestepping jagged pieces of wood with small, light steps that belied his obvious heft. She hoped he had another delicate side, one that might go easy on them once they got out of here.

"Stay right there," Ozzie parroted as he disappeared through the door. "Where we going, dumb ass?" She leaned over the top of the split railing, craning her neck. "Monsie! Where are you? You still okay?"

"I'm okay." Her voice was faint. "I'm just sitting here. Against the wall."

"Are you bleeding anywhere?"

"No." A pause. "I don't think so."

"How's your foot?"

Before she had a chance to answer, the cop reappeared, holding a thick green coil in his right hand. He tossed it up to Ozzie, who caught it deftly. "It's a military parachute cord," he called. "Fasten one end of it to the windowsill, and let yourself down. I'll get your friend here, and we'll wait for you outside the window."

The ensuing twenty minutes, Nora thought later, might one day be described as a comedy of errors as she, Grace, and Ozzie arduously frog-hopped their way down the side of Turning Winds. They would definitely recall Ozzie's agility as she plummeted down along the wall in record time, as well as the terrified whoop that came out of Grace's mouth as she swung the rope too hard, nearly knocking off the old flower box still perched outside the living room window. Nora would remember crawling backward down the side of the old building like some kind of decrepit bug, although she got to the bottom without incident, and none of them would forget the way the moon lit up the night sky like a headlight behind them. But right now there was nothing amusing about Monica's foot injury—which up close, looked gruesome, already swelling and changing color—or the expression on the policeman's face as they stood before him moments later. He was not nearly as old as she'd thought he was,

Nora realized, studying the diamond stud gleaming from his right earlobe. The gold nameplate above his breast pocket read LAWRENCE. She wondered if it was his first or last name. With his blond hair and smooth, apple-cheeked skin, he looked young enough to be in college.

"All right then," he began, fastening the parachute rope with a small plastic clip he withdrew from his pocket. "Now that—"

"Please," Ozzie broke in. "Please, please, don't arrest us. Like my friend told you already, we were just in there reminiscing. We're not criminals. Honestly, we weren't doing—"

She stopped as he held up a hand. "Are you aware that this building is state property?"

"Oh God," Monica whimpered.

"We didn't know that," Ozzie said. "Honest to God, we didn't. We would've never—"

"Let me finish," he said. "Not only is it state property, but it's also getting torn down this coming Wednesday. If it wasn't, I'd have no choice but to arrest you. Especially considering you just destroyed a good piece of it."

"It's getting torn down?" Monica whispered. "Really?"

"Really." The cop pulled out a thick pad from the breast pocket of his shirt and gave Monica a sympathetic look. "You're lucky you weren't killed, ma'am, falling through that staircase. The wood is rotted from the inside out from all the termites. You could've broken your neck." He flipped open the pad with a flourish and wrote something at the top. "They're gonna put a Dollar Store here, I think. Sometime next year. And another coffee place."

Nora watched silently as he scribbled on the front of the pad.

In a few short days, Turning Winds would be erased from the planet, the living, breathing memories inside a thing of the past. She wasn't sure if the lonely sound she heard in the trees just then was a bird calling or the sound of her own heart breaking.

Officer Lawrence tore off the piece of paper and handed it to Ozzie. "Considering the circumstances, I'm going to let you all off with a fine. You can mail this in directly to the Willow Grove Police Department."

"Thank you, Officer," Grace gushed.

Ozzie stared at the paper. "Two hundred and eighty *dollars*?" she sputtered.

"You're lucky it's not double." The cop raised an eyebrow. "We caught a couple kids in here last summer who were boozing it up. They got fined two hundred *each*." He pointed at Ozzie with the tip of his pen. "And don't be late with the payment. After six days, it doubles."

Ozzie scowled as she shoved the piece of paper in her back pocket.

"You ladies have a good night now." The policeman peered at them from behind his flashlight. "You are going to leave the property now, correct?"

"Yeah, yeah." Ozzie swung another arm around Monica, supporting the other side of her as they half hobbled, half carried her back to the car. Nora could feel the cop's eyes on them as they put her inside and shut the doors.

"What a motherfucker," Ozzie said, gunning the engine. "He could've let us go with a warning. Especially since the damn place is going to be fertilizer in a few days. Two hundred and eighty dollars. What a crock of shit."

He lifted his hand as they sped past him, and Nora wondered if the gesture was one of spite or if he was just trying to be polite. Whatever it was, she was glad they were leaving. She didn't want anyone, including the old house, to see the look on her face as they drove away from it for the last time.

Chapter 27

For over an hour, Monica refused to entertain the idea of going to a hospital. She brushed off Grace's insistence that her injured ankle needed to be X-rayed and dismissed Nora's suggestion of a possible concussion, even launching into a long, roundabout explanation of the physical symptoms of concussions (Liam, apparently, had suffered one a while back) and how none of her symptoms were even remotely the same. Besides, it was almost two in the morning! She couldn't bear the thought of having to sit in a dingy emergency room for another two or three hours just so that she could get her foot taped up and be given a few Tylenol. "Please," she said for what must have been the third time. "Please, let's just get into the city. All I want is a hotel room, a hot bath, and a little bit of sleep before I have to go in and face the firing squad."

They stopped pushing. After all, it was Monica's call. Her mind was obviously occupied by a number of other things, namely the litany of events that would take place at the precinct in a few more hours. And since nothing seemed to be horrifically injured and she did not appear to be in agonizing pain, there was no need to add to her stress level, especially if she was insisting otherwise.

They were on the Henry Hudson Parkway, the city on their left, lit up like a carnival, when Monica turned awkwardly, grimacing as she rearranged herself against the seat. It was then that Nora saw the blood, like a smear of blackberry jam against the filmy fabric of her shirt.

"Monica?" She reached over, her fingers hovering just above the spot. "You're bleeding back here."

"I am?" Monica reached around with two fingers, wincing as they came in contact with the wound. "Oh, I got scratched, I think, on the way down. It's tiny. I can hardly feel it."

"Can I see?" Nora asked.

Monica leaned over a little so that Nora could push up her shirt. There were three wounds, each about two inches in length, running just along the outside of her backbone. They were small but deep, the surrounding area already beginning to bruise a sickly yellow color. The one closest to the outside was still moist. As Nora leaned in closer, she could make out weblike trickles of blood leaking out from the bottom. She lifted her eyes, but Ozzie was already watching her in the mirror.

"I knew it." Ozzie made a hard turn into the left lane and then skidded to a halt in front of a red light. A flurry of angry honks rose up behind them, but she turned around in her seat and leaned all the way over until she could see Monica's injury for herself. Her face darkened as she shook her head. "No way. Uh-uh. Monica, you have to get checked out. A sprained or broken ankle is one thing. These are puncture wounds, which are serious even if you hadn't gotten them from a shit-heap like that. Are you up-to-date on your immunizations? When's the last time you had a tetanus shot?"

Monica stared at her blankly. "Um . . ."

"That's what I thought," Ozzie said. "All right, let's go. Grace, will you get your phone out and Google me the closest hospital?"

"No!" Monica gave the effort a final stab, reaching forward with both hands to grab Ozzie's shoulders. "Please, Ozzie. I hate hospitals. I'll call my doctor on Monday. After . . . everything else."

"Forget it," Ozzie said. "You don't have time to screw around here, Monsie. If you got tetanus from some nail in that place, you can get symptoms within twenty-four hours. Fever, stiff neck, even spasms. Now, we're finding you an ER and getting you looked at. End of story."

Monica lowered her hands from Ozzie's shoulders, letting them fall limply into her lap. Then she turned, pushing her face into the seat, and sobbed.

"Monsie." Nora put an arm around her shoulder. "Why are you so upset? It's just the—"

"I don't want to *go*!" Monica wailed. "I hate hospitals! And I'm fine!"

"All right?" Ozzie nodded at Grace, blatantly ignoring Monica behind her. "Where're we going?"

"Lenox Hill," Grace answered. "It's about four blocks away, on East Seventy-Seventh. The ER'll be on your right."

The Escalade shot forward, narrowly missing a parked car, and careened down the street. Nora moved in as close as she dared and patted Monica's thin shoulders, which rose and fell under her staggered weeping. She thought she might know where Monica was right now, at least inside her head. It was a place she'd been many times before, when the threat of one more thing, even a single, unnecessary word, felt as though it might break her completely. It had been a long weekend. And it was not over yet. She smoothed Monica's damp hair back from her head as Ozzie drove through the narrow streets and held on tight.

If the hospital had not been identified by the bright blue LENOX HILL HOSPITAL sign out front, Nora thought she might never have been able to tell it from a high-rise apartment building. With its dull brick exterior and small windows, it took up most of the block and rose so high up above them that Nora could not see the top of it. Inside, the space was all sleek chairs and shiny floors. Wide hardwood walls rose up like fortresses around a row of hanging lights, and the scent of lemon oil and rubbing alcohol hung in the air. Directives were everywhere: QUIET, PLEASE and LINE FORMS HERE and PLEASE HAVE ALL INSURANCE CARDS READY AT CHECK-IN, each one written in neat block letters.

Nora helped Monica into a blue chair against one of the walls as Ozzie walked across the room and launched into a conversation with a red-haired woman behind a desk. Grace stood next to her, still fiddling on her phone. Every so often, Ozzie's voice would rise, and she would lift an arm, pointing in Monica's direction.

"She's the bossiest person I know," Monica murmured, watching Ozzie across the room, "but I think I could be in hell and I'd still be okay if she was with me."

"Me, too." Nora squeezed Monica's hand, wondering how it was possible to reconcile such a statement with the reality of

Ozzie's life back home. It was not so much that Ozzie was in a horrible relationship—such a thing wouldn't have shocked her about any one of them, really—it was that she had stayed for so long. That she had stayed at *all*. Even her explanation about the familiarity of it and being able to navigate through such volatile territory had sounded hollow, as if she had believed such a thing before but now it wasn't quite holding its weight. But maybe that was what saying things out loud did sometimes: it made a situation tangible, forcing you to look at it in a way you never had before. Maybe for the very first time.

After a few minutes, an aide dressed in maroon scrubs and white shoes came out and helped Monica into a wheelchair. His long hair had been tied back into a ponytail and a gold star-shaped earring adorned his right earlobe. They followed him as he wheeled her back into the emergency waiting room. "It'll just be a few minutes," he said, adjusting the wheel brake. "I'll come back for you when they're ready."

"Famous last words," Ozzie muttered, sinking into a chair. "Which reminds me, Mons. You ever get hold of your attorney?"

"I left him another message," Monica said, staring at the floor.

Ozzie looked hard at her and then dropped her eyes.

Nora looked around the waiting room. Two middle-aged men sat a few seats down from them, their heads tipped back against the wall, eyes shut tight. The one closer to Nora had his hand draped lightly over the other's, a gold wedding band glinting on his fourth finger. Next to them was an overweight woman with a pink bandanna over her head and a teenage girl, an emaciated slip of a thing with bright blue streaks in her brown hair and quarter-sized holes in her earlobes. She leaned heavily against the woman, who was reading a magazine, and picked at her cuticles. But it was the woman across from them, dressed in a dirty khaki coat, who held Nora's attention. She was slumped sideways in her chair, either too exhausted or in too much pain to sit up straight. The toe of one black sock peeked out from a hole in her sneaker, and the other shoe had no laces. The combination of a green knit hat pulled low over her forehead and the grime on her face made it impossible to tell her exact age, but Nora guessed she was in her late fifties, maybe even early sixties. Every few minutes, she reached up and yanked at one of the ratty braids sticking out from the bottom of her hat. Nora watched her chew on the end of it, biting down hard and then pulling with her lips, as if trying to suck marrow from a bone, and she wondered with a vague sort of horror if the woman was hungry.

As if reading her thoughts, Ozzie leaned forward. "Anyone hungry?" she asked. "God only knows how long we'll be here. I can try to find an all-night place that delivers."

Monica shrugged. "A little."

"I could eat," Grace said.

Ozzie walked back over to the desk. "You guys have a yellow pages I could look through?" she asked.

"Just use my phone," Grace said, holding it out.

"I hate all those iPhones." Ozzie waved it away. "I can do it faster this way. Trust me."

She tucked the phone book under one arm and gestured toward the front door. "I gotta call Gary, too. I'll be back in a few minutes."

Nora watched as Ozzie let herself out the side door and held the phone to her ear. She wondered what Gary looked like, what kind of expression came over his face, his eyes, when he got angry. If it was anything like the tone of voice she'd heard on the phone, it couldn't be pretty. But was he handsome otherwise? Did Ozzie ever look across the room at a party and exchange a wordless, intimate look with him? Have him come up behind her at the kitchen sink while she was doing the dishes and kiss the back of her neck? Did he do nice things for her, maybe on her birthday or Mother's Day or Christmas, take her to breakfast with all the kids, or book a bed and breakfast just for the two of them? Were the occasional kindnesses how Ozzie justified staying with him? Was that really all she thought she was worth?

Nora looked over at Monica. "How're you feeling?"

"Okay." Monica let her chin drop into her hands. "Tired. What time is it?"

"Two forty-five," Grace said.

Monica shook her head and closed her eyes. Nora watched as she inhaled deeply through her nose, the planes of her cheeks widening like wings on either side.

"I bet we'll be out of here in thirty minutes, tops," Grace said. "There's not that many people here in the waiting room and it can't be that backed up at this hour."

In fact, they didn't call for Monica until 4:26 a.m. By that time, Ozzie's Thai food order had been delivered, everyone had eaten, and Ozzie and Grace had nodded off. The old woman in the khaki coat had been summoned twenty minutes earlier, hobbling across the room as her name was called and then reappearing again just a short time later, only to head immediately for the side door. Nora was filled with an ineffable sadness as she watched the old woman go, one hand clutching the front of her coat as she limped down the street. She thought of running after her, tapping her lightly on the shoulder, asking where it was she was going, just so she could hear her say "Home." But Nora did not move, and when she leaned forward to catch sight of her again, the woman had disappeared into the night.

A young Indian doctor with a red bindi in the middle of her forehead ordered an X-ray of Monica's foot, which turned out to be badly sprained, and tightened an air cast around it. She gave Monica a tetanus shot, as well as something called tetanus immune globulin to prevent further infection, put clean bandages over the wounds, and told Monica to come back in two weeks.

It was almost six a.m. by the time they got to the hotel Grace had found them on East Sixty-Fifth Street. They'd argued on the way from the hospital whether or not it was even worth it to get a room at this point; the hour was so late and since they had to be at the precinct before noon, what little sleep they might get would probably be light and restless. It was Grace who'd insisted finally, convincing them that even four or five hours of sleep would benefit Monica—and the rest of them—more than they might realize. The hotel was only two blocks away from the police station where Monica had to turn herself in, but Nora was more relieved to see that it had recently been cleaned. The bathroom, with its white fixtures and spotless mirror, smelled like eucalyptus, and there was not a trace of dust on any of the furniture. Grace and Ozzie collapsed on the pull-out couch, while Nora helped Monica into the queen-size bed and got in next to her. Thirty minutes later, she could still hear Monica next to her, tossing and turning.

"You okay?" she whispered finally. The room was dark; the heavy curtains over the window obliterated even a hint of street light outside. Still, she could hear the faint sounds of traffic below, the occasional beep and screech of a tire.

"Oh, I'm sorry!" Monica rolled over awkwardly, her casted foot heavy behind her. "Am I keeping you awake?"

"No," Nora lied. "I can't sleep either."

"Not tired?"

"Exhausted." Nora arranged an arm behind her head and stared up into the inkiness above her. "Just thinking."

"Me too."

"About what?"

"About how scared I am," Monica said.

Nora reached down and took her hand. "I know. But you're doing the right thing."

"I am, right?"

"You are."

Monica rolled over so that she was staring at the side of Nora's face. "You know what else I was thinking about?"

"Hm?"

"Running away."

"Running away?" Nora blinked. "From here?"

"Yeah. Well, from tomorrow, actually."

"You can't run away, Monica. That would just make things worse."

"I know. I just like thinking about it."

"Where would you go?"

"I don't know." Monica rolled back over and sighed. "Mexico, maybe. Venezuela."

Nora turned her head a little. "Do you know Spanish?"

"*¿Cómo se llama?*" Monica said. "*Hola. Gracias.* Could get me around for a little while, at least."

"How about Paris?"

"I don't know any French," Monica said. "And they're supposed to be pretty rude to Americans."

"You've never been?"

"Next year." Monica paused. "With Liam. I hope." Her voice broke on the last word.

Nora waited, wincing inwardly at the question on her lips. She closed her eyes. "You really love him, don't you?"

"Yes," Monica whispered. "I do."

"Then you should tell him about this." She squeezed Monica's hand. "Secrets ruin everything. People always find out about them sooner or later."

For a few moments, the only sound in the room was the rush of fading traffic behind the windows.

There was a long pause. When Monica spoke again, her voice was clotted with tears. "I'm still such a little girl," she whispered. "I still need so much."

So much what? Nora wanted to ask. Love? Attention? Forgiveness? She turned all the way over and ran a fingertip over the faint outline of tears on Monica's face. "It's okay," she said. "We all do."

Neither of them spoke again after that. In fact, Nora was pretty sure Monica had fallen asleep; her breathing had shifted to a deeper, lower decibel, and every so often, one of her arms would jerk to the side, as if she were catching herself during a free fall. Maybe the words Nora said next weren't supposed to be heard. Maybe they were just supposed to be put out there, the way so many of the first lines she recalled these days were, so that they might drift along and find their way to the person who needed them next.

But she said them very softly anyway—"*In an old house in Paris that was covered with vines, lived twelve little girls in two straight lines*"—before closing her eyes and going to sleep.

Chapter 28

Nora had been to the city once before with Trudy and Marion to see *Les Misérables*, but they had taken a bus into Port Authority and then driven around in a taxi afterward, looking at the sights from behind the windows. There had been throngs of people swarming their way around and along the sidewalks, impeding their view of anything at eye level, and she'd been able to hear a dull roar of what she thought must have been the bowels of the city itself from behind the taxi window. This was nothing like that, she thought as the cab let them out in front of the precinct that morning. A manual clock on the dashboard read 11:02 a.m., and Nora wondered if the usual swell of people were now trapped behind a desk somewhere, working on their computers. Whatever the case, the street was strangely quiet; a few people hurried to and fro, but not with the breakneck speed Nora had come to attribute to most New Yorkers. The sidewalks, too, had a calm, green appearance, flanked on either side by good-sized trees in a multitude of fall colors.

The Invisibles

"Like a little neighborhood," Ozzie said, widening her arms to encompass the surroundings, and Nora couldn't have agreed more.

The precinct itself was a beautiful building, much more attractive than the hospital, with new brick siding, dark blue wooden trim over an arched doorway, and stone steps. An enormous American flag hung from a pole above the front door, snapping in the breeze, and the words 19TH PRECINCT had been painted on the front door in white cursive handwriting. Still, there was a silent air of authority to the building, a muted weight that made Nora nervous.

"Okay." Monica's fingers trembled as they stood at the top of the steps. "Here goes."

"And your attorney's coming, right?" Ozzie asked, holding her by the elbow. It was the third time she'd asked since they'd gotten up and dressed in the hotel room. "You said he finally left a message? He knows where to come?"

"Right." Monica nodded. "He'll be here."

A muscle pulsed on the side of Ozzie's jaw as she glanced nervously up and down the sidewalk. Nora hoped Ozzie wasn't planning on creating a scene. That was the last thing any of them needed.

"Geez, Louise," Grace said as they stepped inside the glass door. "It looks like Grand Central Station in here."

Nora had never been to Grand Central Station, but she doubted if she would have disagreed with the comparison if she had. The gigantic room they found themselves in was even more impressive than the outside of the building. Everything had the appearance of having been recently renovated; the smooth marble floor looked new, and a black countertop, which ran almost the entire length of the room, had a sleek, burnished quality to it, as if it had been rubbed down the night before with a soft cloth. Still, it was the number of people crammed into the space that caught Nora off guard; countless policemen in uniform, some holding people just above the elbow, others on their cell phones, all swishing by in a stern sea of movement. There were people like them too, regular pedestrians with wide eyes and grave faces, even a young mother with a small child, sitting on a bench along the far wall, waiting, she supposed, for a service similar to theirs. Opposite them was a sign that read: PLEASE CHECK IN AT THE FRONT DESK.

"Over here." Ozzie steered them toward a smaller round desk, behind which an older man with a silver mustache stood.

"Can I help you?" He glanced carelessly at Monica, who had put her crutches to one side and placed her hands neatly on the counter, and went back to shuffling papers.

"I have to . . ." Monica cleared her throat and then stared down at her hands. "Is there, um, a detective here I can talk to?"

Silver Mustache lifted his eyes. He had small blue eyes and loose jowls under his chin. The extra skin swayed lightly as he spoke. "A detective?" he repeated.

"Yes." Monica's voice was barely over a whisper. "Um, I believe his name is Detective Kingston?"

"We don't have a Detective Kingston here."

Monica looked over helplessly at Ozzie, who was turned around, scanning the room behind her.

"Are you sure it was Kingston?" Grace asked. "Maybe it was something that sounded like Kingston?"

"Do you have a detective with a name here that sounds like Kingston?" Monica was pleading with the man now, begging him to look up.

"We have three detectives here," he said, still working on his papers. "Detective Otto, Detective Kyril, and Detect—"

"Kyril!" Monica burst out. "That's it! Detective Kyril. Can I talk to him please? He asked me to meet him here this morning."

"I'll see if he's in." The man picked up his phone and pushed a button. He stroked his mustache with two fingers as he listened a moment and then said: "Augie? There's a woman here to see you." He covered the mouthpiece with his hand and leaned toward Monica. "Your name?"

"Monica," Monica whispered. "Monica Ridley."

"You'll have to speak up." The man winced. "I can't—"

"MONICA RIDLEY!" Ozzie roared. "Her name is Monica Loreen Ridley, for Christ's sake, and she has an appointment here this morning with Detective Kyril!"

The man's small eyes creased around the corners; he took his hand off the mouthpiece, said Monica's name into the phone, and without taking his eyes off Ozzie's face, replaced the receiver.

"Shit, I'm sorry," Ozzie said quickly. "We're all a little jacked up this morning. Everyone's kind of on edge."

"I suggest you get yourself jacked down then." The man picked up his stack of papers once more. "You talk like that to me again, and you'll have more to worry about than finding a detective around here."

"Yes, sir." Ozzie looked genuinely contrite. "I apologize."

Within minutes, a small man wearing wheat-colored pants, a white button-down shirt, and a dark blue vest came out of a side room. "Miss Ridley?" He stretched out his hand as he moved toward her. "Detective Kyril. Thanks for coming in." He surveyed the rest of them with a pleasant expression. "Attorneys?" He smiled a little. "Or family?"

"Oh." Monica touched the side of her face with her fingers. "Neither. They're my friends. Here for moral support."

"Oh." Detective Kyril shoved his hands inside his pockets and rocked back on his heels. He was wearing penny loafers. "Do you have an attorney coming, too?"

"I um . . . I'm not . . ."

Ozzie shot Grace a wayward look and then stepped forward. "She has counsel coming, but he can't be here until noon."

Monica whirled around, staring at Ozzie.

"Okay." The detective nodded. "That's fine. It'll take a while to get you processed anyway. We have to get your fingerprints and all your pedigree information before we proceed to the next step."

Monica whirled back around. "You need my fingerprints?"

"We do." Detective Kyril took his hands back out of his pocket. "You're being charged with a felony here, Miss Ridley, remember? You're going to be put through the system. Just like we talked about on the phone."

Monica dropped her eyes.

"I'll need you to come this way," he said. "Oh, and . . ." He turned, glancing at the rest of them, who had fallen in line. "Just her for now, all right? You can have a seat over there. I'll come get you when we're finished."

Ozzie sighed loudly as Monica and Detective Kyril disappeared through a side door. Grace slung an arm around her shoulders and grabbed Nora's hand, steering both of them over to the small set of benches in the corner.

"What's going on with Monica's attorney?" Grace asked as they settled themselves.

"Did you get in touch him?"

"Nope." Ozzie stared straight ahead.

"Well, she obviously didn't."

"Nope."

"Ozzie." Grace sounded exasperated. "What's going on? Why would she lie about getting an attorney?"

"Because she's afraid Liam's going to find out." Ozzie turned to look at them. "It's why she didn't want to go to a hospital, either. She doesn't want him getting the bills, figuring anything out."

"So you went and got her one?" Grace pressed. "Where, from Legal Aid or something?"

"Something like that," Ozzie said.

Nora stared at the space of marble floor between her feet. They'd all lied—every single one of them—on this trip, hiding things from the very people to whom they'd once bared their souls. She herself was the worst, having held out the longest, still not coming clean about that last night at Turning Winds. She'd opened up a little bit, telling them about the boyfriend situation, even exposing Daddy Ray to Grace, but she still wasn't as brave as the rest of them. She still couldn't go there. Couldn't do it. Couldn't even imagine doing it. It was just who she was. She needed time. Space. More time. More space.

Except that she knew that all the space in the world still wasn't big enough.

And that time was running out.

Chapter 29

It was a silly thing, Nora thought later, a ridiculous thing really, but as they sat there waiting for Monica to come back from her fingerprinting and processing, all she could think about was Elmer, how comforting he would feel just then inside her hands, the slight heat of him against her skin. How was it that such tiny things could carve such deep places inside? How did they manage to fit in there among everything else and still take up so much space?

She caught sight of Monica's blond hair as she emerged on her crutches from another room. Detective Kyril was on her right, his mouth in a tight line. Monica's makeup was smudged, and there were red splotches on her neck where she had been pulling at the skin. Nora stood up quickly as the detective approached, as if anticipating news from a surgeon. Ozzie and Grace followed.

"We're done with the processing," Detective Kyril said. "Is the attorney here?"

"It's only eleven fifty," Ozzie said, glancing down at her watch. Her fingers were trembling. "He said noon."

"All right." The detective stretched out his arm, indicating a door on the left. "You can wait in here until he arrives. I have another appointment though, at twelve thirty, so if he's late, I'm going to have to proceed without him."

"He won't be late," Ozzie said grimly.

They followed the detective into a small room furnished with a wooden table, a water cooler with a paper-cup sleeve, and four chairs. Nothing else. No windows, no pictures, not even an air vent. Nora wondered if the outside was just for show; if the real story of the Nineteenth Precinct revealed itself inside, after they finally grabbed you.

"I'll be back," Detective Kyril said, giving them a nod.

"How'd it go?" Grace asked as the door shut.

Monica shook her head, tears welling up again. Nora could see the black stains on her index fingertip and thumb, the faint whorls beneath them, like pieces of scalp beneath the hair. She was forever marked now. Branded.

"You okay?" Nora asked.

"No." Monica wiped her nose with the edge of her sleeve. "No, I'm not okay." She looked hard at Ozzie. "What did you do?"

"What do you mean?"

"The attorney, Ozzie. Who did you get? Who could you possibly have gotten to represent me in this city?"

The door opened then, eliminating the need for Ozzie's response. "Well, you were right about him being on time," Detective Kyril said. "It's twelve o'clock on the nose."

"Punctuality is the politeness of kings!"

The man's voice behind her caught Nora by surprise, but not nearly as much as the shock that catapulted through her when she caught a look at his face. She sat frozen as Theo swept past, the faint rustle of his silk suit emanating a clean, rich scent. His hair was still parted on the right side, but it was much shorter now, and he wore it brushed back off his eyes. He looked older too, but in a good way, the lines and creases in his face the marks of someone who had already lived a third of his lifetime. Which he had, of course.

"Oh my God," Grace whispered. "Is that . . . ?"

"Yeah." Ozzie's eyes bloomed inside her face. "It sure is."

Nora didn't respond. She was too busy looking from Theo to Monica to Ozzie, trying to determine if this was really happening, and if it was, *how*. Monica's face was a map of confusion, fear, and relief. "Theo?" she said finally. It came out as a whisper.

"And your name again is?" Detective Kyril looked over his glasses as Theo settled a caramel-colored briefcase on top of the table, withdrew a thin sheaf of papers, and slid them in his direction. "Attorney Gallagher, Detective." Theo looked over at Monica and nodded. "I was recently hired to represent Miss Ridley in the charges being brought against her."

Monica's mouth, which was already open, fell slack.

"All right, then." Nora watched dumbly as the detective began scanning the paperwork in front of him. She could feel Theo next to her; his presence was almost otherworldly, as if she were only dreaming of it, but no, there he was, literally inches away. Inches and yards away. Whole football-field yards away.

"I understand all the basic processing has been completed," Theo said. "Fingerprinting, pedigree information . . ."

"All set," the detective said. "Except for the mug shot. They were backed up in the film department."

"Fine." Theo pushed another piece of paper across the table. "I'd also like to request a DAT, instead of having my client sent down to Central Booking."

Detective Kyril looked up. "Your client has been accused of a Class C felony. She stole close to fifty thousand dollars from a charity organization. We don't issue DATs in those kinds of situation."

"What's a DAT?" Monica asked fearfully.

"It stands for desk appearance ticket," Theo said, putting a hand on Monica's arm. "Basically, it means that you can be given a hearing date today to return to criminal court instead of having to go down and spend the night in Central Booking while your date gets set."

"Oh, God." Monica's voice began to rise. "Please, I don't want to spend the night in jail!"

Theo leaned over and whispered something in Monica's ear. She listened, whispered a reply, and hung her head, quiet once more.

"I'd like permission, then, to ride down with my client to Central Booking," Theo said. "She's an upstanding member of the community with no previous record. There's no reason to place her in a holding cell with other criminals while she's forced to wait for her paperwork to be processed in Albany."

"Done." The detective stood up.

Ozzie beamed and squeezed Monica's hand. Theo stood up across from him. "Anything else?"

"She still needs her mug shot," Detective Kyril said. "Follow

me up to the front desk, please, and then we'll make arrange-
ments to have you transported to Booking."

Nora felt her heart slow, the sound of it a dull, thudding roar in
her ears as Theo led Monica out of the room behind the detective.
His arm was around her, and she could hear him talking. "Let's
get the photo taken first, all right? Then we can sit down and
catch our breath for a minute."

Three more feet and she could reach out and touch his sleeve.
Meet his eyes, look into the green light of them.

"Monica," Ozzie said.

Monica paused under Theo's arm, taking everything in for the
first time. Her eyes grew wide, and from the way her mouth contorted, Nora could tell that she understood finally what Ozzie
had done. She fell into Ozzie's arms and sobbed.

Nora saw Theo watching them, saw how his face softened at
the sound of Monica's cries, the lines around his eyes creasing just
as they used to.

He said her name, or at least she thought he did. It could
have been something else: "Hello" or "There you are." She didn't
know. The roaring that had begun in her ears had moved to the
inside of her head, blocking out sound, noise; even, it seemed, the
air around her. She took a step back, bumping into Grace, who
clutched her around the arm. She saw Theo's lips close around
her name—Nora—the orb of it lingering on his mouth before
disappearing again.

"Nora," Grace squeezed her arm. "Honey, are you okay?" Her
voice, loud enough to be heard throughout the station, registered
finally in Nora's ears, and she took a fast, single breath.

"I need air," she heard herself say, pushing past Monica and

Ozzie and Theo too, who stepped back in alarm as she nodded a hello in his direction and, without looking back, raced for the door.

She trotted down the front steps, two at a time. There was nowhere to go, of course, except home. Which was exactly what she was going to do, she realized. It was too much, all of it, like a pile of bricks that had gotten larger and heavier as the trip progressed. She'd withstood as much of it as she could, one thing after the other, her knees buckling, shoulders splitting from the building pressure of it, but now she was underneath, she was trapped inside that pile, and she had to get out before she succumbed to the weight of it.

She flagged a taxi with a frantic wave of her arm, leaping into the street without looking in either direction. An oncoming car swerved at the last minute; the driver leaned on his horn. She stepped back, catching the irate face in the rearview mirror and tried again.

"Nora!"

Theo's voice shot out behind her, a frantic sound edged with a sincerity that belonged only to him. She hesitated but did not turn around, moving farther into the street, begging for a taxi. He didn't need to do this. He didn't! Why couldn't he just leave things alone now, let them be? Didn't he have more to finish up with Monica inside? Her arm waved above her head now, a crazy flag, pleading for surrender.

"Nora, please!" He was running toward her. His shiny dress shoes made a clicking sound against the sidewalk, and the hem of his jacket flapped back on either side like dark wings. "Please."

He caught her around the arm and pulled her toward him, out of the street.

"Hey." She twisted out of his grip and threw him a look. "There's no need to grab."

"I'm sorry." He was panting; his cheeks were flushed. "But why'd you just run out like that? Where are you going?"

"Home." She shrugged, bringing her fingers to her earlobe. "I have to get home."

"Home where?" He looked incredulous. "Do you live here? In the city?"

"No. Back to Willow Grove. I'm still there." The admission flared a stab of anger within her, and she turned around again and lifted her arm. "I . . . I'm sorry I ran out. I have an appointment I forgot about. That I'm late for."

She fluttered her fingers, begging for a cab, a rickshaw. Hell, she'd even take a horse at this point. Anything to leave. To leave and disappear and let it all go. She'd never come back. There was no need to. She'd taken the leap and then sunk like a stone. It had all been a mistake, every single part of it. Every moment, including this one. She was doing the right thing, leaving. It was the only thing left to save herself before she drowned.

"Nora, come on." He took a step toward her, shoving both of his hands inside his suit pockets. "We haven't seen each other in almost fifteen years. Can't you give me two minutes?"

She lowered her arm slowly and stepped back on the curb. His shoes were a rich oxblood leather with dark stitching around the toes.

"You look so—" he started.

"How'd you even get here?" She interrupted quickly, already

knowing the answer but dreading the polite, useless banter that would insult them both if she did not ask. "I mean, here. With Monica."

"Ozzie called me. Last night; around one a.m., I think. She told me where you all were, what was going on, and . . ." He shrugged. "I don't know if Monica'll actually retain me as her attorney, but I was glad to put in an initial appearance until she decides."

She raised her eyes, but only to tie level, a rich cream silk with navy stripes. "How did Ozzie get your number?"

"She said she looked it up in the phone book while you guys were in the ER." He cleared his throat, a nervous sound. "I used to work in Jersey, but now I'm in private practice in Chelsea. I have an ad in the yellow pages."

She nodded slowly, absorbing the information a bit at a time. "Well, it was nice of you to help." She flicked her eyes at him and turned around to focus on the street again. "It was good to see you, Theo."

"Nora." He stepped off the curb and stood next to her. He smelled different, she realized. Older. Stranger. Richer. Which he was, of course, on all counts. How foolish she was to think he would smell the same, that the old Twizzler smell might still be there, lingering around his earlobes.

"Do you have kids now?" It came out before she realized she had formed the thought and hung there in the air between them, a faint bubble.

"No." He squinted at something, toed a bare spot on the pavement. "My wife wanted them, but I . . ." He rolled his teeth over his bottom lip. "It's why we split up."

A yellow cab peeked around the corner at the opposite end of the street. She moved toward it, blinking back tears.

"Nora."

"I have to go. I really do."

"Ozzie told me what happened, Nora. That last week. At Turning Winds."

Her arm froze as she struggled to breathe. The oxygen in the air seemed to have been cut off, and for a moment, her mouth open and shut like a fish. And then as before, a sudden gasp of breath, a surfacing again. She whirled around.

"You *knew*?" Her rage was at a peak now; a new blood coursed through her veins.

"Not until after." Theo swallowed, his Adam's apple as big as a peach pit. "Ozzie wrote me a letter after she got to that ranch in Montana, and she told me. I saw her again totally by accident at a bar a few years back, and we talked about it again." He took another step toward her. "Why didn't you ever tell me?"

The cabdriver had seen her and was moving the vehicle in their direction. "You knew?" she said again. "All this time? And you never called? You never— " She stopped as her voice broke, and she moved over as the cab slid in next to her.

"I tried." Theo took her hand, but she shook it off. "I wanted to come see you when I came home from school that Christmas on break. I drove to the house three different times, but I couldn't do it. I don't know why. I was terrified for some reason. I'm sorry, Nora. I was an idiot. I was dating another girl at school, and I . . ." He stopped, squeezing the space between his eyebrows with his thumb and middle finger. "God, I'm so sorry."

She got into the car, inhaling a strange, spicy scent. The driver was wearing a purple turban and had a black beard that came down into a point.

He'd known?

Theo lurched toward her. "Nora, will you just—"

"Don't." She turned her head and looked straight at him. "You should have said something. Anything." His face blanched as she closed her fingers around the door handle.

He stepped back as the door shut in his face and then knocked rapidly against the window. "Nora, please. Just wait."

"Go," she said to the taxi driver. "Please. Go now."

His tires squealed as he moved away from the curb and shot down the street. She was sitting close enough to the passenger window that she could see Theo in the sideview mirror running after them.

She held on tight to the edge of the seat and forced herself not to look back.

Chapter 30

The taxi driver had dark brown skin and was wearing a turban, but Nora could not tell what his ethnicity was. The ID tag on the front dashboard spelled out the name—Aaquil Shezzbaharrat—but that was no help, although Nora guessed he might be Muslim or Tibetan. It was even more difficult when he began to talk; his words were so thick with a foreign accent that she had trouble making out even a few of them. Still, there was no mistaking the look on his face when she told him where she wanted to go.

"Pennsylvania?" he repeated, although it came out as "Pennsyl-vay-neeya?" He shook his head. "That is too far. Too far. Way out of my your-isdiction."

She held up a wad of bills. "Name your price. I mean it. I'll pay you whatever you want. I just have to get back home. Right now."

Aaquil's dark eyes widened.

She shook the bills under his nose. "I'm serious."

"Four hundred dollars," he said quickly.

"Done." She handed him two one-hundred-dollar bills. "The other half later. When we get there."

Aaquil took the money and held it up to the light. Then he shrugged and turned around. "Crazy American women."

"You have no idea," she muttered as the cab barreled down Interstate 80. "You have no fucking idea."

She was glad Aaquil didn't talk; gladder still that she couldn't understand him even if he had wanted to. She stared instead at the back of his turban, examined the soft folds of material wrapped tightly around his head. What secrets were under that purple slip of silk? How many things would the people in his life never know? And what would keeping those things secret do to them? To him? She'd been right to feel uneasy that first day when Ozzie called and begged her to come to Chicago. Her instinct not to go had been right on the money. None of them were equipped to deal with everything that would come out into the open again; not one of them over the years had developed the skills needed to do such a thing. Nora doubted if any of them even knew where to look for them. It was like putting a bunch of children in a room full of cobras and telling them to duck.

And now Theo.

My God, *Theo*. Coming out of nowhere, like the final blow.

All these years he had known, like the rest of them, and hadn't said a word. Hadn't done a thing. What was wrong with him? What was wrong with them? Or maybe it was her. Maybe with all her quirks and oddities, she'd just been entirely unapproachable. Untouchable.

What had made him blurt out such a thing on the sidewalk?

To a stranger! Which, when all was said and done, was really what they were. Maybe it was all they'd ever been. Oh, he could pretend that they were more. That they'd had some kind of sordid emotional history together, instead of the pathetic fifteen or sixteen months they'd shared. She'd let him have that, if that's what it took. She didn't care.

I tried, but I couldn't do it! I'm sorry!

She brushed the words away with a hand across her eyes and looked out the window. Ozzie had told him, had written a secret letter from out West, telling him everything. She'd broken a vow of confidence, of solidarity. But then they all had when it came to her, leaving her behind the way they had. She hated them all. She really did. She would never forgive them, even if they begged her for an entire lifetime to do it. It was time to leave them all behind. Time to cut the cord, to put on her big-girl panties, as Monica liked to say, and strike out finally on her own. She'd done it with Mama. She could do it with them.

A first line came to her, as they usually did when things began to make sense again, realigning themselves like overturned chess pieces: *"The past is a foreign country: they do things differently there."* Good old L. P. Hartley, who'd written *The Go-Between.* He knew what he'd been talking about. And now she did too.

The past was over.

It was time to move on, to look toward the future now and create a new life.

The cab pulled into Trudy's driveway at three thirty, just as the light was beginning to change. The moon hung low in the sky, full as a womb. Nora gave Aaquil the other two hundred dollars and thanked him, not just for the ride, but for the silence. The stillness was something she had not realized she needed until it ended. It felt enormous now, like a gift he had bestowed upon her without request. He nodded, bringing his hands together against his lips, and bowed his head.

She headed up the steps, her insides quavering for some reason. Where was her previous resolve? Her new determination? The sound of Alice Walker barking as she rang the doorbell undid her, a ball of string loosening from the inside out, and she leaned against the door and wept at the sound of it. How strange that it would come down to this, that an animal should be the one, the only one, who would remain loyal to the end. But of course that was how it should be. It was something she had known from the very beginning. The dog barked once more and then again. She knew it was her. She knew Nora was back.

"All right, all *right*." Nora could hear the impatience in Trudy's voice as she fiddled with the lock, and Nora grasped the doorknob, as if that might help things along, might get her inside faster. Another bark. "Calm *down*, Alice Walker!" Trudy snapped. "I'm going as fast as I can here." The lock jiggled again, followed by a fifth bark. "Yeah, well, *you* get some arthritis in those paws of yours and then you can talk to me about getting a door open."

"Let me, dear." Marion's voice drifted through the door, and the lock gave way all at once, opening so fast that Nora nearly fell in. "Nora?" Marion stepped back in alarm as Nora stumbled and then caught herself. "Oh, darling, what happened? What's wrong?"

"Nothing's wrong." Nora sank to her feet, embracing Alice Walker as the dog jumped up to greet her. She buried her face in the thick brindle of fur along the back of her neck, closing her eyes and inhaling the warm, familiar scent of her. She was home. She was back. This was all she needed. She knew it now. She would never let herself get carried away by anything else again. She lifted her face, regarding her dog's liquid brown eyes between her hands. "You want to go for a walk, baby?" Alice Walker barked, and then reached out and licked the tears from her face.

"Nora?" Trudy was dressed in a blue velour sweatsuit and pink bedroom slippers. Her face was pale.

Nora ignored her, wiping her eyes with the back of her wrist and rubbing the back of Alice Walker's ears. "Let's go," she said to the dog. "Let's go for our walk."

"All right, whoa!" Trudy had her hands out in front of her, palms out, as if Nora were holding a gun in her direction. "Just *whoa,* okay? Do you want to tell me what the hell is going on here?"

"Trudy." Marion sounded hopelessly reproachful.

"Nothing's going on." Nora stood up, looking around the room for Alice Walker's leash. "Can I have her leash?"

"Her leash?" Marion glanced around the room. "Where's her leash, Trudy? Did we leave it outside?"

"Screw the leash." Trudy's eyes were fixed on Nora in the sort of way that made her want to run as fast as she could in the opposite direction. "You burst in here after being gone for three days; you've got no bags, and you're crying your eyes out, and you tell me that nothing's going on?'

Nora shook her head. "I just mean it's nothing I can't handle. Listen, thank you so much for taking care of Alice Walker. I really appreciate it. Can I just have her leash?"

Trudy didn't move. Her eyes glowered and her mouth had reverted into the kind of scowl she sometimes adopted when the occasional rude or nasty person came into the library. It was her no-nonsense look, her "you screw with me and I'll have your ass in a sling" stare. Nora knew it well. It made her nervous.

And then Trudy blinked. Shrugged. "All right. You know what? Have it your way." She whirled on a heel and strode into the kitchen, snatching Alice Walker's leash off the table.

"Thank you." Nora took it from her, avoiding her eyes, and clipped it to Alice Walker's collar. Her hands were shaking. "I really do appreciate— "

"Save it, please." Trudy ushered her toward the front door with the back of her hand. "Glad to help, though. You take care. And keep building those walls, Nora. Keep it up. And then come back and tell me one day how it all worked out for you. What the view behind them looked like."

Nora stood there on the front step for a moment as the door slammed behind her. She could hear Marion whispering and then the faint footsteps of Trudy walking away from her. Trudy had never crept around the edges when it came to saying something about Nora's choice of an isolating lifestyle. But not once, in all the years she had known her, had she ever said something like that. Something with such finality. Such closure, as if the choice was out of her hands now. As if it was too late. Nora felt stunned.

Alice Walker barked again, looking up at Nora with her usual quizzical expression. Nora blinked, jarred out of the feeling. It was fine. She'd already let go of the others. She didn't need Trudy, either. She didn't need any of them.

"All right, baby," she said, starting down the steps. "Come on. Let's go for our walk."

The moon followed them as Nora and Alice Walker moved through the familiar streets of town, the white fullness like an oversize pearl inside a sea of periwinkle blue. Nora could not shake a peculiar feeling that rose inside her as they strode along; it was as if she were moving through some kind of invisible barrier, as if the pages of her life were turning one after the other, beside her. Soon, very soon, she felt, she was going to get to a page where she would be forced to stop and read the words . . . What would the words be? She couldn't imagine.

She picked up the pace, tugging impatiently when Alice Walker paused to sniff the base of a fire hydrant, and hurrying her along when the dog stopped again to stare at a squirrel. It seemed incredible to her that on a night when she *had* to get to the birch grove, when everything she knew, everything she had ever come to understand about her life rested on this moment, that it might take them twice as long.

And then, all at once, like a small door opening, they were there. The three birch trees, their trunks as white as bleached bones, stood tall as sentinels. Fragments of shredded bark peeled back from the sides, and a few remaining leaves, which hung like small yellow coins from their branches, made a faint tinkling sound in the wind. Opposite the trees were the train tracks, rusted now and choked with weeds. The red crossing sign on the corner was chipped and faded, and farther down, a single blinking light clicked on and off like a blue heartbeat. The relief and dread that she always felt filled her now as she headed for the trees. She let go of Alice Walker's leash and then, just as she had done every morning for the last fifteen years, she stretched herself out and lay down beneath them. After a few minutes, the dog came over and lay down beside her. The earth was cold and damp against her cheek, but Alice Walker's body, pressed against her side, was warm.

Nora closed her eyes and let it come.

She had been much farther along in her pregnancy than Max or any of the rest of them had guessed, a gestational length that no oral medication, given by a doctor or otherwise, could fix without serious, potentially fatal risks. The Cytotec—four small white pills shaped like facet-cut diamonds—was meant to be used only in the earliest stages of pregnancy and as a result, took much longer to work. For two days and two nights, Nora bled like an open wound, getting weaker and sicker by the moment.

She refused to be taken to the hospital, and since her cries were getting harder to quell, Ozzie and Monica carried her up to the widow's peak on the roof and settled her inside a nest of blankets. It was the most practical place to go, since they were the only ones who knew about it, and it wasn't going to take much longer for Elaine, who was on duty that night, to question their story about a painful period. It was late June; the dark summer night pulsed around them with a waning heat, and the moon rose like a silver disk in the sky. They tried to keep her as comfortable as possible, but it was difficult. The pain that coursed through Nora's abdomen was like nothing she had ever imagined; finger-knives reaching into her uterus and then twisting, squeezing, burning. Worse, it would not let up, not even to let her take a deep breath, and so barely a moment elapsed without a whimper escaping her lips.

Grace was not helping anything either; she paced around the tiny space, crying endlessly about going to hell. "I'm the most to blame," she kept saying. "I *asked* my boyfriend to do it. It wouldn't have happened if I hadn't asked him. He gave me the pills. It's like giving someone the gun to go shoot someone. I'm as much to blame as anyone else. More, even."

No one refuted her words; even Ozzie, who sat next to Monica, her knees drawn up beneath her chin, stared at the ground, lifting her eyes every few moments to look over at Nora. Grace paused from her rants only when a strangled sob made its way out of the back of Nora's throat. Then she would rush to her, lying down in the space alongside her belly, rubbing the contracting muscles along the flat expanse of her back, smoothing the damp hair away from her forehead. "Okay," she said. "Okay, sweet girl. It's going to be all right. I promise. It going to be all right."

Another hour went by—or was it a day, a month, a year?—before Ozzie finally stood up. "This is crazy," she said. "You're trying to end the life of one thing and killing yourself in the process. I'm calling an ambulance."

Something moved and twisted between her legs then and Nora let out a cry that was so animalistic, so pure with pain, that she felt the hairs on her scalp prickle. She arched her back and groaned again, more softly this time, but with just as much agony, and then sank back to the ground in a heap.

"Oh my God," Monica said. "It's too late."

Even Ozzie, who was already two rungs down the ladder, stopped and rushed back over. "Nora," she said, leaning over her limp form. "Nora!"

Monica let out a screech and pointed to a rivulet of blood seeping out from beneath the blankets. "Oh God," she whispered. "I think it's the . . ."

Ozzie threw back the covers. Nora's legs began to shiver violently under the cool air, but she struggled to sit up, to see. There was so much blood that for a moment she was sure she was dead. But no. It was something different, an emptiness now, a deep and terrible void, as if she were inside some kind of wreckage at the bottom of the ocean. She searched Ozzie's face desperately, watching the planes of her cheekbones tighten and then loosen again. "It's out, I think," Nora whispered. "Oh my God, I think it's out."

She closed her eyes as Ozzie moved her legs farther apart. Monica began to cry and covered her face with her hands.

"Yes," she heard Ozzie say in a hollow voice. "It's out."

"It's just tissue, right?" Grace's voice was too high. "Right, Ozzie?"

"Yeah."

"Throw it out," Grace said. "Throw it out, throw it out, throw it out. I don't want to see it, Ozzie. Please. I don't want to see any of it."

Ozzie grabbed a towel off to the side and moved it between Nora's legs. "It's nothing," she said. "Okay, Nora? It's nothing. It's just blood and . . . stuff. It doesn't even look like anything."

"Where are you going to put it?" Nora tried to sit up, but her body was shaking so hard that it was nearly impossible. Her arms collapsed beneath her, the muscles loose and jellylike. Grace moved in closer, hooking both hands beneath Nora's armpits. Her skin was like ice, the bones in her fingers like sticks. "Tell me, Ozzie," Nora insisted. "Where are you going to take it? Where are you going to put it?"

"I'm going to throw it out," Ozzie said.

"In the toilet?" Nora's teeth were chattering. "You're going to flush it?"

"No." Ozzie swallowed. "I don't think I can flush it."

"Why not?"

"It's too . . . I don't think I can. I'm afraid it'll block the pipes."

Nora's teeth clicked together like the rapid-fire sound of castanets. Her eyes were as wide as spoons, the hollows beneath her cheekbones nearly concave. "Oh my God." It came out as a sob. "Where, then?"

"I'll put the towel in a bag," Ozzie said. "And then I'll take it out back."

The back. Where they kept the garbage. The dumpster.

Nora crumpled against Grace's arms.

"Oh, God." Grace felt Nora's forehead with a shaky hand. She adjusted her blankets and brought her ear down to Nora's lips. "I can hear her breathing," she said. "I think she's just unconscious. She's probably in shock. Just go," she whispered. Ozzie was still standing there with the towel. "Please, just go and do it. I'll stay with her."

Ozzie fought back tears as she turned, still clutching the towel. "Come with me, Mons," she said. "Please. I don't want to do this by myself."

Nora came to again slowly, as if coming up from the depths of the sea. She watched groggily as Ozzie and Monica disappeared down the chimney steps with the towel.

"Hey," Grace said softly. She brought her face down close to Nora's. Her breath smelled like blood. "How're you feeling?"

Nora shook her head and began to cry.

"It's all over." Grace stroked her forehead and ran a finger over the thin line of perspiration standing out along Nora's hairline. She began to rock her upper body back and forth, moving it like the mantra coming out from between her lips. "We'll never think of it again. It's all over now, okay? It's all over."

Nora didn't answer.

Above them, the moon rose like a Communion Host, the white light of it deathly silent. A thought came to her just before she lost consciousness again: would it ever forgive them for what they had just done? Could it ever, in some small way, look the other way?

Nora woke up again in her own bed, disoriented in the dark of the room. Her blankets were wet, and she was shivering despite the heat of her skin, the fire in her mouth. She could hear Grace snoring across the room, and the faint outline of the oak tree branches looked like tentacles behind the curtains of her window. Traces of pain ribboned through her abdomen, pulsing along the insides of her legs like tiny afterthoughts, and a new maxi-pad placed inside her underwear was heavy with blood. Slowly, the night came back to her: the pain, the roof, the towel.

The towel!

She threw back the blankets and staggered out of bed. She had to get to the towel. It was out there alone, in the dark, buried beneath God knows what, for God knew how long. *I'm coming. Hold on. I'm coming.*

She took two steps and tripped over a body.

"Huh!" Ozzie sat up, swaying. "Who's that?"

"Just me." Nora got back up, struggling to keep her voice from quavering. "I have to go to the bathroom."

"Nora." Ozzie's voice was alert; she was remembering now, too. "Are you okay? You want me to go with you?"

"No, I'll just be a minute."

"How do you feel?"

"Better."

"You sure?" Ozzie made a move to stand up. In the dark, Nora could see the outline of Monica next to her. "Let me just come with—"

"Ozzie, please." Nora put a hand on her shoulder. "I'd just like . . . I need privacy right now, okay?"

"Yeah." She could feel Ozzie relax under her hand. "Yeah, sure. Of course."

"Go back to sleep." The room began to spin around her. "I'll be fine."

She waited outside the door for three agonizing moments until she could hear the measured rise and fall of Ozzie's breathing again. The pain was unbearable, razor-knives again, and she was so hot that she was sure she was burning up from the inside out. No matter. The towel came first, above everything else. She paused at the foot of the steps, steadying herself against the railing, and listened. The sound of canned laughter drifted out of the den, which was right next to the front door. Shit. Elaine was watching some stupid show on TV. And there was no way she could use the back door. It squeaked at the slightest movement. There was only one other option.

She moved toward the cellar and nearly stumbled with fright as Grace appeared out of the shadows. Dressed in her shortie pajamas with little blue panda bears, she looked more like a ten-year-old girl than a senior in high school, and her face was so pale that for a moment Nora thought she was looking at a ghost.

"Where are you going?" Grace hissed. "You're supposed to be in bed."

"I have to go," Nora said. "Out there. Please, Grace. Don't say anything. Just let me go. I have to do this. Please."

"Let me come with you." Grace gripped Nora's arm.

Nora twisted out of the hold. "No!" It was a whisper-scream. "Don't you dare! Go back to bed."

"Please." Grace was crying now; big tears rolled down her cheeks, and her nose began to run. "Please, Nora. I can't sleep. Please let me come."

"This is not about you," Nora said, pushing past her. "Now leave me alone, Grace. I mean it."

She opened the door to the cellar steps and looked down. The flashlight she'd spotted on top of the refrigerator trembled in her hand, and she jerked it to the right and then the left, trying to make sense of the steps that led down into the dark. She could hear Grace sobbing quietly as she closed the door behind her and descended the steps. The sound tore at her, but she did not stop. Tiny dust motes hung suspended in the pale beam of light, and a moth flew into her hair. She cried out as her fingers tore at the insect, clawing desperately at it until she realized it was gone. She went down farther, sweeping the space with her flashlight until her eyes fell on the shelves across the room, the neat line of tin cans and glass jars lined up like some kind of artillery. She moved toward them instinctually, knowing exactly what she would do. The Peter Pan box that Theo had given her in memory of their first date was just where she'd left it, placed there after their breakup, pushed in tight behind the row of jelly jars so that she would not have to think of it—or him—again. Now she slid it out carefully, her hands shaking, and cried out as it fell to the floor.

"No," she whimpered, bending down. But the top was cracked, the hinge badly marred. It closed unevenly, the edges misaligned now from the fall. She clutched it to her chest and ran.

She went through the smaller, silver garbage cans first, untying the knotted necks, and then pawing through the contents as quietly as she could—orange peels, coffee grounds, soiled maxi-pads, fast-food containers, and wadded-up tissue paper—but there was no sign of the towel. She stopped short in the middle of the third one when she came across a bag from the grocery store, the ends tied neatly in a bow, but it held only an old chicken carcass. She retched, pressing her nose and mouth into the elbow of her other arm, and threw it back.

The dumpster was a few feet away from the smaller cans; white and black garbage bags rose halfway to the top, their necks throttled with red plastic twist ties. A putrid smell arose as she hauled herself up one side of it and stepped in: rotting food, sour milk, shit and blood, the awful, rancid stench of decay. She began to weep again as she balanced awkwardly on the misshapen forms, trying to maneuver the flashlight with one hand as she held the box in the other. A faint scurrying sounded and Nora bit down hard on the outside of her wrist so that she would not scream. And then all at once she saw it, a brown paper bag perched in the corner between two plastic ones. The paper bag had brown and white stripes on the outside, the word JITTERBEANS stamped in the middle. She froze, holding the light on it, afraid to go any closer, and then crept forward. A section of towel poked out of the top, the rough material clean and unsoiled. It could be anything in there, she thought. Anything at all. She poked at it a little with the flashlight on one side, pushing the material back with the end of it. With a gasping sound, the garbage bag she was standing on split. She yelped as her bare foot sank through it. The smell of chicken grease rose up around her as she struggled to extricate herself, yelping again as her foot came into contact with something cold and slimy. She pulled herself up hard, righting herself, and looked around again. Despite her fall, the bag had not been bumped; it was still sitting there, staring at her like a dead eye. She pulled the towel out all at once, and tore it open with shaking hands.

There, in the middle of a horrifying mass of blood and clotted tissue, lay the tiniest baby she had ever seen. Nothing about it resembled a comma or a lima bean. It was the size of a Band-Aid, ten, maybe even twenty times bigger than anything Max had told them it might be, and while the oddly shaped head gave it a strange, alien appearance, there was no mistaking the tiny arms and legs, or the humanness of its face. It was all there, in all its ineffable, horrific beauty.

Nora knew it was dead. And yet as she sat there, looking at it, she couldn't help but feel as if it might open its eyes suddenly or take a single, staggered breath. But nothing happened. Nothing moved or breathed or even stirred. Even the wind had died down, keeping reverently still.

Somewhere a sound emerged then, and the hairs on the back of Nora's neck stood up. It continued on, a piteous noise that got louder and louder, transforming itself into a rending of something already torn, until slowly, as if waking, she grew conscious of the fact that it was coming from deep inside her, an imploring wail rising to the stars and the planets and all of the heavens beyond.

The towel was too thick and unwieldy to fit in the little box, so Nora tore a piece of her nightgown off at the hem and wrapped the fetus in it before tucking it inside. She clawed at the new tears blurring her vision; she needed to see, to do things just right now, without bumping or disturbing it. She could smell the heat rising from her skin; something inside of her was infected or dying. Maybe she was already dead.

Except that she couldn't be dead, she realized, her bare feet racing along the sidewalk moments later, the ripped nightgown flapping awkwardly at the bottom like a tattered flag. She couldn't be dead. She clutched the tiny box in one hand, her weakened body moving soundlessly through the night air, her breath coming out of her in hoarse, staggered spurts. Her feet smacked against the sidewalk until finally, like the answer to a never-ending prayer, she was there.

The birch trees beckoned like pale soldiers in the night, and the light from the moon bled down from the heavens. She sank down beneath them, pawing at the dirt with her fingers, digging, tearing, until the skin on her fingers turned raw. Her fevered body shook as she placed the broken box inside the little hole and placed a hand over the top of it.

"I'll be back," she whispered. The box felt like a piece of ice, and she leaned over it, trying to decipher its shape in the dark, to impart some kind of warmth from her own trembling fingers. "Every day, I'll be back. I promise."

Chapter 31

She knew logically now that the only thing left after all this time was the old box, that the contents inside had disintegrated into a pile of dust. But sometimes she thought, her cheek still pressed against the cold earth, she could feel it there beneath the dirt and rocks; she could sense it somehow, as though it had merged behind her rib cage, inside her heart.

Yes, Grace, I believe dead people can feel love.

She'd never say it out loud, would never admit it to another living soul, but she knew the child could feel her there, pressed against the blankets of snow and the sheets of rain and the mud and the grass, day after day, week after week, year after interminable year. She knew.

It was then that she realized, with perfect clarity, that the pain she'd been carrying around for so long was not about the girls leaving her behind or their inability to speak of that night. It was about her and the baby in the ground and nothing else. Which meant that this was hers to fix, hers to free herself from. No one else's. She understood, too, that she did not want to live any more of her life with the weight of her decision strung around her neck. Hadn't she just been wondering why she could not find it in her to forgive? Could it have something to do with an inability to forgive herself? And if so, what might happen now if she did?

Nora stretched out the fingers of one hand along the dirt and pressed down, leaving small indentations beneath her fingertips. It took a long time for her to find her voice, and when she did, it came out in a whisper.

"Goodbye, my angel," she said. "Goodbye."

Headlights sliced through the dark. Alice Walker lifted her head as a car pulled in across the street, and pricked her ears. A low growl sounded in her throat as the lights dimmed and then went out. The sound of a door opening and then shutting again brought the dog to her feet, and Nora reached out, grabbing her around the collar. Figures emerged from the other side of the street, two, three, four of them. No, five. Nora squinted as she got up from her supine position, praying that the group was not a bunch of drunk teenagers and that none of them had seen her there.

"Nora?"

She nearly wept as Ozzie's voice came through the dark.

"Nora, are you over there?"

She sat up, holding on to Alice Walker's collar, and tried to steady herself. The dog was growling with abandon now, her danger sensors on overload. "Shhh," Nora said softly. "Shhhh, baby. It's okay."

The women came over slowly, Ozzie first, then Grace and

Monica. Trudy and Marion followed on tiptoe, their faces twisted with anxiety and confusion. Nora drew back as she saw them, drenched again in a new fear, a new hopelessness. She didn't want them to know; she didn't want any of them to know. This was hers alone, and no one else's.

"Norster." Ozzie sank down next to her, one hand going to Alice Walker's head, massaging the dog behind the ears. "Oh, Norster, I thought we'd lost you."

Nora brushed a loose remnant of dirt from her face and tried to compose herself. "What are you doing here?" she asked. "Is Monica allowed to leave . . ."

"I'm okay." Monica hobbled forward, facing Nora. "Theo came with us, too. My arraignment isn't scheduled 'til Wednesday. He made sure it was okay."

Nora shook her head, struggling to understand. This wasn't about Theo. Or was it? She couldn't remember anymore. "I just . . . I don't understand what any of you are doing here. How did you even find me?'

"We went to your house," Grace said. "But there was no one there except Marion and Trudy here, who were sitting on the step. They said they were waiting for you to come back. That you'd left for a walk." She reached out, placing a hand on Nora's arm. "I knew where'd you'd be."

Nora looked over at the older women; they were holding on to one another, as if one of them might fall over if the other let go.

"She's here," Nora heard herself say, holding Grace's gaze. "I brought her here."

Grace nodded. Her eyes filled with tears.

"Who, Nora?" Ozzie sounded faint. "Who's here?"

It was time. Her turn now to peel back the cover she had been hiding under all these years. Her turn to open a vein, to tell the whole truth.

To become visible.

"The baby," she said. "I went back out to the dumpster that night and . . . and got her." Her voice was a whisper. "I put her in a little box that Theo gave me a long time ago and brought her here so that I could put her to rest, bury her the right way." Marion pressed her fingers to her mouth. Trudy's lips were set in a tight line, her eyebrows knitted in a line along her forehead. "I've come back every morning since then to sit with her. So that she's not alone. So that she knows I haven't forgotten. But I think she knows now." Nora nodded. "I think it's time for me to let go."

Monica fell to her knees. Grace sank down beside her. Soft sobs filled the air, the plaintive sounds of grieving and loss, pain and grief, as it all came back again. It was for all of them, these cries, for everything they had lost—and everything that had just been found again.

They surrounded Nora slowly, these women, these mothers, each of them, Trudy and Marion too. One by one, they reached for her above the dark earth and the howling memory of their past.

She opened her arms and let them in.

Monica had only a few hours, she told them, before Theo had to take her back to New York. They had a lot to do before the arraignment on Wednesday. There was no fooling around this time, no way they could dicker around with anything.

"Where is Theo?" Nora asked.

"We left him in the lobby of a Days Inn," Monica said. "You know, the one behind the high school? He wanted to come, but we told him we needed some time with you first."

Nora nodded numbly, trying to visualize him in his beautiful shoes. He was probably sitting in one of those shitty chairs by the window, fiddling with his iPhone. Maybe he'd unloosened his tie, run a hand through his hair. He might be staring out at the window next to the vending machine in the front lobby, wondering if they'd all come back in time. If they'd come back at all.

Trudy and Marion had left, taking Alice Walker with them, and the rest of them were seated around the faintly ridged hill of dirt. Above them, the birch trees swayed and bowed in the cool wind; higher still, the full moon waned.

"We should finish our Invisibles meeting before we go," Ozzie said, staring up into the sky. "We can pick up where we left off the other night. I mean, it's the real thing now, with that goddess staring down at us the way she used to."

"I don't even remember where we left off," Nora said, settling herself down in a circle with the rest of them. "Monica's wine bottle blow job, maybe?"

They laughed a little, and the sound traveled up around them like tiny pieces of light before dispersing again.

"You were just about to share a first line," Ozzie said, holding Nora's hand. "You said it was from some book called *The End of the Affair*. Do you still remember it?"

Nora bit the inside of her cheek. "I do," she said.

"Okay, then." Ozzie squeezed her hand tighter. "Go for it."

Nora took a deep breath. "My first line tonight is from the novelist Graham Greene, who wrote *The End of the Affair*. And it goes like this: *'A story has no beginning or end: arbitrarily, one chooses that moment of experience from which to look back or from which to look ahead.'*"

It had meant something the night she chose it, but now the meaning had deepened to a level she had hardly known existed. She made a mental note to add it alongside her other favorite first line in her notebook, one an artifact from her past, the other a light for the future.

"I'm confused," Grace said. "What's it mean?" She burst out laughing.

They laughed with her, all of them, knowing that somehow tonight they had crossed the deepest of chasms and emerged intact. Somehow, despite their own personal hells, each of them was still holding on to the best part of themselves. And it would be with these selves that each of them would look bravely ahead, into the future.

Stick wishes were next, the final leg of the ritual, thrown out to the full moon in all her glory. Ozzie went first, tracing the air with a small twig she had found, writing her hopes there in desperate, frantic air letters. She turned, finishing, and Nora thought she might sit down the way she always did and concede to the next one in line. Except that she didn't do that.

"I want to say mine out loud this time," Ozzie said, tossing her stick to one side. "Back at Turning Winds, I think I was too afraid to say what I really wanted. Maybe I thought you'd judge me. Or think I was weak, which would mean that one of you might stop loving me. But I'm a woman now. I need to tell each of you my hopes and dreams. Out loud. Because when I tell someone the truth, and she decides to keep on loving me anyway, that's when I know I've found family. That's when I know I'm really home."

The women watched as Ozzie turned around again and faced the moon. She raised her hands the way she had always done, until the milky, orbital belly was centered directly between them and threw her head back. "I want a life of my own," she said loudly. "I want to forgive my mother for the things she did to me and to stop the fucking cycle she dragged me into. I want to reach down inside myself and find the strength I know is in me to leave the man who treats me so badly, to create a life for myself and my children of stillness and love." She lowered her arms slowly, as if the words themselves had gotten too heavy.

Nora stood up and put her arm around her. She pressed her mouth close to Ozzie's ear. "You will," she whispered fiercely. "You will, and we'll help you. Every step of the way."

Ozzie nodded and kissed her hard on the cheek. "I'll need it. After this trip, I know I can do anything. But not without all of you."

Monica was next. She stood up, making a great display of throwing her stick to one side, and shook her hair out. The women laughed encouragingly. It was not easy, saying such truths out loud. There had been a reason for stick wishes, for emitting their deepest hopes in silence.

"I want to own up to the things I've done." Monica's voice was tremulous. "Whether or not that means I have to go to jail. And I want to meet my father, to get to know him, find the good in him, if there is any." She glanced over at Nora. "I've already talked to Liam. I told him what I did. I don't know what's going to happen to us, but he's going to help me set up a meeting between me and my father when I get back." She shrugged, and even there in the dark, Nora could see her lips trembling. "It's a start," she said. "You know? And I've got to start somewhere."

Grace was next. She didn't even bother with a stick, but she turned, facing the moon head-on. She paused for a full minute, as if gathering herself, and something in Nora lurched, waiting for her to object again to the pagan-ness of the situation, to the part that didn't have anything to do with Jesus or Mary.

"I want to accept myself," Grace said softly. "I want to embrace every part of myself, the sick parts and the well parts. I want to open myself to my child, however imperfect I might be, and love her the only way I know how, with my whole, fractured heart." She sat back down again, breathing hard, and Nora flung her arms around her.

"She needs you, Grace," Nora whispered into Grace's shoulder.

"I know," Grace nodded. "And she'll get me."

"Your turn, Norster," Ozzie said.

Nora lifted her face from Grace's shoulder and rubbed her eyes. She had the sensation then of having traveled down a long road, a path blocked with thorns and boulders and somehow, in some way, reaching the end of it. She felt different, if not older somehow, then new again on the inside. She stood up on quavering legs and looked up at the moon, still high in the sky, the edges pulsing faintly with some miraculous light.

"I want to talk," she heard herself say. "I want to talk and talk and talk until everything inside of me comes out and there is nothing else left to say. I don't want to not tell nobody but God anymore. I want to tell you. I want to cradle the past in my arms and feel it there, in all its terrible rawness, and then I want to say goodbye. I want to close the door on that part of my life and move forward under the moon, with all of you. Again."

The women rose as one and surrounded her, their arms like a brick fortress around her trembling shoulders, and she knew it to be true.

She knew it to be the truest, purest thing she had ever known.

They went to the car afterward and Nora slid into the backseat. There was not much room, since a large metal cage placed on the floor took up most of the space, and Nora frowned, angling her legs around it.

"Don't you recognize him?" Grace was looking at her from the other side of the car, her mouth split open into a grin. Nora glanced at Ozzie and Monica, who were watching her from the front seat.

"Who?" she asked.

Grace pointed at the cage, and it was only then that Nora saw Elmer, quivering silently in the corner, nibbling on a bit of hay.

"You got Elmer?" She stared at the women, aghast. "How? When?"

"We stopped in Hopatcong on our way here." Ozzie shrugged. "We thought he'd do better with me on the farm than with those weirdos back at Hopatcong Honey's. The place was a crack den, I think."

Nora hovered over the cage, her fingers sliding through the slots, as if she could reach him from there. The tiny animal shivered and huddled further into the corner at the movement.

"His name means 'noble,'" Ozzie said proudly.

Grace laughed. "I thought you named him after Elmer Fudd."

"That's just what I told you," Ozzie said. "I was trying to keep things light. The cards were pretty much stacked against me at that point, if you remember. I didn't want to get any of you more riled up than you were."

"It fits him," Nora said softly as Ozzie started the car. "I love it."

Her heart was beating like a jackhammer as they drove into the Days Inn parking lot. Even the steady warmth of Elmer, who she had been holding in her hands, did not ease the building anxiousness inside. Horrible orange curtains flanked the wide front windows, blocking anything on the inside from sight, but Nora knew he was in there. She could feel it.

"You want to go in?" Ozzie had parked the car and shut off the engine. She was turned around in her seat, looking at Nora. "Just you?"

Nora paused for a moment and then put Elmer back inside his cage. He scurried toward the far corner again and rubbed his paws against his tiny eyes. And then, as she watched, he looked up at her with a steady, knowing gaze.

"Yes," she said, opening the car door. "I do."

He was standing at the far window all the way across the lobby, his back to her as she made her way inside, but he turned immediately, as if he had sensed her presence. Even from fifty feet away, she could see how tired he was, how the circles under his eyes stood out like small half-moons, how the front of his shirt puckered and bagged in the front. He was holding his suit jacket over one shoulder, the collar of it snug inside the crook of his index finger, but his shoulders sagged, and Nora wondered if he might drop it any moment. A receptionist with pink streaks in her brown hair looked up as Nora walked past the front desk. "Hello there, ma'am! May I . . ." Her voice drifted off as Nora kept going. Theo had not moved, but she did. She moved on steady legs toward him, stopping only when she was a few feet away. Even then, she did not drop her eyes, did not bring a finger up to pull on her earlobe.

"Hi." She was not sure what else to say just yet.

"Hi." His voice was soft as a breath, and his nostrils flared white around the edges. He lowered the jacket from his shoulder and dropped it along the back of a yellow-and-brown-striped couch.

Was there any reason to bring it all up again? Nora wondered. Or had they already said what they'd needed to say? If she turned around and walked away right now, would she be all right? Or would she replay this scene a thousand times in the future, each one with a different verbal combination, each one creating a different portal through which they would—forever after—continue to view each other?

"I'm glad to see you made it home," he said, shifting his feet. "New York taxis aren't always that reliable."

"It was fine. I paid him well."

Theo nodded.

"Are you going back tonight?" she asked.

He glanced at his watch, a heavy silver thing with a dark blue face. "Pretty soon. I haven't slept much, and Monica and I have a lot to do before the arraignment on Wednesday."

"Thanks for bringing her. It meant a lot to me to have her here tonight."

"You're welcome. It was the least I could do."

She could see something dim behind his eyes, and she stepped forward, taking his hand. "Theo." He closed his fingers around hers, pressing just the tips of them against the back of her hand. "*I* should have been the one to tell you about the pregnancy all those years ago. I'm sorry I didn't. I just didn't know how. I was so ashamed of myself, so embarrassed." She could feel the pressure behind his fingers, the steady pull of them against her own as he drew her closer.

"Why?" he whispered.

"Because I was such a mess to begin with. Every time we tried to be intimate, I'd have flashbacks of things done to me as a kid, or things would start resurfacing and . . ." Her tears rose in her throat. "And then you broke up with me, which I don't blame you for, but it just confirmed everything about myself that I thought was broken and unfixable . . ."

"Oh, Nora." He stroked her knuckles with the edge of his thumb. "I thought I was doing the right thing when I broke up with you. Really I did. There'd be times when I'd touch your face or kiss you and you'd seem to go somewhere inside your head. Like something had grabbed you underwater and was holding you there. And then we started sleeping together and things just . . ." He closed his eyes, remembering. "That look in your eyes, your face . . . God, I thought I was killing you somehow. I didn't know what to do."

"It wasn't your fault." Nora's cheeks burned. "You couldn't have known."

"When Ozzie wrote me that letter and told me about the pregnancy and then everything after that, I almost had a heart attack," Theo went on. "I just couldn't believe it. Something like that had never even occurred to me."

Nora nodded, pressing her lips together.

"I would've supported you," Theo whispered. "Whatever you wanted to do. I would've helped you through it."

"I know that now." Nora pressed her forehead against his shirt. "I'm sorry I didn't give you that chance back then."

They stood there for a moment, lost in thought, each of them unraveling the threads that had led them inside an old movie theater, atop a thick sheet of ice, beneath a set of striped sheets, and back around again. It was baffling how life worked, Nora thought, how the holes found their way inside everyone. Some were larger than others, some deeper, more treacherously sloped. But no one got off without them. No one, at the end of their story, emerged intact.

And maybe that was the beauty of it after all. Maybe it wasn't about how few holes we ended up with, but how we taught ourselves to see through them, how we learned to look at our lives from another angle, maybe discovering a light that had not been there before.

"We were so young," Nora whispered. "Weren't we? So young and so hopeful."

"Yes." He nodded, pulling her all the way into him, and wrapped his arms around her. "Nora," he said, his voice breaking. "Oh, Nora, Nora."

Ozzie had told her once that her name meant "light."

And it was true she thought now, as the words coming out of his mouth drifted above them like tiny stars.

It was true.

Chapter 32

That Friday, she took Alice Walker with her to see the razed building at the corner of Magnolia Avenue. It was dusk, and the air, purple and fragile, hung around them like iris petals. She stood across the street for a long time, gazing at the space where Turning Winds had once been. Except for a few small piles of rubble off to one side, the lot was empty. A small white board hammered into the dirt read WIDEMAN'S CONSTRUCTION, indicating the only past sign of life. There was nothing of them anymore. Nothing at all. She waited for the sadness, or maybe even anger, to surge up within her, but neither one came. She thought back instead to the past week, a series of days strung along one of the most miraculous fragments of her life, and how it had all begun on her thirty-second birthday, when the quote by Anne Rice had popped into her head: *"Once upon a time, there was a woman who discovered she had turned into the wrong person."*

But not me, she thought now. *Not me.*

The truth was she could hardly believe how much her life had changed. It felt limitless in some strange way now, as if she had discovered herself on the first blank page of the rest of her life. She felt a thrill, thinking of it.

And what of a first line? What would her own first line be? Maybe it wasn't something she needed to know just yet; maybe she would surprise herself one day as a string of words came to her when she least expected it. That was how they worked after all, wasn't it? Sitting there neatly in the middle of a page that one just happened to turn to? Taking your breath away? And then toeing the line, and jumping straight into the abyss, taking you with them?

That was how Nora felt now: as though she had jumped, not into the abyss but over it. It would take time to secure her footing, maybe even a while to focus her gaze, but there was nothing as green as the horizon ahead, no light above so luminous as the moon's.

Acknowledgments

First thanks goes to my extraordinary agent, Stacey Glick, who believed in this book from the very beginning and remained devoted to seeing it through to the end. Words fail me, friend. You are the real deal.

Every writer on the planet should be given at least one opportunity to work with the brilliant Emily Krump, who not only created a path for me to walk down while editing this book, but remained steadfast company throughout the entire journey.

Thank you to the art department at William Morrow for creating such a beautiful cover, and for everyone at HarperCollins for contributing their talents toward this book. I am forever grateful.

I wrote this book because when I was a little girl, I belonged to a tribe of children who knew and loved me before anyone else did, much like The Invisibles. It is difficult to recall a time since when I have felt as authentic as I did then; being seen by this band of souls was, and remains to this day, one of my life's most precious treasures. My endless gratitude goes to Amy, Maria, Ruthie, Ani, Josie, Michael, Joey, Lucy, Catherine, and Mark.

It was because of you that I continued on.

It is because of you that I still do.

About the author

About the book

Insights,
Interviews
& More . . .

Read on

Meet Cecilia Galante

Herbert William Plummer, 2015

CECILIA GALANTE is the author of three young adult novels, three middle-grade books, and a children's chapter-book series. She is the recipient of many awards, including a NAIBA Book of the Year and an Oprah's Teen Read Selection for her first novel, *The Patron Saint of Butterflies*. Her books have been translated into Japanese, Turkish, and Polish. ∽

The Story Behind
The Invisibles

WHILE I WOULDN'T CHANGE the odd, frightening circumstances of my childhood (born and raised for the first fifteen years of my life inside a religious commune), there are a few details I wish had worked out differently. It would have been nice, for example, if someone from law enforcement had shown up one day to inquire why children were forbidden to live with their parents, or why extended, brutal punishments were an acceptable form of discipline. Since most of my novels begin with the question "what if?" I found myself imagining the answers to these questions when I sat down to write my first novel, *The Patron Saint of Butterflies*. It wasn't an accident that Agnes Little, the shy, fourteen-year-old protagonist in the novel, was born and raised in a commune similar to the one I had lived in, but her resulting escape and the agonizing decisions she made afterward (which led to a police intervention) were completely fictitious. While I was on tour for the novel, a woman asked me if I wished the end of the story had happened in my real life. Well, yes, actually. That was exactly why I wrote it. Without getting too psychological here, it was a way of reclaiming my past. Doing things my way this time, instead of being forced to follow the litanies of a madman. Or, as the great writing teacher Natalie Goldberg once said, "writing to live twice." ▶

The Story Behind *The Invisibles* (continued)

I found myself in a similar situation when I first began to think about *The Invisibles*. The bonds between the children of the commune were some of the most powerful human links I've ever experienced—both then and now. Having to leave the only home I'd ever known and start over again in a new world was difficult, to say the least. But being physically separated from this child-tribe of mine was like losing an arm—two arms, actually, since most of the time we were holding one another. As I began to write, I found myself drawn to the main characters in the book, each of them inspired by a girl from my past with whom I had been raised and, because of drugs, death, and other irrevocable circumstances, I have since lost contact. It was a deep, deep loss, one that reverberated through my early adulthood, and one that still aches when I think about it now.

I started with that ache, imagining the group of us meeting up again. There was the pale, thin one I fashioned Monica after, who twirled her hair when she was nervous and was so painfully sweet that it brought tears to my eyes. Would she still clutch for my hand the way she'd always done back then, rubbing a thumb along the edge of mine until I shook it loose again? And what of the girl who inspired Ozzie—loud, obnoxious, standing up in the face of authority, even to her detriment? Would she be different? Or had time softened some of her edges, granted her a different outlook on the world? Grace was the girl I remembered as drawing all the time, once creating an entire scene of birds out of bits of tightly rolled paper, and Nora (although not all of her) was based on me. What would bring us together? What would we say? Was I the only one who still had nightmares about the commune? Had any of them found a way to put those demons to rest, to rise above the nightmare of our childhood and not just survive, but thrive?

I knew I didn't want to set another novel inside a commune, and so I began to think of other circumstances in which similar shared relationships might blossom. The girls' home came to mind immediately. Not only was the parental void there, but the girls would have the opportunity to bond in much the same way my friends and I had inside the commune. The rest of the story is fiction, dreamed in the fluid way that is sometimes granted when you start with vivid characters. It unfolded piece by piece as I was writing, sometimes taking me in one direction and sometimes in another. Often, I found myself completely off course, and I would have to go back and start again, to try to retrace the steps these characters might have taken if they were in such a place and time.

Secretly, I hope that each of these women from my past will recognize pieces of themselves in my story. If they do, I hope they remember a time when they were mine, when as little girls, we ▶

The Story Behind *The Invisibles* (continued)

created a whole world unto ourselves
inside another, darker one. It's why
I write, after all. To connect with the
things I've lost. To find a way back.
　A way home. ～

Questions for Discussion

1. The book opens with Nora's birthday, which she had forgotten. What is the significance of Nora forgetting her own birthday?

2. One of the first lines that Nora quotes is "Once upon a time, there was a woman who discovered she had turned into the wrong person." Do you think Nora has turned into "the wrong person"? How does she let this feeling of leading a misguided life affect her?

3. *"Leave it in the past, Ozzie had said, where it would get smaller and smaller until one day it would just disappear altogether."* How has this pact changed Nora's life, given what we know? What do you think Ozzie was referring to when she said this?

4. Why do you think Nora is so hesitant to welcome the old friends she's missed back into her life? Why does she continue to resist opening up to them about her past and her life?

5. As an adult, Nora still clings to her love of the moon and first lines of books. What does this signify about her development into adulthood? Why do you think she still looks to the moon for guidance?

6. The girls decided on the name "The Invisibles" for their group. In what ways do you think each of ▶

them felt invisible in their lives as teenagers? What about now as adults?

7. The novel moves between the past and present. What does this structure reveal about the characters? How does it affect your interpretations of them both then and now?

8. Nora reveals that she broke off both of the longest relationships she had as an adult and afterward turned down most offers to go on dates. She also has few friends. Why do you think she's so hesitant to let new people into her life?

9. What do you think happened to change Ozzie from the fierce girl she had been in high school to the woman she is now? How do you think reuniting with her old friends will affect her?

10. We find out that Nora's mother had tried to contact her after Daddy Ray died. Why do you think Nora never wanted to confront her mother?

11. In what ways is Ozzie's determination to find the rabbit's mother significant? How about Nora's refusal to give up the baby rabbit, despite numerous demands from Ozzie to do so? What might the baby rabbit represent to her?

12. Why do you think Nora shows such resistance to going back to Turning

Winds? What makes her different
from the other women, who are
eager to go back?

13. In what ways are the women still the
same people they were as teenagers?
In what ways are they different? Do
you think they've changed for the
better? ～

On Books and Reading

HARPER LEE once described reading as akin to breathing, and I'm pretty sure that's exactly right. From the moment I discovered books, I couldn't get enough of them. I read endlessly as a kid, devouring whatever I could get my hands on, and plowed my way through the library during my teen and adult years. Since the age of twenty, I have had a stack of books next to my bed that is nearly as high as the bed itself, and into which I dip at random depending on my mood that night. I buy books the way some women buy shoes, and there are few things in my life that compare to the anticipation of beginning a brand-new one. I believe that reading is the most essential tool for a writer—more important than any teacher or graduate program in the world—but books are also one of the truest sources of joy I've ever known, portals into the worlds and minds of people I will never meet except on the page. Books are the best of everything; they are solitude and company, student and teacher, stranger and friend.

Here are some of my favorites.

Olive Kittredge, by Elizabeth Strout

The winner of the well-deserved 2009 Pulitzer Prize, this novel-in-stories follows the acerbic, cantankerous Olive Kittredge through the eyes of her fellow neighbors in Maine. I love central characters who possess strange, ornery personalities but with whom you fall in love anyway. Olive is such a person, a one-in-a-million character that you wish you knew personally. I feel similarly about Elizabeth Strout, who has written some of the most beautiful sentences I've ever come across.

A Visit from the Goon Squad, by Jennifer Egan

Another Pulitzer Prize winner (2011) and another novel-in-stories. Like Strout, Egan knocks it out of the park with her deeply felt characters and fresh, beautiful prose. I'm drawn especially to writers who get right to the point and say what needs to be said, but in a way that makes you wonder where in the world he or she got such an idea in the first place. Egan is one of those writers. Also, not many authors can force me to put a book down so that I don't finish too quickly. This one did—and still does.

Tiny Beautiful Things, by Cheryl Strayed

This isn't a novel, but a collection of Strayed's writings from when she used to maintain an advice column at Salon .com. Strayed (who also wrote the blockbuster *Wild*) is one of those rare writers who can evoke the purest type of honesty in their work without sounding preachy or oversentimental. Each of these pieces is a window into her own life, as well as a basket overflowing with the generous lessons she's learned along the way. It's a wise, brave little book from a woman who's been there and back again. ▶

To Kill a Mockingbird, by Harper Lee

It's no accident that I teach this book every year to my eighth-grade students at Wyoming Seminary Preparatory School. It was one of my own favorites as a kid, and I relish the shared excitement each semester as study of the novel comes to a close in my classroom. The layers within this book, as well as its riveting themes of racism, courage, and empathy, continue to keep it as pertinent today as it was when it first came out. Maybe even more so.

Talk Before Sleep, by Elizabeth Berg

I love Berg's style of writing—clean, simple, with the kind of details that make me think, "Oh, I'm not the only one!" This novel, which deals with a woman battling cancer and the friends who rally around her, has all those traits and more. Berg is wonderful at humanizing her characters in such a way that they become almost intimate by the novel's end, and her books, which almost always deal with things like relationships, marriage, and the search for self, continually strike a chord with me. ～

Discover great authors, exclusive offers, and more at hc.com.